THE IRON KNIGHT

A MEDIEVAL ROMANCE
PART OF THE DE RUSSE LEGACY SERIES

BY KATHRYN LE VEQUE

Dedicated to all of you who have had, or needed, a second chance in life. Even in the darkest hour, there is always hope. Take it from me.

Author's Foreword

Welcome to the story of The Iron Knight!

This was such a fun story to write. Very different from most of my others in that the hero is different. To put it frankly, in Medieval terms, Lucien de Russe is an old man.

He's forty years old. Now, that's not old by today's standards, but when you're a Medieval knight and you've just spent the past twenty years in various battles, exhausting yourself and beating your body up, forty is OLD. But I like Lucien because he's wise and seasoned. He's seen a lot and done a lot. He's got a stellar reputation as a warrior but the truth is that his personal life is a mess. You'll find out why.

A couple of things to point out – Richmond le Bec appears in the prologue ten years after his battle with Hotspur on the Welsh Marches. He, too, was forty years old in his novel, GREAT PROTECTOR, so this book is set about ten years after that. Richmond is nearing fifty. That's ancient for Medieval times.

Also, there is a young knight in this book who has a fairly important role – Colton de Royans. He's twenty years old in this novel and he's got his father's wisdom and fighting ability. Remember Colton from TO THE LADY BORN? He was about two in the book and just a pistol. He tried to steal goats. He wanted everything he saw. Yes, he was spoiled, but that little toddler has grown up into a hell of a man. See if you don't think so. And his father, Weston, hero of TO THE LADY BORN, makes an appearance at the end. Weston is one of my all-time favorite characters.

The usual disclaimers/clarifications here, too – Spelthorne Castle is fictional. Sherborne Castle is real – I've actually been there. It's a giant place and, oh, the stories I imagined for it! It has also appeared in THE QUESTING. The garrison commander in this book is a direct descendant of Cortez de Bretagne, the hero of THE QUESTING. Looks like the de Bretagnes made Sherborne their legacy (although in real life, that was not true. Sherborne Castle was held by the Catholic Church).

Just a few fun facts before you delve into this story. I truly hope you love Lucien and Sophina's story because I loved writing it.

Love,
Kathryn

PROLOGUE

February, 1408 A.D.
Bramham Moor, Yorkshire

G OD, HE WAS so frozen he could hardly lift his hand.

The battle at Bramham, which had first involved knights on horseback, was now a mass battle of men on foot, hand-to-hand combat in the middle of an icy moor, with snow falling and ice building up so fast that once a man had fallen, the blood spilling from his body turned to ice crystals in mere seconds. Chain mail was freezing up, particularly bad when blood or water came into contact with it, making for a thoroughly miserable experience.

It was brutal as well as slow, this battle. Men were slogging through red-tinted mud in slow motion, trying to kill each other but barely able to fight because the weather was so bad. Between slashing swords, flying flails, and thrusting fists, it was turning into more of a shoving match. At least the movement was helping them stay warm. Once in a while, a dagger would come out and someone would grunt as a frozen blade was shoved between his ribs.

The smell of death was in the air, too, mingled with the smell of smoke from the fires from both Henry IV's encampment, led by the High Sheriff of Yorkshire, and the Earl of Northumberland's encampment. Death always smelled like smoke, something like dirty, gritty embers mingled with old blood. It was the smell of lives being wasted.

There was nothing pleasant or victorious about that smell at all.

But here he was, in the middle of another battle in a long line of innumerable battles that had seen the King of England fending off a rebellion from the great house to the north, the House of Percy. Northumberland had been very active over the past ten years trying to wrest the throne from the former Henry of Bolingbroke, and because he was loyal to the king – and a favored of the man – he was always expected to be right in the middle of whatever conflict happened to be occurring.

Well, he was just getting too damn old for such things. He'd been doing this kind of thing for nearly thirty years, ever since he had been a squire. There was no glory any longer, nothing to be proud over. It was just men dying for a cause that didn't make any sense any longer.

He didn't want to do this anymore.

"Lucien!"

The shout came from behind, jarring Sir Lucien de Russe from his unhappy thoughts. He turned to see a man approaching him through the crowd of fighting, wrestling men. It was a man he knew extremely well, a very close friend, and an older knight who had no real business being in the middle of this mess. Slugging his opponent squarely in the face, Lucien pushed his unworthy adversary to the ground as he turned for his friend.

"Richmond," he said with disgust, pointing to the outskirts of the battle where men were not fighting and dying. "Get out of here. Are you trying to get yourself killed?"

Sir Richmond le Bec grinned at his friend, his bright blue eyes twinkling wearily. "I was going to ask you the same question," he said. "Rokeby needs you. Come out of this mess."

They were referring to Sir Thomas Rokeby, the High Sheriff of Yorkshire and the man orchestrating this battle on behalf of Henry. At least, that was what everyone was told even though the truth was something they all knew – le Bec and de Russe were in charge of it. Rokeby didn't make a move without them.

As le Bec remained on the perimeter of the battle, watching the movements, Lucien was in the middle of it, fighting. *The Iron Knight*, they called him, a mixture of intelligence and strength that was uncommon in men. There was no one tougher, mentally or physically, and no one with more determination or sheer force of will anywhere in Henry's army.

Lucien de Russe was invincible.

But that mental strength had been wavering as of late, a discontentment that had not gone unnoticed. Perhaps it was his advancing years or perhaps it was even the fact that he seemed to have developed a distaste of war in general. No one seemed to know and when le Bec had asked him about it, Lucien wasn't sure himself. All he knew was that he was unhappy with it all. Still, his fighting resolve had never wavered. No one had ever expected that it would, not from The Iron Knight. No matter what he felt, he still had a job to do.

Now, he had an excuse to get out of the fighting with le Bec's summons. He began following Richmond out of the mess of men but he soon took the lead and began shoving men aside, men who were trying to take a swipe at le Bec. Richmond had served Henry for more years that Lucien had and, now in his fifth decade, he'd earned the right not to have to fight any longer. His experience and tactical knowledge were invaluable, but the very big man with the broad shoulders was no longer expected to fight.

In fact, Lucien didn't like for him to. He was always afraid that someone was going to catch le Bec unaware and then Lucien would have to explain the man's death to his widow. Consequently, he was very protective of the man. Richmond's demise wasn't a thought he found particularly pleasant.

"God, this is miserable," Lucien grunted, kicking one man aside and watching him fall face-first in the red mud. "We shall be lucky if this is all finished by dusk."

Richmond belted some fool who came too close to him. "I know," he said grimly. "We have been watching from the ridge. Northumberland has rotating troops, allowing most to fight but some to rest. Then he puts in the rested troops and rotates out some of the wearier men. This will go on all night if we let it."

Lucien looked at him with some impatience. "Then we roll mounted knights in on the northern flank where Northumberland has been changing out his men," he said. He threw up his hands. "I have been watching, too. Why have you not done this, Richmond?"

Richmond lifted his eyebrows. "Because Carlisle is coming," he muttered, hoping none of Percy's struggling men had heard him. "He has been sighted about two miles to the north. We also have de Cleveley moving in from the west. They should be here shortly; they were detained by the weather but their messengers assure us they will be here before dusk. Percy's strength is limited, Lucien. We have fresh men coming in that will finish the job we started."

Lucien wasn't so impatient any longer. He was coming to see that whatever Percy did was futile. "Is that so?" he said, finally pleased about something. "Then what does Rokeby want to see me about?"

Richmond put a hand on his shoulder, pulling him away from some particularly nasty fighting. "Because he wants you to ride in with Carlisle and direct the army," he said. "You know what needs to be done, as you have been in the heart of it."

Lucien glanced around him, at the dead and at the dying and at the fighting. He grunted. "I have been in the heart of it far too long," he murmured, watching as a very young Percy soldier was dispatched by one of his men. So, so young. *The waste of it all.* "I have never been out of the heart of it, Richmond. This is all I can remember, days like this and death like this. Is there really something else in life other than this? If that is true, then I cannot recall it."

Richmond looked at his friend, feeling the despair. "I am sorry," he said. "You have shouldered the majority of the burden of these wars for so long. I have been a fool, remaining outside of the lines while you fight. You have been fighting for all of us, Lucien. But, hopefully, you will be able to rest after this. If we can pull a decisive victory out of this battle, Percy will have no choice but to retreat to the north to lick his wounds. That means we will have peace for a time. You can return home to see your children then."

Lucien grunted, making sure to stay out of the way of any fighting as they moved. "My son is fostering at Kenilworth," he muttered. "He is fifteen years of age and a man grown. The last time I saw him, he would not even speak to me. As for my daughter, I have not seen her in almost a year. She still lives at home with her nurse. I have no idea how she will receive me when next we meet."

Richmond eyed the man; they all knew that Lucien's wife had died in childbirth with a young daughter who was born with limited use of her legs. The birth had been destructive and difficult on both mother and child. Lucien had been quite in love with his wife, Laurabel de Reyne de Russe, and her death had shattered him. He'd been a bitter and morose man for the past seven years, far from the congenial and humorous soul that Richmond had known for years. Laurabel's death took something out of him, something that he would never regain. It was as if Lucien didn't want it back, that spark that had made him so likable and warm.

Nay, the spark was gone and Lucien didn't seem to care. These days, he didn't seem to care much about anything. Everything he did was duty-bound and nothing more.

Richmond missed his old friend.

"Children are strange creatures," Richmond said, putting a hand on Lucien's shoulder as they cleared most of the fighting. "Young men are especially strange. I have two of them, you know. I can vouch for how odd they can be, so I would not worry over Rafe. I am sure he loves and admires you, just as we all do."

Lucien thought on his tall, dark-haired son who was already an old and wise soul at his young age. It was a much more complicated relationship than Richmond made it out to be, a son who would not even speak to his father, but Lucien didn't go into any details. Frankly, he didn't have the mental strength to do so at the moment.

"Mayhap," he said. "In any case, I look forward to this battle being over so that I can return home for a time. I may barricade myself in and never leave again."

Richmond grinned. "Not even for me?"

"Especially not for you."

Richmond laughed softly. "Then I may not let you go home," he said. "In fact, I…."

He was cut off by the soft singing sounds of flying projectiles. Yew-shafted arrows suddenly landed in the mud around them and both men whirled to the Northumberland lines to the east only to see a new volley of arrows rising into the cloudy sky. Both of them began to run.

"Damnation!" Richmond roared. "I thought we eliminated his archers!"

Lucien, being faster, was ahead of Richmond. "We did," he grunted. "This must be a new contingent. Did we have reports of reinforcements arriving for Percy?"

Richmond narrowly dodged being hit by an arrow as it plunged into the ground beside him. "Nothing," he huffed as he ran. "We have had scouts out for weeks and no one has said anything about rein-forcements."

It was a deadly slip in intelligence with an arrival of fresh archers. The problem was that they were launching into the mass of fighting men, hitting their own soldiers as well as Henry's. Sloppy tactics at best.

Confused and very concerned, Richmond and Lucien continued to run, seemingly escaping the barrage of arrows that were pummeling the men in the moor down below. They had come to the crest of a frozen rise with Henry's command off to the west. They paused to turn and see the damage the hail of arrows had done.

More men were down and more blood was spilled onto the frozen tundra. As many Percy men were down as Henry men and Lucien shook his head grimly as he surveyed the damage.

"Fools," he hissed. "Does Percy even realize he is killing his own men?"

Richmond sighed heavily. "It is a very bold move," he said, "and a ridiculous one. One does not fire on one's own troops."

"He did."

"Aye, he did."

Lucien's gaze lingered on the group below before turning towards the west. "Come," he said. "Let us discuss this with Rokeby. And I want something to eat before I ride out to meet Carlisle."

Richmond turned to follow him. "Understood," he said. "You should have a little time. Carlisle is still well away at this point. I would guess that you will not have to leave for at least a...."

An abrupt sound from Lucien cut him off. The man grunted as if he'd been punched in the gut, a sharp and blunt exhale, and suddenly he pitched to his knees. Startled, Richmond looked down at his friend to see one of the spiny Yew arrows projecting from the lower portion of his back. As Lucien fell forward, Richmond dropped to his knees beside him, throwing his arms around the man so he wouldn't fall face-first into the frozen earth.

"My God," Richmond gasped, trying to hold on to Lucien and get a good look at the arrow location at the same time. "Easy, Lucien. Be easy. Let me see where you've been marked."

Lucien groaned, trying to stifle it. "Great Bloody Christ," he cursed softly. "Is it true? Did the bastards truly get me?"

Richmond held fast to Lucien, his heart pounding with apprehension. "I do not know how they managed to do it, but they did," he said, finally getting a look at the area of penetration. It was down by his right kidney, thankfully away from the spine, but that was still a very vital area. From the blood that was already pouring out, it was clear that something important had been hit. "I must get you out of here. I'd hate to have another barrage come sailing into us both. Can you stand, Lucien?"

The man with a reputation for being as tough as steel lurched to his feet even as Richmond tried to help him. But Lucien shook him off. He wouldn't take the help, not even from his dear friend. There was a massive spiny arrow sticking out of his back but Lucien began to walk, putting his hand back to feel at the arrow as Richmond followed alongside, astonished that the man was walking under his own power. It was a sheer tribute to the man's strength.

"Bastards," Lucien hissed, feeling the arrow as it was firmly stuck in his back. "Those bloody clodheads. If they think they can kill me, then they had better think again. No Percy arrow is going to strike me down."

He was charging forward but it was clear that he was weaving even as he walked. He was unsteady. Richmond didn't want to grab him, to insult him by insinuating that he wasn't strong enough to walk without assistance, but it became increasingly apparent that the arrow had done some damage. Lucien was losing blood in copious amounts and Richmond fought down his panic.

"You have faced worse than this," he said, trying to sound as if the strike wasn't as bad as it looked. "Let the physic remove the arrow and you shall be up and about in little time. In fact, I will call you lazy if you stay down any longer than an hour or two."

Lucien was starting to lose color in his face. "It is nothing, then?"

Richmond lied to him openly. "Nothing at all."

Lucien believed him. At least, he seemed to but it was difficult to tell. The color was draining from his face and his lips were turning an odd shade of blue. Just as they crested the rise over the battlefield and Henry's encampment was in sight, Lucien came to a staggering halt.

"God's Bones, Richmond," he muttered. "I… I do not believe that I feel very well."

He fell like a stone, unconscious. The Iron Knight, the man who was renowned for his durability, was suddenly human. He wasn't a statue made out of sinew and stone. He was a man of flesh and blood, and that blood was mingling with the frozen ground, pouring from his wounded body. The cry that rose from Richmond's lips at that moment could have been heard all the way to London.

Men came running from all directions.

CHAPTER ONE

Year of Our Lord 1410, the month of July
East of the village of Tisbury, Wiltshire, England

"WILL WE BE there soon, Mama?"

"By the setting of the sun. Continue with your sewing, sweetheart. It will make the time pass quicker."

On a gloriously warm summer's day, the fortified carriage rolled along the dusty road, escorted by four armed soldiers from the House of du Ponte. It was nearing noon and the day was in full bloom, with birds in the trees overhead and a cavalcade of insects hovering happily in the fields.

In fact, the season was almost too warm. Being this far south, there was the matter of the humidity along with the heat, and that combination tended to breed an unpleasant smell in both man and beast. Even now, the older woman in the carriage could smell that musty scent and she kept sniffing at her armpits and hands, discreetly of course, thinking that it might have been her. But she wasn't the smelling sort, which led her to believe it was the carriage itself. It wasn't *her* carriage.

It was the carriage of the man she was betrothed to.

It wasn't exactly a betrothal, in truth. The man in whose carriage she was traveling was a man that her father hoped would agree to a marital contract. Having been widowed for six years, Lady Sophina Seavington de Gournay had been living in her father's home in

Andover for that length of time and her father, a practical man, was displeased with the fact that he found himself supporting his adult daughter and young granddaughter.

Sophina knew her father had been impatient with her burden. He'd never made it any secret, which was unfortunate because Sophina's daughter, Emmaline, had grown up thinking no one wanted her or her mother.

Amory de Barenton, Lord Andover, had spent six years trying to find a husband for his widowed daughter, a widow without much of anything to induce a perspective husband other than a pretty face. A pity she is not well supplied, people would say as they clucked their tongues and shook their heads. Lady Sophina would make a fine wife were it not for her lack of fortune.

It was a fairly shameful way to exist. Sophina didn't like feeling like a burden; a proud and intelligent woman, she ran her father's house and hold, was smart with money, and was an excellent hostess to her father's business associates and friends, but she really wasn't needed any longer because her father had remarried himself two years ago and the new Lady Andover hated Sophina with a passion. Therefore, when a potential betrothal came up with St. Michael du Ponte, an extremely wealthy merchant with a prosperous import business, there was no question that Sophina should be sent to the man for his inspection.

It wasn't as if she'd had a choice.

So now Sophina found herself in a well-appointed carriage that reeked of body odor and four armed soldiers who seemed to be eyeing her with some curiosity. One of them even winked at her and when she didn't respond, he winked at her daughter. Sophina wasn't the nervous type but she was nervous around these soldiers, men she didn't know. She couldn't believe her father had sent her along without so much as an escort from his house. He'd never made it plainer that he was glad to be rid of her. Like unwanted baggage, she had been happily – and hastily – shipped out.

Therefore, the journey itself, although blessed with lovely weather, wasn't a particularly welcome one. It was wrought with anxiety. Sophina watched the countryside pass by, wondering what she was going to find at the end of the road. She'd never met the man who her father had suggested a marriage to and now she felt like she was to be a prize mare trotted out for a potential buyer.

"Oh!" Emmaline suddenly gasped. "Oswald, cease this moment! *Cease!*"

Diverted from her train of thought, Sophina looked at what had her daughter flustered and caught sight of a long, fluffy tail as it disappeared in the folds of her daughter's dress. Emmaline was trying to grab the creature it was attached to and, suddenly, a long and furry body came into view as Oswald the Ferret made his presence know.

Oswald was a nibbler; that is, he liked to put his teeth on everything. Not hard enough to bite, but enough to chew. Now, he was chewing at her daughter's fingers and the needlepoint the girl was trying to work on. He evidently wanted the bone needle she was working with and Emmaline was trying to push the beastie away.

"I thought he was sleeping," Sophina said, a faint smile on her lips as she watched her daughter wrestle with the pesky pet. "Mayhap he is hungry now."

Emmaline frowned as Oswald chewed on her finger. "Can you give him something to eat, Mama?" she half-asked, half-begged. "He is biting me!"

Sophina laughed softly as she dug around in the basket of food they had brought with them, pulling forth a small pork bone with meat still attached. She then pulled the ferret away from her daughter and held the bone up in the creature's line of sight. The reaction was instantaneous; the ferret grabbed the bone and happily planted itself between the ladies as it noisily bit into it. Pieces of pork began to fly.

Sophina watched the ferret gnaw enthusiastically on the bone. "My furry child is now satisfied," she said wryly, turning her attention back towards the basket. "Are you hungry, Em?"

Emmaline shook her head. "Nay," she said. "Not now."

Sophina glanced at her daughter, noting the girl's gaze had moved to the green summer landscape beyond the window. "You should eat something," she said. "You have not eaten since before dawn."

Emmaline shrugged, her needlework ending up in her lap. "Mama, are you afraid?"

"Of what?"

"Of meeting your new husband."

"He is not my husband, yet."

Emmaline sighed. "Not yet," she agreed quietly. "But he will be. Grandfather will see to that, no matter what you think of him. Even if you hate him or even if he is a terrible ogre, you will still have to marry him."

Sophina was careful in her reply. At sixteen years of age, Emmaline was astute, brighter than most. She had fostered in her younger years, in a good house, but that ended when Sophina's husband had died. The lord where Emmaline had been fostering tried to broker a contract between Emmaline and his son of the same age, a lad who had been born with the mind of an infant. Evidently, the lord thought Emmaline would have been a good match for the boy now that she was fatherless and the lord believed he could play upon Sophina's fear for her daughter's future now that her father was dead. But Sophina would not be bullied. She had her daughter sent home immediately and far away from the unscrupulous lord.

Now, as Sophina looked at her child, she was coming to think that Emmaline had seen a good deal of strife in her young age – her father's death, devious lords, and a grandfather who barely acknowledged her. Now the girl was facing the prospect of her mother marrying a man neither of them knew and the good Lord only knew what kind of man St. Michael du Ponte was. This wasn't the type of life Sophina had wished for her lovely, smart daughter. She wanted something so much better for the lass.

It was difficult not to fear the future for them both.

"I am sure Grandfather would not have sent us to the house of an ogre," Sophina said evenly. "I am sure he is hoping for a satisfactory marriage."

Emmaline wasn't so sure. Her mother had a way of glossing over things and Emmaline knew that it was because her mother was trying to protect her. But she was a young woman now and she was not afraid of the truth – the truth that women were pawns in the world. Sometimes they were welcome, sometimes they were not. They had no rights and no say in their lives. She thought that was a rather terrible existence.

"Mayhap," Emmaline said, glancing at her mother for a moment before looking away. "I suppose anywhere we go will be better than where we were."

She sounded depressed and defeated. Sophina hated hearing that tone in her daughter's voice. She was too young to sound as if life held no joy for her. But the truth was that it didn't; it hadn't for a while. Reaching out, Sophina patted her daughter's hand, squeezing her fingers, giving her silent encouragement that all would be well. They would find a place where they were wanted. She was about to tell her daughter so when a loud clamoring sounded against the side of the carriage.

The entire vehicle rocked sideways and the women could hear the soldiers yelling to one another, shouting about something the ladies couldn't quite make out. By the tone of their voices, however, they were agitated. Something had happened and as the women looked at each other in apprehension and confusion, something, once again, hit the side of the carriage. It sounded like pebbles being thrown until an arrowhead pierced the wooden side. Emmaline saw the sharp tip about six inches from her head and she let out a scream.

"Get down!" Sophina yanked on her daughter's hand, pulling the girl to the floor of the carriage. "Get down and put your hands over your head!"

Gasping with fright, Emmaline clumsily threw herself onto her belly on the floor of the carriage, putting her hands up to cover her strawberry-blonde head as her mother came down on top of her. Emmaline grunted with the force of her mother's weight, which was fairly insignificant, in truth. It was simply that Sophina had come down right on top of her, trying to protect her. As more projectiles hit the side of the carriage, Sophina had the good sense to grab Oswald and shove the beast inside of the food basket to protect him. Outside of the carriage, a full-scale war took place.

Men were yelling and horses were nervously yelping. In fact, the four horses that pulled the carriage were dancing about so that the carriage was jerking around, tossing Sophina and Emmaline around carelessly. Sophina ended up being bounced off of her daughter as the carriage threw them about, slamming into the side of the carriage and hitting her elbow.

Darts of pain shot up through Sophina's arm as she struggled to get back to her daughter, but just as she reached Emmaline and grabbed the lass by the sleeve, the entire carriage suddenly tipped over, spilling them about like rag dolls. As the women screamed, the men fought around them. There was chaos and pandemonium everywhere.

The carriage was still being dragged by panicked horses tethered to harnesses that were still attached to the cab and it was now imperative that the women keep their arms and clothing away from the open side of the carriage that was now on the ground. If anything got caught up in that opening, the carriage would have been dragged over it, possibly breaking limbs or even strangling them. Sophina pushed her daughter onto one of the benches, now sideways, and she leapt onto the other one, trying to stay away from the dragging ground.

"Mama!" Emmaline screamed.

Sophina held out a hand to her daughter to stop her from moving. "Stay where you are," she commanded. "Hold on to something until this carriage comes to a halt!"

But that wasn't to be. The soldiers driving the carriage team were fighting for their lives as the terrified horses plowed down the side of the road and towards a lake that was at the bottom of it. Usually an idyllic lake, one with reeds and fish and small birds that would hunt for their meals beneath the lilies, now was looming ahead like a death trap.

And neither Sophina nor Emmaline could see it coming.

༄

Spelthorne Castle, Dorset
Seat of the Tytherington Barony

"WHERE ARE YOU going?"

A young knight asked the question with concern and puzzlement, but Lucien didn't reply right away. He simply pushed past him, quickly, as if he had some place to be.

"Away," he finally said. "*Out.* I am going out to clear my head."

The young knight, Sir Colton de Royans, was nearly bowled over by his liege, no easy feat considering the size of Colton. A very big man with enormous shoulders and hands, he was a blindingly brilliant young warrior of twenty years and had been with Lucien since eleven years of age when his father, Weston, had personally delivered his eldest son to his friend and comrade to foster.

Weston de Royans, Baron Cononley and Constable of the North Yorkshire Dales, had been very emotional trusting his beloved son to The Iron Knight, but it had been necessary. Colton had been a spoilt, outspoken, gifted, and humorous youth who had been vastly overindulged by his adoring father. It had been up to Lucien to remove the spoilt edges and help mold the boy into one of the best young knights of his generation.

It had worked, but it hadn't been without a struggle. Colton had been headstrong and stubborn, but Lucien had been patient. Patience, and a few fatherly beatings, had helped turn the unruly boy into a confident man. Colten grew to adore Lucien, which had turned their relationship into a fond one. They adored each other, to be truthful.

Colton was the son that Lucien had always wanted.

But Colton also interacted with Lucien in a way that Lucien's other knights wouldn't dare. He told the man what he thought and, most often, he didn't hold back. He was quite bold and had the fighting skill to back up that boldness. Like now; he grasped Lucien by the arm before he could completely get away.

"Go where?" he asked. "You cannot leave when Lord de Saix and his daughter are due to arrive any moment. They will expect you to greet them."

Lucien came to a halt, mostly because Colton was dragging on him. He turned to look at the blonde-haired knight, a very handsome young man and also a very tenacious one. He knew very well that Colton might hang on to him and not let him leave and then he would find himself in a fight. He sighed heavily, looking at Colton's hand on his arm.

"Let me go," he said quietly.

Colton refused. "Lucien, you cannot leave," he said quietly but firmly. "I know you have no interest in this contract, but Henry himself arranged it. It was Henry who personally sent you the missive about gifting you with a very wealthy bride and because he is taking such an interest in this betrothal, if you run out now, you will not only insult the lady and her entire family, but the king as well. You *know* this."

Lucien was, indeed, aware. He could feel that formidable de Russe anger swelling in his chest. "I do not need you to lecture me," he said, jerking his arm and breaking Colton's grasp. "I am well aware of what is at stake."

"And yet you would still leave?"

"I did not say I was going forever!"

Colton pursed his lips wryly at him. "You did not say that you were *not* going forever, either," he pointed out. "Lucien, truly. You simply cannot leave because you do not want to face them. You will have to face them sooner or later."

Wise words from the young knight that halted Lucien in his tracks. He lost some of his fight then, feeling foolish for having been reminded of the truth from a man young enough to be his son. He visibly relaxed, sulking now.

"I know," he muttered unhappily, running his hands through his long, dark hair. "But... with God as my witness, Colton, you know that I did not want this. I never wanted it. I never asked for it nor did I ever make any mention of anything having to do with a betrothal. This is all Henry's idea and, although I know he believes he is rewarding me, the opposite is true. I do not want a wife. I am too old for one and I am especially too old for this one. She is younger than you are and, from what I've heard, a spoilt little minx. I do not want that in my midst much less married to it."

"Who told you that?"

Lucien's eyes narrowed. "I have friends. Men who know her father have told me such things."

Colton wasn't sure he believed him but he didn't say so. He knew that Lucien would do anything to remove himself from having to face this unwelcome betrothal. He had been with Lucien when, two weeks ago, the man had opened a missive from the king only to discover he was soon to be a husband. It had not been a happy moment in the life of a man who had known more than his share of unhappiness.

Colton felt a good deal of pity for Lucien; he truly did. The man wanted nothing more than to live a quiet life, alone, and die old and warm in his bed. But that was evidently not to be. The king had other ideas about one of his favorite warriors.

Ideas that this particular warrior was not receptive to.

"Well," Colton said thoughtfully, "I can always have a horde of soldiers ambush her and her father on the road and chase them home. Would that be your pleasure, my lord?"

Lucien scowled. "It would be, but I would be in a good deal of trouble if I let you do that," he said. Then, he lifted his dark eyebrows as if a thought had just occurred to him. "Why don't you charm her, Colton? You are much better looking than I am. Why don't you make her fall in love with you so that she will not want to marry me?"

Colton saw very little humor in that suggestion. "Not I."

"Why not?"

"Because I am too young to marry."

"I could command it, you know."

"Nay, you cannot. I will refuse."

"You would refuse a direct order?"

Colton nodded firmly. "I will run straight to Henry and tell him what you have done." He pointed a finger at Lucien. "You may be able to force me into submission, but Henry shall have the last laugh, Lord Tytherington. Mark my words."

Lucien's scowl grew. "Cheeky bastard," he grumbled. He watched Colton stand there with a rather triumphant expression on his face and it infuriated him. "Do what you like, then. I am going on a ride to clear my head before this... this *succubus* arrives with her father. She is going to bleed me dry, I know it."

Colton bit off a grin. "She very well may be a nice girl."

Lucien simply growled and rolled his eyes, turning to quit the chamber. Colton, now grinning, followed.

They were in the keep of Spelthorne Castle, a bastion that had been built much in the style of Sherborne Castle to the southwest. The land in the area, as a whole, was rather flat with great groves of trees and wild growth. There were no hills to speak of, at least hills enough to constitute the high ground, so Spelthorne had been built in the middle of a flat plain, built up on a mound of earth that had been dug out from the moat which surrounded it. Twenty-foot walls surrounded the grounds, which were comprised of a three-storied keep, square and broad, a hall, stables, an enormous troop house, kitchens, and even a garden. The garden, however, was for vegetables and herbs, not flowers, and the kitchen servants tended it. It was fairly extensive.

In all, Spelthorne was the seat of the Tytherington Barony, something Lucien was quite proud of. The king had gifted it to him several years ago as a reward for meritorious service to the crown and Lucien kept the peace for Henry from Shaftesbury to the west and Salisbury to the east, Warminster to the north and Fordingbridge to the south. It was quite a large territory but Lucien had over a thousand men sworn to him alone, plus he also housed another one thousand of Henry's troops. Combined, he had more than enough men to cover the territory and the Tytherington Barony was one of the most powerful in southern England. Where The Iron Knight reigned, men were naturally respectful.

Men were naturally wary, too, of a knight who was more apt to show action first and talk later. Lucien had that reputation. He always brought might to any disturbance or contention to secure the situation before getting to the meat of the crisis. Lucien had lived too long and had seen too many things to behave in any other fashion. He hadn't time for men's foolery or politics. His job was one of service and peace, and he did both admirably.

At the moment, however, he was in a situation where his usual forthright manner or an armed force would do no good, unless he wanted Colton to send out men to ambush his betrothed and her father, which he did not. His hands were tied and he knew it. Purging himself from the innards of Spelthorne's powerful keep, he made his way to the stables with Colton on his heels.

"Did you hear me?" the young knight called after him. "She may very well be a nice girl and if you leave, you will be insulting her for nothing. Is this really how you want to start off your marriage?"

Lucien came to an abrupt halt and Colton nearly smashed into the back of him. "Enough," Lucien snarled, holding up an angry finger. "Give me time to digest this situation. I do not need your ridiculous chatter. You are making me angry."

Colton stepped back, trying very hard not to smile. Lucien wasn't beyond throwing a punch when riled and the man had a devastating blow. "I am sorry," Colton said contritely. "I am simply trying to help you see the entire situation, not simply your perspective alone. I do not want you to anger Henry and I do not want you insulting your future relations. They will think you a cad and a boor, and you are neither of those things."

Lucien pursed his lips irritably; the lad was right and he knew it. He took a deep breath, struggling for calm.

"I will not insult anyone," he said, less anger in his tone. "I simply want to clear my head and think. If the lady and her father arrive while I am gone, you will simply tell them I had business to attend to and apologize for my absence. But say no more; make them comfortable and I will return… when I feel like it."

Colton couldn't help but chuckle, then. He watched Lucien march off towards the stables, wisely choosing not to follow him. He'd already pressed his liege as much as he was willing. In truth, he could do no more. The rest was up to Lucien.

In spite of what he'd told Colton, Lucien wasn't entirely sure he would return at all. As he made his way into the stables for his horse, he found that he was quite willing to forsake all of this simply to be free of an unwanted marriage. He'd built Spelthorne Castle into a great military might but he wasn't beyond abandoning it. His freedom and his sanity meant more to him than a few blocks of stone did. Well… not really, perhaps. But his convictions sounded good in theory.

So he had the stable master saddle his big dappled rouncey, the one with the big arse and hairy hooves. It was a formidable beast, one he'd traveled with and taken into battle innumerable times. He had several chargers, temperamental and powerful beasts, but he preferred the company of his old friend, Storm. He and Storm thought alike, acted alike. In fact, the big horse greeted Lucien like an old friend, nuzzling him, licking his shoulder and neck, until Lucien gently pushed the big horse's head away and vaulted into the saddle.

Thundering out from the big gatehouse of Spelthorne, Lucien headed south under fair skies and moderate winds. It was a warm day, breezy, and as he gently rode along the countryside, he could feel his stress easing. Surely nothing could be so terrible on a glorious day like this. The road wasn't particularly bad, as the summer season hadn't been terribly wet, so the ground upon which Storm trod was even and dry. The big horse lifted his hooves in a prancing way as he loped, his hairy tufts on his legs waving in the breeze along with his big silver tail. He was happy to be out and about.

So was Lucien. He felt much like the horse, happy to flee Spelthorne for the moment. The place belonged to him and as much as it was his refuge, it was also his hell. He thought on his prospective new wife and what she would mean to his way of life. He thought of his daughter who, at ten years of age, ruled the house and hold, but not in a good way. Perhaps in a sense, he was running from her, too.

She was, in a word, a terror.

Susanna Isobelle de Reyne de Russe had been born with a weak spine and legs as the result of a difficult birth, a birth that had killed her mother. Susanna was bright and beautiful, but her behavior was atrocious. But it was his own fault; Lucien had made her what she was. He'd catered to her and spoiled her until she was positively unmanageable. There was no one else to blame. Guilt and remorse beat into him on a daily basis because of it.

He couldn't help the shame... Laurabel's death, Susanna's injury. He was the man of the family, wasn't he? Hadn't it been his job to protect his wife and daughter? He'd failed miserably. Surely there was something more he could have done.

But there hadn't been. Even Lucien knew that, deep down, but he still couldn't shake the guilt. Now he found himself wondering if his new betrothed and his daughter would be able to co-exist. Would a female influence help Susanna's behavior? Or would it make it worse? He could only imagine that his daughter wouldn't react well to another woman at Spelthorne and, quite frankly, Lucien wouldn't react well to it, either.

He couldn't even control the one he had.

With thoughts revolving around his betrothed and his daughter, Lucien continued to make his way south, enjoying the day, trying to feel some joy for the life and blessings he had. He had many things, in truth, far better than most. A lucrative and powerful command and the respect of all of England. But a pain in his back reminded him of the fact that he wasn't as strong as he liked to pretend he was; the injury from the battle at Bramham still hadn't fully healed and rides such as this, and any extensive exertion, quickly exhausted him.

That arrow to his back had nicked a major blood supply vessel and destroyed his right kidney, and his body, at his age, still hadn't healed correctly, especially from the infection that followed. Poison had taken over his body and damaged his innards badly. He still had pains and weakness because of it.

But he ignored those symptoms. At least, he tried to. He couldn't submit to anything that made him feel or appear anything other than completely healthy and in control. The truth, however, was that the strong, healthy man known for his iron constitution before Bramham was quite different following the injury in battle. It was simply the way of things, but Lucien hated the weakness. He hated that he wasn't the same any longer. Still, he did his best to mask that fragility. Only those very close to him knew of it, or could see it, but to everyone else, he was still the same.

Inside, however, so much of him was dying, beaten, or already dead.

So much of him was already gone.

Lost in thoughts of his injury and his destiny, Lucien slowly eased Storm back, slowing the animal's pace. They were far enough south of Spelthorne now and away from the major road junctions that he was certain to miss the arrival of his betrothed and her father. That had been his goal. Now, he was free to ride about and enjoy the scenery, reconciling himself to what was to come. He was too old to appreciate change these days. That was his primary problem; he didn't want to change. He didn't want to assume more burdens than he already had.

The town of Tisbury appeared off to the southeast, a village he was quite fond of and where he was the administrative justice. It was part of his barony. Tisbury was a bustling place and there was prosperity there, something Lucien was proud of. He'd worked hard to eliminate any undesirable element, crime and outlaws, leaving the town for the good folks. The villeins were mostly farmers and tradesmen, although there were a few merchants who imported goods from Ireland as well as the continent. There was a good deal of trade coming in from the ports of Southampton, which was only a day's ride to the southeast.

The breeze was picking up a little now, stirring the trees overhead, and he caught sight of a fallow deer and fawn off in the shrubbery. He reined Storm to a halt, taking a deep breath, inhaling the placid moment. So much of his world was wrought with warfare or politics or stress, so a moment like this, in the warmth of the day, beneath the shading canopy, was unusually tranquil for him. It was needed. Over to his right was a thick bit of foliage and a small lake beyond. He thought that the shore of that lake looked just right for a nap. So what if the succubus and her father were arriving at Spelthorne at this very moment? He would take his time returning.

God only knew, once he returned, he would probably never be allowed to leave alone ever again.

Using pressure from his thighs, he turned Storm through the thicket and towards the lake. Just as the horse moved off of the road, however, he began to hear screaming. Puzzled, he thought he heard it coming from the direction of the lake and he pushed the horse through the brush, his eagle-eyed gaze moving across the water, the shore, and the surrounding area. It didn't take him long to see a carriage sliding down the shoreline towards the lake and landing in the water with a jarring splash.

More than that, he could see panicked horses attached to the carriage and a gang of men fighting all around it. The screams were coming from inside the carriage. As he watched the carriage settle into the water and begin to slowly sink, he swung into action.

Storm bolted across the shoreline, thundering towards the fight and the sinking carriage. Lucien was fully aware that he didn't have his broadsword, but that didn't matter at the moment. He had two daggers on his person as well as fists that could drop a grown man in one punch. He didn't much fear what he was getting himself in to but the frightened female screams had his attention. The carriage was sinking, taking on more water now, and an auburn head suddenly popped up from one of the carriage windows as the vehicle lay on its side.

Lucien didn't wait. He ran Storm right into the water and dove off of the saddle, straight into the lake. He came up, swimming furiously towards the carriage as the auburn-haired woman struggled to pull another woman out of the carriage behind her.

Lucien was a good swimmer and he made it to the carriage in little time, heaving himself up onto the axel and climbing up onto the side of the carriage where the auburn-haired woman was. The moment he moved next to her, however, she shrieked and lashed out at him, knocking him in the face. Off-balance, Lucien fell back into the water below.

Shaking the stars from his eyes, he surfaced on the water and climbed up onto the axel again. This time, he made no move to climb up next to the panicked woman.

"Lady," he said, wiping blood and water from his nose. "I mean you no harm, I swear it. Let me help you away from here before you drown."

The woman was terrified; he could see it in her face. A rather exquisite face, in fact. "Stay away," she cried. "I have nothing of value for you to rob me of! Stay away or I will kick you before you can get near me again!"

Lucien looked around, seeing the fighting going on. There were six soldiers bearing blue and yellow tunics and then host of very poorly dressed men, fighting the soldiers. One of the soldiers was down and another was struggling with the carriage horses, cutting their harnesses free from the weight of the carriage. That left four to fight off at least ten poorly-dressed men and, in that state, they were sorely outnumbered. It didn't take a genius to figure out what was going on. Lucien turned back to the woman, who was now pulling a young girl from the window.

"I assure you, lady, that I am not an outlaw," he said. "I do not know who attacked you but I am not part of it. I was riding by and heard your screams. Please allow me to help you and your friend before you both drown."

The auburn-haired woman was still very wary. She clutched at the younger woman, who was now out of the carriage and weeping. It was evident that they were both terrified. Before the woman could threaten him again, Lucien extended a hand.

"Please," he said, softly and gently. He had that ability to be tender when he wanted to. "Let me help you. I swear to you that my intentions are noble."

The auburn-haired woman eyed him, her expression quite torn. Given the carriage had sunk substantially into the lake, however, she had little choice. It continued to sink as she pondered Lucien's offer.

"We cannot swim," she finally said. Suddenly, she thrust the young girl at him. "Take my daughter. Save her, please."

Lucien still had his hand extended to her. "I can save you both," he said calmly. "Come down her with me. Climb down carefully and I will take you to safety."

With a moment's further hesitation, the auburn-haired woman relented and helped her daughter towards Lucien, who took the girl carefully, helping her to climb down the axel and into the water. Lucien couldn't quite stand in the depth so he held on to the carriage as the girl climbed down, weeping softly as she lowered herself into the water. Lucien took hold of her.

"Come over here, love," he said gently, coaxing her over to him. "Come and hold on to my neck. Grab me from behind; that's it. You are doing very well."

The young girl was barely a feather's weight holding on to him. Her small hands were cold and wet around his neck. Looking up, Lucien could see the mother beginning to descend.

"Come along, my lady," he said. "Watch your step; do not slip on the grease. That's right; carefully, now."

The auburn-haired woman was moving very slowly, very timidly. It was clear that she was terrified of the water, as she kept looking at it thinking she was descending into a pit of fire. Lucien put his hand up when she drew close, helping guide her as she lowered herself into the water. Once she was in, she looked at Lucien with such terror that he was struck with pity. The woman was nearly panicking but managed to keep herself under control. He took her hand, pulling her towards him.

"Hold on to my neck, just as your daughter is doing," he said steadily. "Hold fast and I shall remove you from this water with all due haste. It will take no time at all, I promise."

The woman gripped his hand tightly enough to break bones but Lucien managed to steer her towards his neck. She threw one arm around his neck and shoulders while the other held on to her softly-sobbing child. It was then that Lucien let go of the carriage and began to swim for his life, away from the shore where the fighting was and over to the shore where Storm was ripping up soft, green grass.

The water was cold as Lucien plowed through it, swimming with all of his strength, dragging the women behind him. They were holding on to him with a death-grip but at least the young girl had stopped weeping. She was still sniffling; he could hear it, but he could also hear the auburn-haired woman speaking sweetly to her, comforting her.

"'Twill be all right, sweetheart, she said. *We are almost to the shore. See how close it is? We are almost there. You are being very brave."*

Such sweet and gentle words in a voice that was liquid and soft, like flowing honey. God, he could have listened to that voice all day. He could feel the woman's arm around his right shoulder, her hand on his neck. Her flesh was cold but there was something different in her touch, something electric and intense. It was like being branded without the searing heat. He couldn't explain it any better than that.

Soon enough, his feet hit the soft bottom of the lake and he began to walk, trudging up to the shoreline to the point where the women could also put their feet down. They let go of him but *he* didn't let go of them. He kept a grip on them both, helping them out of the water and onto dry ground. Only when he was certain they were clear of the lake did he finally let go. Exhausted and feeling quite weak now that the crisis was over, he sank down to his knees, breathing heavily, coughing to clear his lungs.

Next to him, the auburn-haired woman and her daughter also sank into the grass, holding on to one another, grateful to be alive. The young girl clung to her mother as the woman sat and rocked her, her hand gently stroking the young girl's head. Lucien, who had been looking over at the fighting on the opposite shore, heard a soft voice beside him.

"We owe you a great debt, my lord," the auburn-haired woman said. "I do not know if we can ever fully repay you for risking your life for us. You have my unending gratitude."

Lucien looked at her. Her long auburn hair was wet from the shoulders down, a dark and rich shade of red that glistened in the sunlight. The woman had skin of porcelain, a sweetly oval face, and eyes that were the color of red brick. Such incredibly beautiful eyes. For a moment, he was actually struck speechless by her beauty as he looked at her but, realizing she had spoken to him, he cleared his throat softly to reply.

"I am happy to have been of service, my lady," he said. Then, he threw a thumb in the direction of the fight, which was dwindling. Men were mostly running away at that point. "Is your husband in that battle? Do you wish for me to assist him?"

The woman shook her head. "My husband is long-dead, my lord," she said. "You have done quite enough. I would not trouble you further."

As they watched the fighting, the last of the blue-garbed soldiers ran up the embankment, evidently chasing the outlaws, and grabbed their horses. They could hear shouting and the rumble of horses' hooves as the animals began to run off. It was a commotion, with everyone scattering, and abruptly, they were all alone. The soldiers, the outlaws, and all of the horses, including the carriage horses, suddenly vanished. Everything was very quiet now. The young girl, still in her mother's arms, suddenly let out a shriek.

"Oswald!" she cried, lurching to her feet and running towards the water. "Mother, it's Oswald!"

Lucien had no idea what she was talking about until he saw a furry head above the water, swimming frantically for shore. Curious, he watched as the head came closer and closer, and the young girl dared to take a couple of steps in to the water. She reached out and grabbed the head, which was attached to a long and wet furry body. The girl scampered out of the water, the ferret clutched to her chest.

"Praise God," the auburn-haired woman gasped, holding up her arms to both her daughter and the pet. "He survived; I was afraid he was trapped inside."

The young girl was back to weeping. "Oh, Ozzie," she sniffled, kissing the wet head. "I do not know what I would do without you. You are safe now."

Lucien watched the exchange closely. He thought this reunion to be rather sweet and, now that everyone was safe, there was a huge sense of relief. But it didn't change the fact that the lady's escort had evidently run off. Stiffly, he rose to his feet.

"Who were the men you were with, my lady?" he asked, scanning the trees on the opposite shore to see if he saw any sign of them. "Where were you traveling?"

The auburn-haired woman could see that her escort had vacated, too. The half-sunk carriage was in the lake with no sign of any soldiers or outlaws. Leaving her daughter cuddling the pet, she stood up, trying to brush off her sopping gown, trying not to look so completely disheveled.

"I am sure they will return," she said. "You need not trouble yourself further, my lord. You have already been a tremendous help today. We are eternally grateful."

Lucien looked at her. "I will not leave you until I know the situation," he said flatly. "*Who* were those men and where were you traveling?"

The auburn-haired woman seemed rather embarrassed to explain. "They... they serve a man whom my father hopes will become my husband," she said. "I was traveling to meet him."

"Where were you going?"

"Gillingham Castle, my lord."

He stared at her a moment. "Gillingham?" he repeated. "That is St. Michael du Ponte's home. Are you going to meet with him?"

The auburn-hair woman nodded. "I am, my lord," she said. "Do you know him?"

Lucien eyed her; did he know St. Michael? Indeed, he did. He knew the prick of a man who was one of the more unscrupulous bastards around. Du Ponte was a lord by background, a gambler by trade, and a lowlife by reputation. Rumor had it that he funded outlaws in Dorset and Devon, taking a portion of their ill-gotten gains in exchange for protection.

Men had been trying to prove the accusations for years but, so far, no one had been able to levy charges against du Ponte because there were very few witnesses willing to testify against him. People weren't apt to turn on a man who could make their lives truly miserable.

"Aye," he finally said. "I know him. But you do not?"

"Nay, my lord. I have never met him."

"How does your father know him?"

She shrugged. "They both travel in the same social circles," she said. "They have met on many occasions."

"Who is your father?"

"Amory de Barenton, Lord Andover."

Lucien knew of the man. He'd heard the name and knew he was a staunch supporter of Henry but beyond that, he didn't know much about him. He couldn't imagine why the man would be associating with the likes of St. Michael du Ponte. But he didn't say anything to that regard, or give way to what he was thinking, because the lady was looking up at him quite curiously with those spectacular eyes. He smiled thinly.

"I have heard of your father," he said. "Forgive me for not introducing myself before this moment. My name is de Russe. I realize it is socially incorrect for us to be introduced without an intermediary, but it seems we find ourselves in rather extenuating circumstances."

The auburn-haired woman grinned. "We do, indeed," she said as she dropped into a practiced curtsy. "It is an honor to meet you, my lord. I am Lady Sophina de Gournay and this is my daughter, Lady Emmaline."

Sophina. Her name was as beautiful and unusual as she was. Lucien's smile turned genuine. "You forgot to introduce the furry fish your daughter is holding."

Sophina grinned, turning to look at her daughter, who was holding the ferret tightly. "That is Sir Oswald," she said. "He is our entertainment on this journey."

Lucien couldn't take his eyes off Sophina; she had a smile that positively lit up the sky. It was bright and beautiful. As he looked at her, he realized that his heart was beating just a little faster, perhaps even fluttering, and he thought it quite an odd reaction to a woman. He'd never known anything like it in his life, at least not that he could remember. He seemed to recall a similar feeling with Laurabel, but that had been a very long time ago. He thought he was beyond any such excitement when it came to a woman. But seeing Sophina smile made him want to smile. It made him want to sigh with delight at the sheer beauty of the gesture.

"Ah," he said, trying to cover for the fact that he was quite blatantly staring at her. "A loyal traveling companion, I see. But it is unfortunate that your journey came to such a violent pause."

Sophina's smile faded. "It could have been much worse," she said. "We have our lives and that is truly all that matters. However, I am concerned that we have been abandoned. I do hope du Ponte's soldiers return for us soon."

Lucien looked around; there wasn't any hint of soldiers returning. He couldn't see or hear anything and he certainly couldn't leave the women alone in this wilderness. He realized that it gave him great pleasure to ponder the possibility of them returning with him to Spelthorne because he wasn't finished basking in Lady Sophina's beauty, not in the least. She wasn't some silly, giddy girl; she was a mature woman with a young lady for a daughter. Even through the panic of the carriage crash, other than punching him in the nose at the onset, the woman conveyed maturity and a calmness that only came with age. She had grown up, she had lived, and she had experienced.

He liked that.

"It is my sense that the soldiers may have run off to chase down the bandits," he said. "They may have returned to Gillingham altogether. In any case, I cannot leave you and your daughter here, alone. You will return with me to my home where I will send word to du Ponte on your whereabouts."

Some anxiety returned to Sophina's expression. "I am greatly appreciative of your concern, my lord," she said hesitantly. "I insist that we would be perfectly fine at an inn in town."

"Do you have coinage?"

Embarrassed, she averted her gaze. "I do," she replied, eyeing the sunken carriage. "But it is at the bottom of the lake along with all of our possessions."

Lucien turned to look at the carriage in the lake; only a corner of it and part of a wheel were visible. "Then we shall return to Spelthorne Castle and I will send my men back here to retrieve your possessions," he said decisively. "Even if I fished them out, I have no way of carrying them back. They are safer underwater right now than they would be sitting on the bank for anyone to take."

Sophina was reluctant to agree. "I suppose you are correct," she said, watching him as he turned and whistled for his fat horse. The horse was off foraging in the thick grass several feet away. But it was clear that something more was bothering her and she summoned her courage to speak of it. "My lord, I pray you do not think me foolish or ungrateful, but we do not know you. It would not be prudent to return to the home of a man I am not acquainted with. I am sure du Ponte's men will return for us shortly so, with your permission, we will wait here."

She was being cautious, as she very well should be, but Lucien didn't have time for such nonsense. She was sopping wet, as was her daughter, as was he. They all needed to get before a warm fire and put on dry clothing. Moreover, he wasn't about to leave her and he certainly didn't want to leave her for du Ponte's men to take her on to Gillingham. That thieving wretch wasn't nearly worthy of a woman like this.

Although Lucien didn't know much about her, he didn't really have to – he could simply tell what kind of character she had by looking her in the eye. Her manner, her behavior, and their conversation had confirmed his observations – she was a woman of integrity and strength. He had a gift to know such things, an intuition, and it had never steered him wrong.

He didn't want to let her get away.

"You said you've never met du Ponte, yet you were clearly heading for his home," he pointed out. "You, at least, have met me. If I have not introduced myself correctly, then allow me to do so. I am Sir Lucien de Russe, eldest son of Sir Aramis de Russe, Duke of Exeter. I am, by birth, Baron Exminster, but I am also Lord Tytherington, Sheriff of Cranborne, a title bestowed upon me by King Henry, and the seat of my fiefdom is at Spelthorne Castle. I am the pinnacle of law and order in this area and if anyone is able to protect you and your daughter ably, my lady, that would be me. Now, are you still reluctant to return home with me?"

By this time, Sophina was looking at him with some awe. "Nay, my lord," she said quickly. "You... you are really the sheriff?"

"I would not lie to you."

She recovered quickly. "I did not mean to imply that," she said. "It is simply that it was quite fortuitous for you to be here when we needed help."

"Indeed, it was."

"I am sorry we have been so much trouble."

Lucien was pleased that his litany of titles had achieved the desired effect. She was impressed, as he meant she should be. She was also willing to comply with his suggestions and he was thrilled. He reached out to grasp the horse as it came near.

"You have been no trouble at all, my lady," he said. "You and your daughter may ride the horse and I will walk. It is not a long journey back to Spelthorne."

There wasn't much more to say at that point and Sophina pulled her daughter to her feet, watching protectively as Lucien lifted the girl onto the horse. Then he turned and put his hands around Sophina's small waist, lifting the woman onto the saddle behind her daughter. It had been so long since he felt a woman in his hands that he thought he might have lingered on her a little longer than he should have, quickly removing his hands when he realized that he should have long taken his hands from her. But there was something about the feel of her against his flesh, that branding feeling again, that he found both fascinating and magnetic.

Not only did he like the look of her, he liked the feel of her as well.

The long walk back to Spelthorne turned out to be one of the more pleasant experiences of his life.

CHAPTER TWO

Spelthorne Castle

"LOOK AT ALL of this, Juno," a man with a graying beard and wildly bushy eyebrows spoke. "All of this shall be yours when you marry de Russe. Does this not please you?"

Lady Juno de Saix had just emerged from her fine carriage into the dusty bailey of Spelthorne Castle. She was dressed in her finest, silk with gold threading, jewelry that had belonged to her mother, and her cousin had dressed her hair in an elaborate style that displayed the thickness, color, and length.

It was her crowning glory, this head of luscious brunette hair that she cultivated, and she was very proud of it. It had brought her many a compliment, so she smoothed at her hair, carefully, as her cousin climbed out of the cab behind her. Her cousin began brushing furiously at the red silk that already had dust on it. Summer breezes kicking up in the bailey already had a fine coating of dirt around the bottom, but the cousin would have none of it as Juno tried to push her away. She didn't want to be beaten like rug in front of everyone.

"It… it *is* big," Juno said hesitantly, looking up at the mighty keep and the complex of buildings that clustered around it, including a great hall. "It is a very impressive."

Wardell de Saix, Earl of Holderness, pulled off an expensive glove and scratched at his forehead. As a man who valued political connections above all, he was thrilled at the prospect of being related to Lucien de Russe by marriage. De Russe was old for his daughter, that was true, but Juno had seen seventeen summers and she was wise beyond her years. She was also lovely, graceful, accomplished in the areas of painting, singing, literature, and religious practices, and she could speak three languages. Therefore, she made a fine match for a man who held more titles than most and would inherit the dukedom of Exeter upon the death of his father. It would be a great political marriage.

Even so, Holderness knew that his daughter was oppositional to the marriage. Juno had been subdued since they'd left their home but he wouldn't resort to discussing her issues with her. He knew what they were and they were of no concern to him. Holderness had plans for his daughter regardless of her personal feelings on the matter. With his own son in line to inherit the Holderness earldom, it was Holderness' intention that his daughter should marry very well also. The dukedom of Exeter was marrying exceptionally well, in his opinion, and he intended to do all he could to ensure the marriage happened. Moreover, he had to get her married off and married quickly.

There was a little matter of a secret she was hiding.

"It has been long time since I have been here," a big, dark-haired knight walked up beside Holderness, a warrior bearing the red and green colors of Holderness. Sir Laurent de Saix looked over his surroundings as he loosened his heavy leather gauntlets. "The last time I was here was sometime around the Battle of Shrewsbury, I believe. De Russe was gathering troops for a northward march at the time."

Holderness wasn't particularly interested in his son's recollections. His head bobbed around like he was looking for someone. "Where *is* de Russe?" he demanded. "I would expect the man to greet us immediately."

Laurent looked around as well. "He will come," he said. "In spite of what you think, Papa, the man isn't waiting around to throw himself at your feet the moment you enter the gates. Lucien de Russe is a very busy man."

Holderness looked at his son with outrage. "Too busy to greet his future wife?" he said hotly. "Deplorable behavior. He should be right here, right in front of us, to…."

"Greetings, my lords, my lady." A big, handsome blonde knight interrupted. Having approached from the direction of the hall, he bowed politely to the group. "I am Sir Colton de Royans. I have been asked to see to your comfort, as Lord Tytherington is indisposed at the moment. He begs your forgiveness but he shall join you as soon as his duties permit."

Holderness couldn't decide if that smooth explanation placated him or not. "Where is Sir Lucien?" he asked. "I expected him to greet us the moment we arrived."

Colton cleared his throat softly. "He sends his sincere regrets that duties have kept him, my lord," he said. It was then that he noticed Laurent standing next to his father. He grinned at the man. "It is agreeable to see you again, Laurent. You are looking well."

Laurent beamed, flashing straight white teeth. "And you are looking ugly," he teased. "But it is nonetheless a pleasure to see you. It has been a long time, de Royans"

Colton nodded. "Almost two years to be exact," he said. "I last saw you at Bramham."

"How is Lucien these days?"

He meant after his terrible injury. Every fighting man in England, and especially those who served Henry, had heard of the nearly life-ending wound. Colton's smile faded.

"It did damage," he said. "But you would never know by looking at him. He is the same as he has always been."

"That is good to know," Holderness put in, not the least bit concerned with an old war injury on his daughter's future husband. All he cared about was that the man didn't die before he married Juno. "I am pleased to hear that the baron is not weak enough to fall victim to an old battle wound. What duties have kept him away from greeting us?"

He wasn't going to let the subject go and Colton glanced at Laurent, who simply rolled his eyes. Laurent was a good man, seasoned and reasonable and moral, but this was the first time Colton had ever met the man's father. He could already see that the Earl of Holderness was not a lord to be denied anything, including a personal greeting by the son of a duke.

"Trouble in the village, my lord," Colton lied. Well, it wasn't *exactly* lying... there could be trouble in the village, couldn't there? "He will return as soon as it is settled. Now, may I show you inside? We have a great variety of refreshments awaiting you, including St. Cloven ale from Norfolk because Lucien heard that you liked it."

That seemed to ease Holderness' offense. Truth be told, St. Cloven ale was the preferred drink of England's nobility so Colton simply said that Lucien had heard the ale was a preference of the earl because, more than likely, it really was. He was trying to ease the earl's anger against Lucien and, luckily enough, it seemed to work, so he held out an arm, indicating the direction of the hall.

Holderness took the hint and moved towards it with Laurent behind him. Colton met Laurent's gaze and the two of them fought off mutual grins as Laurent took his father inside. They both understood the needs of a demanding lord. As Laurent and his father headed for the hall, Colton waited politely for the ladies to act as their escort.

"My lady?" he said evenly. "May I show you inside?"

Juno looked at the big, blonde knight. He had a square jaw, close-cropped hair, and the deepest blue eyes she had ever seen. He was quite young, too; not as young as she was, but certainly a young knight. Still, he had a deep voice and a manner about him that suggested maturity. Moreover, he was quite attractive. She flushed around the ears, grasping at her cousin's hand as if she needed support while speaking to the handsome young knight.

"Thank you, my lord," she said, hardly able to look him in the eye because she was terrified he would see her flush. "You are very kind."

Colton smiled at the rather pale but pretty young woman. "It is my pleasure, my lady," he said. "Please permit me to formally introduce myself – I am Sir Colton de Royans. Your brother and I have fought together on a few occasions. I consider him a friend."

Juno dipped into a practiced curtsy. "I am Lady Juno de Saix and this is my cousin, Aricia." She indicated the very slim young woman next to her. "I hope it is agreeable with Sir Lucien that my cousin has come with me. She is my maid."

Colton nodded. "I am sure that Sir Lucien will be quite agreeable," he said. "Now, I can show you to the hall or, if you prefer, a chamber has been prepared for you and I can take you there to rest, instead. What is your preference, my lady?"

Juno looked at Aricia, who whispered in her ear. Juno nodded before returning her focus to Colton. "I would be very grateful if you could show me to my chamber," she said. "And… and hot water would be very welcome."

Colton began walking, motioning her along. "Of course, my lady," he said. "I will have a bath sent up to you. Follow me, please."

Juno didn't need any prompting to follow the man; she rather liked looking at him as he walked, as did her cousin. They made quite an odd pair – while Juno was elegant and stylish in her dress, Aricia was quite different – she had an elaborate hairstyle that also involved a scarf, which she kept wrapped around her neck and the lower portion of her face. It was strategic, to cover her bad skin eruptions, and she was literally covered from head to foot with fabric. Only the eyes shone through – bright blue eyes that were also focused on Colton. In fact, the two ladies exchanged interested glances as they followed the big knight towards the square keep.

Across the bailey they went, passing by soldiers heading to their posts and other inhabitants going about their business. There was even a young boy chasing chickens about, catching them to bring them back into the kitchen yard. Spelthorne, as a whole, seemed very busy and prosperous, which would certainly please Holderness. All the while, however, the ladies were mainly focused on Colton in front of them, watching his gait, which was really more like a swagger. It was most attractive to behold. They were nearly to the entry of the keep when they were met in the doorway by a servant girl.

"Sir Colton," the pale, young woman said anxiously. "Lady Susanna is asking to see the new lady. Will you present her?"

Colton shook his head. "Not yet," he said. "Lady Juno wishes to refresh herself after her long journey. Tell Lady Susanna that she will meet the lady once she has rested."

The servant girl looked at him with fear in her expression. "She will not be pleased," she whispered loudly, looking at Juno and Aricia fearfully. "Just… just a brief moment? Can you just bring her for a brief moment? It shall not take long."

Colton sighed heavily. "I will speak with Lady Susanna," he said, "after I settle Lady Juno and her cousin."

With that, he pushed past the jittery servant, taking Juno and Aricia into the dark, cool keep. Three stories tall, not including the lower storage level, it had two big rooms on the entry level and a spiral staircase built into the thickness of the wall that connected the living levels.

The second level also had two big chambers while the third level had four small ones. This was the level for guests and their servants, and it was this level that Colton intended for Lady Juno and her cousin. As they were passing the second level on their way to the third, however, they could hear someone shouting from one of the chambers.

"Who is there?" It was a girl's voice, shouting. "*Tell me who is there!*"

Juno looked at Colton, who soundly ignored the cries. He simply continued up the stairs and they followed, listening to the girl on the second level as she continued to shout. Once on the third level, however, the voice was blocked by the heavy stone walls of the castle. Colton led Juno and Aricia to one of the small chambers and pushed open the door.

"Here you are, my lady," he said. "The room is small but it is comfortable and well appointed. I will send servants up with water and food and kindling for the fire. If you require anything else, please do not hesitate to ask the servants or send for me. We will make your stay here as comfortable as possible."

Juno looked around the room. It was tiny, indeed, but it had two lovely windows facing north and west, and a rather large and fluffy bed shoved into a corner. There was a chair, a small table, and a small wardrobe against one wall. The wardrobe was painted with flowers and it was quite lovely. There was also a small modesty screen next to it, painted with the same flowers that were on the wardrobe. She turned to smile at Colton.

"It is all quite lovely and cozy," she assured him. "Thank you for being so gracious, Sir Colton. We are grateful."

Colton nodded. "It is my pleasure, my lady," he said. "I will have your bags sent up shortly."

Hand on the latch, he started to pull the door shut but Juno stopped him. "My lord," she said quickly, preventing him from leaving, but the moment he looked at her with polite curiosity, she felt quite foolish. Her cheeks were starting to flush again. "The crying we heard when we came up the stairs… is that someone we should be introduced to? That is to say, is that the Lady Susanna the servant spoke of? I am concerned that she believes me to be quite rude not to come at her bidding."

Colton shook his head. "I would not worry about it," he said. "That is Sir Lucien's young daughter and any introduction should come from Sir Lucien himself. She knows that. Is there anything else, my lady?"

Juno simply shook her head, not wanting to trouble the man further. Colton smiled politely at her before shutting the door, leaving Juno and Aricia to settle in to their small chamber. Once the door closed, however, Aricia turned to Juno excitedly.

"He is *so* handsome!" she exclaimed softly. "'Tis a cruel twist of fate that he cannot be your husband."

Juno's thoughts lingered on the attractive young knight. "I would be just as averse to marrying him if he was the man I was pledged to," she said quietly. "His degree of comeliness does not matter to me."

Aricia's gaze lingered on her cousin's dark head. "I know," she said, her voice considerably softer. "I did not mean it as it sounded. Forgive me."

Juno knew that. Aricia was very kind, usually very tactful. More than that, she knew what was in Juno's heart… and it wasn't fine young knights or even an older, prestigious one.

"There is nothing to forgive," she said, forcing a smile as she began to remove her delicate doeskin gloves. "Besides… Papa would not dare permit me to marry anyone who was not an earl or better. Nothing but the most prestigious husband in England will do for me and to the devil with my wants. You know this as well as I do. He has never listened to me."

Aricia nodded faintly and began to remove the scarf from around her face and neck. "I know," she said. "His wants take precedence over all."

"That is true."

"*L'homme est avide et moyenne,*" Aricia hissed. "*Il ne te merite pas.*"

Juno smiled faintly at her cousin. "Ambition has always ruled Papa," she said, pulling off the second doeskin glove. "It is not a matter of greed. I do not believe he is deliberately cruel. He simply wants the House of de Saix to be more prestigious than anyone else. That is why he sought this marriage with de Russe; regardless of how I felt or who I wanted to marry, he pestered the king and begged until Henry finally relented. I do not know if de Russe knows any of that. Mayhap it is better if he does not. This is all some grand move in Papa's game of politics."

Aricia finished pulling the scarf away from her face, revealing badly marred skin with great redness and pustules. It was particularly bad around her mouth and beneath her cheekbones. She was very pale, with pale lashes and eyebrows, and a rather angular face and big jaw. Aricia was from Juno's mother's side of the family, and that entire family was from France in the Bordeaux region, very pale and wispy people.

But Juno didn't share those family traits. Though her hair was dark, her skin was pale and clear, and she was rather pretty. Not wildly beautiful, but she had a pale and lush beauty she very carefully maintained with expensive creams and oils, things she had learned about whilst fostering in some of the country's finer castles. They were expensive potions but her father bought them without hesitation if he thought it would make her more attractive to a wealthy husband.

Therefore, Juno knew how to make her skin soft and her teeth clean, and she even knew how to use cosmetics but all she would really use was lip rouge on occasion, just enough to give her pale face some color. With all of her knowledge from the worldly houses she had fostered in, she tried to help Aricia with her terrible skin but that type of skin seemed to be allergic to everything. It was an awful condition that also affected the back and shoulders and chest. White willow powder, when applied, seemed to be the only thing that would calm the flare-ups but, for the most part, Aricia was resigned to a life of covering up. She had quite a lovely collection of scarves and veils to do this with, but Juno felt very sorry for her cousin.

Still, Aricia's attitude was one of resilience. She hadn't fostered in the fine houses that her cousin had. In fact, she'd never really fostered at all. She had lived for most of her life in France at her grandmother's home, raised by women when her father abandoned the family. She had learned to dress finely and cover her skin cleverly. She had also acquired the talents of dressing hair and sewing the latest fashions, and Juno happily allowed her cousin to dress her in every way. Aricia always made her look quite beautiful. They made a companionable pair, the two of them, now in residence at Spelthorne Castle for the inspection of the great Sir Lucien de Russe.

Juno had to admit that she wasn't looking forward to it.

Lost in thoughts of the coming introduction to her potential husband, Juno set her gloves aside and was preparing to loosen her sleeves when there was a knock at the door. Aricia gasped, as she was without her scarf covering her face, so Juno waited until Aricia was properly covered before opening the door.

Two servants were standing outside, women, and they were carrying food and wine. Juno admitted them and the women rushed in, putting it all upon the small table, before dashing out.

When Juno went to close the door behind them, she could see two more servants, male this time, carrying a big tub between them, so she opened the door wide as the men brought the linen-lined copper tub into the chamber and set it carefully on the floor.

In fact, Juno stood back, and Aricia pressed herself into a corner, as a cavalcade of servants came in and out of the chamber, not only bringing food and tubs, but water and wood as well. People scurried in and out as Juno and Aricia watched it all, watching the efficiency of Spelthorne's servants. In fact, they moved swifter than any servants they had ever seen, almost a panic to the movements, as if fearful they would not be just as fast and competent as their master wanted them to be.

The man known as The Iron Knight.

As Juno watched the last of the hot water poured into the tub, she was coming to wonder if the nickname of the man she was betrothed to meant more than simply his durability on the field of battle. She wondered if it was in his manner, too. Was he a man so old and battle-hardened that there was a sword where his heart should be and a shield and chain mail where his soul once rested? For servants to be so swift, and so rigidly efficient, surely Sir Lucien de Russe was far more in his manner than simply a man who fought for the king and administered justice in the name of the crown.

Perhaps he had an iron fist, as well.

With that frightening thought, she went about preparing to meet the man with a reputation that was coming to consume her thoughts.

Papa… who is this man you have pledged me to?

Cଓ

"IT IS FORTUNATE the day is warm," Lucien said. "I believe our clothing has dried sufficiently. At least, I am no longer dripping."

He'd meant it as a joke, smiling, because his heart was lighter this day than it had been in a very long while. What had started off as a very bad day had, after a few rough patches, grown into one of the better days of his life.

Spelthorne Castle was in the distance and he had already pointed it out to the ladies, which had conveniently caused him to turn and look at them. Truthfully, he really *wanted* to look at Sophina but he was pretending that every glance in her direction or ever word out of his mouth had some sort of greater purpose. It didn't. He was just trying to be very casual about speaking with her.

All he wanted to do was speak with her.

As for Sophina, the past two hours had seen her struggling not to warm to the man who had saved her and her daughter. She was, indeed, trying very hard not to but it was oh-so-difficult.

What wasn't to like? He was tall, broad, strong, and very handsome, she thought. She liked his long, dark hair with streaks of gray at the temples. She liked his square jaw with the big cleft in the chin, and his eyes... they were an odd color, a sort of muddy brown, but they were beautiful. At least, she thought they were. In fact, there wasn't one thing about Lucien de Russe that she didn't find handsome or charming, and it made her sick to her stomach. Why couldn't her father have pledged her to someone like de Russe? The answer was obvious, of course.

Lucien de Russe was far too good for her.

But that didn't stop her from dreaming. They'd covered two hours, chatting about a variety of things, but it seemed like two minutes. She felt as if she had known him forever but the truth was that she didn't know him at all. She very much wanted to. Her thoughts were lingering heavily on the man when Oswald the ferret suddenly slithered out of Emmaline's arms and onto the dusty road.

In response, Emmaline slid off the horse to run after her naughty pet, leaving Sophina alone on the big gray beast, watching her daughter as she chased down the cavorting ferret. At the horse's head, Lucien snorted at Emmaline's antics.

"I thought all young ladies had tame and obedient pets," he commented. "I hesitate to say that your ferret friend does not seem very obedient."

Sophina laughed softly. "He is very affectionate and loving," she said. "But he has not learned much obedience. It is my daughter's fault, truly; she does not have the heart to discipline him."

Lucien was watching the young girl romp around in the grass beside the road where the ferret was giving her a good chase. "And you think you could do better?"

Sophina feigned insult. "Of course I can," she insisted. "I am a mother. It is my job to discipline."

Lucien lifted his eyebrows. "Is *that* your job?" he teased. "It is my understanding that a mother's only job is to teach her daughter how to catch a husband. Was I misinformed? Because if you have schooled your daughter in catching something, you have failed miserably because she cannot even catch the ferret."

He was jesting with her but Sophina didn't say anything. Hesitantly, fearing that she might not have understood the jest, Lucien turned around to look at her only to see that she was giving him such a hateful expression that he broke down into laughter. Because he was laughing, she broke into laughter as well.

So much for scowling at him.

"That was a dastardly comment, my lord," Sophina said. "I am not sure I can forgive you."

"Even if I say please?"

"Mayhap. But it is questionable."

Lucien's gaze lingered on her a moment before turning around to watch the road. Truth was, he was having a hard time keeping his focus off of Sophina and each time he looked at her was better than the time before. That giddy heart in his chest was thumping a mile a minute. But further thoughts of the beautiful woman riding Storm were cleaved as Emmaline captured the elusive ferret. Triumphant, she walked back in their direction, cradling the animal in her arms. Seeing the girl with her pet, hugging it, suddenly reminded Lucien of his own daughter.

He found himself wishing he had a daughter as sweet and sociable as Emmaline. Instead, God had seen fit to gift him with something much, much different. If only Susanna had been born with a sweet disposition, but she hadn't. She was a demanding and terrible child, far from her sweet and noble mother, and he struggled against the depression that thought provoked. Here he was, enjoying an unexpectedly splendid afternoon and he didn't want morose thoughts to spoil it.

Those morose moods occupied too much of his time as it was.

"Then I will ask your forgiveness once again for my dastardly comment," he said, fighting off thoughts of Susanna. "For, clearly, you have raised your daughter well. Surely you know I was jesting with you."

Sophina softened. "Of course I knew," she said. "I did not think you were serious. I hope you did not think I was serious, either."

Lucien shook his head. "Never."

The mood was warm and light between them as Emmaline came to walk beside the horse now that she had her pet in her arms. She scratched the animal's head affectionately.

"Your castle looks very big from afar, my lord," Emmaline said. "Is it truly so large?"

Lucien could see it off in the distance, the big walls built of gray stone gleaming in the late afternoon sunlight. "It is big enough for my needs," he said. "Because I am a garrison for the crown, I have about two thousand troops stationed at the castle. You will see once you go inside. The castle is, essentially, a military fortress for the region."

Emmaline thought on that; things like crown troops and sheriffs and even the rebellions that had been sweeping the country weren't really part of her world, so she was very curious about such things.

"And your family?" she asked. "Do they live with you even though it is a military fortress?"

Now Sophina was very interested in where the conversation was going. In the two hours they had casually conversed, she'd not yet had the nerve to ask him of his wife, if he even had one. It really wasn't her business so the event of Emmaline's unexpected question had her listening with great eagerness. Perhaps she couldn't get away with asking such a question, but innocent Emmaline certainly could. Lucien was immediate with his answer.

"My son is fostering," he said. "He has seen seventeen summers and he serves his master at Kenilworth Castle. My daughter, however, does live with me at Spelthorne. She is ten years of age. I would like for you to meet her."

Emmaline nodded. "I would be honored, my lord," she said. "Does she have pets, too?"

Lucien shook his head. "Nay," he replied. "My daughter was injured at birth and she has a great difficulty in walking, so we try to keep things like cats and dogs and ferrets, things that she can trip over, away from her."

It made some sense but a world without pets, to Emmaline, was a sad world, indeed. "I see," she said, somewhat troubled. "I am sorry to know that. But what does she do all day if she does not have a pet to tend?"

Lucien cocked his head thoughtfully, thinking on the question. He didn't give Emmaline the first answer that came to mind – *she screams and throws tantrums and makes us all miserable.* Nay, that was not the answer to give her. He tried to think of something less horrific but, in truth, it was difficult.

"She likes to draw," he said. "She has a nurse who has been with her since she was born. Her nurse has taught her to draw and play the harp. She also sews very well."

Emmaline thought of the sewing she left submerged in the carriage. "I like to sew, also," she said. "So does my mother. You should see the beautiful things she sews. But what of your wife? Does she live at the military fortress, too?"

Lucien glanced over at the nosy young woman. "My wife died when my daughter was born."

Emmaline looked stricken. "Oh," she gasped softly. "I am sorry, my lord. I did not mean to… I did not know."

"Emmaline," Sophina said from atop the horse. She'd heard what she'd needed to hear and she was embarrassed to have been so curious over something so personal and tragic. Now, she felt foolish. She couldn't even manage to feel relieved. "Mayhap you should ride with me now. Do not exhaust Sir Lucien with your chatter."

Lucien waved her off. "She is not exhausting me," he said. "It is refreshing to speak with an intelligent young lady for a change. I spend my days talking to ugly men. Bah!"

He made a face and both Emmaline and Sophina laughed at him. Sophina's gaze lingered affectionately on her daughter.

"She will talk you into your grave if you let her," she said. "You are very patient with children. Your son and daughter are very fortunate to have such an understanding father."

Lucien's smile faded as he looked at Emmaline, who was hugging her pet, smiling at him. Was it really true that there were children like her? Children who were full of love and laughter, not animosity and angst? It seemed so unbelievable considering the behavior of his own children and he was coming to think that it must have been a mother's influence on a child that made them pleasant and happy.

Had Laurabel lived, perhaps things would have been different with his children. Perhaps they would be kind and well-behaved, and they would love him. Perhaps he wouldn't be resigned to a son who hated him and a daughter who was horrific at best.

Perhaps the problem had been him all along.

"We will be at Spelthorne shortly," he said, turning away and catching sight of his fortress in the distance, now looming closer. "Mayhap I should send word to your father, as well, my lady. He will want to know that you have suffered a mishap on your trip."

Sophina couldn't help but notice that her mention of his children had brought about some change in his mood. He had been smiling and kind one moment, sullen the next. It was an odd reaction, she thought. Surely the man would be very proud of his children but from his response to the mention of his offspring, one might wonder otherwise. Quickly, she hastened to ease whatever melancholy might threaten to settle.

"Although I thank you for your thoughtfulness, my father will not want to be bothered with any mishaps on our trip to Gillingham," she said. "All that matters to him is that we arrive whole and safe. I will send him word once we have met with Lord du Ponte."

Lucien cast her an odd look. "I would hardly think that telling him of your trouble and reassuring him that you and your daughter are well is hardly a bother. If it was a situation involving my daughter and granddaughter, then I would surely want to know."

Sophina smiled thinly. "You do not know my father very well," she said. "He only cares for important information. Small details, and tribulations that have no bearing on his life, do not matter to him."

Lucien digested her statement. She was painting a rather callous picture of her father. He glanced at Emmaline to see what the girl's reaction was, but she was focused on her pet, nuzzling him and rubbing his belly. She didn't seem much interested in what her mother was saying about her grandfather.

"But *you* matter to him," he said to Sophina. "You and your daughter."

"I wish that were true," Sophina muttered. When she saw Lucien turn to look at her, curiously, she realized she had commented before she could think of a polite reply. She had become so comfortable with the man over the past couple of hours that replying truthfully had been her first instinct. It had been a mistake; she knew that. He would think she was either bitter or unwanted, or both. Quickly, she scrambled to smooth over her slip. "I simply mean to say that my father is a very busy man. He has a new wife now and many things that require his attention. Emmaline and I are unscathed, thanks to you, so there is no need to concern my father over it."

Lucien wasn't sure he believed her glossed-over explanation but he didn't dispute her. He was still under the impression that there was something careless or unpleasant, or both, between the lady and her father. It shouldn't have concerned him in the least but he found that it did. It intrigued him. He couldn't imagine a father not caring for his daughter.

Not caring for Lady Sophina.

Lost in thought, he caught sight of one of his patrols riding along the road. They always traveled in pairs and when he saw them moving down the road towards him, at a distance, he lifted his hand to catch their attention. Suddenly, the patrol was thundering in his direction and Storm, at the sound of rushing hooves, began to get excited. Still in the saddle, Sophina held on tightly as Lucien calmed the horse down.

"Not to worry, my lady," he told her. "Storm will not throw you. He is simply excited when he hears the charge of horses. He thinks that he is supposed to be part of it."

Sophina wasn't so sure, holding on to the saddle nervously. "He is a very big horse," she said. "I would imagine he is quite formidable in battle."

Lucien patted the horse's face affectionately. "He is," he said. "I have other warhorses that are more aggressive and more deadly, but Storm is very smart. He senses danger and goes out of his way to avoid it. He has saved my life on more than one occasion."

Sophina watched Lucien stroke and pat the horse and it was clear that he loved the beast. "Then I am glad to know you have such support in your profession," Sophina said. "Surely, if you serve the king as you do, then it is most important for you to have the very best of everything, horses included."

Lucien grinned. "If the king expects me to defend his throne, then you are correct. I must have the best of everything. I am fortunate enough to have the means."

Sophina tore her gaze away from him because the patrol was drawing very close, heavily armed men on big horses. Emmaline, walking next to her, seemed a bit intimidated by the approaching pair and Sophina reached down, touching her child reassuringly.

"This is all very new to us," she said to Lucien. "My father's home of Thruxton Castle is significantly smaller than Spelthorne. We do not have great armies. There are no heavily-armed knights. My father's existence is not as grand as yours."

Lucien turned to look at her. "Your father does not have the need for big weapons and big armies, I am sure," he said. "Out here, I am the law, so heavily-armed men are a necessity. You saw how you were attacked back by Tisbury – outlaws are very well armed, too. It is a violent world in general, my lady."

At that point, the patrol was on them, coming to a halt in front of Lucien. One of the men dismounted and greeted Lucien formally.

"My lord," he said. "De Royans told us to keep watch for you. He wanted to let you know that Lord de Saix and his daughter have arrived."

Lucien's good mood was shot full of holes in that short statement. The past two hours had seen him forget about the arrival of his betrothed. In fact, for the past two hours, he had been a widower who found great attraction in a widowed lady. He had been a free man, free to dream about a future he never believed possible. His future had been a dark, dreary place until the introduction of Sophina de Gournay, who had been on her way to meet a potential husband.

Truth be told, Lucien wasn't going to let St. Michael du Ponte get in the way of what he wanted. He would make a far better husband for Sophina than the criminal, du Ponte. Was he truly thinking of marriage after only knowing the woman for two hours? As impulsive as it seemed, he was. He truly was, for in that brief span of two glorious hours, he could see a future that was no longer dark and dreary. He could see hope and happiness and light. Of course, he didn't know Sophina well at all but what he had seen, he had liked very much. He didn't want to let her get away.

But that was not his choice.

Now, the reality of his own betrothed, a gift from the king, had arrived at Spelthorne. Briefly, he considered turning around and fleeing with Sophina and Emmaline. He really did. He didn't want to marry a child bride he knew nothing about. He didn't want to return to Spelthorne where a hopeless and dark existence waited for him. He didn't want to go back there, back to darkness. He wanted to wander the roads forever, carrying on a light and delicious conversation with a beautiful woman and watching her sweet daughter chase her ferret about. That was what he wanted. Such a brief, shining moment of delight in a life that had been void of such things.

Now, reality had hit him.

He couldn't run.

"Very well," he grumbled. "One of you return to Spelthorne and tell de Royans I am on my way. You will also seek the majordomo and tell him that I am bringing two guests and they are to be made as comfortable as possible. Additionally, tell de Royans to have twenty men assembled, heavily armed, and prepared to ride out with me immediately upon my return."

The men were nodding eagerly. "Aye, my lord," the one man said. "De Royans will want to know where you are riding to."

Lucien threw a thumb in the direction of Sophina and Emmaline. "These ladies were set upon by bandits," he said. "We must retrieve their belongings, which are at the bottom of a lake, before the bandits can get to them. In fact, you'd better have forty men prepared to ride. This may be a big task."

The first man nodded smartly and snapped his fingers at his companion, who reined his horse about and took off for Spelthorne. But the first man remained, glancing at the women behind Lucien.

"Can I be of further assistance, my lord?" he asked. "I can take the girl with me on my horse and we can make haste back to Spelthorne."

It made sense. They were still about a half-mile out and it might be better for the ladies to tuck them safely away in the bosom of Spelthorne, the sooner the better. But that would mean the end of the two most blissful hours of Lucien's life. Still, it would be better for the ladies to get them to safety and food and dry clothing. With a faint sigh, he nodded.

"Aye," he replied. Then, he turned and held out a hand to Emmaline. "Young lady, this is Ranulf Gray. He has served me for many years and is a competent and trustworthy man. He will return you to Spelthorne while your mother and I follow."

Emmaline was reluctant. She looked up at her mother, who smiled and nodded, before placing her hand in Lucien's. Lucien then led her over to the soldier's horse and easily lifted her into the saddle. Both he and the soldier waited until she was settled before the soldier leapt on behind her. He put an arm around her and the wriggling ferret, gathered his reins, and then took off back towards Spelthorne.

Meanwhile, Lucien had made his way back to Sophina. Without a word, he mounted the horse, sitting behind her, but so close that she was sitting on his lap. It was the first time Lucien had gotten particularly close to her and, immediately, he knew it had been a mistake. She was soft and warm in his arms and he could feel her tender buttocks on his lap, which caused immediate arousal.

But he fought it. Sweet Jesus, did he fight it. He hadn't been this close to a woman in years and his reaction was instantaneous. This luscious, beautiful woman with the dark red hair had his entire body on fire, so much so that his hands were beginning to shake. He tried to cover it, gathering his reins and spurring Storm after the soldier and Emmaline, but he was quite certain Sophina could feel him tremble. He was sure of it. Trouble was, he wasn't sorry in the least. He liked the feeling.

Sophina's trip back to Spelthorne was considerably slower than her daughter's.

CHAPTER THREE

SUNSET OVER THE vibrant summer landscape was sweet and warm, with gentle breezes blowing up from the south, carrying the scent of the sea along with them.

All around Spelthorne, the inhabitants were preparing for the coming night. As the sky overhead bled colors of dark blue, purple, pink, and orange, men on the walls of the castle were lighting torches and feeding the dogs, dogs that patrolled the walls and perimeter of the fortress. Night sentries came on duty as day sentries surrendered their posts. With the walls secured, the hustle and bustle of the castle continued in the bailey below.

The doors of the great hall were open and servants went about their duties. Soldiers looking for an early meal wandered in and out. Unlike many halls, the floor of the great hall was made from great wooden planks, held in place by massive joists over a vast storage area below. The wooden floor made for a great deal of noise as people moved in and out. Straw thrown about the floor to absorb spills and hold in some heat helped with the sound, but not enough. The hall could be a loud place at any given time.

A vaulted roof crowned the great chamber and small windows all around the top of the ceiling allowed smoke from the two enormous hearths to escape. There were three massive feasting tables, each one of them seating at least fifty people, plus there was enough standing room in the hall for a few hundred more. It was an expansive place because here, Lucien held court on the last Friday of every month. The tables were moved aside and he sat at the end of the room, with his scribe and several armed men, hearing cases from his fiefdom and deciding justice.

It was all part of his duties as Sheriff of Cranborne, a position given to him by Henry about ten years before when the rebellions against Henry's reign were in full swing. Henry needed men loyal to him stationed throughout the country, and Lucien held parts of Wilshire and a good chunk of Dorset secure for the king. Much power came with his title, power that Lucien, so far, had used wisely.

Sophina had heard all of this from a very talkative servant. In her borrowed chamber on the top floor of Spelthorne's enormous keep, a chatty woman with bad teeth and thick, bristly hair had brought food and drink, and much conversation. She also brought two oversized robes, both of them evidently made for a man, while taking the lake-smelling clothing from the ladies to wash out.

Those had been Lucien's instructions and the servant was more than willing to tell Sophina that Lord Tytherington had made it clear that the lady and her daughter, as his guests, were to have everything they needed to make their stay comfortable. Sophina was very touched by Lucien's hospitality, kindness she was unused to, so when asking for hot water to wash her body with, she had been rather timid. She didn't want to seem demanding. The servant, however, was most apologetic, explaining that someone named Lady Juno had use of the tub at the moment. That didn't mean much to Sophina, who had no idea who Juno was, and she insisted that any hot water and soap would be most welcome. With that request, the servant fled.

Once the servant was gone, both Sophina and Emmaline put on the heavy, dry robes that were left for them. The garments were most definitely made for a man because not only were they huge, they were very long and smelled of wood of some kind. Sophina thought it might have been cedar, a precious and aromatic wood, and that perhaps the robes had come from a chest made out of such wood. She had seen such chests, luxuries though they were. In any case, it was lovely to be dry as they waited for the Spelthorne servants to wash their clothing.

Climbing onto the rather small but very comfortable bed in the chamber, Emmaline snuggled down with Oswald, who had been slithering around the bed, and promptly fell asleep, exhausted from her busy day, as Sophina watched the world outside of the window. Their chamber overlooked part of the bailey and most of the stables, and the smell of hay and horses drifted in on the wind now and again. Down below, she could see men moving about in the course of their duties, soldiers on the wall, and dogs running through the bailey, barking. There was actually a good deal to see and she was quite interested in her surroundings.

But what she was really looking for was Lucien.

Truth be told, she had been very sorry to be separated from him once they'd reached the bailey of Spelthorne. He'd dismounted his horse and pulled her down after him, his hands lingering on her perhaps a bit longer than they should have. Or was that her imagination? Certainly a man as great and prestigious as Lucien de Russe wouldn't be interested in her. She had already established that. But she was still dreaming that such a thing might be possible.

Sophina had been struggling against her attraction to Lucien since nearly the beginning of their association but, now, she found she couldn't rail against it at all. Lucien had her attention, which was unfortunate considering she was due to meet the man her father wanted her to marry. She tried not to give in to the disappointment that thought provoked. For the moment, she was here at Spelthorne and, for the moment, she would give in to her little fantasies about Lucien de Russe. Until the time came where she was passed on to du Ponte, never to see Lucien again, she would continue to indulge her secret attraction to him. In this new and unexpected world of Spelthorne, she was content to live the fantasy.

She'd never had such a fantasy before, ever.

As the afternoon passed with Emmaline sleeping and Sophina sitting at the window, dreaming of Lucien, a soft knock finally rattled the door. Sophina crossed the room to open the panel, revealing the servant with the bad teeth. The woman had returned with two big men lugging a copper tub between them. Bath time had finally arrived.

It was actually a small tub, about the size of half of a barrel, with taller sides and a seat built into it so one could sit in the tub and pour water over his or her body without splashing it over the sides. There was no real submersion of the body at all. It was quite fascinating, really, to see the latest form of bathing in, of all places, a military fortress, but it was extremely welcome. Sophina opened the door wide and admitted the servants, who set the tub down by the hearth.

Next, hot water was poured into the tub, about halfway, and the female servant also produced a hard, white bar of soap that smelled heavily of rosemary, and a separate mixture of salt and vinegar for further cleanliness. She even brought pieces of fabric to dry off with. When the male servants fled the chamber, the female servant remained and offered to help Sophina bathe, but she turned the woman down. Bathing was something she had always done alone. Once the door to their chamber was shut and locked, Emmaline leapt off the bed and was the first one into the tub.

Oswald jumped in, too, turning it into a splashy experience. Sophina helped her daughter bathe in the hot water, inhaling the strong rosemary scent of the soap as she washed her daughter's hair with it. Even Oswald received a lather. It was lovely and luxurious, and after Emmaline sufficiently bathed, Sophina ordered her daughter and the ferret out of the tub and took her place in it. The water was still quite warm and the scent of the rosemary strong, as she scrubbed herself from head to foot, removing the smell of the lake scum and the general dirt from travel.

It was a heavenly afternoon spent luxuriating in a warm bath with food and drink aplenty. Sealed up in their borrowed chamber, Sophina and Emmaline were comfortable, clean, and well-fed. It was the best ending to the day that they could have asked for even though the entire experience had been most unexpected. The day had begun with the intention of making it to Gillingham before the end of the day, but outlaws, and Lucien, had changed those plans.

Not that Sophina was upset about it. She wasn't upset in the least. In fact, she had never been quite so comfortable or quite so happy. Wrapped up in the big, borrowed robe that smelled of wood, she imagined that it was Lucien's robe. She imagined the robe touching his skin just as it was touching hers, caressing his naked flesh. As she lay down on the bed where her daughter had so recently napped, she had thoughts of Lucien's bare flesh against hers. Wildly inappropriate, and even silly, but her thoughts lingered on a naked Lucien just the same. As Emmaline sat at the small table and ate small purple grapes, white cheese, and a hunk of freshly-baked bread, Sophina drifted off to sleep with naughty thoughts of Lucien de Russe.

Emmaline knew when her mother fell asleep because the woman snored softly. Just little puffy snores, actually, but it told Emmaline that her mother was in an exhausted sleep. The woman slept like the dead, anyway, and very little could wake her once she was sleeping. As Emmaline shoved food into her mouth and fed Oswald cheese, she looked around the room before standing up, grapes in hand, and wandering over to the same window her mother had been parked beside. In the bailey below, there was a lot of activity, including a big horse that was very unhappy. Men were trying to put a blanket on him, or a saddle, but the horse wanted none of it. Emmaline grinned as the horse kicked a man and he went flying.

It was pure entertainment in her world. She wished she could tell her mother about it but she would have to wait until the woman was coherent. Quickly becoming bored now, with nothing to do, Emmaline moved back over to the small table to collect more grapes when she heard soft voices outside of the chamber door.

Curious, she went to stand next to the door, listening, and she could hear what sounded like two female voices. At her age, everything had her interest. She wanted to know who was on the landing. Very quietly, she unbolted the door and cracked it open, peeking into the area beyond.

It was dim in the landing outside but she could make out movement. The door across from her chamber was open. She could see into it and the fact that it was utterly jammed with trunks. It looked like there had been an explosion of clothing because she could see garments everywhere – on the bed, on the floor, and piled on the trunks themselves. More than that, two young women were standing just outside of the chamber, speaking in loud whispers. Emmaline could hear them. One was about her age, she thought, but she couldn't see the features of the other one because she was holding a scarf up to cover the bottom portion of her face.

Bored, and vastly curious about the young girls outside of her door, Emmaline slowly opened the panel and stepped through, silently closing the door behind her. When she looked up from the door latch, it was into two surprised pairs of eyes. She smiled weakly.

"Greetings," she said quietly. "Do you live here?"

The pretty, pale girl without the scarf across her face shook her head. "Nay," she said, somewhat nervously. "Do you?"

Emmaline shook her head. "Nay," she said. "My mother and I were traveling to Gillingham Castle and we were set upon by outlaws. Sir Lucien saved us and brought us here."

The pale girl's brow furrowed. "How horrible!" she exclaimed softly. "Were you injured?"

Emmaline shook her head, taking a timid step or two towards the ladies. "Nay," she said. "But our carriage tipped over and fell into a lake. Sir Lucien swam to the carriage and then had us hold on to his neck. He swam all the way back to shore with us hanging on to him. It was positively heroic!"

The pale girl blinked as if startled by the story. "He *did*?" she asked, awe in her tone. "And he brought you here to safety?"

Emmaline nodded. "He did," she said. "My mother and I cannot swim so if he had not come to our rescue, we surely would have drowned."

The pale girl's mouth popped open in utter astonishment. She looked at her companion with the scarf across her face and the two of them stared at each other with wide-eyed looks. Emmaline looked between the girls, seeing that she had duly impressed them with her horrific afternoon.

"I am Emmaline," she said. "It was rude of me not to introduce myself. Are you Sir Lucien's guests, too?"

The pale girl looked at her, still with that same wide-eyed expression. It appeared like she wasn't sure how to answer the question. "We are," she said. "I am Lady Juno de Saix and this is my cousin, Aricia."

Emmaline bobbed a curtsy to the ladies, the polite thing to do. She was looking at the embroidered fabric across Aricia's face. "My," she said with genuine appreciation. "Your scarf is quite lovely. Did you make it yourself?"

Aricia nodded; she was always nervous when in the presence of someone new, nervous that they would see how terrible her skin was.

"I did," she said. "I am honored by your admiration, my lady."

Emmaline smiled. "I sew but I do not sew nearly as well as you do," she said. "If we are here a very long time, mayhap you will show me how you sewed something so beautiful."

Aricia nodded eagerly, feeling flattered by Emmaline's kind words. Flattery, in her isolated world, was rare. "I would be happy to," she said. "How... how long will you stay?"

Emmaline shrugged. "I am not for certain," she said. "My mother is on her way to meet her betrothed, Lord du Ponte, but we were ambushed and our carriage wrecked. I believe that Sir Lucien is going to send word to Lord du Ponte and he will come and get us. It could take days, at least."

Juno cocked her head thoughtfully. "Du Ponte?" she repeated. "I do not believe I have heard of him. I must ask my father tonight at sup if he knows of Lord du Ponte."

"Your father is a guest here, as well?"

"He is, indeed."

Emmaline dipped her head in thanks. "Then I thank you," she said. "My mother has never met Lord du Ponte because the contract was arranged by my grandfather. If your father knows Lord du Ponte, I am sure my mother would like to hear what he knows of him."

Juno lifted her eyebrows. "Then your mother and I have something in common," she said, "for I have not yet my betrothed, either."

Emmaline was interested. "Oh?" she said. "Who is your betrothed."

"Lucien de Russe."

Emmaline's mouth popped open in astonishment. "Sir Lucien is your intended?"

"Aye."

"And you have never met him?"

"Nay."

"But how long have you been a guest here?"

Juno shrugged. "We only arrived today," she said. "We were told that he was detained by trouble in the village and now I find out that trouble was you. It seems that Sir Lucien was quite noble in saving your life. I am glad he was of assistance to you."

It was a kind thing to say and Emmaline smiled, but she still wasn't over the fact that this young girl, no more than her age, was betrothed to a man old enough to be her father. Certainly, it was not unacceptable in society and, more often than not, encouraged so that old men could have young brides to have many more children with. Still, Lady Juno was very young and, to Emmaline, Sir Lucien was quite old. He had to be at least twenty or more years older. She began to feel some pity for the girl.

"Thank you," she said sincerely. "I am sorry if we took Sir Lucien away from meeting you. I would not have knowingly done that."

Juno smiled. "Of course not," she said. "I understand. Saving a life is more important. I will be introduced to Sir Lucien tonight at sup and all will be well."

Emmaline nodded. Then, she sniffed the air. "I think I smell sup already. I am quite famished. I hope they will bring our meal soon."

Juno's eyebrows lifted. "Bring your meal?" she repeated. "Will you not attend the meal in the hall?"

Emmaline looked down at herself, wrapped up in a heavy dressing robe made from wool. "When our carriage went into the lake, so did our clothing," she said. "All I have is the dress I was wearing and the servants took that away to wash it. I would not presume to think that I could go out in public in this clothing."

She made a face, causing Juno and Aricia to giggle. But in that giggle, they were also sizing up her, looking at the robe she was wearing. It was bulky and hideous. Aricia finally turned to Juno.

"She is taller than you are but I am willing to wager that she would fit into your clothing," she said. "Why not lend her something until her clothing can be retrieved?"

Juno nodded eagerly. "Of course!" she exclaimed. "I am certain I have something to fit her."

Emmaline was torn between refusing the generosity and giving in to it. She had few friends, living with her mother and cruel grandfather as she did, so she was quickly being swept up in Juno and Aricia's excitement.

"I... I do not wish to be a bother," she said. "Sir Lucien said that he would send his men to retrieve our possessions, so I am sure I will have my own things returned to me very soon."

Juno frowned. "But you said they were at the bottom of a lake."

"They are."

"Then they will be smelly and wet," Juno pointed out. "I will loan you something dry to wear until your clothing can be returned to you in wearable condition. Oh, do let us dress you!"

It was a lovely, thoughtful suggestion and Emmaline couldn't honestly think of a reasonable excuse to refuse her. Besides, there was an allure in spending time with two girls her own age, girls who seemed kind and generous. A timid smile crossed her lips and she opened her mouth to thank Juno, but the words never came froth. A screech from the floor below interrupted her gratitude, whistling up the spiral stairs and filling the air with its unhappy wheeze.

"Stop talking!" a young girl's voice shouted for all to hear. "Stop talking up there! Come down here to me this *instant!*"

The three young women froze, looking at the stairwell with shock and dismay. The faceless young girl screamed again, with frustration, positively lifting the hairs on the back of their necks. Frightened, Juno reached out and grasped Emmaline.

"We heard this girl earlier today when we arrived," she hissed. "We were told that she was Sir Lucien's daughter. I've not met her. Have you?"

Wide-eyed with fear, Emmaline shook her head. "I have not," she said. "What should we do?"

Juno didn't know. "I do not want to anger Sir Lucien," she hissed. "The knight that showed us to our chamber – de Royans was his name – said that Sir Lucien should introduce me to his daughter, so I do not want to disobey the man's wishes."

More screaming hurled up the stairs followed by something banging against the stone down below. The screaming was accompanied by demands again, demands that the young women come to the source of the screaming. Whoever was yelling had strong lungs because she was very loud, but the three young women on the level above had no intention of obeying the commands. They stood there, simmering in uncertainty, when the door to Emmaline's chamber suddenly opened.

Sophina was in the doorway. Wrapped in a heavy brown woolen robe, she appeared sleepy but alert. Even though the woman was a heavy sleeper, the screaming going on downstairs was loud enough to wake the dead. As more yelling and banging wafted up the stairwell, she frowned deeply.

"Who is that?" she demanded softly. "What has happened, Emmaline?"

Emmaline ran to her mother, grasping at her. "I do not know, Mama," she said honestly. "We were simply talking when someone down below started yelling. Lady Juno believes it is Sir Lucien's daughter."

It was then that Sophina focused on the two girls her daughter was standing with. One was pale and pretty while the other one covered most of her face with an embroidered red scarf. They looked to be about her daughter's age and she smiled politely.

"Ladies," she greeted. "I am Lady Sophina, Emmaline's mother. Are you guests here, too?"

Juno nodded, her gaze moving over the lushly gorgeous older woman with the dark red hair. She was rosy-cheeked, with smooth skin and beautiful eyes. In truth, Juno was a bit in awe for a moment, as she had never seen such a lovely woman of that advanced age. Surely the woman had seen well over thirty years, but it was difficult to know for sure. She looked positively ageless.

"Aye, my lady," Juno replied. "I am Lady Juno de Saix and this is my cousin, Aricia. We are here at Spelthorne with my father, the Earl of Holderness. Lady Emmaline told us of your misadventures today. I was sorry to hear of your troubles."

Sophina thought that Juno seemed like a pleasant young lady on the surface. At least, she was well spoken and had polite manners. Her smile turned genuine. "It is kind of you to say so, my lady," she said, turning her attention once again to the shouting and banging below. "Has anyone gone down to see what the screaming is about? Mayhap the girl is in some kind of trouble."

All three young ladies shook their heads. "Nay, Mama," Emmaline said. "She has screamed at us to stop talking and attend her. There is no trouble, only that she wants us to go to her."

Sophina was puzzled. "*Go* to her?" she repeated. "And she is Sir Lucien's daughter, you say?"

All three girls were nodding to varying degrees. "Aye, my lady," Juno said. "I was told that Sir Lucien would personally introduce me to his daughter and I do not want to anger him by heeding her call. I must wait."

The screaming was now turning into crying. Loud, unhappy crying.

Bewildered at the behavior, Sophina left her daughter and the two ladies and made her way to the stairwell, peering down to see if she could see anything. Since it was spiraled, there wasn't much to see except some shadows on the wall where the dim light was silhouetting a figure, moving about. There was more banging against the wall. Now deeply curious, Sophina made her way cautiously down the stairs.

The second level was configured a little differently than the third level with two or three large rooms; Sophina had noticed when she'd been shown to her chamber earlier. As she came down the stairs, she could see a young girl with long, dark hair sitting on the floor near the stairs. In her hand, she had two steel rods of some kind with claw's feet at the base. Sophina had no idea what they were but she was banging them about, crying unhappily. Sophina paused four or five steps from the bottom, watching the girl slam the rods around.

"Are you hurt or injured?" she asked politely. "Do you require assistance?"

The young girl instantly stopped banging and looked up at her, astonishment on her tear-streaked face. In that moment, Sophina instantly knew that what the girls had told her had been the truth – this was Lucien's daughter, for she looked exactly like him. She had his long, wavy dark hair and muddy brown eyes. She even had the shape of his chin, with a big cleft in it. The moment she laid eyes on Sophina, however, she gasped and struggled to roll to her knees.

"Who are you?" she asked eagerly, scrambling to get up from the floor. "What is your name?"

Sophina remained on the steps. She didn't want to get in range of those rods that the girl was holding on to, rods that she was using to stand up with. Sophina could see that they were canes of some kind, although she'd never seen canes like that before. She wasn't entirely sure the girl wouldn't start swinging those canes at her.

"I am Lady Sophina," she said. "I am a guest of Sir Lucien's. What is your name, child?"

"Susanna," the girl said immediately. "There are more girls here, aren't there? I asked them to come and visit me but they will not come. They are mean and cruel, and I shall have them punished!"

The short outburst was petulant but Sophina remained even. "I am sorry you are angry, but I assure you that the girls are not being rude," she said. "They have been instructed to stay to their chambers. I am sure you will meet them soon enough."

Susanna's eyes bugged as if she'd just been told something completely outrageous. "But they must come to me *now*," she insisted. "I cannot travel the stairs. Therefore, they *must* come to me!"

She began to cry again, slamming the rods about violently, and Sophina was quickly coming to understand something about the girl – she was badly behaved, spoilt even, and it occurred to Sophina that all of the banging and crying had been a tantrum. She was, in fact, having one now. Her gaze flicked off to her right where an older woman, wearing a tight wimple, cowered in a chamber doorway. The older woman was looking fearfully at the child on the ground. Now, those screams were beginning to make some sense.

"Susanna," she said, loudly, so she could be heard over the screaming. "Why are you banging about so? Do you think this will make the girls come to you?"

Susanna slowed her actions as if confused by the fact that someone was pointing them out. She looked at Sophina, angry tears on her face. "But they *must* come!" she insisted. "How am I to see them if they do not? *They must come!*"

Sophina shook her head. "They will most certainly *not* come," she said, bordering on stern. "Did you think they would not be frightened by the crying and banging you have been doing? Of course they are afraid. They will not come to you if they are afraid you might try to scream and bang on them, too."

Susanna came to an abrupt halt, mulling over what the strange woman had told her. She couldn't decide if she was even more outraged by it or embarrassed. "But...," she sputtered, "but they must do as I say."

"Why?"

Her eyes flew open wide. "Because I wish it!"

"*Why* should they do as you say?" Sophina repeated. Then, she shook her head. "A well-behaved young lady will invite friends without even trying. A young lady who screams and bangs about will only chase people away. They will be afraid of you. Now, I am sure if you are quiet and politely ask them to join you, they will want do to it much more than if you scream at them. Do you understand?"

Susanna was still weeping, softly, but at least she wasn't screaming. Lower lip trembling, she wasn't entirely sure how to respond. In truth, no one ever questioned her. She was always allowed to do as she pleased. She was a very bright girl and knew that her demands would always be met, but in this case, people were not running to do her bidding and she could not adequately handle her frustration.

The more she thought on the situation, however, the more she began to see things from only her perspective – she wanted the young women upstairs to come to her and they would not. That was all she could understand. It had always been that way in her world and her wishes had never been denied. Suddenly, she brought the metal canes in her hands down with a violent crash.

"Tell them to come to me *now!*" she screamed. "I am sick and wretched, and they must come and play with me! I demand it!"

Sophina didn't react other than to watch the child throw another tantrum. For as kind and wonderful as Lucien had been, she found it rather shocking that the man's daughter was so terribly behaved. She didn't understand it, frankly. But as she watched the girl practically kick and scream because she wasn't getting her way in all things, she thought there was something quite pathetic about her. She was clearly a very unhappy child.

"They will not come to you if you behave like this," Sophina said steadily. "What is your sickness, child? What is the matter with you?"

Susanna wasn't much interested in talking about herself. "I cannot walk very well, you fool," she snarled. "Can you not see my canes? Are you blind?"

Now she was hurling insults, which Sophina didn't take kindly to in the least. She adored children and was very good with them, and no matter who this child's father was, she wasn't going to let the little chick insult her. Her manner cooled as she backed away, moving for the stairs.

"I can see quite clearly," she said. "In fact, I see a screaming, ill-tempered child who does not deserve anyone's friendship or attention. The fact that you cannot walk well does not give you the right to be so terribly rude. I will tell the young ladies upstairs not to come down here no matter how much you scream, so scream until your head explodes. No one will listen to you. Until you can politely speak to those around you, I will ensure my daughter, at the very least, does not heed your call. Good day, Lady Susanna."

With that, she turned and headed up the stairs, listening to a sudden silence from Susanna before the screaming began again in earnest. By the time she reached the top of the stairs, Emmaline, Juno, and Aricia were gathered there, eyes wide as Sophina emerged from the stairwell. The howls that were coming up after her now were loud and unearthly.

"What happened, Mama?" Emmaline demanded. "Who is making those terrible noises?"

Sophina cocked an eyebrow. "Lord Lucien's daughter, as you suspected," she said. "She is an unfortunate child. I would suggest we all retreat our rooms now so that we will not antagonize her. She can hear us quite clearly down the stairwell, so mayhap it is best if we retreat to our rooms for now."

Juno and Aricia nodded quickly, fearfully, and started to hustle to their chamber. Juno came to a halt, however, once she put her hand on the door latch. "Lady Emmaline?" she whispered loudly in the hopes that the mad child down the stairs would not hear her. "Would you come with us so that we may properly dress you until your clothing can be washed?"

Emmaline looked at her mother with big, begging eyes, but Sophina was a bit confused about the request. Before she could ask what Juno had meant, Emmaline grabbed on to her mother.

"Please, Mama?" she asked passionately. "Please, may I go with them?"

Sophina had to grin at her extremely eager daughter. "I would like to give you permission, but what, exactly, will you do?"

Emmaline tugged on her mother's arm, eager for the woman to give her consent. "I told Lady Juno that our clothing is being washed," she said quickly. "She offered to let me borrow some of her clothing until ours is returned to us so I do not have to wear this terrible robe. Please, Mama?"

Gazing into her daughter's eyes, Sophina couldn't help but relent. It wasn't often that her daughter was around young women her own age and she knew the girl was desperate for friends. She really didn't have any. Sophina looked over at Juno and Aricia, who were looking at her with the same hopeful expression that Emmaline had. She figured her daughter couldn't get into any trouble if she was in the chamber next door. Patting her child on the cheek, she nodded.

"Go," she said. "Enjoy yourself. And thank Lady Juno for her generosity. It is very kind of her to share her possessions with a young lady she does not know."

Emmaline let out a little squeal of delight and kissed her mother on the cheek before dashing off to be with her new friends. As the door to Juno's chamber shut quietly behind the giggling girls, the howling from the floor below was still in full swing. The smile faded from Sophina's face as she retreated into her own chamber and shut the door, shutting out the screams of the ill-behaved child.

But the fact remained that she suspected she might have to face Lucien's daughter again, at some point, and she braced herself for that moment. She was fairly certain the girl would tell Lucien about the terrible lady who said terrible things to her. She wondered how she was going to explain her way out of that one but, truth be told, there wasn't much she could say in her defense. The girl was horrible and Sophina didn't regret what she'd said, but she was certain she would be disappointed when Lucien threw her and Emmaline from Spelthorne as a result.

Until that time, Sophina would have to dream of Lucien all she could, including the fact that she was still wrapped in the man's robe. She rubbed the heavy wool, feeling it against her flesh, as she went to lie down on the bed. Once she lay back on the fluffy mattress, she inhaled the fabric draped on her arms, smelling the heady scent of wood mixed with what she imagined was a man's smell. Lucien's smell.

More fabric touched her belly and her breasts, and she couldn't help but rub the material against her nipples, imagining what it would feel like for Lucien to touch her nipples. It had been years since she'd been with a man, since her husband had died, so the thought of a man on her flesh, between her legs, brought heat to her loins like nothing she had ever experienced.

The scratchy wool on her woman's center brought chills and she raised her knees, gently rubbing the fabric on her woman's center, imagining that it was Lucien's manly touch. It was enough to bring her the greatest of pleasure to her trembling body. With the wool rubbing against her nipples, she tossed the robe open and began to stroke herself, giving herself pleasure, eyes closed and a smile on her lips when she remembered an old nun from her childhood speaking of the sins of the flesh and discouraging young girls from even bathing.

A bath is a temptation to evil, the old crone had said, but that had never stopped Sophina from pleasuring herself. She never saw any harm in it and, frankly, she had done it quite often. She still did. Like now; inserting a finger into her already wet sheath, she trembled with delight at the sensation as her free hand came up to caress a naked breast, visions of Lucien de Russe dancing in her head.

Thoughts of the man with the big shoulders and long, dark hair was enough to send her panting. The finger in her sheath began to work in and out, stroking the pink flesh, stimulating, and in little time, a powerful release rolled through Sophina. She knew if she kept stroking, another climax would come so she did, playing with her tender core, coaxing forth two more releases before finding some satisfaction. Breathing heavily, she lay upon the bed, her left hand wet from her slick body.

With thoughts of Lucien heavy in her mind, she wiped her hand off on the inside of his robe, in the general location of where his buttocks would be. She smiled to herself, knowing it would dry before he would ever wear it again, but knowing that even when she left, a small part of her would remain behind, secretly to touch his skin.

It was a nasty little secret, but she didn't care.

She rather liked nasty little secrets.

CHAPTER FOUR

L UCIEN HAD BEEN listening to Holderness spout his mouth off most of the afternoon, ever since he had returned to Spelthorne with Sophina and Emmaline. Entering the gates of his fortress, with Sophina so deliciously on his lap, he'd run right into the man, who had been in conversation with de Royans near the keep. God help him, he hadn't been fast enough to avoid the man. He'd had little choice but to turn Sophina over to his majordomo and greet the man whom Henry wanted to be his future father-in-law.

But Lucien had other ideas.

Playing the perfect host, which he was very good at doing when he wanted to, he took Holderness into the great hall of Spelthorne where he and de Royans and a very big, dark-haired knight known as Gabriel of Pembury, proceeded to ply Holderness and his son with a good deal of very expensive wine. Lucien didn't have many vices but fine wine was one of them, and he had a special sweet, dark red wine imported from Spain, made of grapes grown near the town of Toledo. He'd discovered the wine through the king and had a standing order for the stuff, which he usually hoarded greedily.

But not today – because the wine was rich and very sweet, it tended to get one drunk very quickly and the aching head the next day was something only told of in horror stories. So Lucien had his knights fetch the strong wine, whereupon he made sure Holderness' cup was always full, topping it off constantly, while he and his men drank it at a much slower pace.

Laurent caught on fairly early that Lucien was trying to get his father drunk but he said nothing. He wasn't exactly sure why Lucien was keeping his father's cup full but it soon began to occur to him that he simply wanted his father out of the way, which wasn't surprising. But he was fairly certain that Lucien didn't know that his father had a great tolerance for alcohol, so the more he poured, the louder and more animated his father became.

Eventually, Laurent had to whisper something to Gabriel, who in turn muttered something to Colton, who was sitting next to Lucien. The next time Lucien tried to re-fill Holderness' cup, Colton stopped him. A brief shake of the head to Lucien's curious glance halted any further attempts to fill up the earl's cup. But at that point, it was too late.

The plan had backfired.

Holderness became loud and opinionated, berating everyone from the king to the French. Not even the pope escaped his wrath as an ineffective man presiding over the most powerful religion in the world (or the only religion, as Holderness put it). Lucien kept a straight face as Holderness turned his rage on Lucien, scolding the man for not having been waiting at the gates when he had arrived earlier that day. The man then went on to extoll the virtues of his daughter, Juno, who was a truly accomplished and obedient girl. Lucien did everything but yawn and Holderness was incensed that Lucien didn't show more interest in his only daughter.

Lucien could take the scolding. That didn't bother him in the least, for the truth was that he brought it on himself by trying to get Holderness drunk. So he took the pounding without uttering a word, but that inactive stance changed when Holderness began to bring up Henry and the past ten years of active rebellions against the king's reign. At that point, Holderness began his opinion of several of the past battles and past rebels – Henry Percy, for one. Percy, also known as Hotspur, was a huge topic of debate and the more Holderness ranted, leaning towards support of Percy but stopping just short of actually advocating the man, the more Lucien's mood sank and the more his passive stance threatened to come to an end.

Laurent, as well as the others, must have sensed this. Knowing that Lucien had been at the head of every battle for the past ten years, and also knowing how the last battle at Bramham had not only ended his career but very nearly his life, Laurent began to intervene in his father's rant, talking the man down, distracting him with other subjects and trying desperately to get him off of the subject of Henry and the rebellions against him. It was a wide and general subject Holderness was tackling, with a variety of factors and players that spread out like a spider's web, but Holderness didn't seem to care that he was verging on insulting the man he wanted his daughter to marry. The wine had seen to that.

Lucien had all he could take when Holderness ventured into the taboo subject – the battle at Bramham Moor, the last and most decisive battle in the rebellion against Henry. As soon as the man started in on it, in spite of Laurent's struggles to prevent it, Lucien simply stood up and walked from the table. He had to get clear of Holderness before the man said something that Lucien would violently react to, but Holderness, in his drunken state, wasn't apt to let him leave.

"De Russe!" he yelled as Laurent tried to intervene. "Where are you going? I am not finished with you yet!"

Lucien wasn't known for his infinite patience. Moreover, he didn't want the man hounding him in his drunken state. Abruptly, he whirled on his heel and marched over to Holderness as Laurent tried desperately to put himself between his father and de Russe. Even Colton and Gabriel leapt up, also placing themselves between their liege and the Earl of Holderness.

"He is drunk, Lucien," Colton said quickly, quietly. "You know this. It is your own fault for feeding him wine as you did. Keep that in mind before you take his head off."

Lucien didn't even look at Colton. He didn't even acknowledge the man. A massive hand shot out, plowing through the knights that were standing in front of him, and grabbed Holderness by the neck. Now, the knights were pushing Lucien back before he could do any real damage.

"One more word from your foolish mouth and I will snap your neck," Lucien snarled. "Do you hear me?"

Holderness wasn't so drunk that he didn't realize he was suddenly in a very bad position. "Let go of me," he hissed. "Let go of me, I say!"

Lucien squeezed and Colton and Gabriel, shoving hard, broke his grip on Holderness, but Lucien didn't like being manhandled by his own knights. He pushed himself away from them, angrily.

"Listen to me, de Saix," he growled. "I will not be related to a man like you. I will not have you in my circle or in my family. You cannot hold your wine and you do not know when to shut your mouth, and both of those failings are stupid and deadly in my world. Take your daughter and get out of here. There will be no marriage."

With that, he turned away, waving Colton off when the man tried to follow him. As he left the hall, with Holderness sputtering and gasping in outrage, he was rather pleased with the situation. Getting Holderness drunk had worked out even better than he'd hoped because it had given him an excuse to get out of the marital contract. He would make sure to send Henry a missive that very night stating that Holderness, and his daughter, were unacceptable because now he had a reason to refuse the bargain. That sweet Spanish wine had given him an even greater and unexpected gift.

Out in the dusk, his mood was actually a good deal lighter than it had been moments earlier. He was free of his marital contract! It was all he could think about, as if a giant weight had been lifted from his shoulders, but in the very next breath his thoughts turned to Lady Sophina.

A goddess divine....

And that goddess was in his keep, sealed up in a chamber, and he would keep her there until the day he married her. Well, perhaps not literally, but figuratively. He had not, and would not, send word to du Ponte. He wouldn't even send word to the lady's father, Lord Andover. He would marry her tomorrow and then send his happy wedding announcements all around, Henry included, as Holderness and his daughter returned to Surrey in shame.

It was all he could do to keep from shouting his glee. He still had to feign anger for his men and any of Holderness' men who happened to be watching. On the outside, he was still disgusted and furious with Holderness. But on the inside, he was as light as a feather.

Smells from the kitchens wafted on the warm breeze, reminding him that the evening meal was an hour or two away. He would see Lady Sophina at the meal and spend the entire evening in conversation with her and only her. It was with thoughts of Lady Sophina heavy on his mind that he headed for the keep, hoping to see the woman again. He'd so enjoyed their time together and now he wanted to enjoy more time with her. It was all he could think of.

Entering the ground floor, the first thing he heard was wailing and he knew exactly who it was. He'd heard that wailing before. Usually, it killed his good mood like an arrow through the heart, but this time, he refused to let it get to him. He took the spiral stairs up to the next floor only to see his daughter on her buttocks, banging her canes around and screaming. He could see her nurse over in the doorway to her chamber, nervously wringing her hands, and he frowned.

"What goes on here?" he demanded. "Susanna, cease you screaming. What is the matter?"

Susanna came to an instant halt at the sound of her father's voice. Her big brown eyes turned to him, red from weeping.

"There are girls on the floor above and they will not come and talk to me," she sobbed. "Make them come, Papa! Make them come to me!"

Lucien put his hands on his hips. "Is that what this is about?" he asked irritably. "You are screaming over something so foolish?"

Susanna banged her canes on the floor again. "It is *not* foolish!" she wept angrily. "I have no friends, Papa. It is your fault I have no friends.

Yet you have brought girls to Spelthorne and you will not even allow me to make friends with them!"

She was off on a crying jag and Lucien sighed heavily, struggling against the inherent guilt that Susanna always brought out in him. *It is your fault.* Aye, everything was his fault. He knew that. But today, he would not give in to her screams. Silently, he bent over and swept her into his arms, cradling her little body against his broad chest as he took her back into her chamber.

It was perhaps the most lavish chamber in all of England. A very big room, it had a massive bed frame, painted with beautiful flowers and animals, and heavy brocaded curtains that hung all around the bed. There were fur rugs all across the floor, meant to cushion her feet when she did, in fact, decide that she wanted to walk, and there was an entire area where a painting easel and other art supplies were neatly kept. Yet another corner had poppets and toys, including a doll's house built like a castle, which had been imported all the way from France.

In all, it was a stunning room for a treasured child, but Susanna saw it as her prison. She always had. She screamed and clung to Lucien's neck as he tried to set her down on the bed.

"Nay, Papa!" she wept. "Do not leave me!"

Lucien didn't give in to her plea. He gently pried her arms from around his neck. "I must leave you for now," he said. "You will see me later, I promise. Will you please let me go now?"

She did, reluctantly, deliberately giving him the most pathetic expression that she could manage. "But you did not agree to bring the girls to me," she demanded. "You *must* bring them. And tell them that they must entertain me. I want to hear stories and I want them to sing for me!"

Lucien stood back, hands on hips, as Susanna's nurse rushed up to help her charge. The woman fussed over Susanna so frantically that Lucien knew the nurse was part of his daughter's problem. The woman catered to her and encouraged her tantrums when she should not. But the woman, Lady Leonie, had been with her since she was born and

Lucien couldn't bring himself to discharge her. If he did, not only would his daughter be even more miserable, but so would he because there would be no one to tend her and he would have to go through the effort of finding someone new.

It was a horribly selfish reason, but his reasoning nonetheless. Lady Leonie, at least, kept some measure of peace where his daughter was concerned. The truth was that his daughter scared him and mentally exhausted him, so the less contact he had with her, the better.

"I will not bring them here if you are going to make such demands on them," he said frankly. "Listen to what you are saying, Susanna – you want them to entertain you and sing for you. Such imperious demands are rude. Do you not understand that?"

Susanna's lip stuck out in a pout. "But I do not have any friends to entertain me!" she insisted. "What else are they to do when they come to me?"

Lucien shook his head. "They are not obligated to entertain you," he said. "Be polite and be kind. Be interested in who they are. Ask them about their lives and where they were born. Let them talk to you. That will be entertainment enough."

He made sense but it was all a foreign concept to Susanna. She had very little social skills because everyone at Spelthorne mostly kept away from her. Therefore, meeting new people, and especially girls her own age, was difficult for her. She genuinely had no idea how to behave. Her brow furrowed, although it was clear that she was mulling over his words.

"But what if they will not tell me where they were born?" she asked. "What if they will not tell me anything at all?"

He cocked an eyebrow at her. "And you think a tantrum is going to force them to speak?" he shook his head. "You must learn to control your anger, child. You cannot always have everything that you want. Sometimes, kindness and politeness will get you much further than anger. If you want them to be your friends, then you must show them that you are worthy. No one wants to be the friend of a screaming child.

Will you at least try to be kind?"

Susanna's frown deepened, torn between guilt and confusion and defiance. But she nodded hesitantly. "I will," she said. "Now, will you bring them to me?"

Lucien didn't have time for that at the moment. His wants were more pressing. But he couldn't ignore his daughter completely; he did that enough. He sighed reluctantly.

"If you behave yourself, then I shall allow you to attend sup tonight," he said. "We have many fine guests and I think you would like to meet all of them, the girls included. So no more screaming, no more fits – behave yourself and be a kind, thoughtful young lady and you shall be rewarded."

Susanna's features lit up. "Can I, Papa?" she gasped. "Can I really attend sup in the hall?"

"If you promise to behave."

She nodded eagerly. The incentive of eating with the adults in the hall was a very big lure. Too often she ate in her room, kept from the knights and adults at Spelthorne. Lucien told her that he did it for her own protection but Susanna was convinced he did it because he didn't like her. She knew her own father was ashamed of her. That only fed the tantrums she was so capable of.

Susanna was a very sad, confused young lady.

"I promise I shall be polite," she insisted. "Will you come for me when it is time for sup?"

"I will."

"I can hardly wait!"

She was rosy with glee. Lucien left the chamber, feeling great relief as he shut the door behind him. He always felt a great deal of relief when he left his daughter's presence. That relief, however, was also coupled with guilt. As the child's father, he felt as if he should want to spend time with her, not run from her, but the dynamic between them had always been this way. He had never known anything else. She screamed, he ran. If he really wanted to admit the truth to himself, deep-down, he couldn't stand to look at Susanna because the child's birth killed her mother. He'd lost a lovely, gentle woman and gained a screaming, spoiled creature, instead.

It just wasn't fair.

There was that guilt again, blaming Susanna for her mother's death and feeling horrible because he had such thoughts. But he shook off the familiar remorse and sadness, instead focusing on the lovely woman on the floor above. He was very eager to see Lady Sophina, eager to see if those two wonderful hours he spent with her were just a fluke. He wanted to talk to her again to see if, indeed, it was still the same lady he remembered.

Taking the stairs two at a time, he ended up at the top of the stairwell and was faced with four doors – two of them were immediately to his right and to his left, chambers that were used to house female guests, which was a rare occurrence, and then two doors directly in front of him. Those closed off chambers were where possessions and trunks were usually stored, or where servants slept. Therefore, he knew Sophina was in one of the doors immediately to his left or his right; not having settled the woman personally, he didn't know which door she was behind, so he chose the one to his left. Rapping on the heavy oak panel, he called softly.

"My lady?" he said. "It is Lucien. May I speak with you?"

He could hear some shuffling going on inside the room and his heart was beating firmly against his ribs with excitement. The anticipation of seeing her again was causing his palms to sweat and he suddenly ran his hands through his shoulder-length dark hair, smoothing at it, hoping he looked neat and attractive enough. He never gave a second thought to his longer hair or stubbled face, but he was now. He wished he had at least shaved. When the door rattled, he stood straight, bracing himself for the sight of that beautiful face. But when the door finally opened, he felt as if a bucket of cold water had been thrown on him.

A young, unfamiliar woman was facing him.

"Sir Lucien?" she said timidly. "How... how good of you to come and introduce yourself. I thought mayhap we would be formally introduced tonight at the evening meal but I am glad you came when you did. It is an honor and a privilege to meet you, my lord."

She dipped into a curtsy and Lucien noticed, standing several feel behind her, another woman covered nearly head to toe in fabric. But Lucien's gaze moved back to the young woman still in a polite curtsy in front of him and it suddenly occurred to him who she was. He should have remembered that, somewhere in this keep, Holderness' daughter would have also been lodged. He very nearly clapped a hand to his forehead with the force of his mistake. He could hardly believe what he'd done.

Damnation... I chose the wrong door!

"My lady," he greeted through clenched teeth. He didn't even know her name, only that her surname was de Saix, like her father's. He didn't even know what to call her. "I... I came to apologize that I was not in attendance when you arrived today. I had duties that kept me...."

Suddenly, coming into his line of sight, was a young lady that he *did*, in fact, recognize. The mere sight of her cut him off quickly. When Emmaline saw him, her face lit up.

"Sir Lucien!" she exclaimed. "I did not think we would see you until tonight. Lady Juno and Lady Aricia have been excellent companions this afternoon. We have been getting along splendidly."

She pointed to the ladies as she said each name, indicating which lady was which. Lucien blinked, rather startled by Emmaline's unexpected appearance. "I am pleased to hear that," he said, hoping he didn't sound as off-balance as he felt. "Is... is your mother in here with you, too?"

Emmaline shook her head. "She is in the chamber across there," she said, pointing directly across the landing. "Did you wish to speak with her?"

Lucien looked at the three young ladies in the chamber, wondering why he felt so nervous. Of course it was because of Lady Juno; his betrothed now had a name. Well, his *former* betrothed had a name.

After the incident in the hall with Holderness, there was no longer a betrothal but he wouldn't tell Lady Juno that. He would leave it to her father.

His gaze moved over the girl quickly; she was small and slender, and not unattractive looking. She had pretty eyes. But she was a shadow compared to Lady Sophina's beauty – a colorless and faded shadow. He took a step back, away from the door.

"Aye," he said after a moment. "There are a few things I wish to, uh, discuss with her. Do not be troubled. I will see you all at the feast tonight. I will call on Lady Sophina myself."

With that, he reached out and grasped the door to close it, but Emmaline was already bounding through the door, rushing to the chamber where her mother was and pounding on the door.

"Mama?" she called. "Mama, Sir Lucien is here! He wishes to speak with you!"

Lucien couldn't believe the situation he found himself in; standing on the landing, he had his former betrothed to his left and Emmaline to his right, banging on the door of the woman he very much wanted for his own. What was he to say to all of the women standing there if it came out that Lady Juno was his intended? What would Lady Sophina think?

For the first time in his life, Lucien resisted the urge to run from a conflict for not even he could survive the wrath of angry or confused women. He considered his options and how fast he could make it down the stairs before they tried to follow him and beat him to death, but as he mulled over his choices, the door in front of Emmaline suddenly jerked open and like a vision of angels, Lady Sophina was standing there.

He swore that he was blinded by her radiant light.

"Greetings, Sir Lucien," she said, her eyes riveted to him as she held his old robe close about her body. "I apologize for greeting you in this manner of dress, but our clothes have not been returned to us yet. Have our trunks been retrieved?"

God, how Lucien wished he was that robe right now, embracing her body, clinging to tender areas that deserved touching and stroking and caressing. It was difficult for him to move past that thought.

"Not yet," he said. "But I expect my men back at any moment. I am sorry I could not provide you with something more appropriate to dress in, but it has been some time since a woman lived here. All of my wife's clothes have long since been given to the poor."

Sophina smiled faintly. "You are most generous in all aspects, my lord," she said. "What you have provided is more than sufficient until our clothing is returned."

Lucien smiled in return, utterly forgetting that there were three girls standing around, watching his reaction to Sophina. But he was jolted from that blissful connection with Sophina's lovely face when Emmaline suddenly spoke up.

"Mama," she said, catching everyone's attention. Then she twirled around in the deep blue surcoat she had on, very pretty, with a soft white shift underneath. "Look at the dress Juno has loaned me. Is it not beautiful?"

Sophina's smile turned in her daughter's direction. "Beautiful, sweetheart," she said. Then, she looked at Juno, who was still standing back by her chamber door. "You have my thanks, my lady. You are very kind and generous to loan my daughter such a lovely garment. She will take very good care of it, I promise."

Juno smiled timidly. "I would be happy to loan you a garment, too, my lady," she said. "I heard what Sir Lucien said about your clothes having not yet been returned. I have more clothes than I can wear in a month. Papa told me to pack for a long stay, so that is what I did."

Sophina shook her head politely. "You are very kind to offer, but I would not dream of depriving you of your lovely clothing," she said. "What you have done for my daughter is enough. I am grateful."

Juno took a timid step away from her chamber, towards Lucien and Sophina and the twirling Emmaline. "It is truly no trouble at all," she insisted. "I would be honored to help. I have so very much to offer and until your clothing can be retrieved and cleaned, I am more than happy to loan you serviceable items. It may take a day or two for your clothing to be cleaned and dried, will it not, Sir Lucien?"

Lucien was forced to tear his attention away from Sophina when Juno addressed him. He nodded shortly. "It is very possible," he said. He quickly returned his attention to Sophina as if unable to look at anything else. "If the young lady is offering, it may be wise to agree. I should like you and your daughter down in the hall tonight for the evening meal and you cannot come wearing my old woolen robes."

So this robe does belong to Lucien, Sophina thought. She also thought of what she'd done in that robe, of her scent now marked on the interior of it. It was enough to make her flush at the mere thought but she fought it, not wanting anyone to see color in her cheeks.

"I can see your point," she said to Lucien, trying to keep her head down a little because she could feel the heat around her ears. "Lady Juno is very generous to be so kind to strangers. If it not too much trouble, my lady, then I accept your offer."

Juno beamed. "It is no trouble at all, I assure you," she said, her manner turning eager. "My cousin has a wonderful eye for dressing and fabrics and colors. She loves to dress women."

Sophina smiled at the enthusiasm of the girl. "Then I am grateful to your cousin, as well," she said, glancing at the girl with the scarf all around her face. "I will be sure to tell your father what a remarkable daughter he has when I see him at the evening meal. You have obviously been raised in a kind and generous house."

Juno smiled demurely; she was quite practiced at being modest. "I have fostered in two very fine homes," she said. "When I was young, I fostered at Prudhoe Castle in the north but when the Lady d'Umfraville died, the lord sent all of the female wards away. My father was able to place me at Wellesbourne Castle after that and I remained there until about three months ago, when my father recalled me home because he had brokered a marriage contract with the help of the king."

Lucien felt as if a giant hand was squeezing the breath out of him.

He could hardly breathe, struggling to come up with a change of subject because he most certainly did not want to discuss Lady Juno's marriage contract, but Sophina was politely interested in the conversation and spoke before he could say a word. It was her conversation, after all. She had every right to continue it, even on the dangerous path it was progressing on.

"Ah," Sophina said knowingly. "My father has made a marriage contract for me as well. In fact, that was where I was going when our party was attacked and Sir Lucien so ably saved us. Are you traveling to your betrothed's residence as well?"

Juno shook her head. "I have already arrived," she said. "Sir Lucien is my betrothed. I have not met him until today."

The smile on Sophina's face turned into something of a grimace. She had been living in a dream world for the past several hours, a world where Lucien was the object of her desire, and to hear he was betrothed to this… this *child*… was like an arrow to her heart. She knew she had no right to feel that way; no right at all.

Still, she found that she couldn't help the disappointment. In those few words, that pale, slender girl had shot her hopes and dreams full of holes, and everything was draining out of her, leaving her feeling hollow. God, she felt so foolish.

So very foolish.

"I see," she said after a moment, her voice sounding oddly strained. She didn't dare look at Lucien. "I am sure you will be very happy. I wish you the best in your new life together."

Juno smiled, but it was forced. It was clear that she wasn't sure how she felt about her betrothal to a much older man. "Thank you, my lady," she said. "And I wish you the same with your coming wedding. Does your intended live close by?"

Sophina realized that she felt very much like crying, her disappointment was so great. It was a struggle to stay focused on Juno's polite question.

"I do not think it is too far," she said, turning to look at Lucien full-on. There was no use in acting as if he'd done anything wrong, or jilted her, because he certainly had not. Her silly dreams had been her own and now they were dead. "Gillingham is not too far from Spelthorne, is it, my lord?"

Lucien had a rather sickened expression on his face; something around his eyes looked sad and defeated. "Not too far," he echoed quietly. "About twelve miles from here. It will take an hour on a good horse, at most. You will be quite... close."

Sophina stared at him. There was something in his tone that might have led her to believe that he wasn't entirely happy about the marriage arrangement with Juno, either. In fact, neither one of them looked particularly happy about the marriage, but more than that, if she didn't know better, she might have thought he was feeling the same disappointment in the betrothal that she was.

But no; she shook herself inwardly. Surely he was pleased with the bride, the daughter of an earl. As she'd known from the beginning, Sir Lucien de Russe was far too good for her, as she was a nearly penniless widow with a daughter. Sir Lucien required a fine wife who could provide him with status and wealth.

He deserved better than her.

"Then mayhap we shall be good neighbors to one another," she said. There was a lump in her throat she couldn't seem to swallow down so she turned away, back for her borrowed chamber. "If you will excuse me, I would like to rest before the evening meal. I look forward to meeting your father, Lady Juno. Thank you again for your kindness and generosity towards my daughter and me."

She was slipping away rather swiftly and Juno called after her. "Would you like me to send a dress to you, my lady?" she said. "I will have Aricia select one. She is never wrong about how a garment will fit on someone. I shall have her bring you something."

Sophina forced a smile; God, it was one of the hardest things she had ever had to do. She felt like weeping. Nay, she felt like bawling. A big explosion of tears and disappointment. That was what she felt like.

But Juno, sweet Juno, was truly trying to be kind. Sophina could not hate the girl, no matter how much she wanted to.

"That would be most kind of you, my lady," she said hoarsely. "I will look forward to seeing you again at the meal."

With that, Sophina entered the chamber and shut the door behind her. It was just in the nick of time, too, because the tears were already falling. She couldn't stop them. She could hear shuffling and talking outside of her door, and Lucien's deep voice on occasion, but soon everything faded away and it was purely quiet.

She was thankful. She didn't want to hear Lucien's voice anymore or see him with that girl he would soon be marrying. Soon, he would be touching that young woman's body in a way that Sophina wished he would touch hers. She was a woman grown and had been married for several years, and she knew how to respond to a man's touch. She knew how to please him.

But it wasn't so much the physical aspect as it was the emotional one. Sophina had been attached to her first husband, Emmaline's father. He had been a bit older and his health had never been particularly good, but he had been wise and gentle and kind. She had grown to love him, so she understood what it meant to love someone and she desperately missed that emotional connection, so rare when it came to marriages. Most of the marriages she knew were those of convenience. There was no love in them, only polite regard.

But Sophina didn't want that in a marriage. She'd had love before and she wanted it again. Perhaps it was selfish of her, but she couldn't help it. She wanted her heart to flutter when she looked at her husband and she wanted to crave his touch. She didn't think that was too much to ask and she was hoping against hope that there would be some kind of connection with her and du Ponte. But now, with the introduction of Lucien de Russe, she couldn't even think of du Ponte. She didn't want to meet him. She was dreading the day he would come for her.

Distraught, she made her way over to the bed and lay down upon it, sobbing softly. For her, dreams of Lucien de Russe had come to a very sudden end and she was deeply disappointed. But better they come to an end now than later, when it would be even more difficult to shake the man.

Truth was, even with this very brief association, she wasn't entirely sure she could ever shake him.

CHAPTER FIVE

Two miles northeast of Tisbury

IT WAS A vicious battle from the onset.

Having been informed by his men regarding the ambush of the carriage carrying Lady de Gournay and her daughter, St. Michael du Ponte took a precious hour to berate and beat his men before demanding they return him to the scene of the ambush so they could, at least, collect the carriage.

Du Ponte was fairly certain that the ladies had been taken by the outlaws but he at least wanted his carriage back. It was expensive and made a good presentation when arriving at the homes of friends or potential allies, even if it had been stolen from the north and brought far south to him as a prize. St. Michael didn't miss a trick when it came to making himself look better than he was. Therefore, he wanted his carriage back.

The women were of little concern at that point. Screaming and yelling the entire time, he rode from Gillingham with forty of his men, racing back the six or seven miles back to the small lake where the ambush had taken place. He had expected to find a sunken carriage and a scattering of possessions, but what he found when he arrived was quite different – more men were swarming the wreckage and he quickly realized that he wasn't the only one who had an interest in the half-submerged carriage and its cargo.

The lake was crawling with soldiers and at least one knight when he returned with his men. Outraged, du Ponte didn't even stop to ask who they were or what they wanted; they had the carriage half-out of the lake at that point and men were bringing wet trunks to the shore.

It was clear that they were claiming St. Michael's prize and he ordered his men to attack without any planning whatsoever. He hoped to overwhelm the thieving soldiers by the sheer surprise of the move, but what he didn't realize was that there had been about twenty more soldiers he hadn't seen, hidden by a line of trees. Once his men attacked, they were immediately outnumbered.

But du Ponte didn't back down. He wanted his ill-gotten carriage and he would fight for it, so he put his men on swarming the vehicle, enough to chase away the soldiers who were trying to steal it. He didn't care about the trunks belonging to his potential wife and he didn't particularly care about her in general. In fact, he was rather relieved that she was gone. He didn't want to marry, anyway, and his agreement to look over the widowed woman had come to him in a moment of weakness when the lady's father had gifted him with a butt of Malmsey wine.

But that had been months ago and his interest in the widowed Lady de Gournay had cooled. The wine was long gone and so was his honor as far as his promise went – he didn't want a wife and certainly not a widow with a child. He must have been mad to consider it. The promise of Malmsey will do that to a man.

So du Ponte remained somewhat behind the battle as his men went to work and the fight ensued. He mostly shouted orders to them, berating them for not making short work of the men trying to steal his carriage, but a few minutes into the skirmish he noticed something interesting – he was noticing the tunics worn by the enemy and he recognized the colors. In fact, he was very familiar with them – the colors of Lord Tytherington, Lucien de Russe, who was a nearby neighbor. The tunics were brown with a gold Teutonic cross on the front, signifying the men of The Iron Knight.

The Iron Knight!

Everyone knew that tunic as one of the most recognizable in England and the awareness that de Russe was behind the thievery infuriated du Ponte. How dare the man try to steal from him! Was it possible that de Russe was behind the initial ambush and that the women in the carriage had been confiscated by him? The thought caused du Ponte to jump into the fray without thinking, enraged by his neighbor's boldness, but he was very quickly driven back by a de Russe knight, a big and very skilled man. He very nearly cut du Ponte's head off and it was at this point that du Ponte realized he was fighting a losing battle. De Russe's men were winning and he was about to lose his precious carriage.

Damnation!

Frustrated, du Ponte was forced to back off. At least four of his men had been badly injured and he knew if they continued that more would be hurt. He didn't want to lose men, not now. He would have to return to Gillingham and regroup, to plan for his next move against de Russe, and he would need every healthy man he had.

So he barked commands to the two knights he'd brought with him, men who weren't particularly reputable but they were loyal. As long as he continued to pay them well, they were extremely loyal. Those knights, in turn, relayed commands to the others and soon, the du Ponte men were retreating, skulking back into the trees and fields from whence they came, heading back towards Gillingham Castle like insects retreating back into their nests. The swarm, so quickly descended, was now equally as swiftly gone.

The group raced back to Gillingham, carrying their wounded, frustrated that they'd been forced to retreat. But no one was more frustrated than du Ponte; he was positively livid and utterly blamed the failure on the weakness of his men. If they had done their duty and protected the carriage in the first place, none of this would have happened. That was du Ponte's attitude all the way back to Gillingham, where the great portcullis lifted to admit him and his men, lowering with a resounding clang once everyone had come through. Dust flew and dogs scattered as the contingent came to rest inside the bailey.

It was dusk now at the small, fortified castle next to the River Stour. It was essentially a manor house surrounded by a giant wall with an equally giant gatehouse that would have been better suited to protecting a much larger castle, but all it protected was an eight-room manor house, kitchens, and a fairly large stable area because du Ponte liked horses. Still, it was du Ponte's domain in all of its small scale and du Ponte marched into the house bellowing for wine and food. Behind him, his two knights trailed.

"Damnation!" du Ponte roared as he entered the great common room, strewn with old rushes and more dogs. He kicked one out of the way as he plopped onto his seat at the head of the big feasting table. "Do you know who that was? Did you *see* who that was?"

The two knights had the countenance of scolded children. They were older men who had seen a good deal of action but men who had never made a name for themselves. They were mediocrity personified. The first knight, a heavy-set man with shaggy graying hair, nodded reluctantly.

"De Russe," Ossian de Fey said. "I saw the colors."

Du Ponte sighed sharply. "So did I," he said as if Ossian was an idiot. "Was it *his* men who ambushed the carriage with the women inside? John, you were there – was it de Russe?"

Sir John l'Evereux stood up straight when he was addressed. He was a big, strong man but something of a simpleton. Only a fine family name had managed to get the man his spurs.

"Nay, m'lord," he said. "Those who attacked us were not organized. They came from the trees like… like animals. They rushed us without reason. They were not de Russe men."

Du Ponte was drumming his fingers impatiently on the tabletop. "How do you know for certain?"

John blinked at the question as if he didn't quite understand it. He looked at Ossian, confused, before finally replying. "Because they were not wearing de Russe colors, m'lord."

Du Ponte stopped drumming his fingers. Then, he smacked the worn table in frustration. "He has my carriage," he said. "He probably has the woman meant for me, too. I cannot simply allow him to take them both. I must get them back. I care not for the woman but I care for my carriage. Still, it will look ridiculous if I lay siege to Spelthorne simply to regain my carriage. I suppose I shall have to ask for the woman's return, too."

Ossian and John were listening carefully, which is something they had learned to do. Often, their orders were in du Ponte's ramblings and they had to be vigilant. Asking questions only served to enrage their volatile liege.

"I will gather the army, then," Ossian said, thinking that was what du Ponte wanted him to do. "We have five hundred men. However, de Russe carries thousands. We will not get very far if we attack him."

Du Ponte looked at him, his jaw ticking furiously. "Then we need more men," he said simply. "Sherborne Castle is a half-day's ride from here. I will go to the garrison commander and tell him what de Russe has done. Surely he will help me regain my possessions. Surely he will act on my behalf and we may not even have to lift our arms against de Russe. Sherborne will do it for me."

Ossian nodded, relieved. He didn't want to get into a futile battle against de Russe. "I agree that would be the better course of action," he said. "Shall I ride for Sherborne?"

Du Ponte pondered the question. He was feeling a bit calmer now as he thought on having the entire garrison of Sherborne Castle behind him. It was a very big garrison of crown troops, men that would undoubtedly be loyal to de Russe, but men who might be swayed if du Ponte could convince them that de Russe had stolen from him. It was a chance he was willing to take.

But he had to sweeten the deal; he had to make it worth their while, at least for the garrison commander, whom he did not know. Bargaining and sweetening deals were simply the way his mind worked.

"Go to the stables, Ossian," he said thoughtfully. "Select one of our younger stallions. Not the best, but a very good one. We shall bring the horse along as a gift for the garrison commander at Sherborne. Surely the man will be flattered enough to see my problem and help me do something about it."

Ossian watched as du Ponte went from wildly angry to quite calm all in a matter of seconds. As long as the man felt things would go his way, his anger was often sated.

"Aye, m'lord," he said. "When will we leave?"

"Tomorrow before dawn. I want my things returned and I do not want to wait any longer than necessary."

Ossian was already heading from the room, leaving John behind to absorb any more of du Ponte's anger. But du Ponte wasn't angry any longer; he was actually very sedate and confident at the moment, a man with mood swings that were both violent and swift. Therefore, John still stood out of arm's length because that was the safe thing to do.

"What would you have of me, m'lord?" he asked.

Du Ponte eyed the big knight. "It is your fault we have to go to this trouble to begin with."

"Aye, m'lord."

"If you had only put up a stronger fight, I would not be chasing my fine carriage all over Wiltshire."

"Aye, m'lord."

Du Ponte rolled his eyes irritably. "Leave me, idiot," he said. "Arrange for a party of twenty men to leave at dawn. We should make Sherborne in a few hours if the weather holds."

John simply turned and walked away, leaving du Ponte alone at the head of the big feasting table. It was quiet at this hour, before the evening meal, and the dogs were milling about, growing hungry, but du Ponte ignored the beasts just like he ignored everything, and everyone, else. There was nothing more important in his world than his own wants and desires, and he was frankly humiliated that de Russe had managed to capture his fine carriage.

But not for long. He would have it back soon. Even if Sherborne refused to help him, he had an entire network of outlaws and brigands in the area that might have the opportunity to get it back for him. That's what was so odd about all of this; usually, the outlaws near Tisbury worked for him. There were two roving gangs in that area and he had done business with both of them, so for one of the gangs to attack his carriage didn't make sense to him. It was true that they weren't, as a whole, the most trustworthy bunch, but he'd never had a gang turn on him.

Until now.

Still, he found it hard to believe that they would, which made him think with more certainty that de Russe was behind the ambush. But for what purpose? What could the man possibly get out of it other than two worthless women and a fine carriage? Given de Russe's honorable reputation, it was a baffling question.

One that kept him up most of the night.

Ↄ

"WE WERE ATTACKED by du Ponte," Gabriel of Pembury was saying. Exhausted, in full armor, he had just climbed off of his horse to be met in the bailey by Lucien. "One moment we were lugging the carriage out of the water and in the next, du Ponte and his men swarmed us with weapons drawn. I tried to yell to the man, to tell him of our mission, but he either didn't hear me or didn't care. I could not get close enough to him to tell him to cease his attack because he remained on the outskirts for the most part, bellowing orders."

Lucien was listening to his frustrated knight, his expression grim. "But you are certain it was du Ponte?"

Gabriel nodded, pulling his helm off and handing it to his squire when the boy darted near. "I know him on sight," he said, "as do you and de Royans and many other men here at Spelthorne. I have no idea why he attacked us but he seemed particularly upset that we were pulling the carriage from the lake. He attacked the men and horses that

95

were pulling it forth. It was almost as if… as if he did not wish to have the carriage pulled free. As if he wanted us to leave it in the water."

Lucien was baffled. "But why?" he asked. "Why would he want us to leave the carriage in the water?"

Gabriel had no idea. He was frustrated and had taken a goodly cut on his left forearm during the skirmish that needed tending. What was meant to be a simple mission had turned into a life-threatening situation most unexpectedly.

"It makes little sense to me, either," he said. "We brought the trunks forth and managed to bring them with us back to Spelthorne, but the carriage is where we left it – half-in, half-out of the water. I thought it best if we simply brought the trunks back at this point."

Lucien wasn't hard pressed to agree. "So du Ponte became angry because you were trying to salvage the carriage," he muttered thoughtfully, making sure he had the facts of the incident correct. "He tried to discourage you from the task. And he would not respond to you when you tried to speak to him?"

"Nay, Lucien. He did not respond in the least."

It was very puzzling and Lucien stroked his chin, pondering the situation, as his men brought forth the wet, algae-covered trunks they had carried on horseback and took them around to the kitchen area to the washerwoman who also did double-duty as the brew wife. Lucien watched his men haul away the trunks as he tried to make sense out of everything.

"Du Ponte's men must have rushed to Gillingham to tell him of the ambush, but in the process, they left the women behind," Lucien muttered. "So du Ponte returns but instead of demanding the women, he tries to prevent you from salvaging the carriage. That makes absolutely no sense at all, not even from a fool like du Ponte."

"Nay, it does not."

Lucien's brow suddenly furrowed as a thought occurred to him. "God's Bones, Gabriel…," he said. "Do you think it possible that he thought the women might still be inside the carriage and did not want for you to disturb it? That he wanted to leave them in the lake?"

It was a rather horrifying thought. "This I cannot know," Gabriel said. "It is possible that may be true, but didn't any of his men see you rescue the women?"

Lucien shrugged. "The entire carriage was swarmed and men were fighting all around it," he said. "It is possible that du Ponte's men were so concerned with their own hides that they never saw me. It seems unlikely, but it is entirely possible."

"So du Ponte does not know you have the women?"

Lucien shook his head. "He must not," he said. "He returned for the carriage first. If he knew I had them, then surely he would have come to Spelthorne at the very first to claim them."

Gabriel mulled over the path the conversation was leading them down. It was a strange and unsavory path, indeed. "Do you think he wanted the ladies dead?" He was almost fearful to ask. "We know he is in bed with the outlaws in the area... what if he paid them to stage the ambush in order to kill the women?"

A light of realization went on in Lucien's dark eyes. "So he returns to the scene of the crime to ensure that it was properly done, sees you trying to salvage the carriage, and has his men attack you in order to prevent you from pulling it from the lake and thereby revealing the victims inside."

Gabriel lifted his eyebrows ominously. "It is as good a theory as any," he said. "But to what purpose?"

Lucien cast him a long and knowing glance. "Mayhap he intended to write the lady's father and tell him that she had been killed," he said. "He would still be entitled to receive her dowry. No wife, but his wife's money. From what we know of du Ponte, I would not be surprised if that was the motive."

Gabriel hissed quietly. "If that is true, then you cannot send him word that the lady is here," he said. "He would only try to kill her again and possibly the next time he would not fail."

Lucien had thoughts of the lovely Sophina at the hands of the unscrupulous du Ponte. That sweet, lovely woman an innocent victim to his wickedness. The mere thought made his blood boil.

"Agreed," he said, trying not to sound as if he had some kind of personal stake in keeping Lady Sophina under his roof. "Mayhap I should send word to Lady Sophina's father with our suspicions. Surely he would want his daughter sent back to him and away from that bastard."

Gabriel simply nodded, thinking that all of this intrigue and murderous intentions was a bit too dramatic for his taste. He was a man that relished peace and quiet, a strange preference considering his violent profession. He was growing weary and restless, standing there as Lucien mulled over the situation with Lady de Gournay and St. Michael du Ponte. But Lucien caught the man fidgeting out of the corner of his eye and waved him on. Lucien didn't want to appear like he was giving the situation, and Lady de Gournay, far too much consideration.

"Go, now," he told Gabriel. "Make sure the washerwoman begins the cleaning process of Lady de Gournay's clothing and then you will make yourself presentable to escort the lady and her daughter to the evening meal. And make no mention of your troubles this day, Gabriel. I do not want the lady to know our thoughts on the matter of her betrothed."

Gabriel nodded smartly. "Aye, my lord."

Lucien watched his knight depart, heading swiftly for the kitchen yards. But as Gabriel walked away, Lucien found that his thoughts grew more and more heavy on the matter of Sophina and St. Michael du Ponte.

What if the man had, indeed, tried to kill her and make it appear as an accident? With du Ponte's mercenary reputation, Lucien wouldn't put anything past him. Now Sophina found herself mixed up in some kind of murder plot so the man could gain her dowry without gaining a wife. It was dastardly at best. That being the case, Lucien had no intention of sending du Ponte any word at all, just as he'd told Gabriel. Instead, he would send word to the lady's father and inform him of his suspicions. And then he would ask for the lady's hand in marriage. In truth, du Ponte had just given him a perfect excuse to do so.

Perhaps this situation hadn't turned out so poorly, after all.

CHAPTER SIX

"**M**ERCIFUL... *HEAVENS!*"

It was a very loud exhale from Sophina as both Juno and Aricia tried to shore up a girdle that was meant for a very tiny woman, someone Emmaline or Aricia's size. Even though Sophina wasn't heavy in the least, she wasn't skinny or bony, either. She was healthy and curvy in all the right places, so the girdle that Aricia had selected for her was just a bit too small. Still, the girls were trying to make it fit because it matched the dress.

And what a dress it was – a soft, pale blue shift went on beneath a blue brocade that glistened like starlight. With Sophina's auburn hair and pale skin, the picture was absolutely stunning. Sophina kept trying to politely tell the young women that the garment was too tight but they wouldn't listen, instead, cinching up the matching girdle to the point where Sophina could hardly breathe. She was certain that her eyeballs were bugging out.

But the girls didn't notice any of that. They were so pleased with their handiwork that she didn't have the heart to tell them how tight it was. They were thrilled with the beauty and, when they produced a small bronze mirror, so was Sophina. She had to admit that she looked fairly lovely with a tiny waist and big bosom. She hadn't thought of herself as lovely in a very long time.

But there was more to it tonight. She hadn't been able to shake thoughts of Lucien even after she'd been informed of his betrothal to Juno, so she was at the point of giving up trying to forget about the man. There was something magnetic about him, something she was unable to resist. Therefore, she would have to suffer her admiration in silence because she would not, in any way, try to usurp Juno's place as Lucien's betrothed. That would have been unfair and unkind.

Still... that didn't stop her from secretly longing after the man. She'd never had an obsession before but she felt as if this was very quickly turning into one and she further knew that the longer she remained at Spelthorne, the less healthy it would be for her. Every time she looked at the sweet, kind Juno, she just wanted to cry. How that young girl became so lucky as to be betrothed to a man like Lucien would haunt her until she died.

It just wasn't fair.

But she kept her thoughts to herself as Juno and her cousin cinched her into her borrowed clothing as tightly as a sausage in casing. Emmaline, still in the lovely dress that Juno had loaned her, was excited about the clothing and even more excited when Aricia dressed her hair in braids and ribbons. Sophina had to smile at her giddy young daughter, surrounded by young women her own age for nearly the first time in her life. She'd never known companionship like this on a peer level. It was an awakening of sorts for the sheltered young lady.

Once Emmaline's hair was finished, Aricia went to work on Sophina's hair. As a widow, she should have been properly wimpled, but Sophina had never liked wimples nor had she any desire to cover up her head, which she found hot and uncomfortable. Mostly, she wore it gathered at the nape of her neck and it was this elegant but simple style that Aricia followed. Somehow, it seemed to fit her. The style highlighted Sophina's graceful, swan-like neck and her slender shoulders as the neckline of the shift and surcoat revealed a good deal of Sophina's porcelain-white skin.

With their new friends dressed, Juno and Aricia now hurried to finish dressing themselves before the meal. Sophina and Emmaline left the chamber to give them privacy and space to work. After all, they were already dressed to the hilt. Now it would be a matter of simply retreating to the great hall and dazzling everyone. Sophina still couldn't breathe very well but it wasn't too terribly bothersome, at least not bothersome enough to loosen the stays. She was afraid the entire vision might be ruined if she tried and the girls had worked too hard for her to do that.

So she stood on the landing, trying to keep her breathing steady, as Emmaline rushed into their chamber to make sure Oswald was tended before they went to the evening meal. Since ferrets tended to use corners of rooms to relieve themselves, Emmaline had trained Oswald to use the ashes in the heart, so the girl made sure that what fire there was in the hearth was banked and pushed off to one side so that Oswald wouldn't get burned if he had to relieve himself. Sophina could hear her daughter banging around in the chamber, speaking to the beastie.

"Mama?" Emmaline suddenly stuck her head out of the chamber. "Do you think Oswald will be hungry while we are away? Mayhap we should have food brought for him."

Sophina thought on the fat little ferret who liked to eat. "He has a bone to chew on and meat scraps left over from the food that was brought to us earlier, does he not?" she asked. "I do not believe he will need anything more."

"Are you sure?"

"I am sure."

Emmaline still didn't seem convinced but was precluded from saying anything further as a shadow appeared on the stairs below. It was a man in boots, for the footfalls were heavy as they came up the stairs, and Sophina found herself looking into the handsome face of a young knight. He was very tall, with black hair and cornflower blue eyes. Those eyes were focused intensely on Sophina.

"Lady de Gournay?" the man asked, watching her nod. He smiled politely. "I am Sir Gabriel of Pembury. I have been asked to escort you and your daughter to the evening's meal. Are you prepared to retreat to the hall, my lady?"

Sophina nodded. "Indeed, my lord," she said. "My daughter and I are well and ready."

Gabriel simply smiled and held out his hand in preparation for helping Sophina down the stairs. A man of very few words, his introduction was about all he could stomach with someone he didn't know. Truth be told, Gabriel was painfully shy when it came to unfamiliar situations or new people, an odd characteristic considering he was one of the fiercer knights on the field of battle. He wouldn't hesitate when it came to arms or protection, but when it came to new people – and especially women – the big knight was quite nervous.

But he acted with poise he didn't feel as he assisted two of the female guests that Spelthorne now housed. Since Spelthorne was almost always comprised of soldiers and knights, as a military garrison would be, the event of guests and of women in particular was rare. Now they had four of them, which would undoubtedly make the evening meal much more pleasant. As least, some of the seasoned men seemed to think so. Staring at men across the table all of the time grew painfully boring. Gabriel had even heard rumor that Lucien himself had bathed for the occasion. Women came around and, suddenly, the men didn't want to smell or look so much like animals.

Including Gabriel. He had to admit, he had washed up as well before coming to collect Lady de Gournay and her daughter. The washerwoman who also brewed the strong, tangy beer they drank here at Spelthorne made soap from tallow, honey, oatmeal, and wood ash that was used by everyone, including the local villagers who did business at the castle. Gabriel was fairly certain that more soap was being used at this moment than had been in months as men washed away the dirt that might offend their dinner companions.

As Gabriel and the ladies emerged from the keep, de Royans was coming in. Clean-shaven and with washed hair, he flashed a grin at Gabriel as he passed in and Gabriel passed out. Colton had been tasked with escorting Lucien's betrothed to the meal and he, too, had made use of the oatmeal and honey soap.

Oblivious to the knights laughing at each other because they'd all seen fit to bathe for the occasion, Emmaline gave Colton a second look as he headed into the keep. Her gaze lingering on his proud form in a simple tunic and breeches; he wasn't even wearing his mail. It appeared to her as if he'd cleaned up because his skin was smooth, as if he had shaved.

Colton de Royans, in her opinion, was a handsome young man and a smile played on her lips as he disappeared from her view and she faced forward, trailing behind her mother and the very tall knight who was their escort. On this night, Emmaline felt more beautiful and happy than she had in a very long while, now facing the exciting prospect of supping in a room full of men. She was sure de Royans would end up in the hall and, perhaps, she might even have a chance to speak with him. Her stomach quivered giddily at the thought.

The night was mild as they moved to the great hall, positioned very close to the keep. The cavernous door beckoned them and there were already people inside, a vast room filled with smoke and bodies and dogs prowling the wooden floor looking for scraps. Straw was scattered all over the floor, gathering in big drifts beneath the three great feasting tables that filled the hall. And it was a loud place, as conversations were carrying, echoing off of the vaulted roof.

Even though Emmaline was following her mother and the big knight, she was awed by the sight of the big, noisy hall. Men were standing about, cups of drink in hand, watching her and her mother as Pembury escorted them inside. He walked both ladies down the center of the hall, as if parading them for all to see, but it seemed that he had a purpose – he was taking them to the big table at the far end where men in fine clothing were already gathered. As the trio approached, one man with dark hair and a strong, angular face stood up and smiled.

"So there you are," he said to Gabriel. "I thought my father and I were to be dining alone tonight. Where is Lucien?"

"Undoubtedly escorting Juno to the feast," the older man, seated beside him, spoke without enthusiasm. He had his head in one hand, leaning against the top of the table. "Where is my daughter? He has not taken her somewhere without an escort, has he?"

Gabriel had little patience for Holderness, who was nursing a massive headache after his afternoon of drinking. He was still somewhat drunk but at least he was coherent. Without answering the man's question, he indicated the ladies by his side.

"This is Lady de Gournay and her daughter, Lady Emmaline," he said. "My ladies, this is the Earl of Holderness, Lord de Saix, and his son, Sir Laurent."

Sophina and Emmaline curtsied, a polished move. "My lords," Sophina spoke for both she and her daughter. "It is a pleasure to make your acquaintances."

Laurent was gallant. "My ladies," he said. "Please, sit. It has been a long time since we have had such lovely dinner companions. I had no idea we were going to be so honored this evening."

Sophina and Emmaline took their seats across the table from them as Gabriel motioned to the servants, who rushed forward with drink. Emmaline didn't like wine, or ale, so one of the servants rushed off to fetch her something more to her liking. Meanwhile, Sophina settled down with a big cup of rich, red wine and Gabriel sat down as well, a proper distance from Emmaline.

"My lady, how long are you to be a guest of Lord Tytherington?" Laurent asked politely.

Sophina was watching a puppy come up to her daughter, noting Emmaline's delight and thinking that, already, they were in for a rough evening when she told her daughter that she could not keep the dog. Emmaline was the type that would take every animal home with her if she could.

"I am not entirely sure, to be truthful," she said. "My daughter and I were set upon by outlaws not far from here and Lord Tytherington saved us. He brought us back here until my father can be notified of our troubles."

"And who is your father?"

"Lord Andover," she said. Then, her gaze shifted to Holderness, who was still sitting there with his head in his hand. "I have met Lady Juno and Lady Aricia, my lord. You are to be commended for such a lovely and thoughtful daughter. She is a delight."

Holderness didn't move until Laurent elbowed him. Then, the man's head came up, his pale face turning in Sophina's direction. "Aye, she is," he muttered, feeling terrible and not entirely ready to become sociable. "Who did you say your father is?"

"Amory de Barenton, Lord Andover."

"Of Thruxton Castle?"

"The same, my lord."

Holderness was showing signs of being more interested in the conversation. "I know him," he said. "I have met him in London on several occasions."

"I will give him your best wishes when next I see him, my lord."

Holderness seemed to be looking at her more closely as if realizing what a beautiful woman he'd been in conversation with. He hadn't really been looking at her, at least not closely, until now.

"What are you doing at Spelthorne?" he asked.

Laurent cleared his throat softly. "The lady and her daughter have run into trouble on the road," he said. "Lady de Gournay was explaining that Lucien saved her and her daughter, and brought them here."

Holderness grunted. "Unfortunate," he said. "Where were you going?"

"To meet my betrothed, my lord."

"Who is that?"

"St. Michael du Ponte."

Holderness' bushy eyebrows flew up. "*That* man?" he said as if disgusted. "Are you serious?"

Sophina had no idea why he seemed so outraged. "Aye, my lord," she said. "My father has a tentative contract with him based upon his inspection of me. My daughter and I were traveling to Gillingham

Castle for that purpose."

Holderness shook his head. "Your father is mad," he declared. "St. Michael du Ponte is an unscrupulous character if there ever was one. How much did he pay your father for your hand? It must have been a great deal because no decent family would give over their daughter to that man. Take some advice, Lady de Gournay – go home. Go home now before it is too late."

Shocked and dismayed, Sophina stared at the man. "But... but why would you say such a thing?"

Holderness smacked the tabletop as if to emphasize his point. "Because it is true," he said, jabbing a finger in her direction. "Du Ponte is a nephew of Henry's wife, Joan. The entire family is corrupt and greedy. Du Ponte was given Gillingham simply to keep peace with Joan and her relatives, but there is nary a decent thing to say about the man. Rumors of his thievery and greediness abound. Do you not know any of this? Your intended is a hated man."

Sophina had no idea how to react to what was practically being shouted at her. She was deeply shocked at the information, information she had never heard before. There hadn't even been a hint. Her father had never told her, nor would he have been inclined to – all he cared about was ridding himself of his widowed daughter. Certainly, he would have taken any offer no matter who it had come from. So he delivered her into the hands of a disreputable man.

As long as his daughter was no longer his problem, Amory de Barenton didn't much care beyond that.

The realization was starting to make her physically ill. *Dear God, Father... what have you done?* As Sophina struggled to compose herself, more people approached their table and when Sophina glanced up, she could see de Royans approaching with Juno and Aricia. She was far too embarrassed and off-balance to speak to them or even acknowledge them, however, and as de Royans sat the ladies down, with Holderness demanding that his daughter sit beside him, Sophina stood up and quickly slipped away from the table.

Losing herself in the smoke and crowd of men, she could hear someone calling her name but she ignored the cries, desperate to be free of the room and of the people who now knew that she and her daughter were destined for a horrible life with a horrible man. Trying to evade those who might try to follow her, Sophina ducked out of a small servant's door near the hearth and out into the night beyond.

The night was soft and mild, a brilliant casting of diamonds against the black sky overhead. Sophina had emerged into a small, square courtyard buried in the middle of the complex of buildings that comprised Spelthorne. In fact, it looked as if she had trapped herself because all she could see were walls surrounding her until, off to her left, she saw a small archway with an iron grate. She went to it, unlatching the grate, and entered the dark doorway beyond. She didn't even care where it went, only that it took her away.

She wished she could run forever.

Stairs led her down between the buildings and she emerged into a wide, grassy area between the stables and the kitchen yard. The stables and their strong smell were to her left while the kitchen yard was to her right. She would rather go through the kitchens than the stables, so she headed in that direction, struggling to keep the tears from her eyes and the fear from her heart. It was true that she had left Emmaline behind in the hall, but she wouldn't have done that had she not seen the arrival of Juno and Aricia. Now, Emmaline was with her new friends, safe and happy, and had hopefully forgotten about what the hateful earl had said.

Or perhaps he wasn't as hateful as he was simply truthful. He'd told her the truth when her father hadn't. She began to seriously wonder if Lucien had known of du Ponte's reputation and simply hadn't told her. Perhaps he didn't think it was any of his business. Perhaps he simply sat back and kept his mouth shut, silently laughing at what she was about to face.

But no. She couldn't imagine he would have done that. In the brief exchanges they'd had throughout the day, she had never gotten the impression that the man was silently laughing at her plight. She didn't truly believe that. But the truth was that it wasn't any of his affair and he had rightly stayed out of it, whereas the Earl of Holderness hadn't. Now, she was embarrassed and frightened, frightened of what she and Emmaline were about to face. It wasn't as if she could return to her father; he didn't want her back. But did she truly want to marry a man who had a hateful reputation? She wasn't sure there was any choice because she had no money and nowhere else to go.

... or did she?

There were many things she could do. Being a common servant wasn't a particularly attractive role in life, but Sophina had to be pragmatic about the situation. She was an excellent chatelaine who could count money, was thrifty, could sew, and she could even cook and make household things like soaps and salves and medicines from herbs. She was very quick to learn and had, over the years, learned a great deal from anyone who would teach her. She would, therefore, make an excellent chatelaine or even a nurse to any worthy family or lord who might be seeking such a person. Perhaps Sir Lucien could even help her find such a position, a place that would take both her and Emmaline. Perhaps....

"It is a pleasant evening, is it not?"

The voice, deep and male, came from behind and Sophina whirled around to find Lucien standing a few feet away. Their eyes met and he smiled into her startled face.

"I was just entering the hall with my daughter when I saw you leave," he said. "Did you get lost?"

Sophina could feel her cheeks growing warm, now caught in her wanderings. She didn't want to explain to the man why she ran, at least not at the moment. Still, it would come up at some point and she suspected it be fairly soon. She could only keep the truth of her actions from him for so long.

"I... I suppose I did," she said, looking around. "I was... that is to say, I had hoped to find the garderobe or a privy, but I seem to have ended up out here."

A smile played on Lucien's lips. "It is much nicer out here than it is in the hall," he said. "But I will be happy to show you the privy if that is what you are truly looking for. You should not be wandering alone, anyway."

She tried to keep up a good front. "Why would you think that was not what I was truly looking for?" she asked. "I said I was."

"I know."

"And you do not believe me?"

He cleared his throat softly, averting his gaze because he was about to call the woman a liar. Far be it from him to insult a woman, but in this case, he had to. He knew why she was out here and it wasn't to find the privy; therefore, he tried to insult her the politest way he could.

"I may have heard rumor to the contrary," he said. "It is possible that I was told that the Earl of Buffoonery chased you from the hall with his unguarded words about du Ponte."

Sophina stared at him a moment. He had called her a fabricator in the nicest way possible but he knew, just as she did, that she hadn't been looking for the privy. Rather than continue to argue with him, she easily gave up. There was no use in denying it because she already looked like a fool more than she cared to. After a few moments, she simply broke down in an ironic snort.

"The Earl of Buffoonery, is it?" she grinned. "That is not a very nice thing to say."

"Am I wrong?"

She shook her head, still smiling. "From what I saw, more than likely not."

Lucien was pleased that she had at least let her guard down a little; she was smiling and that was something. He was relieved that she wasn't overly insulted by his contradiction. "I came out here to see if I could be of any service," he said. "I must apologize that a guest in my hall offended you so. I am truly sorry."

She was touched that he should concern himself so. "You need not apologize," she said. "It was not your failing."

"I could have at least slapped a hand over his mouth had I been present."

He was jesting. Or, perhaps he wasn't. Sophina couldn't be sure. In any case, she shook her head. "I am flattered that you would trouble yourself so, but I am sure there is nothing you can do in the face of the earl's ramblings," she said. "Were you told what he said, then?"

Lucien nodded. "I came into the hall just as you left," he said. "Gabriel told me what Holderness said to you."

"Is it true? What he said – is it true?"

Lucien hesitated a moment before nodding his head. It was clear that he was reluctant to admit it. "It is true that du Ponte does not have the most stellar reputation," he said evenly. "Beyond that, I will not say anymore."

"Why not?"

"Because you are to be his wife. I do not want you repeating to him what I have told you."

She cocked her head, unable to decide if he had just insulted her. "I would not repeat anything to him that you told me," she said. "I am not a silly young woman who cannot keep my lips shut."

He shook his head. "I did not mean it that way," he said. "I simply meant that the burden of such knowledge might be difficult for you to bear when you do not even know the man."

"Do *you* know him?"

"A little."

"And based upon what you know of him, would you allow *your* daughter to marry him?"

He shook his head, slowly and deliberately. "Nay, my lady, I would not."

"Why?"

He sighed faintly, drawing in a deep and thoughtful breath before releasing it. "What I know of du Ponte, I do not like," he finally said. "Let me see if I can give you an example – last year, there was a tournament in Shaftesbury, not far from here. Du Ponte competed in it, as did many of us, but his tactics were underhanded and when he lost a bout in the joust, he not only challenged the field marshals, but the man he was competing against. He threatened everyone because he felt he had been unfairly treated when the truth was that he had been treated most fairly in the situation. He was caught using a joust pole that had been banned for years – a spear-tipped vehicle that could have easily killed a man. He had it camouflaged. When he was discovered, he accused everyone of acting unfairly against him. I had never seen a grown man throw a temper tantrum up until that time."

Sophina was listening closely, horror mounting at what she was being told. "Then what the earl told me inside really was the truth," she said. "St. Michael du Ponte is a hated man."

Lucien nodded faintly. "We do not have many dealings with him, for good reason."

Sophina simply shook her head, sickened at what she was hearing. Perhaps there was some small part of her that had hoped the earl had been exaggerating, but hearing Lucien's story, she could see that her hope had been futile. But in his answer, she also felt a measure of frustration.

"When I asked you if you knew St. Michael du Ponte, why did you not tell me this?" she asked softly. "Why did you not tell me what you knew?"

"What would you have me say?"

"The truth!"

Lucien scratched his forehead. There was a good deal on his mind, not the least of which was the lady's situation with du Ponte. He had been planning out what he was going to say to her for the past few hours but now that he stood in front of her, he was almost embarrassed to say what was on his mind. Yet, he knew he had to.

"Will you walk with me, my lady?" he asked quietly. "I have a need to speak with you further. Let us stretch our legs beneath this night sky."

Sophina nodded her head for lack of a better reply and Lucien reached out, taking her elbow politely. Beneath the moonlight, they began to walk towards the torch-lit kitchen yard.

"You would like the truth," he said softly, almost rhetorically. It sounded like he was talking to himself. "There is a good deal of truth to go around, my lady. Where shall I start? Mayhap I should start with a question – are you expecting to continue on to Gillingham Castle even after what you have been told?"

She looked at him, sharply. "Would you?"

"Nay."

"Nor do I."

He glanced at her as they strolled across the soft earth. "Then what do you intend to do?"

Her gaze lingered on him a moment before averting her eyes, looking at her feet as they walked. "Strangely enough, I have been thinking on that very subject," she said quietly. "My father does not want me or my daughter returned. He has a new wife he supports above me and a home cannot have two queens. Believe me when I tell you that he was more than happy to be rid of me and even though this trip was meant for St. Michael to inspect me before accepting my father's offer of marriage, I know in my heart that I was never going home again. Whether or not St. Michael approves, my father will not accept me home."

Lucien's brow furrowed. "Why would you say that?" he asked. "Surely he would want his daughter home if a potential husband does not approve. Where else would you go?"

She laughed bitterly. "That is a very good question," she said. "As I said, I was pondering that dilemma this very moment, right before you found me. I have decided that I am not going to continue on to Gillingham. I will not put my daughter in that situation, having a stepfather who is, from what I have heard, a terrible man. Furthermore, I am not going home. That leaves little options for me. However, I have many skills that would be of great value to someone who is looking for a chatelaine or a nurse, and I would like to ask for your assistance in finding a placement for my services. I am money-wise, I can run a kitchen and house most efficiently, I can sew, and I can also nurse the sick and young. I am very good at that. So, you see, I am not entirely worthless. I do have some value. I am hoping you can help me find a place where I will be most useful. You have been so kind to me already that I feel terrible for asking for this great additional kindness from you, but I hope you will consider it. I do not know where else to turn."

By the time she was finished, Lucien was smiling faintly at her. They had reached the wall of the kitchen yard with its old iron gate and Lucien came to a halt.

"Strange," he muttered. "I was thinking today how much I need a chatelaine. I have a majordomo, but he is simply an old soldier who is not much good in the field any longer. He runs my house and kitchens because he is old and gruff and bossy, but I was never so much in need of a chatelaine than today when I had four female visitors delivered to my front door. Having a majordomo tend to women's needs is most improper."

Sophina looked at him, surprised and puzzled. "But…," she sputtered, stopped, and started again. "But you are betrothed to Lady Juno. She will be your chatelaine when you marry. That will solve your problem."

Lucien shook his head, some of his humor leaving him. "There will be no marriage," he said flatly. "I am not agreeable to marriage, at least not to that child. That last thing I need is a wife who is young enough to be my daughter."

Sophina struggled to ignore the joy in her heart in hearing the news. Just because he didn't want to marry Juno didn't mean that he wanted to marry someone else… her, for example. Nay, it didn't mean that at all, but he had just said he needed her as a chatelaine. Would she willingly be one for him even if they were not married?

She was more willing to do that than she had been willing to do anything in her life, ever.

"Does Lady Juno know?" she asked softly, realizing that her hands were practically quivering with excitement.

He shook his head. "Unless her father has told her, I would suspect she does not," he replied. "But her father was a drunken mess this afternoon, so it is possible he has not even thought to tell her yet."

"So she still believes the marriage will proceed?"

"More than likely."

Sophina thought on that, inherently feeling some pity for the polite young woman. "I spent some time with Lady Juno this afternoon," she said. "She is a kind and thoughtful girl. She did not strike me as silly or flighty."

He grunted in disapproval. "Be that is it may, I have no intention of marrying her," he said. "Her betrothal was a gift from Henry who thought to reward me for my years of service and sacrifice, but I do not see this marriage as a reward. I see it as a prison. Moreover, I do not wish to be related to Holderness; the man is an arrogant boor. Therefore, there will be no marriage."

The more he spoke, the giddier Sophina felt and the harder it was to control it. "I see," she said, pretending to be neutral about it. "So you need a chatelaine, do you? Would you like to hear of my qualifications again?"

He shook his head. "Nay," he replied. "You have already told me your skills and I do not believe you would lie to me. If you did, I would find out soon enough and I am sure you would not take that chance. That being said, I really did not have the role of chatelaine in mind for you."

Sophina was deeply and instantly embarrassed. "Oh," she said, unable to look at him. "I... I apologize, then. I thought you meant... well, it does not matter what I thought. I hope you will still consider helping me find a position, then. It is either that or I will have to commit myself and my daughter to the nearest convent, for we have nowhere else to go."

He could see that she was disappointed that he had denied needing her as a chatelaine; it was in everything about her – her tone, her movements. And in that disappointment, his heart began to sing. Was it possible she truly wanted to be his chatelaine? Did she think enough of him to want to stay at Spelthorne? God, he could only hope.

"You did not let me finish," he said. "I did not have the role of chatelaine in mind for you for several reasons – first, you technically belong to du Ponte until he either accepts you or rejects you. Correct?"

She nodded glumly. "Correct."

"Yet you have told me you have no intention of completing your journey to Gillingham, which means you are rejecting him before he rejects you. Am I correct again?"

"You are."

"But, as a woman, you really have no say in the matter, do you?"

She shook her head. "None at all, but I still will not go to him."

Lucien's gaze lingered on her lowered head. "Then I must write your father and tell him," he said. "He must understand that you have no intention of marrying du Ponte. He must further understand that I am offering for your hand and would make a far better husband to you than du Ponte ever could. That is why I said I had not considered you for the role of chatelaine – I have considered you for the role as my wife. Would this be of interest to you?"

Sophina's head snapped up and she looked at him, wide-eyed, in the moonlight. She started to speak but she was so overcome that she choked on her words and ended up coughing. As Lucien grinned, amused by her reaction, she struggled to catch her breath.

"*Me?*" she gasped. "*You* want to marry *me?*"

He nodded. "If you will have me."

She still didn't believe him. "But… but you have only just met me!"

"That is true, but I know what my instincts are telling me. They are never wrong."

She stared at him, a hand going to her head in utter astonishment. "Are you *sincere*, my lord?"

"I have never been more sincere about anything in my life."

Sophina's jaw dropped; she couldn't help it. She had no idea what to say but, suddenly, she was flying at him, her arms going around his neck and her lips on his. It was a spur of the moment reaction, something that hadn't even crossed her mind until she was aloft in his big arms, his lips devouring hers, his arms wrapped tightly around her body. It was heaven, it was bliss, it was sheer delight. It was a kiss unlike anything she had ever known. But as soon as she realized what she had done, she was terribly embarrassed and struggled to pull away from him.

"Where are you going?" he murmured, his lips against her cheek. "You cannot throw yourself at me like that and expect me to let you go so easily."

Truth was, she didn't want him to let her go so easily, either. Confused, embarrassed, but wildly happy just the same, she ended up huddling against him as he nuzzled her neck and jaw. The contact between them, flesh to flesh, had all of the subtlety of a raging fire. There were sparks between them and smoke from scorched skin; everything heated and carnal was flaming up between them. The more he touched her, the more she quivered.

"I am sorry," she breathed. "I did not mean to do that. It was entirely improper of me."

He laughed low in his throat. "I care not," he said. "I would have said all of that much earlier today if I thought you'd have the same reaction."

She could feel his hot breath against her flesh and it caused her to tremble violently. "I should not have done it," she whispered.

"Do you regret it?"

She tried to shake her head but his hands were on her, preventing it. "Nay," she breathed. "But we are not formally betrothed. A young lady who believes she is still your intended bride is in the hall. If we were to be seen...."

She had a point. With a final gentle kiss to her cheek, Lucien reluctantly let her go, disappointed when she moved out of arm's length. She appeared to be having trouble standing, her knees weak from their encounter. He, too, was having much the same reaction; as he looked at her, his heart was beating so strong, so fast, that he could hardly catch his breath.

"Please tell me that this means you will consider my marriage offer," he said, his voice full of emotion. "I realize we have only just met, as you have said, but I knew within the first few hours of knowing you that you were the woman I wanted to marry. Look at us, Sophina... we are not young and new. We have lived a good deal of our lives and we have the children and the battle scars to prove it. We are two of a kind, people in the autumn years of life, who understand things from a perspective of having lived and having been loved. I was loved, once, and I loved in return. When she died, something went out of me that I thought I would never regain. But when I saw you today and came to know you a little, that which I thought had died is now threatening to come back to life. Does that make any sense or am I rambling like a madman?"

Sophina could hardly believe what she was hearing. It was a reflection of everything she had been thinking, of secrets and thoughts long-buried in her heart. Was it really true that Lucien had the same dreams and aspirations that she did?

"If you are mad, then let us be mad together," she said softly. "I, too, knew love. I was very much loved by a kind and noble man. When my husband died, my life was over. Up until a few moments ago, I still believed it to be over. You are correct when you say that we are no longer young and idealistic. We are lived many years and understand life more than most. I should like to get to know a man who has thoughts and hopes and ideas as you seem to have. If you will share them with me, I should like to share mine with you."

Lucien just stood there, smiling in a way he'd never smiled before. There was such warmth and feeling behind the smile, an expression that no one had seen on him since the death of his wife. Those days of joy had vanished when she was buried. But now, that joy, that consuming happiness that he'd known once before was threatening a resurgence. He should have been cautious about it but he found he was too damn happy to be cautious about anything.

"I would like to share them with you," he whispered. "I would be honored to share them with you."

"And I with you."

His gaze lingered on her a moment, glittering in the moonlight as he reconciled the direction his life was taking. He'd never considered himself a giddy man, but this day had seen that opinion of himself change drastically. He wanted very much to hold her again, simply because he'd missed the feeling of a soft, warm body in his arms for so long, but he refrained. There would be time enough for such things later.

"Well, then," he said, struggling to focus on what needed to be done because his thoughts naturally wanted to linger on her. "The first thing I must do is rid myself of Holderness and his daughter. After that, I shall to write Henry and then to your father to inform them of the coming changes."

Sophina was feeling the same giddy delight that he was, struggling to keep it under control. "Truly," she said, putting a hand on his arm gently. "Lady Juno is a very kind girl. Emmaline likes her a great deal. I should not like to see her hurt by all of this."

He smiled faintly, taking her warm hand in his. "You have a tender heart," he said quietly. "I can see it. You do not like to hurt others."

Sophina shook her head. "Not intentionally, I do not," she said, feeling his fingers against hers with the greatest of delight. "I am sure you will be tactful and kind, whatever you do."

He kissed her hand gently. "I shall try."

Before she could reply, they heard clamoring over by passageway that had led from the small central courtyard that the hall door had opened in to. Lucien dropped Sophina's hand quickly and by the time three small bodies appeared, running towards them, Lucien and Sophina were standing a few feet apart from each other, quite respectably. As Sophina watched curiously, her daughter's running form came into view.

Emmaline was heading straight for Lucien. It took Sophina a moment to recognize Juno and Aricia behind her. They were all running like the wind, skirts blowing out behind them.

"Sir Lucien!" Emmaline gasped as she reached him. "You must come! It is your daughter!"

Lucien's brow furrowed but, immediately, he was moving swiftly with the ladies clustered around him, heading back for the hall.

"What has happened?" he asked steadily. "Is she injured?"

Emmaline shook her head; it was clear that she was over-excited. "Nay!" she said. "Your daughter was screaming because you were not there to eat sup with her and she hit the earl in the face with one of her metal canes! Blood is everywhere!"

Lucien didn't know whether to laugh or rage. It was so typical of Susanna to do something like that, which is why she never ate in the hall. He simply couldn't trust her behavior. Rolling his eyes, he continued on, following the path they had all come, back up the stairs and through the courtyard into the side entrance to the hall.

Emmaline had been right. Blood *was* everywhere.

CHAPTER SEVEN

Sherborne Castle
Dorset

"I KNOW LUCIEN de Russe," a tall, black-eyed knight said. "He is incapable of what you are suggesting."

Du Ponte was in the gatehouse of Sherborne Castle, a massive three-storied structure that was staffed by heavily-armed sentries, all looking at him very suspiciously. In fact, du Ponte and his men had not been allowed past the gatehouse and now stood inside a guard's room, a very small chamber that was barely big enough for two men. There was an unusually large hearth, now spitting out a great amount of heat and smoke into the room, as du Ponte faced the garrison commander.

Du Ponte's men had been kept outside of the castle, huddling in an angry group on the field just outside of the drawbridge, while du Ponte was the only one allowed to meet with the garrison commander, a legacy knight by the name of Jorrin de Bretagne. He was a big man, rugged and dark, and he didn't seem too inclined to leap to du Ponte's immediate defense. In fact, if anything, he was on de Russe's side.

Already, the meeting wasn't going well.

"My lord, I assure you, it is the truth," du Ponte pushed now that he found himself on the defensive. "The man ambushed my betrothed and her daughter as the carriage traveled just west of Tisbury. I know it was him because when I returned with my men to save the women, de

Russe had an entire contingent of men dragging the carriage out of the lake that it had fallen into during the ambush. He was looting all of the trunks that the carriage had contained. I have many men who will swear to this, my lord. You must believe me."

De Bretagne folded his arms over his broad chest, his expression suggesting impatience. "I have fought with de Russe numerous times," he said. "I have found him to be honorable and talented. What you are suggesting is slanderous at best. Do you have proof of this betrothal you speak of?"

Du Ponte nodded emphatically. "I have brought it with me," he insisted. "A missive from the woman's father suggesting the marriage. It is in my possession."

De Bretagne simply shook his head, still in great doubt. "Who is to say you did not forge the missive?"

"It has Andover's seal on it!"

"And de Russe has custody of the woman, you say?"

"He does! He stole her!"

"I do not believe that he did."

Du Ponte was at a loss. He'd not expected this reaction. "Then you will not help me?" he pleaded. "My betrothed and her daughter are at stake and you will not help me? God's Bones, who can I turn to if you will not help me? There is no one else! My betrothed is in great danger and you will not help!"

De Bretagne shifted on his big legs, irritably, holding up a hand to silence the wailing that du Ponte was doing. "Why don't you simply go to Spelthorne and ask de Russe to return your betrothed?" he asked as if du Ponte was an idiot. "Did you even think to do that?"

Du Ponte threw up his arms. "How can I ask him to return her when he is the one who ambushed her in the first place?" he fired back angrily. "Do you not understand? Lucien de Russe has taken that which belongs to me and I want it back!"

He was shouting, which didn't sit well with de Bretagne. He wasn't one to be shouted at. He had the fiery Spanish temperament in his blood and that never reacted well to shouting.

"Speak in a civil tone or I will not lift a finger to help you," he growled.

Du Ponte could see that he'd offended the man. He moved towards him, imploringly, coughing when the smoke from the overly-large blaze in the hearth got in his throat. "Please, my lord," he said, calmly and more quietly. "I would not have come here if I did not believe this to be a terrible and serious matter. I need men to go with me to force de Russe to return my betrothed and my belongings. He has my carriage, in fact, and I want it all back. Will you not give me a few hundred of your men so that I may go to Spelthorne prepared?"

De Bretagne's eyebrows lifted. "A few hundred?"

"A few thousand."

"A few *thousand*?" de Bretagne repeated, disgusted. "Of course I will not give you my entire army to march on Spelthorne. I know for a fact that de Russe would not have done any of those things that you have accused him of. There must be another explanation."

Du Ponte could see that the situation was slipping away from him. Shouting hadn't worked; perhaps pleading and sorrow would.

"If there is, I am in fear for my life to go to Spelthorne to seek it," he said. "We are speaking of The Iron Knight, a man with such a reputation that those who do not fear him are foolish men, indeed. I tell you that de Russe stole my betrothed and my carriage, yet you will not help me. I am perfectly willing to speak to de Russe in a calm manner, but he will laugh at me if I go with only the men I employ. Yet... if *you* will ride with me to Spelthorne, he will see your numbers and he must speak civilly to me. Mayhap you can even convince him to return my carriage. And my betrothed, of course. Will you at least do this? I only ask for your mediation, my lord, and nothing more."

De Bretagne pursed his lips irritably. He suspected that if he didn't do something, this wouldn't be the last he saw of du Ponte. He knew of the man; it was hard not to know of him and his shady reputation. All good men in the southwest of England kept an eye on du Ponte, knowing what the rumors were about him, and this included de Russe.

De Bretagne was coming to think that if de Russe had ambushed the man, it was to gain back property that had been stolen. Perhaps that was the real reason behind this. In any case, de Bretagne was coming to think he needed to agree to at least mediate whatever problem du Ponte thought he had with de Russe. Anything to keep this fool from hounding him.

Frustrated at the situation and at du Ponte's howling, he shook his head reproachfully.

"Very well," he said. "I will go with you and I will discover the truth of your accusations. But you will let me handle this situation my way, do you understand? Any interference from you and I will cut all ties."

Du Ponte was very eager. "Of course, my lord," he agreed swiftly. "Bless you for your assistance. Bless you."

De Bretagne grunted. "If anything, I should take you to Spelthorne so you can beg de Russe's forgiveness for slandering him so," he said. "You are a fool, indeed, if any of what you have told me is not true."

"All of it is true, I swear it."

"We shall see."

Much to du Ponte's annoyance, de Bretagne was slow to move. It wasn't until the next morning that he even began to assemble his troops as he kept du Ponte and his tiny contingent of men outside of the walls, unwilling to allow them inside.

Du Ponte swore that once he was finished with de Russe, he would make sure that de Bretagne paid the price for his apathy.

CHAPTER EIGHT

I T WAS ALL very exciting....

At least, Emmaline thought so. She was with her two new friends, Juno and Aricia, being escorted by none other than Colton de Royans while chaos went on in the hall. Lady Susanna de Russe, the same young girl who had screamed at them for most of the day from her chamber below, had belted Juno's father in the mouth with one of her canes in a fit of anger.

After fetching Sir Lucien, Emmaline and Juno and Aricia had followed him, and Sophina, back into the hall and straight into the heart of the chaos. In fact, there was so much going on that Sir Lucien asked Sir Colton to usher the young women from the hall. The young knight quickly complied.

There had been a great deal of cursing and yelling going on, which was why Emmaline suspected de Royans had been asked to remove the impressionable young ladies. He'd taken them out of the smoky, loud hall and back into the keep, into a ground-floor solar that was directly off the entry. From the madness of the hall to the sudden quiet of the keep, it was as if they had entered another world. Things were peaceful and quiet again.

The solar was cold, dark, and cluttered, and de Royans summoned a servant to build a fire while he quickly cleaned up the mess that was on a very large, heavy table. As the fire in the hearth gained steam and the young women huddled back by the chamber door, Emmaline thought she saw maps and written documents in the pile of things that de Royans cleaned from the table. In fact, as the light in the chamber grew, she could see weapons and armor and other items suggesting war and weaponry all around the room, crowding the walls and corners. Clearly, this was a man's chamber. Once the table was cleared off and the fire was burning in the hearth, de Royans sent the servant for food and drink.

Emmaline, Juno, and Aricia sat very close together on one end of the table as de Royans tried to coax more flame from the hearth. Aricia was whispering to Juno, who kept shaking her head. They both looked a little shocked at what had happened. Emmaline couldn't hear what Aricia was saying but whatever it was, Juno was either disagreeing with her or denying her. She kept shaking her head. But finally, perhaps after too much prodding from Aricia, Juno cleared her throat softly.

"Sir Colton," she said, her voice timid. "Mayhap I should return to the hall to tend my father. He will wonder where I have gone."

"My mother will tend him quite ably," Emmaline assured her before Colton could reply. "She is a very good healer."

Juno looked at Emmaline with both concern and relief on her features. "Are you sure?" she whispered. "It may be too much for her to handle. My father can be... difficult."

Emmaline shook her head. "She is very good," she repeated. "Do not worry."

Juno seemed to relax further. In fact, there was *too* much relief. "Then I am grateful," she said. "It is not that I do not wish to tend my father, but... well, the sight of blood makes me ill. I thought I should offer to tend him so that I did not look like a careless daughter."

Emmaline grinned. "He was yelling very loudly."

"And blood was spraying!" Aricia put in.

Juno put her hand on her stomach in disgust. "I know," she said. "And then my brother grabbed a servant's apron and shoved it into my father's mouth to stop the bleeding. It looked like he was trying to kill him!"

Aricia snickered, as did Emmaline. Soon, all three of them were giggling as Colton stood up from the hearth and eyed them all most critically. "A man has lost teeth and all you three can do is laugh?" he said sternly. "I am shocked, ladies. Terribly shocked."

He said it with enough exaggeration that it was evident that there was some manner of jest in his statement. Emmaline lifted her chin at him.

"Well," she said, "it *did* look like Juno's brother was trying to kill him, stuffing that rag in his mouth as he did."

"He was trying to stop the bleeding, my lady."

"I am aware of that."

Emmaline and Colton eyed one another, his deep blue eyes against her green ones. She was no wilting flower, this girl. She wasn't afraid to speak her mind. Colton's lips finally twitched with a smile, something Emmaline saw before he turned back to the hearth.

"So your mother is a healer, is she?" Colton asked. "Where did she gain this knowledge?"

Emmaline watched his broad back as he fussed with the fire again. "She learned the art from her mother," she said. "She has tried to teach me but I do not seem to have a talent for it as she does. Sir Colton, may I ask you a question?"

"Indeed."

"What is the matter with Lady Susanna that she cannot walk without those canes?"

Colton positioned the flaming logs against the fireback. "She was injured at birth."

"Does she often use her canes as weapons?"

Colton turned around to look at her. "That is a peculiar question," he said. "Why do you ask?"

Emmaline looked at Juno and Aricia, perhaps for silent encouragement, before answering. "Because she was screaming all afternoon, demanding we visit her," she said. "We heard great banging, *something,* and I would assume it was her canes. Then, tonight she hit the earl in the mouth with them. Is she always so violent?"

It was a question Colton didn't want to answer. He had been at Spelthorne for many years; consequently, he had been around when Susanna was born. He had seen her grow up from a spoilt child into an even more spoilt young lady. But the subject of Susanna was a forbidden one with Lucien so it was something that was very rarely discussed. Colton knew the relationship dynamics between father and daughter; they all knew. They knew of the guilt Lucien felt with regard to his wife's death, letting his daughter do whatever she pleased because of it. Some men even thought Lucien let her do as she pleased because he hated her. But it wasn't something any of them was allowed to discuss.

"Lady Susanna has many problems," he finally said. "You must tolerate her, as we all must. She is beyond reproach, disciplined only by her father."

Emmaline was increasingly curious, only fed by Colton's answer. "Then she may behave as she pleases?" she asked. "Will she not be punished for striking Juno's father?"

Colton stood up from the fire again, brushing off his hands. "That will be for Lucien to decide," he said. "Now, let us forget about the madness in the hall, shall we? I have asked the servant to bring you food and drink, and once you have had your fill, you will retire to your chambers for the evening."

It seemed like an order. Emmaline and Juno and Aricia looked at each other curiously but also with some disappointment. They were hoping for a big feast tonight with great food and entertainment. Instead, thanks to an unruly young girl, they were sequestered in what appeared to be a solar. That didn't sit well with them, and most especially with Juno. She had come to Spelthorne with a purpose and it wasn't to be separated from the man she was supposed to marry.

"Will Lord Tytherington not join us in our meal?" she asked. "I fail to understand why we have been removed from the hall."

Colton faced the pale young woman. "Because Lucien felt the chaos and sight of blood was too off-putting for a sensitive young woman such as yourself," he said. "This chamber is much quieter and cozier. I am sure it will be much more to your liking."

Juno was getting the impression that they were deliberately being kept away from the hall and, in particular, Lucien. She hadn't come to this place to be kept in a chamber, away from everyone. Abruptly, she stood up.

"It is *not* to my liking," she said flatly. "Lady Emmaline and my cousin may remain here, but I, for one, am returning to the hall. If I am to be the future Lady Tytherington, then it is my right."

She stormed off and Colton, with a heavy sigh, took off after her, leaving Emmaline and Aricia sitting alone in the small chamber. It was heating up very nicely, a nice bit of warmth against the cool night. Even though the day had been warm, night temperatures could drop dramatically. Hearing Juno and Colton bickering near the entry, Emmaline turned to Aricia.

"I do not mind being in here, to tell you the truth," she said. "I have never been fond of feasts with guests I do not know. I simply do not know what to say to them sometimes."

Aricia, behind her striking scarf embroidered with hummingbirds, nodded eagerly. "Nor I," she said in her husky voice, the accent heavily French. "I would much rather eat in my chamber and not be forced to socialize."

Emmaline studied the girl a moment. She had spent a great deal of the afternoon with her, coming to know her and her cousin, but the entire time, Aricia had kept the scarf over the lower part of her face. They had laughed and chatted, but still that scarf remained. It appeared that Aricia was hiding herself from the world. Emmaline had to admit that she was curious as to why. She was coming to think that Aricia had a good deal to hide. A deformity, perhaps? Or was she just so terribly shy? She wondered.

"Juno said she fostered in some very fine houses," Emmaline said. "Did you?"

Aricia shook her tightly-wimpled head. "I lived in France with my mother and grandmother for many years," she said. "I came to live with Juno and my uncle, the earl, a few months ago. It has been my task to help prepare Juno's trousseau for her marriage, so I have been helping select fabrics and sew garments. When Juno marries Lord Tytherington, I will remain as her lady-in-waiting."

Emmaline tilted her head thoughtfully. "You do not wish to marry, too?"

Aricia quickly averted her gaze. "Nay," she said, a hint of sadness in her voice. "I will not marry."

"But why?"

Aricia shrugged. "It is simply not something I wish to do," she said. "People have never paid much attention to me."

Emmaline could understand why. In truth, it didn't take a great intellect to figure it out. "But you cover your face," she said gently. "You hide your beauty. You must let them see your face in order for them to pay attention to you."

Aricia shook her head. "I cannot."

"But why?"

Aricia sighed faintly, eyes still averted. "Because... I simply do not have the beauty that most women do," she said. "So I wear colorful scarves. That is the beauty I wear, the beauty I wish to show to the world."

Emmaline was coming to feel some pity for the girl because it was clear she was being evasive about her features or showing her face in general. Emmaline's curiosity grew.

"You have lovely eyes," she said helpfully. "I am sure the rest of you is equally lovely. Will you not show me so I can see for myself?"

Aricia kept her head down. She didn't reply right away but after a moment, a hand came up and she lifted one corner of the scarf, enough so that part of her left cheek was exposed. Emmaline could immediately see the marred skin, red and angry, covered with bumps and pustules.

At that moment, she quickly understood why Aricia kept her face covered but she showed no horror in the revelation. Instead, she reached out to lift the scarf higher, seeing the extent of the damaged skin.

"Ah," she said, gently dropping the scarf back to its original position. "Now I understand. I did not mean to push."

Aricia shook her head, clearly embarrassed for having revealed her secret. "You did not," she said. "It is a natural question considering I keep myself covered as I do. But now you know why."

Emmaline wasn't sure what to say to her. She really didn't have an answer. But she truly felt sorry for her because, from what she'd experienced from Aricia, the girl was very helpful and thoughtful. It was a sad state that she couldn't even uncover her face because of a terrible skin condition.

"Mayhap it is something that will pass when you get older," she said helpfully. "Was your skin always this way?"

Aricia shook her head. "Not always," she said. "This condition came about a couple of years ago."

Emmaline wanted to help the girl, just as Aricia had helped her by lending her clothing. Emmaline had learned something of generosity over the course of the afternoon, something she had never really experienced before.

"Then mayhap it will go away when you get older," she said again, trying to sound positive. "But my mother is a great healer... would you allow her to see if she can help you? I am sure she can do something."

Aricia looked at Emmaline with some fear. "I... I do not know," she said hesitantly. "There is a physic at Thruxton Castle and he has tried to help, but it never did. Sometimes it made things worse."

Emmaline wasn't deterred. "I am certain my mother can help," she insisted. "You must let her try. Will you? She will be very kind and gentle."

Aricia was reluctant but the lure of help was too much to refuse. The skin issues had essentially ruined her life. Therefore, if there was a chance that something might help her, she was willing to try anything.

"Very well," she said after a moment. "If you think she can help."

"I think she will do everything she can."

It was settled. As Emmaline and Aricia sat in silence, they could hear more bickering out by the entry as de Royans evidently blocked Juno's exit from the keep. Juno was quite unhappy about it, unusual for the girl who seemed to be very even-tempered. She marched back into the solar where her cousin and Emmaline were. She grasped Aricia by the wrist, pulling the girl up from the table.

"Come," she said stiffly. "We are going to our chamber."

Aricia didn't resist. She allowed Juno to pull her away from the table but not before she cast Emmaline a rather concerned but curious look. Sedate Juno was angry at de Royans and refused to remain where she had been asked to remain. She was showing some defiance. Emmaline waved at Aricia as the woman was yanked from the chamber, her attention moving to de Royans as the man stood in the doorway, watching the pair retreat up the narrow spiral stairs. When they were finally out of his line of sight, he turned for the solar to find Emmaline looking at him with big eyes. Perhaps even accusing eyes. He smiled weakly.

"Obviously, she does not like to be denied her wishes," he said, somewhat quietly. "She must understand that she cannot go into the hall if Lucien has ordered her away."

Emmaline watched the young knight as he came back into the solar. His movements were slow and thoughtful, and it didn't even occur to Emmaline that she was now alone with her object of youthful lust. It was just the two of them in that small, low-ceilinged room.

"She has a point," she said, shrugging. "She is to be Lady Tytherington so she has a right to go where she wishes."

De Royans shook his head. "Not in this case," he said. "Unless Lucien tells me differently, she is to remain here."

Emmaline thought that sounded rather final. Not wanting to push the issue, as it really wasn't any of her concern anyway, she changed the subject.

"You call your liege by his given name?" she asked curiously.

"I do."

His answer was almost in the form of a challenge, as if he had perfect right to do it, so she didn't pursue that line of questioning, fearful that it might anger him for some reason.

"How long have you served Lord Tytherington?" she asked.

Colton perched his taut buttocks on the end of the table, far down from where Emmaline was sitting. "I have been with him for ten years."

"Where were you born?"

"At Hedingham Castle."

"Where is that?"

"Essex."

"Do you have family there?"

He shook his head. "My father is Baron Cononley, Constable of the North Yorkshire Dales," he said. "My entire family is from Netherghyll Castle in Yorkshire. It was my mother's family who held Hedingham and, consequently, where I was born. My mother is a de Vere and her brother was the Duke of Ireland."

Emmaline thought that was an impressive lineage for the handsome young knight and, now, it was starting to occur to her that she was, indeed, alone with him. With Juno and Aricia out of the way, there was nothing standing in the way of her coming to know the young knight better. It was better than she could have hoped for. *Ah, sweet victory!*

"Will you stay with Lord Tytherington forever, then?" she asked. "Or do you ever plan to go home?"

He raked his hand through his short blonde hair, scratching his scalp. "I must return, someday," he said. "I will inherit my father's titles and lands upon his death. But I hope that will not be for a very long time."

"You love your father?"

"I adore him."

Emmaline smile faintly. "I loved my father, too," she said. "I was very sad when he passed away. 'Tis strange... his death seems so long ago, yet it also seems like it was just yesterday. It has only been a few years but I feel greatly panicked when I think that I cannot remember what his face looked like."

Colton looked at her. She was a pretty thing, like her mother, and she had a rather deep, honeyed voice for one so young. She didn't seem giddy or particularly silly like most young women were. She seemed to have a fairly level head.

"What did he look like?" he asked quietly.

Emmaline had been thinking on her father's features when Colton asked the question. Surprised at the rather gentle question, she looked at the man only to see that he was looking at her quite intently. Their eyes locked and her face flushed a deep shade of red. Perhaps, she wasn't so ready to be alone with him as she thought. Quickly, she lowered her gaze.

"He... he had brown hair," she stammered, feeling his eyes on her. "But it was light brown, not dark. He had green eyes that crinkled when he smiled. He liked to hug me and rub his scratchy beard on my face until I screamed."

She was grinning as she said it, something that made Colton smile as well. "That sounds much like my father," he said. "My father is a hugging man. He would hug me until I cried to be released. He still hugs me, even today, but I do not run from it like I used to."

Emmaline dared to look up at him. "You should not," she said quietly. "Someday he will no longer be there to hug you and you will miss it."

Before Colton could reply, the entry door to the keep opened up and Lucien blew in, carrying a wailing Susanna in his arms. They made their way swiftly past the solar and up the spiral stairs that led to the floor above. Close on Lucien's heels, Sophina entered the keep as well, following Lucien's path up the stairs. Their movements had been very hurried, as if both Lucien and Sophina had a purpose, perhaps having to do with Susanna and the events of the night. Emmaline looked at Colton with some alarm but he merely shrugged as if whatever was going on had nothing to do with them. His casual attitude calmed her alarm immediately.

But they were prevented from discussing it as the servant Colton had sent for food also entered the keep, heading into the solar with a heavy tray in her hands. The woman was struggling with the weight so Colton stood up and went to her, taking the pitcher and cups from the tray, setting them on the table. With the tray balanced, the servant proceeded to set a big knuckle of boiled beef on the table along with pickled turnips, boiled peas and beans, and bread with a big glob of butter next to it. She brought three big metal spoons and a knife, but there were no trenchers or anything to put the food on for individual servings.

Silently, the servant fled the solar, leaving Emmaline and Colton there with only three big spoons and nothing to serve the food on. Colton simply picked up a spoon and handed it to Emmaline.

"Eat," he said. "I will see if I can have the servant find some trenchers."

Emmaline shook her head. "That is not necessary," she said. "There is no one else to eat the food but me. I do not mind spooning it out of the bowls and into my mouth."

He was about to insist on trenchers but thought better of it. If it didn't matter to her, then it didn't matter to him. But she might feel differently with what he was about to say. He picked up one of the spoons as well.

"I have not yet eaten, my lady," he said. "I was planning on sharing this with you since your companions have gone to their chamber. Should I seek the trenchers now?"

Emmaline didn't look at him. She thought it was rather romantic, sharing the meal with the knight with only spoons to eat from the same bowls. She knew it was very forward of her to think so, but she was coming to have something of an obsession for Colton. And why not? He was handsome and well-spoken. She liked that. She also liked the way he looked at her. Coyly, she shook her head in response to his question.

"Nay," she said, putting her spoon into a bowl of steaming green pea pottage. "If you do not mind sharing from the same bowl, then I am not troubled, either."

Colton almost insisted that he go and get the trenchers but something made him pause. He was rather flattered that she didn't mind. She was young, this one, but not too young. She was only four or five years younger than he was, or so he thought. He really didn't know.

But something made him want to find out.

CHAPTER NINE

"T HIS IS WHY I do not allow you to sup in the hall," Lucien said, his jaw ticking with restrained anger. "You cannot behave yourself, not ever. Even when you promise me you will behave, you never keep that promise. What you did was extremely serious. Do you even comprehend that?"

Sitting small and pale and defiant on her bed in the middle of her opulent bed chamber, Susanna's face was set in a permanent frown. Her father had just brought her back from the disarray that was the great hall, disarray that was her fault no less, and she wasn't happy in the least. The child was defiant until the end.

"I… I did not mean to hit him," she said. "He put his face in the path of my canes. It was not my fault!"

Lucien looked at her, his jaw continuing to tick. He was so angry that he was genuinely afraid of what he would say to the girl. *The girl.* He couldn't even call her his daughter. Was he truly so detached from his own flesh and blood?

"He did not put his face in the path of your canes," he said, hardly able to control his rage. "You had a tantrum. You hit the Earl of Holderness. Susanna, I am at my end with you. I did not discipline you when I should have and I have indulged you far too much, thinking that gifts and patience would buy your good behavior. But it has not. You are unruly and uncivilized, and now you have shamed me in front of a peer. You are too simple to understand just how serious this is. Therefore, I am going to do what I should have done years ago. I am going to send you away. It is obvious that I have no control over you."

Susanna's eyes widened. "You will send me *away*?"

"Aye."

"Where?"

"Cranborne Priory."

"The church of the Blessed Virgin and Saint Bartholomew?"

"Aye."

Instead of screaming, Susanna stared at him in shock. It was clear that she had no idea how to react, but soon enough, the lower lip began to tremble. Tears began to form.

"You hate me," she hissed. "You are sending me away because you hate me."

Lucien refused to give in to the pity and the guilt that her accusations so frequently brought on. "I do not hate you," he said. "I am your father. But it is clear I have made a terrible decision in keeping you with me all of these years. Mayhap the nuns at Cranborne can do something with you for I, surely, cannot."

Susanna burst into soft tears. "You hate me," she repeated. "You hate Rafe, too. That is why he stays away and will not come home. He hates you, too!"

Lucien's composure took a hit at the mention of his son, a young man he'd not seen in years. It was Rafe's choice, of course. Lucien had never really made the time for the boy after his wife's death, instead, burying himself in the politics of the king. It seemed better for him to forget he'd had a family because grief threatened to overwhelm him. But the consequences were serious in that Rafe de Russe had grown to resent his father so much that, to this day, he would not speak to him. He would not return missives sent. Lucien had stopped sending anything to his son about a year ago. He knew now that his relationship with his children was entirely his fault. In trying to forget about his beloved wife's death, he'd alienated both of them.

"Rafe is a man grown and can make his own choice on the relationship he has with his father," he said quietly. "You, however, are not grown. You are still a child and a badly behaved one at that. I will have Lady Leonie begin packing your things."

With that, he turned for the door, leaving his daughter sobbing quietly behind him. He couldn't even spare the energy to comfort her, fearful he would go back on his decision as he fell for her sorrow. Nay, he couldn't do that at all. He had to remain strong because she had to be sent away.

It was the best thing for both of them.

Shutting the chamber door softly behind him, he caught movement out of the corner of his eye, on the stairwell leading to the floor above. With lightning speed, he grabbed the dagger at his waistband, turning to confront the movement, but relief flooded him when he saw Sophina stepping off of the stairwell.

She was smiling at him in the dim light. The sight of her lightened his heart in ways he could not describe; from the hell of dealing with Susanna to the glorious sight of Sophina, his emotions were swinging wildly.

"I am sorry," Sophina said softly as she came off the stairs. "I did not mean to startle you. I came to see how your daughter was faring."

Lucien's manner was soft on her. "That is kind," he said, sheathing the dagger. "She is well. Better than the earl is, at least."

He said the last sentence with some irony and Sophina's smile broadened. "He permitted me to look at his damaged mouth," she said. "He has some loose teeth but nothing was knocked free. Most of the blood we saw was from his teeth cutting the tender interior of his mouth. He will heal."

Lucien nodded in understanding. "My thanks to you for tending the earl," he said. "That was generous, my lady."

She shrugged. "It was no trouble," she said. "But I will say that he is quite angered by what happened. Mayhap... mayhap you should go and speak with him, to ease him."

Lucien cocked his head curiously. "Did he say something to you?"

She shook her head. "Not to me, he didn't," she said. Then, she eyed him. "But he said a good deal to his son. Things I should not repeat to you."

"Tell me. Please."

She was reluctant. "He will know that I have told you."

"Then if he did not want me to know, he should not have said it for you to hear."

Sophina could see that he wasn't going to let it go. The truth was, he should probably know what was said so he knew just what the earl thought of him. Hesitantly, she spoke.

"He questioned your ability as a husband and father based on the behavior of your daughter," she said quietly. "I should not repeat these things, my lord, but...."

"Go on," he encouraged her. "I would know what the man has said. It is only fair."

Sophina sighed faintly. "He spoke of your son," she said, her voice low. "He said that the boy spouts his hatred of you and that the son's rantings should be an indication of your true character. He is not entirely sure he wants his daughter to be married to such a man."

Lucien's eyes narrowed. "I have already broken that betrothal."

"Then the earl must have forgotten."

Lucien's jaw began ticking with anger again. That and the throbbing veins in his temples were usually the first indications of a coming storm. But he kept himself in check, mulling over what he'd been told. He realized that his main concern was whether Sophina believed any of it or not. He didn't want her thinking he was an inept man hidden behind the guise of an honorable reputation. Nay, he didn't want that at all.

"I am sorry you had to hear such things," he said after a moment. "I have been painted in a rather unflattering light."

Sophina tried to smile but what he said was true; the earl's rantings were not flattering. "The earl was angry," she said in defense of Lucien.

"As you have pointed out, he is not the most tactful man. I am sure that what he said was not true."

Lucien nodded. "But it is," he said. He sighed faintly, moving for the stairs where she was standing. Never in his life had he had any inclination to explain his relationship with his children, but he did now. He wanted Sophina to understand that he wasn't a completely terrible father, merely a guilty one. "It is true, Sophina. My son will not speak to me and my daughter... well, you have seen how she is."

"That does not make you an inept husband or father."

He looked at her, sorrow in his eyes. "I suppose not," he whispered. Then, he averted his gaze, rubbing the heel of his big boot on the floor. It was a pensive gesture. When he spoke again, it was barely above a whisper. "Her name was Laurabel. She came from the House of de Reyne, a great family to the north. Oh, we were in love. Giddy, wonderful love. I adored her. She was petite, with blonde hair and an infectious laugh. When my son was born, we were overjoyed. Rafe was everything we could have hoped for and he was my pride and my joy. When he was around eight years of age, I sent him to foster although it was difficult to part with him. Still, it was necessary. Right before that time, Laurabel became pregnant with Susanna. We were thrilled. But in that happiness came my worst nightmare."

Sophina knew what had happened to his wife and she was deeply sympathetic. Silently, she sat on the steps, tugging on his sleeve so that he sat down on the step below her. Her hand rested on his shoulder as he continued.

"Susanna's birth was traumatic," he said, his voice full of sorrow. "She was stuck inside my wife's womb, unable to come free, and the physic had to struggle to bring her forth. You can see the results of the birth on my daughter, as she cannot walk properly. Although her mind is very much intact, her body is damage. But Laurabel... she bled to death. There was naught the physic could do to save her. After that... after that, it was nearly impossible to face life without her. I suppose I found solace in my duties for the king. There was a great deal going on and it was easy to distract myself with war. But in the process, I neglected my children, both of them. The results are what you see – a daughter with terrible behavior and a son who will not speak to me. It is my fault and I know it. Lo, that I had handled the situation differently. But grief – and guilt – has created my own private hell. So, you see, the man they call The Iron Knight is only hard and invulnerable on the exterior. Inside, there is nothing left."

It was a painful confession, painful to express and painful to hear. The man was laying himself open and Sophina understood that. She was sensitive to it. "It takes a brave man to let me see into his soul as you have done," she said softly. "I understand grief, Lucien. I understand it as you do. I understand wanting to hide from it. I do not fault you for doing what you felt you had to do in order to keep your sanity."

He looked up at her, into those beautiful eyes that had sparked a resurgence of life within him. He reached up, cupping her sweet face with a gentle hand. "I am sorry for the grief you have also experienced," he said, caressing a cheek with his big thumb. "Tell me of your husband. I should like to hear of him if you can manage it."

She smiled faintly. "You have bared yourself to me," she said. "It is only right that I do the same. My husband had been a great knight, once, many years ago. But his heart was bad and his career as a warrior was cut short about the time I married him. Edward de Gournay had seen forty years when I married him and I was about Emmaline's age."

Lucien smiled faintly, his dark eyes twinkling. "I have very bad news for you, indeed."

"What?"

"That your next husband shall also be forty years of age," he said. "Do you go around seeking old men to marry, then?"

Sophina giggled. "Not intentionally," she said. "And I am not sixteen years of age any longer, so I am older as well."

"How old are you?"

"I have seen thirty-five summers."

He continued to stroke her cheek with his thumb, a faint smile on his lips. "You are ageless and beautiful," he said softly. "Please; continue telling me of your husband."

She relished the feel of his hand on her face, distracting her from her tale. It was a struggle to focus. "Edward was a kind man," she said. "In truth, I almost looked at him as a father figure. He was kinder to me than my own father had ever been and I very much wanted that male element in my life. He taught me things, he gave me sage advice, and I was happy. He would have been so very angry to see how my father treated Emmaline and me after his death."

"How was that?"

She shrugged, averting her gaze as she thought of her father. "With indifference," she said. "I believe I alluded to that before. My father did not want us around and I did my best to run his home in an efficient manner, but when he married again, his wife saw me as a threat. That is why he was so quick to explore the contract with du Ponte and that is also why I can never return home."

Lucien suspected as much from what she'd hinted at during the course of their conversations. He dropped his hand from her face, moving to claim her hand, instead. "You have a home with me forever," he said. "It is unfortunate how your father behaved, but it is of little matter. In fact, I am grateful."

She looked at him queerly. "Grateful?"

He nodded, a smile on his lips. "Indeed," he said. "Had he not sent you to pass du Ponte's inspection, I would have never met you. So, you see, your trip to Gillingham was destiny. It was meant to be, only not in a way either of us had imagined."

Sophina hadn't thought of it that way and she met his smile, in complete agreement. "That is very true," she said. But soon, her smile faded. "But it seems we have a few obstacles to overcome. You must first make it clear to the earl that you are refusing the betrothal with Juno."

Lucien grunted, the warm spell of their conversation broken as Holderness was mentioned. "Aye," he said. "I must do that now, tonight. Where did you leave the man?"

"In the hall," she said. "The last I saw of him, he was there with his son."

"And the young women?"

"Your knight – I believe his name is de Royans – is still with them," she said. "He took them away from the chaos of the hall when you asked him to."

"You see where they went?"

"I have not looked. Emmaline thinks he is quite attractive, by the way."

Lucien snorted, rising from the stair and holding out a hand to pull Sophina to her feet. "He is far too young for whatever Emmaline has planned for him," he said. "Tell her that she must wait if she has her sights on de Royans."

Sophina laughed softly. "I am not entirely sure she has her sights set on him and she has not even mentioned him to me, but I have seen the way she looks at him. She is young and he is handsome. Why would she not look at him?"

Lucien waved his hand as if to wipe away that entire suggestion. "I can barely manage my own personal life," he said, teasing. "I cannot think of de Royans'."

"Mayhap, at some point, you will. Emmaline will need a husband, too, soon enough and if you and I marry, that will be your duty."

He wiped a hand over his face. "When the time comes, I shall simply force de Royans to marry her at the tip of a sword and be done with it. That will be the end of my negotiations."

Sophina chuckled. "How romantic."

Lucien cast her an impatient look. "I am too old," he said. "I do not have time for romantic betrothals."

"Get it done at the end of a sword."

"It is much faster that way."

Sophina continued to chuckle at him. "I hope you still have time for the woman you intend to marry, Lucien."

His eyes glimmered at her. "You will be where all of my time is spent, so that is not an issue."

She couldn't seem to stop smiling at him. Such sweet words from the man had her feeling something deeper and broader than what she ever felt for Edward. But not in the negative sense; it was simply different. Joyful and different.

"That is good to know," she said quietly. "Now, if you have duties to attend to, I would like to ask for your permission to speak with your daughter."

His smile faded. "Why?" he asked. "You should know that I have made the decision to send her away from here."

Sophina's manner turned to one of great concern. "Where?"

"Cranborne Priory. I have obviously failed to raise a proper child. The nuns at Cranborne will not fail."

He didn't sound cold about it, merely resigned. Sophina's gaze trailed to his daughter's chamber door. "May I at least speak with her?" she asked quietly, politely. "I have a daughter of my own, you know. I understand them."

Lucien hadn't thought of that, but she was absolutely correct. She had a very well-behaved and sweet daughter, and he was embarrassed that he did not. He sighed faintly.

"I cannot let my failings fall upon you," he said. "Susanna is my problem. I do not want her to become yours."

"Please?"

She was pressing in the sweetest way possible and Lucien folded. He could already see that he would fold to anything she wished, but he was not troubled by that realization in the least. He took her hand and gently brought it to his lips. "As you wish," he murmured. "I shall be in the hall. If you need me, send for me."

Sophina merely nodded, feeling his kiss against her flesh like a branding iron. Everything about the man was hot. She watched him leave the keep, her focus lingering on the doorway long after he'd left. Even though he was gone, somehow, he was still with her. It was an odd sensation but the most comforting one she'd ever known.

Inevitably, her attention turned towards Susanna's chamber door. The mother in her was determined to speak to the motherless girl who had her father at his wit's end, so much so that he was about to send her away. That didn't solve the problem, in Sophina's opinion. It only made a lonely girl more lonely.

Taking a deep breath, she rapped softly on the chamber door.

CHAPTER TEN

"I TOLD YOU this afternoon and I will tell you again now," Lucien said steadily. "It is in my right to refuse this betrothal and I have done just that. My decision is final."

The great hall of Spelthorne was cloyingly hot, creating a rather sweaty and uncomfortable atmosphere. Lucien was seated at the same feasting table where Susanna, an hour earlier, had smashed Holderness in the mouth. As Sophina had indicated, Holderness had not left the hall, nor had his son. They had remained and when Lucien went looking for the man to reiterate his position on the betrothal to Lady Juno, that is exactly where he found them.

Holderness' mouth was swollen and there were bloodied rags on the floor and on the table still, but the damage to his mouth hadn't impeded his ability to drink. He was doing it in excess as he had earlier. Lucien was coming to realize that Holderness was simply a drunkard and he silently cursed himself for wasting all of that good Spanish wine on the man. He could have given the cheapest wine possible and it would have had the same effect.

Still, he'd come into the hall with a purpose. He was concerned that Holderness had evidently forgotten about the afternoon's drinking session when Lucien had broken the betrothal. Lucien was more than perturbed that Laurent had not reminded his father of what had transpired, but perhaps Laurent was hoping Lucien would forget about the incident. Lucien, however, forgot nothing. Especially in a situation like this, his wants would be abided.

"That is *outrageous*," Holderness sputtered. "By what right do you say such a thing? You have not even formally met my daughter yet. If you knew her, you would not say such things!"

Lucien remained cool. "I have met her and she is a polite young woman," he said. "But the fact remains that earlier today, you embarrassed yourself and your entire family with your drunkenness and I will not be related by marriage to you. Do you not remember any of this?"

Holderness' eyes were wide with both outrage and confusion. "Of course I do!"

"Then I do not have to remind you that it was you who instigated this situation, not I," Lucien said. "Furthermore, your daughter is far too young for me. This was Henry's idea, not mine. I am, therefore, dissolving this betrothal. Are you sober enough to understand me now?"

Holderness turned red around the ears, furious and embarrassed. "I understand that you are a dishonorable man by breaking what the king himself has decreed," he said. "The contract was brokered with Henry. You must abide by it."

Lucien wasn't happy that the man had called him dishonorable. In fact, it was about the worst thing Holderness could have said. He looked at Laurent, standing next to his father.

"Must I explain to your father that calling me names is not going to force me to change my mind?" he asked the man. "If anything, he has just insulted me beyond repair. Remove him from this hall before I do something you will both regret."

Laurent was in an awkward position. He was a knight, and a very good one, and had served under Lucien several times. He liked and respected the man, but his father was becoming something of an embarrassment. Still, the man was his father and had moments of goodness. Laurent was walking a fine line.

"Lucien, may I speak with you privately before you throw us all

THE IRON KNIGHT

out?" he asked quietly. "Only a moment of your time, please."

Because he liked Laurent, Lucien agreed. But as Laurent started to Lucien's side, his father grabbed on to him.

"Nay," he said angrily. "If there is to be any discussion on this subject, I will hear it. This is not your business, Laurent. This is between Tytherington and me."

Laurent was starting to lose patience. "Do you truly believe he will want to speak to you after you called him dishonorable?" he asked. "Lucien de Russe is one of the most honorable men I know. You had no right to accuse him otherwise."

Holderness didn't like to be reprimanded by his son for all to see. His jaw ticked angrily as he spoke, turning to Lucien. "I did not mean to call you dishonorable," he said. "I meant to say that what you are doing is dishonorable. My daughter will be shamed because you have broken the contract. No decent man will want her if they know The Iron Knight has refused her."

Lucien remembered what Sophina has said about Lady Juno – *she is a kind and thoughtful young woman.* Lucien had no desire to malign the girl; he simply didn't want to marry her. Therefore, Holderness may have had a point, as much as Lucien hated to admit it. But the truth was that he was anxious for this to be finished. He simply didn't want to waste the energy dealing with a betrothal he never wanted, especially when a woman he very much wanted to marry had his attention. Nay, he didn't want to deal with this at all.

"I have not told anyone of this marriage contract and unless you have spouted off for the entire world to know, then it shall be between us and Henry," Lucien said with more patience than he felt. "If anyone asks, you can tell them that you refused the betrothal, not I."

Holderness snorted. "Who would believe that?" he asked, frustrated. "Only a madman would refuse to allow his daughter to marry The Iron Knight."

Lucien fixed on him, his dark eyes glittering coldly. "Earlier this evening, I was told that you were questioning my ability as a father," he

149

said. "I was further told that you questioned whether or not I would make a good husband to your daughter. Suffice it to say that you are correct; I will not make a good husband to your daughter. She is blameless. Now, pack your things and be gone by morning. I have no further need to discuss this."

Holderness was shocked, feeling cornered because someone had repeated what he'd said in anger about Lucien. Now, he'd cooked his own goose and Lucien had every right to be angry.

"There is no negotiation?" he asked, stunned. "As quickly as that, you will order us to leave?"

"Aye."

It was a simple answer, one that had Holderness' head spinning. He could hardly believe what had happened. "You will do this without even getting to know my daughter?" he pushed, incredulous.

"Why would you want her to know a man whose credibility as a husband you have questioned?"

Holderness threw up his hands. "I was angry!" he insisted. "Your daughter had just knocked me in the mouth!"

Lucien wasn't going to argue with the man any longer. He had said what he needed to say. Looking at Laurent, standing next to his father, he spoke directly to him.

"Put your father to bed," he said. "Come find me in my solar when he is bedded down for the night. You and I must speak."

Laurent nodded, grasping his father by the shoulders and pulling the irate man away from the table. No good could come of any conversation or negotiation between Lucien and his father this night, but Laurent felt hopeful in Lucien's summons to his solar. Perhaps there was something more to discuss to salvage the situation.

For his sister's sake, he hoped so.

℃℥

"WHY ARE YOU here?" Susanna demanded. "I did not summon you."

Sophina was standing just inside the door of the child's lavish chamber. It was pretty and soft and all things a girl's chamber should be. But this chamber did not house a girl; it housed a monster.

Quietly, Sophina closed the door behind her and faced the petulant child.

"Nay, you did not," she said steadily. "I asked your father for permission to speak to you and he has given it."

Susanna eyed the woman who had spoken boldly to her earlier in the day. She wasn't happy to see her. She wasn't happy to see anyone who wasn't catering to her every whim.

"I do not want you here," she said, turning away. "Get out."

It was a rude command but Sophina fought off a smile. "Such impertinence," she scolded softly. "Who has given you the right to behave so?"

Susanna wouldn't look at her. "Get out," she said again. "I have given you an order. You must obey."

Sophina caught sight of the child's nurse in the shadows. She wondered if the woman would try to physically throw her out, but when the woman didn't move, Sophina returned her attention to Susanna. As long as the nurse was going to stay out of it, Sophina had an idea about how to get through to Susanna. She had been thinking about it all afternoon and, in particular, when she saw how the child behaved in the hall tonight. It was just a hunch she had, and probably a bad one, but the child was a hard case. Incorrigible, to be truthful, so Sophina suspected she really had nothing to lose at this point by going with her instinct. Susanna was on her way to Cranborne Priory according to her father, so she already had one foot out the door.

This was her last chance.

"I do not have to obey," Sophina said. "I want to speak with you. I have heard that you are going to Cranborne Priory. Does this please you?"

Susanna began thumping those canes again. It was a tick, something to do with her angry hands and a threat of what was to come if she was not obeyed. "I am *not* going," she said flatly. "My father will not send me. He always does as I wish and I do not wish to go."

It was a bold statement. Sophina began to move in her direction, slowly, not wanting to get hit by one of those canes. "Tell me something, Susanna," she said. "Are you not ashamed of your terrible behavior? You hit an earl of the realm tonight. Do you understand how serious that is?"

Susanna stiffened; Sophina could see it. "My father came to me, did he not?" she said, turning to look at Sophina. "When I scream, he comes."

The light of recognition went on in Sophina's head; *so she knows how to control him.* It was infuriating, actually. Susanna was in complete control of her father, in every way, and she knew it. Without another word, Sophina walked up to Susanna and ripped both canes from her hands, tossing them far away. Shocked, Susanna screamed in fury.

"Give those to me!" she yelled. "I need them!"

Sophina shook her head. "Nay, you do not," she said. "You only need them to hit people and strike fear into them. That is your only need with those canes. Now you do not have them."

Susanna was furious. She tried to stand up but Sophina pushed her back down by the shoulder, certainly not hard enough to hurt her but hard enough to cause her to fall back into her chair. Susanna screamed again and tried to kick at Sophina with one of her spindly legs, but Sophina grabbed it easily. Giving a yank, she pulled Susanna right down onto the floor.

The child yelled her anger, infuriated at the treatment, but Sophina had a point to make. She hadn't hurt the child nor would she, at least not in a brutalizing manner, but the girl had to have a taste of her own medicine. Sophina suspected that was the only way Susanna would understand just how abominable she had been. Sophina only hoped that Lucien wouldn't be angry at her for it. Still, if it would help his relationship with his daughter, she was willing to take the chance.

"Now," Sophina said as Susanna sat on her bum a few feet away.

"How did you feel to have your canes taken away? How did it feel for me to pull you onto the floor?"

Susanna was beginning to cry, so angry that she couldn't control it. "You are a terrible woman!" she hissed. "I am feeble and ill and…!"

"Nay, you are not feeble and you certainly are not ill," Sophina countered, cutting her off. "You are a strong, smart young lady with a nasty streak. You delight in tormenting your father and then blaming him for your problems. But the truth is that *you* create your own problems, Susanna. Your father has decided to send you to the nuns at Cranborne and do you know what they will do to you if you misbehave? They will beat you and your father will not be there to protect you. No one will. Do you understand that?"

Susanna wasn't quite sure how to react. She rolled onto her knees in an attempt to stand. "I am going to get my canes," she snarled. "I am going to get my canes and hit you with them!"

Sophina, very casually, moved over to the wall where she had tossed the canes. There was no possibility that Susanna could move faster than she could. Without a word, she collected the canes and went to the lancet window overlooking the northern portion of the bailey. Quite calmly, she tossed both canes out of the window.

"Nay, you are not going to touch me with them," she said. "I will make sure you never see those canes again. You are going to learn to behave yourself and the first part of that will be taking away your weapons. You do not use them to walk. I have not even seen you try. You only use them to hurt people."

As Susanna realized her canes were gone, she began to turn red in the face. Eyes full of tears, she opened her mouth and wailed as loudly as she could.

"I hate you!" she screamed. "Get out of here! I will tell my father and he will punish you!"

Sophina crossed her arms. "I am not leaving," she said, her voice low and steady as Susanna wailed. "I want you to understand what I have done. By taking your canes and pulling you to the floor, I did to you what you have been doing to everyone here at Spelthorne and, in particular, your father. I have intimidated you. I frightened you. Is that how you feel right now? Are you afraid of me? It is not a good feeling, is it?"

Susanna was on her knees, screaming and beating her hands against the floor. "You are a terrible, hateful woman!" she cried. "My father will punish you! I hope he makes you scream and cry as you have done to me! You are horrible and hateful!"

"So are you."

Susanna looked at Sophina as if the woman had struck her.; She wasn't used to being insulted. Still red in the face, with tears all down her cheeks, she grunted and groaned and gasped as she struggled across the floor, over to a section of the room that held her poppets and other toys. Sophina watched her curiously, thinking that the girl at least had some strength to her, when Susanna settled down next to a small table with a miniature set of pewter dishes on it.

It was truly a beautiful little set, and undoubtedly expensive, but Susanna immediately picked up a little cup and hurled it at Sophina's head. Only a swift movement avoided contact. Shocked that the child not only threw the cup but had good aim in doing it, Sophina shook her head reproachfully.

"I would not do that again if I were you," she said quietly. "You will not like my reaction if you do it again."

Susanna's answer was to shriek and throw another cup, one that Sophina easily avoided this time. She was prepared. Susanna picked up a little plate now and threw it as Sophina came in her direction. The little plate hit Sophina in the thigh harmlessly and clattered to the floor as Sophina swooped over Susanna and picked her up from behind.

Scooping the child up beneath her arms, she hauled the fighting, snarling child over to the bed. Sitting down on the mattress, Sophina put Susanna over her knee but not without a fight. It was a bitter struggle until the very end.

As the nurse wept in the shadows and Susanna screamed as if she was being stabbed, Sophina spanked Susanna within an inch of her young, naughty life.

CHAPTER ELEVEN

"**S**HE SPANKED HER!" Emmaline gasped, rushing into the chamber that Juno and Aricia shared and slamming the door. She was electrified with excitement. "I listened from the stairs and I heard when my mother spanked her!"

Juno and Aricia had wide eyes on Emmaline. "Lord Tytherington's daughter?" Juno clarified, astonished. "Did she *really*?"

"She did!"

The girls stared at each other in shock for several long seconds before bursting into laughter. Juno tried to shush them but she was laughing, too. It was such sweet justice for a terrible child. Juno pulled Emmaline and Aricia away from the door and over to the bed where they could huddle and whisper. She didn't want their joy to be overheard. She was to be Lady Tytherington, after all – it wouldn't do to rejoice in the misfortunes of her soon-to-be stepdaughter.

"Your mother is very brave," Juno said sincerely, holding Emmaline's hand as the girl giggled. "Lord Tytherington's daughter has excellent aim with her canes. I wonder if she tried to hit your mother with them."

Emmaline shook her head. "I do not think so," she said. "But I could not hear for certain. I am sure my mother would not make an easy target."

She continued to giggle but there was more behind her jubilation than just a shocking situation. She had just come from Colton de Royans and, after having supped with the man, she was fairly certain she was deeply, irrevocably in love with him. The meal had been an interesting mix of silence peppered by spells of chatter, and Colton was a brilliant conversationalist as far as Emmaline was concerned. She had enjoyed every minute with the man even though she had done most of the talking.

Therefore, she was slightly giddy at the moment. She'd only been passing by the second floor after just having left de Royans when she heard her mother's voice and the spanking going on. Now, she was breathless for more reasons than just one.

But if Juno noticed that Emmaline was more effervescent than usual, she didn't say anything to that effect. In truth, she seemed both humored and appalled by Susanna's spanking, and that was the full focus of her attention at the moment.

"I wonder why your mother is spanking her," Juno wondered seriously. "Do you suppose Lord Tytherington gave her permission to spank his daughter for what she did to my father?"

Emmaline shrugged. "I saw Sir Lucien leave the keep a little while ago," she said. "It is possible he did. Mayhap he asked my mother to do it."

"But why did he not do it himself?"

No one had an answer for that. Now that the giddy shock of the spankings of that terrible little girl had worn off, they were left to sit in wonder of what had occurred. But Emmaline was also thinking of de Royans and the last time she saw him. She couldn't help that her thoughts kept drifting to him.

"I am sorry that you did not remain for the meal," she said to Juno. "Sir Colton promised he would send food up to you."

Juno's features stiffened. "He is a rude knight," she said. "He does not seem to understand what is expected of me here at Spelthorne. He is supposed to obey my commands just as he would obey Lord Tytherington, but he would not do it. I will make sure Lord Tytherington knows."

Emmaline didn't want Colton to be punished but she also didn't want to let on that she had a full-blown obsession with the man. She wasn't sure how Juno or Aricia would take it, especially now that Juno was wishing hate upon the knight. It might make her hated, too, and she didn't want to ruin this new friendship so soon. Colton wasn't anything to her and she wasn't anything to him, so she wasn't willing to jeopardize her budding relationship with Juno. Quietly, she cleared her throat.

"Until you are married to Sir Lucien, I do not believe his knights have to obey your commands," she said hesitantly. "But Sir Colton was just doing as he'd been commanded. He would be in for a great deal of trouble if he let you back into the hall when Sir Lucien told him to take you away from it. Moreover, why would you want to go back in there where there was all of that blood? I thought it made you ill."

Juno looked at her with uncertainty, realizing that she was probably correct for the most part. "It does," she said. "But I still should have been there. Instead, your mother had to tend my father's injury. It should have been me."

Emmaline shook her head, baffled. "But you said it makes you ill to see blood!"

Juno was ashamed. "I know," she said. "But... well, Lord Tytherington will think me foolish and weak now. Those are not good qualities in a wife."

Emmaline waved her off. "He more than likely does not even care," she said, although she really wasn't certain. Her gaze lingered on Juno for a moment because the girl seemed so torn and nervous. "Do... do you *really* want to marry him, Juno?"

Juno looked at her, sharply, showing that it was a tremendously invasive question. But she quickly backed off, returning to her ashamed and subdued demeanor. "He is a great man," she said. "It would be an honor for any woman to be his wife."

It was a practiced answer, as if she had rehearsed it. As if someone had *made* her rehearse it. Emmaline looked at Aricia, who gazed back at her with some doubt. There was definitely doubt in the girl's eyes.

"You can tell her the truth," Aricia said to her cousin, quietly. "She will not tell anyone."

Emmaline shook her head, looking to Juno. "Of course I will not tell anyone," she insisted. "You do not wish to marry him?"

Juno sighed heavily, looking at her hands. "Well...."

"*Tell* her," Aricia pushed.

Juno didn't say anything. She continued to stare at her hands. Finally, it was Aricia who spoke because Juno seemed unable to.

"It is no reflection against Lord Tytherington, but my cousin does not wish to marry him," she said quietly.

Emmaline looked at Aricia, most curious about her statement. "But why?"

Aricia's blue eyes softened. "Because she loves a young knight who served her father," she said sadly. "He is a good man from a good family but they are not wealthy. They do not have connections. My uncle knows this, which is why he pushed so hard for the betrothal between Lord Tytherington and Juno. He cares not for her feelings. He only wants to make a wealthy marriage for his daughter."

Emmaline was greatly disturbed by the story. She looked at Juno again. "Is this true?" she asked. "You love another man?"

Juno nodded faintly. "When my father found out, he dismissed Reid from his service," she said quietly, tears forming in her eyes. "My brother was kind enough to send him to friends of his, the House of Wellesbourne, but the fact remains that... that...."

She turned red in the face and Emmaline looked at her, very puzzled. "What *is* it?"

Aricia couldn't stand it any longer. "She is pregnant with Reid's child," she hissed. "My uncle knows this. That is why he is pushing this marriage – he wants Lord Tytherington to marry her quickly so he will believe the child to be his."

Emmaline gasped, a hand flying to her mouth in shock. "Sweet

Mary!" she gasped. "Is *that* why he wants you to marry Sir Lucien?"

Juno nodded, a stray tear falling from her face and onto her lap. "The betrothal with Lord Tytherington was already in the process, months ago," she said. "The more I told my father that I did not wish to marry anyone other than Reid, the more adamant he became that I must marry well. Reid's family is honorable but modest, you see, and my father does not want that. You see… we have lost most of our wealth, too. My father sees a marriage with Sir Lucien as a way to gain financial resources."

Emmaline was still horribly shocked at the truth. "Then he only wants it for the money!"

"Aye."

"But… but the pregnancy?"

Juno lifted her head, looking at Emmaline without a shred of regret. "Reid and I love one another deeply," she said. "I thought the fact that we have consummated that love would force my father to abandon his quest to find me a wealthy husband, but it did not. It only pushed him into demanding such a thing immediately. He wants Lord Tytherington to believe the child is his."

Emmaline couldn't possibly feel worse for her new friend as she did now. It was a horrible, heartbreaking story, not only for Juno but for Lucien as well. Holderness was trying to trick the man into raising a child that was not his.

"Your pregnancy cannot be very far along," she said. "You do not have a rounded belly."

Juno shook her head. "A month or mayhap a little more, at the most," she said. "It is still very early."

"And it was very difficult traveling all of these miles here to Spelthorne," Aricia said, her sympathetic gaze on her cousin. "She has not been feeling well at all but my uncle has no care for her. It does not matter to him if she is ill or not."

Emmaline was overwhelmed with horror and sorrow for the situation. "Your brother came here with you, did he not?" she asked. "Does he know of your condition?"

Juno nodded. "He does."

"And he sides with your father?"

"Nay, he does not. But, like me, he has little choice in the matter. Laurent has been very kind and considerate to me."

Emmaline was truly saddened by everything. Reaching out, she grasped Juno's hand because she didn't know what else to say. It seemed that they were all caught up in the game of marriage betrothals and politics, one way or another – her mother with du Ponte and Juno with Lucien. As the three ladies sat on the bed, pondering the devastating situation, there was a soft knock on the chamber door. Aricia went to answer it.

Sophina stood in the doorway, smiling pleasantly at the young ladies inside, and the girls seemed to sit up and take notice. They didn't want to appear as if they had been in deep conversation with something quite shocking.

"Good eve, ladies," Sophina said. Her gaze moved to Emmaline. "I came to find you, young miss. It is time to retire for the night. Bid your friends a fair evening now. We will see them on the morrow."

Juno lowered her head and wiped quickly at her eyes as Emmaline went to greet her mother. If her mother happened to see Juno weeping, she didn't want the woman asking questions, so she said the first thing that came to mind.

"Did you really spank Sir Lucien's daughter?" she asked.

Sophina's smile vanished. "Who told you such things?"

Emmaline gave her a mother a wry expression. "I *heard* you," she said. "Did Sir Lucien give you permission to spank her for striking the earl?"

Sophina gave her daughter a long look, reaching out to grasp her hand. "That is none of your affair," she said. "Come along, Em. Bid your friends a good sleep."

Emmaline would not be dragged away so easily. Before Juno's revelation, she had been waiting to see her mother or, more specifically, for her mother to see to Aricia. She hadn't forgotten about their conversation earlier where Aricia had showed her the terrible state of her skin. All thoughts of pregnancies and forced marriages aside, she pulled her mother into the chamber.

"Wait," she said. "Mama, I have been telling Lady Aricia what a great healer you are. Can you spare a few moments before we retire? It is important."

Sophina wasn't as patient as she normally was. She was weary from an extraordinarily eventful day and having just come from her battle with Susanna, she was weary. She wanted to go to sleep. But the soft plea from her daughter naturally had her complying. She was never one to refuse help to anyone, no matter how exhausted she was.

"Of course," she said steadily, looking to the young woman with the veil across her face. "Is there something I can do for you?"

Aricia stood there, twisting her hands nervously, and didn't say a word. Truthfully, she was embarrassed and unsure. Emmaline stepped in to take charge when she saw that Aricia couldn't, or wouldn't.

"Aricia has a skin condition, Mama," she said as she led her mother over to the girl. "She said that the Thruxton physic tried to help her but that it made it worse. That is why she wears these beautiful veils, to hide her skin. Can you look at it to see if you can help her?"

Sophina was the least bit curious now. Her gaze on Aricia was calm and reassuring. "Will you remove your veil so that I may look, my lady?" she asked politely.

Aricia was horribly embarrassed. No one but Juno had really seen her face as of late, so to show it to women she had just met, no matter how kind they were, rattled her. She was so very uncomfortable. But she liked Emmaline and she liked what she knew of Emmaline's mother. Having no real older female figure in her life, it was easy to latch on to someone respectable and kind. Still, it was difficult to lower her guard, so with the greatest hesitation, she reached up to unfasten one end of the veil. Carefully, she lowered it, averting her gaze as she did so. She didn't want to see the disgust in their eyes when they looked at her skin.

But there was no disgust to be had, only great curiosity in the best sense of the word. It was curious concern as Sophina got her first look at Aricia's angry skin. The young woman's forehead was filled with red bumps but her entire face, both cheeks, chin, and neck, were literally full of terrible red lumps, rashes, and pustules. She was very pale-featured, very plain, with a long jaw and a dimpled chin. Sophina peered closely at it for a brief moment before motioning towards the bed.

"Sit," she commanded softly. "I must get a closer look. Em, will you and Lady Juno please bring candles? I will need light."

Emmaline and Juno scattered, hunting down tapers in the small chamber. Juno collected a tall bank of tapers that was near the table in the room while Emmaline took the taper next to the bed. They brought them over, leaning the tapers near so they shone brightly in Aricia's face.

Meanwhile, Sophina was getting a very close look at Aricia's jaw and chin and something occurred to her – the girl had a beard. In fact, she had a beard all the way under her chin and down her skinny neck. It wasn't thick, but it was definitely a beard that had been covered up by the veil so it wouldn't have been noticeable at all. But the more Sophina looked at it, the more the obvious occurred to her.

Aricia wasn't a girl at all.

Her neck had a bulge in the middle of it, the same bulge that men had once they went from being a boy to a man, and Sophina glanced at Aricia's long, firm fingers. They were a man's fingers. It was very puzzling and rather astonishing revelation, but Sophina wasn't apt to say anything about it.

If Aricia wanted to pretend to be a girl, there must be a reason be-hind it – fear, sickness, or even a preference. Perhaps she simply liked the way girls dressed. In any case, it wasn't Sophina's business. She'd lived long enough to know that there were many different kinds of people in the world. Aricia had proven herself to be a very kind and generous person, so what she wanted to do with her life, or more correctly his life, was of no concern to Sophina. The world was full of wonderful and unusual people.

"May I see your chest?" she asked gently. "I would like to see how much of your skin is affected, if I may."

Reluctantly, Aricia pulled back the top of her surcoat, showing the top portion of her chest and all of her shoulders. Sophina checked her neck and back, noticing more red bumps but not nearly as bad as what was on her face. But as she inspected, it was becoming abundantly clear that Aricia was male – a patch of faint, white hair on her chest and then more patches of fine hair on her back. She had no breasts at all and her build, as Sophina was looking at her from the rear, was sinewy and very slender. Unlike most girls, who at least had some feminine lines to their body, Aricia had none.

Still, Sophina said nothing. She went back to inspecting Aricia's face, focusing on the task at hand and not her suspicions. She thought that she could, indeed, help her.

"My mother was a healer," she told Aricia. "When I was younger, my skin would flare just a little and my mother would have me eat fish if it was available, accompanied by apple cider vinegar. I know it sounds strange, but she said that we must make sure our insides are working well and that would help the outside. For my skin, she would make a mask of honey and cinnamon to ease the redness and then she would also make a potion from honey and clotted milk to wash my face. It helped a great deal. I will ask Sir Lucien if I may procure these ingredients for you and you must cleanse your face every morning with honey and cinnamon, and then every night with honey and clotted milk. Once you have done that, then you will rinse your face with vinegar made from apples. Are you willing to do this?"

Aricia nodded eagerly. "And you think it can help?"

Sophina nodded. "I believe it might," she said. "But watch what you eat, as well. Fish and fowl are preferable to beef and mutton. Try to eat green vegetables. No cheese. See if that helps make a change in your skin. By my mother's advice, those things helped me, so it is worth a try."

Aricia was awed by Sophina's suggestions, her face glowing with gratitude. She nearly broke down in tears. "The physic at Thruxton told me that it was sin that caused my skin issue," she said. "He also said it was bad humors in my body. He even bled me a few times but it did not help. It simply made me ill. He said... he said that God was punishing me."

It was an emotional delivery and considering the young woman's secret, Sophina had a feeling that the physic at Thruxton had discovered it, too. It sounded like the man was less than understanding or accepting of someone who was simply different from the rest, viewing it as a strict and narrow-minded man would. It was sad, really. Sophina could see how much it had hurt Aricia simply from the way she spoke and Sophina naturally felt some compassion for the young woman.

"Sometimes men like to preach of sin when the truth is that they are not without it," she said. "I do not believe God has visited a pox upon you, my lady. Let us see if those things I told you of will help. I will obtain the ingredients on the morrow."

Aricia didn't know what to say. She wasn't used to having someone be so kind and understanding with her. Blinking her eyes of the tears that had been forming, she quickly put the veil back over her face, once again hiding behind it.

"I do not know how to express my gratitude," she said, her voice trembling. "I promise I will be very careful in what I eat and I will use your potions faithfully. May... may I help you procure the ingredients and watch how you mix them? I should like to be able to do it for myself."

Sophina smiled faintly. "Of course you may," she said. "I would be happy to have your help."

Emmaline, who had been watching her mother with pride, smiled at Aricia. "She means that she would like to have your help because I am inept at anything she tries to teach me," she said, watching Aricia and Juno giggle. "My poor mother did not bear a daughter she is able to pass her skills along to."

Sophina grinned, putting her arm around her daughter's shoulder and kissing her head sweetly. "You are good for other things, my love," she said. She gave her a final squeeze before returning her focus to Aricia and Juno. Not strangely, she was looking at Aricia through new eyes now that she knew the girl's secret. "We shall start on the medicines for your skin in the morning. For now, I think we should all get a good night's sleep so we will be fresh on the morrow. It has been a rather busy day for all of us."

Juno and Aricia agreed as Sophina pulled her daughter to the chamber door. As she opened the heavy panel, she heard Aricia's voice behind her, softly.

"Thank you, my lady," she said, her eyes moist once more. "For your generous nature... I am very grateful."

Sophina smiled her reply, ushering Emmaline out into the landing and closing the chamber door quietly behind them. It was only a matter of a few steps across the dark landing before they came to their chamber door and Emmaline opened it, stepping through with her mother behind her. As Sophina shut the door and bolted it, Emmaline spoke softly.

"Mama?" she asked.

"Aye?" Sophina said as she went to light a taper in the dark room.

Emmaline didn't reply immediately. She picked up Oswald from where the ferret had slithered out from under the bed. She hugged the creature, cooing to him. When she finally spoke, her voice was very soft.

"Does... does Aricia have a hair on her face?" she asked.

Sophina struck the flint and stone, lighting the taper. The soft glow filled the room before she answered. "Aye," she said softly.

Emmaline pondered the answer. "I saw it in the light when you were looking at her skin," she said. "Is that part of her skin problem?"

"Nay."

"Then what?"

Sophina went to the hearth, bending over to stir up the embers and throw on another piece of peat. She wasn't sure her daughter realized that Aricia was male and she didn't feel it was her place to tell her. It was clear that Aricia had gone to great lengths to conceal her sex, for whatever reason, but Emmaline considered her a friend. She had been so very excited to have friends. Sophina knew her daughter well enough to know that her daughter was generous and accepting, but she really couldn't be sure how she would react to a new friend who was concealing a fairly serious secret. She might be hurt by it.

Therefore, Sophina thought that Aricia should be the one to tell Emmaline the truth behind her identity. That kind of information needed to come straight from her.

"Does it matter?" she finally asked.

Emmaline shook her head. "Nay," she said honestly, watching her mother stir up the fire. The small room began to fill with some light and warmth. "Is it just the way she was born, then?"

"Aye, Em. It 'tis."

Emmaline considered poor Aricia and the body that seemed to be betraying her. It hadn't crossed her mind that Aricia was male – nay, it never did. She simply thought that her new friend was different. She had some issues. But Emmaline realized that she didn't much care. She set Oswald down on the bed and began to unlace her girdle, preparing for sleep.

"I like her," she said decidedly. "She has been very kind to me and I will slap anyone who teases her for skin eruptions or her beard."

Sophina stood up, brushing off her hands. "Mayhap it is not necessary to slap anyone," she said. "But I have a feeling that Lady Aricia could use an understanding friend. She is different, that is true. The truth is that we are all different, Em. That does not make any of us better or worse than each other; it simply makes us different. And differences are nothing to fear."

Emmaline liked the way her mother put things. She was always very logical, helping Emmaline to see things more broadly than most. When

Emmaline had fostered those years back, she'd been forced to deal with some very petty girls, although the Lady of the Manor had been kind enough. All Emmaline knew was that she didn't want to be like those silly girls who were only concerned for themselves. Even if she didn't have the acumen for healing like her mother did, she still liked to help people. She liked the feeling she got when she was kind to someone and they appreciated it.

"Aricia is very talented, don't you think?" she asked, pulling off the girdle. It was embroidered with flowers. "She made this. I think it is beautiful."

Sophina could see the sympathy her daughter had for Aricia and it was touching. There was admiration there for a girl who had been so very kind to her.

Sophina finally ushered her chatty daughter into bed, stroking the girl's hair to calm her down. That usually worked with Emmaline and had since she was a baby. Soon enough, she settled down with Oswald in her arms and drifted off to sleep, leaving Sophina wide awake and alone with her thoughts.

As the fire in the hearth snapped and hissed, Sophina found her thoughts drifting to the events of the day. So very much had happened, from the ambush of the carriage to the walk back to Spelthorne, and to meeting Lady Juno and experiencing the insanity of Susanna. So very, very much, but the most important thing of all was in meeting Lucien.

Lucien....

Her heart leapt at the thought of him. She had spent so many years being immune to men, to the thoughts of loving again, that the introduction of Lucien de Russe still had her reeling. So much of what he said rang true to her; neither one of them were terribly young any longer. They had known love at one time in their lives. They were both resigned to empty futures.

But now, meeting one another by chance as they had, it seemed that life would no longer be lonely for them. Had they only really just met today? Had it been so short a time? Perhaps it *had* happened so quickly, but in truth, nothing had ever felt so right. It felt real and hopeful and joyful. Sophina didn't need weeks or months to tell her that Lucien was a man of his word, a man who she could quite possibly find love with again. She knew that now and, for the first time in many years, she was looking forward to what the future would bring.

For the first time in many years, she was actually happy. Once, she'd cursed her father for sending her to du Ponte, but this evening, she was thankful that he had. For once, her father did something good for her and didn't even realize it.

With thoughts of Lucien on her mind, she finally slept.

CHAPTER TWELVE

Dawn, the next day

L UCIEN HADN'T SLEPT much the night before.

Thoughts of Sophina had been heavy on his mind, so heavy that every time he closed his eyes, she was all that he saw. He could feel her in his arms again, that soft and delicious feminine warmth that he'd missed all of these years. Her luscious auburn hair and creamy skin were glorious in his eyes, a striking combination on a striking woman. She was all things alluring. He simply couldn't believe how much she captivated him when he'd only just met her. Perhaps he was just an old fool, after all, now rushing headlong into something because of his attraction to a beautiful woman.

Or perhaps he was simply a man who knew what he wanted.

The previous day had been eventful, to be sure. That was more than likely a good portion of why he hadn't been able to sleep. After his encounter with Holderness in the great hall, Lucien and Laurent had spent some time in Lucien's solar along with Colton and Gabriel. It was just the four of them, men who had fought together, who had support- ed one another, and, for a time, Lucien missed that which he'd walked away from. After Bramham, he'd not seen another battle. Two years without a battle for a man who was born and bred for them was a long time, indeed.

He felt old and useless as he'd talked to Laurent, who had spent some portion of the previous year in a variety of skirmishes and military actions. They had been on Henry's behalf and as Lucien listened to Laurent talk about the particular strategies of certain battles, he began to miss it very much. It had been part of his life for so many years that he realized he felt rather empty not being in the thick of things.

But it had been necessary for him to retire. His gilded spurs, scuffed and worn, sat on a shelf in his solar. To some, the spurs had been symbolic but to him, they were as much a part of him as his sword or his shield. When he'd taken them off and shelved them, permanently, he hadn't realized just how much it had taken out of him. He lost the best part of himself.

But his health still wasn't as strong as it should be. He knew that. Even sitting and listening to Laurent after the strenuous day he'd had, his back hurt and his guts hurt, organs that had been damaged by the arrow that had penetrated him. He was exhausted, feeling drained like an old man would. It was shameful. He truly hated that thought, that he was just an old man now with his glory days behind him. In talking to the young knights around him, he didn't like that thought one bit.

Unfortunately, it was the truth.

Much of the conversation with Laurent had been about Holderness and the betrothal to Lady Juno. Lucien repeated that he had no aversion to Lady Juno and that Holderness was free to tell everyone that he, in fact, had declined the marriage to Lucien, and Laurent understood. He was a reasonable man, unlike his father. But Laurent also stressed that he did not believe his father would surrender his claim so easily because he was set on being a relation to The Iron Knight. Holderness wanted that prestige in his family. Over any protests, Holderness would stick to the bargain he very badly wanted.

Therefore, the matter wasn't settled. Laurent told Lucien that his father had no intention of leaving Spelthorne, at least not until he'd had the chance to hammer Lucien into changing his mind. But Lucien's mind would not be changed and he was frustrated at Holderness' lack of respect towards his decision. That only made him more adamant to adhere to it. The immovable object had met the mountain and they would continue to push at each other until one or the other gave.

Lucien knew for a fact it wouldn't be him.

The conversation eventually turned from Holderness and they spoke of trivial things for a while, bringing about soft laughter and fond memories. Then, about two hours before dawn, Colton and Gabriel excused themselves, Colton to sleep and Gabriel to the wall. He was the commander of the night watch at Spelthorne and thought it best to make his rounds. Laurent also excused himself to go and check on his father, who was supposed to be sleeping but whom, Laurent suspected, had found more drink. He always did. Lucien was, therefore, left alone in the solar, finally dragging his weary body out of his chair to go and seek his bed for an hour or two. It was at this point he slept fitfully, visions of Sophina filling his brain.

"Lucien! *Awake!*"

Lucien was already sitting up in his bed before he even realized he had moved. He started grabbing around for his broadsword, a broadsword that was down in his solar with his spurs, only his sleep-hazed mind didn't realize that quite yet. He was in his tent, on the edge of a battlefield, and someone had just awoken him in a panic. Battle was imminent. Blinking his eyes, he realized that Colton was standing in his dark chamber. He wasn't in his tent or on the verge of battle. He was in his own bed and the sun wasn't even up yet.

"What is it?" Lucien said as he staggered to his feet, wiping his hands over his face. "What is amiss?"

Colton was handing him his boots. "You will not believe it," he said. "An army is approaching Spelthorne. A very big arm."

The words sank in and Lucien took his boots from Colton but didn't make any move to put them on. He simply stood there, looking puzzled.

"An army?" he repeated. "What army? Have you seen banners?"

Colton nodded. "Our scouts say that they bear Henry's banners," he said. "They are coming from the west."

That didn't clear up Lucien's confusion in the least. "Henry's banners?" he repeated. Then, he began to think. "Who is located to the west that would be bearing Henry's banners? Waldour is closest, but they are to the south, and Sherborne and Exeter are to the west."

Colton was quickly indicating the boots in his hand, to put them on, and Lucien took the hint, sitting on his bed so he could put his shoes on. He was more awake now but utterly puzzled. With the boots on, he grabbed his tunic and pulled it over his head on his way out of his chamber. Colton was fast on his heels.

"Did our patrols contact them?" Lucien asked as he took the narrow spiral stairs.

"Nay," Colton said. "They thought it best to return and report the approach first."

Lucien hit the ground floor of the keep, practically running past his solar and out into the dark bailey of Spelthorne.

"That was probably wise," he said, heading to the gatehouse. "They did the right thing. But I am vastly curious as to who would be marching to Spelthorne bearing Henry's colors. Where is Gabriel?"

"Rousing the troop house," Colton said. "Shall we sound the horn? I did not want to do it on the chance that you were aware that we were to be visited by a crown ally and had neglected to tell us."

The horn was the alarm. They ran practice drills on that horn, every man to his post, and Lucien nodded his head swiftly. "I know of no ally that should approach my fortress today," he said firmly. "Sound the horn. Get the men moving in case this is to be something very bad."

Colton was off. Lucien wasn't feeling any great anxiety but he was curious. Who would be marching an army to Spelthorne? He could only think of one man – du Ponte possibly – but the only fallacy in that theory was that he would not be flying Henry's banners. So the question remained – *who* was it?

Truth be told, Lucien was feeling some excitement. It had been so long since he'd faced a hint of a battle that it was all he could do to keep the smile from his face. He was secretly hoping that he was about to be attacked.

The heart of The Iron Knight began to beat again.

Somewhere around the side of the hall, back towards the troop house, a horn sounded. It was a clear, loud peal that roused all of Spelthorne to its sorrowful cry. To Lucien, it was like the voice of God. It brought confidence and power to his weary body, feeding his soul. Old knights never retired, no matter how much they said they did or how much they should. Feeling the familiar scent of battle in the air was all they needed to feel young and powerful again.

Ready to go to war.

The gatehouse of Spelthorne was only two stories and the height of the wall. It was comprised of two towers that each housed a tightly spiraled staircase that led from the bailey to the wall walk. It did, however, have a double-portcullis to trap an invading army. Lucien reached the gatehouse and mounted the northern stairwell, making it up to the wall so that he could see for himself the incoming threat.

As the sun began to rise in the east, turning the sky shades of deep purple, Lucien could, indeed, see a black tide on the western horizon on the road that led to Spelthorne. He couldn't see much more than that because of the darkness but he could see the pinpricks of light that the incoming army was carrying. *Torches.* The moon had set and since they were moving in the darkness, they needed the torches to see. That meant they were determined to come. As he stood there and watched, still not particularly concerned, he noticed a few of the sentries standing around him, watching, too.

"They are flying Henry's banners, my lord," one older soldier said to him. The man had been with Lucien for several years. "They've not sent us a messenger to announce their approach."

Lucien grunted. "Why would they?' he said. "They know we can see them. But if they were going to attack us, the element of surprise is gone."

The old soldier's gaze lingered on the army in the distance. "So is their sanity," he muttered, turning away. "Who would attack the stronghold of The Iron Knight?"

Lucien kept his focus on the incoming army, but inside, he was swelling with pride and anticipation. He was the warrior who had endured almost all of Henry's rebellions without a scratch. He had fought every fight, manned every battle, and he had mostly come through unscathed. Some said that God Himself protected him, but God had been sleeping the day of Bramham when the arrow had found its mark. Still, the old soldier's words meant something to Lucien. There was an army coming, evidently led by a madman.

Lucien would meet them head-on.

He left the wall with the intention of heading back to the keep to don his armor and whatever weapons he could still find. Halfway across the bailey, now lit under a dusky-blue sky, he ran in to Laurent and Holderness, having just come from their lodgings in the knight's quarters. While Holderness simply looked unhappy, Laurent was alert and interested.

"What is happening, my lord?" Laurent asked Lucien. "We heard the alarm."

Lucien nodded. "An incoming army," he said. "I would suggest you stay to the hall for now until I can discover their purpose. No sense in putting yourselves in danger."

Holderness frowned. "An attack?" he asked. "We are facing an attack?"

Laurent immediately turned to his father. He knew that Lucien would have no patience for his foolery this day. "Papa, retreat to the hall," he said, his patience limited. "You do not need to be out in the midst of this. Retreat to the hall and I will come and tell you what is happening when I know."

Holderness' head hurt so badly that it was threatening to explode, creating a foul mood. He eyed Lucien. "Is this usual?" he asked. "Is Spelthorne often a target of surprise attacks?"

Lucien kept his temper in check although it was difficult. "We have not been attacked yet," he said evenly. "Do as I say. Retreat to the hall."

"May I attend you, my lord?" Laurent asked quickly. He was a warrior and didn't want to be relegated to the hall. "Give me a command and I shall follow it."

Lucien nodded. "Indeed," he said. He was happy to have Laurent's service. "Go to the wall. Gabriel should be there by now. If he is not, I want your eyes up on that wall. Watch the incoming army. I will want a report as soon as I finish dressing."

"Aye, my lord."

Laurent dashed for the wall and Lucien headed for the keep, leaving Holderness standing in the middle of the bailey, feeling abandoned. Frustrated, he threw up his hands and headed for the hall as he'd been instructed. Maybe there was good drink there, even at this time in the morning.

All around Spelthorne, men were dashing about to their posts, but inside the keep, the women were awake and watching the activity from their windows. The horn, which had been on Juno and Aricia's side of the building, woke them up immediately and, sleepy-eyed, they stood at the window, watching the activity below. They could see men running about but they had no sense of panic. In fact, Juno, in early pregnancy, wasn't feeling well so she crawled back into bed while Aricia stood at the window and watched the happenings. It was most curious.

In Sophina and Emmaline's chamber, only Sophina was standing at the window, watching the activity below as her lazy daughter lay in bed and snuggled with Oswald. Emmaline was a sound sleeper, like her mother, but in this case, Sophina had awoken because she suspected the sound of a horn over a military fortress wasn't a good thing. There was a great deal of activity below and also on the wall walk, which she had a clear sighting of. Men seemed to be running about as if they had a purpose. Sophina seriously wondered what that purpose was.

"Mama?" Emmaline yawned over on the bed. "What is happening? Why did they sound that horn?"

Sophina could see the south and western side of the wall from where she was standing. She could also see a small portion of the gatehouse and even in the dim morning light, she thought she might have seen Lucien upon it, but it was difficult to tell. Puzzled, she shook her head to her daughter's question.

"I do not know," she said. "But I think that I should find out. You stay here. I will return."

Emmaline didn't argue with her. She didn't want to leave her warm and cozy bed, so she fell back asleep as her mother pulled on the heavy robe from the day before, the one that belonged to Lucien. Securing the robe around her slender body, she slipped from the chamber and closed the door softly.

It was very dark in the keep as she made her way down the spiral stairs, trying very hard not to trip and break her neck in the darkness. The floor below seemed to have a light emitting from the chamber across from Susanna's, whose door remained closed. Timidly, Sophina went to the door where the gentle light was streaming from, peering inside the crack of the door to see who was inside. She could hear someone banging about and it was only a second or two before Lucien came into her line of sight.

He was settling a coat of mail over his big frame, tugging at it, as he passed out of her line of sight again. Quietly, Sophina knocked.

"Lucien?" she called softly.

The door opened so swiftly that she nearly fell backwards as Lucien was suddenly standing in front of her. He smiled, seeing that he had startled her.

"What are you doing awake?" he whispered loudly. "You should still be in bed."

She cocked an eyebrow. "With the archangel Gabriel blowing his horn at dawn?" she asked, watching him grin. "I thought Christ and his angels were about to make an appearance."

Lucien snorted, reaching out to take her hand and pulling her into his chamber. He very quietly shut the door.

"Nay, not Christ, at least not yet," he said, heading over to a table where there was a variety of wardrobe items on it; heavy leather gloves, a dark tunic, a belt, a few daggers, and a large broadsword in a scabbard. He picked up the tunic. "I am sorry the alarm awoke you. There is an army approaching and it was a call for my men to assume their posts. But you should not worry. The army is flying Henry's banner so I am fairly certain they are not here to attack us, but my men are prepared all the same."

The smile faded from her face. "That seems strange," she said. "Why would an army be traveling here at dawn?"

He shook his head. "I suppose I shall find out," he said, pulling the tunic over his head and straightening it on his big body. "That being said, you will stay to the keep. It is my suggestion that you go to the kitchens and have the servants bring food into the keep, for you will lock it up and bar the door until I tell you it is safe for you to open it. There are six women in this keep now and I would have all of you protected."

Sophina nodded. He was calm and confident, and therefore she was not afraid. Moreover, she wasn't one to scare easily. "As you wish," she said. "Then I suppose I should go put on some decent clothing so I may conduct business outside of these walls."

He glanced at her, looking at the robe she wore. *His* robe. He tried to steer clear of thoughts of fabric that had touched his skin and was now touching hers, because thoughts like that would get him into trouble. As much as he would like to have that kind of trouble, he simply didn't have the time.

"I would hurry if I were you," he said, trying to distract himself from thoughts of her flesh. "The army is less than an hour away. Do not delay."

Sophina had her task set before her and she faced it with her customary resolve. "I will not," she assured him. She watched him as he collected his belt and moved to put it on. "Is there anything I can do for you? Do you require any help?"

For some reason, he thought those were beautiful words. It had been years since he'd heard such words, meant only for him. Caring words, as if she... *cared*. When he looked at her, she was gazing up at him with confidence and eagerness, prepared to do whatever he needed. God, he loved that. Setting the belt down, he went to her and took her face between his two big hands.

"Your presence here, at this moment, is all I require," he said softly. "I could not sleep last night for thoughts of you and now that you are here, standing before me, I am joyful to realize that yesterday was no dream. I rescued you from a lake and somehow during the day, my attraction to you became overwhelming. You are under my skin and I do not even know how it happened, only that it did. I want to wake up to you every morning, Sophina. I want your face to be the first one I see in the morning and the last one I see at night. At this moment, having you so near me... something within me is whole again. It is alive again. I am not sure I can explain it any better than that."

Sophina's heart was fluttering wildly against her ribs, making it difficult to breathe. "I can hardly believe that yesterday was not a dream, either," she said softly. "Much like you, I did not sleep very well last night."

"Why?"

"For the same reasons you did not," she said. "I cannot stop thinking of you and what you said last night. You said that we are not young and new, and that we understand things from a perspective of having lived and having been loved. That is true, all of it, and because it is true, I worry that we are being impetuous in our actions. We are old enough not to act on impulse. But the truth is that I do not care what common sense tells me. I care what my heart tells me, and my heart tells me that this is where I belong. With you."

His smile broadened and he kissed her lips, sweetly. "You do," he murmured. "You belong with me and to me."

"But what of Lady Juno? Did you speak with her father?"

His smile faded. "I did," he said. "He is like a dog with a meaty bone. He refused to accept that I do not want to marry his daughter but the unfortunate fact is that he is going to have to accept it when I marry you."

Sophina sighed faintly, thinking of heartbroken Juno. "I wish there was an easier way to do this, something that would not crush Lady Juno," she said. "She is such a kind girl, Lucien. I do not want to see her hurt."

He loved that she was such a soft-hearted woman. Rather than be jealous or petty towards the girl he was betrothed to, all she could think about was the girl's feelings. It was the true mark of maturity.

"I know," he said. "Would it make you happy if I speak to Juno and tell her of the situation? I was going to leave it to Holderness to inform her of the change in plans, but if it will make you happy, I will tell her myself. Mayhap that will ease her pain a little if I explain that my heart belongs to another. Surely she will understand that."

Sophina's heart skipped a beat. "Your... your heart belongs to another?"

His eyes twinkled. "It does."

"Me?"

He grinned and kissed her on the forehead, releasing her face and turning back to the table with his tack on it. He picked up his leather belt again.

"More than likely," he said, trying to sound glib, embarrassed that he was already talking about his deep feelings. "It is too early to say. You have not yet earned it yet although you are well on your way."

Sophina could see that he was being evasive, but it wasn't a bad thing. He was simply trying to jest his way out of a very serious subject. She fought back.

"You have not earned mine, either," she pointed out. "But I will give you every chance in the world, so fear not. There is still the opportunity."

He cast her a sidelong glance. "Cheeky wench," he muttered. "I had better have your heart by sunset or I will not be a happy man."

She lifted her eyebrows. "Oh?" she said innocently. "Pray, what will you do if I withhold my affections?"

"Dare you taunt me?"

"Never, my lord. It was simply a question."

He couldn't keep the smile off his face. "It is too horrible to speak of," he said as he fastened the leather belt around his waist. "I will not tell you so that you can wonder all day long and be afraid. You will have no choice but to surrender to me."

"That hardly seems fair."

He burst out into soft laughter. "Mayhap it is not fair, but it is the way of things," he said, finishing with the belt. The broadsword scabbard was next. "I must say that I am looking forward to spending the coming years bantering with you. You lighten my heart."

Sophina's eyes glimmered at him. "And you make mine sing," she said, her expression rather coy when he looked at her. It was a sweet gesture. "Now, I must go to the kitchens and you must go to the wall. I will ensure that the keep is locked up tightly until you tell me otherwise."

"Have you been through this before, then?"

She shrugged. "Many years ago when I was fostering," she said. "But, as I said, my father's home is peaceful. I cannot say that I ever remember it having been attacked."

He nodded, hating that they had to get back to the business at hand. But there would be all the time in the world in the future to laugh and joke as they just did. He'd never looked so eagerly towards something in his life. He finished tying off the scabbard.

"Excellent," he said, moving towards her. "I know the keep is in good hands with you in charge. And speaking of being in charge... I did not have an opportunity to ask you what happened with Susanna yesterday. I have not seen you since I left you here in the keep,"

"I know."

"Did you speak with my daughter?"

Sophina was reluctant to answer him, for obvious reasons, but she had little choice. If she didn't tell him what had transpired, Susanna surely would.

"Aye," she replied evenly. "I did speak with her. I tried to explain how good behavior is much respected and bad behavior is loathed."

"What did she say?"

"She threw pewter cups at me."

He grunted, embarrassed. "I am very sorry she did that. She is…."

Sophina cut him off. "I spanked her for it."

His eyes widened. "You did?"

She nodded, unable to tell if he approved or disapproved of her actions. She decided to give him the all of it, her reasoning behind what she did. "Lucien, I am under the impression that Susanna has never been disciplined in her life," she said. "She is spoiled, willful, and deceitful, and when speaking of what she did to Juno's father last night, she was very plain in telling me *why* she did it. She was angry you were not in the hall with her and she knew if she hit Holderness, you would come to her. She wants what she wants and she does not care who she hurts in the process."

Lucien was trying not to look too embarrassed and foolish. "Aye, I did go to her, didn't I?" he asked, but it wasn't a question. It was a statement of resignation. "She told you that she hit him so that I would come?"

"She did."

He sighed faintly, turning back to the table that still had daggers on it. His movements, so sharp only moments before, were now slow and pensive. "I am afraid I have not been a good father to her," he finally said. "You know what happened when Laurabel died. I have told you all of it. With my son, I fear it is a lost cause. He hates me and has every right to. But with Susanna, I did what I thought I needed to do for her. I bought her everything she wanted. I never denied her anything. But I have created a monster and I know that, so nowadays, I try to spend as little time with her as possible. It is difficult for me to admit, even to myself, that when I look at her I see my worst failure. I fear that Laurabel would be very ashamed of how I have raised our daughter."

Sophina went to him, putting a gentle hand on his arm. "She would have done what I did, I am sure," she assured him softly but firmly. "She would have put that girl over her knee and spanked her. Susanna needs spankings and she needs them often until she understands there are penalties for her behavior. And she is not to have those canes back, Lucien. I threw them out of the window and she is not to have them back. She uses them as weapons and she must not be allowed to terrorize people with them."

He looked at her, still feeling deeply ashamed in spite of her words. "You did what with them? Oh, it is of no concern. You are correct, of course," he said. "I will make sure she does not have them returned. It is ironic; I command thousands of men who jump to do my bidding but I cannot command my own child. I will admit that she has been my greatest source of shame. I pray you do not think too badly of me upon realizing this"

Sophina shook her head. "We all have weaknesses," she said. "You are no different, but I admire you for your admission. I do not think badly of you at all."

He nodded faintly, feeling comforted by her reaction. Knowing she did not view him unfavorably, it gave him the courage to ask for help. "Then I will ask you," he said, "how can I fix my failure? I am not one to ask for help, but I will ask if you will help me with her. I do not know what to do with her any longer and the older she becomes, the worse she becomes. You have such a lovely daughter so it is clear you know more about childrearing than I do. I would consider any advice a personal favor."

Sophina touched his cheek, a sweet gesture. "Of course I will help," she said. "I am willing to believe there is a sweet child under all of that naughtiness. I will help you find her if I can."

Lucien was feeling a tremendous amount of hope and gratitude in her reply. So many emotions were swirling around in him that he reached out and pulled Sophina into his arms, his warm mouth slanting over hers. She fell against him, his hard mail against her tender body, but it didn't matter. She snaked her arms around his neck, pulling herself closer to him even as he nearly crushed her in his embrace. He was seriously regretting the fact that he'd put his mail on because he very much wanted to feel her against him, her warmth to his.

Her scent. Something sweet and musky filled his nostrils as he kissed her, causing instant arousal. God's Bones, it had been years since he'd bedded a woman who meant something to him. Not since Laurabel, really. He'd had women since then, of course, whores who would follow the armies and were simply a warm body to release himself into, but to lie with someone he felt something for... it had been a very long time, indeed.

Lucien was consumed with the smell and feel of her, his mouth on hers, his arms around her, but soon enough, his grip loosened and his hands began to roam. She was wrapped up in his big robe but that that did not deter him; he was a man used to getting what he wanted. He was not subtle. His lips still fused to hers, he pulled open the robe, exposing the shift that she had slept in. It was Juno's pale blue shift, finely woven, and her hard nipples pushed through the fabric. Lucien could feel them when he dragged his palms across her breasts and it drove him mad.

Something in him unleashed.

With a growl, he grabbed her by the waist and lowered his head, suckling her hard nipples through the fabric. Sophina gasped as he suckled and bit and tugged at her breasts, her hands finding their way into his long hair, holding his mouth against her breast as if to nurse a starving child.

Still gripping her waist, Lucien lifted her up onto the table that had so recently held his war tack. He wasn't sure what he was going to do with her up there, but it was something instinctive. *Needful.* Her legs were parted as he yanked her to the edge of the table, wedging himself between them. One hand left her waist and snaked underneath her shift, moving for the unfurling flower between her legs. She didn't stop him. The moment he touched her, he groaned.

"God's Bones," he muttered, his mouth still on the wet fabric against her nipples. "You are as wet as rain."

Sophina didn't have a chance to answer as he thrust fingers into her quivering body, first one and then two. She groaned softly, throwing her head back as she lifted her knees higher, giving him unhindered access to her tender core.

Her movements blinded him. All Lucien could think of was thrusting himself into her slick folds and he fumbled with the chain mail, trying to pull it up, trying to untie his breeches at the same time as his painful erection strained against them. He managed to push the mail coat aside, untying his breeches and working them down as much as he could to free his erection. Yanking Sophina forward so that her buttocks nearly hung off the side of the table, he arched his big body over hers and thrust into her willing, waiting body.

Sophina was so highly aroused that she bit off a cry into the side of his head as he plunged into her. It was the most wildly pleasurable thing she had ever known and, almost immediately, her body began trembling with what was the first of several releases.

Lucien, feeling her body react to his in a most erotic way, didn't wait to extend his pleasure. He could feel her body milking his, demanding his seed, and he was so wildly stimulated that in little time, he was answering her, climaxing so hard that he bit his lip in the course of his pleasure. But, God's Bones, it was worth it. Every move, every grunt, and the terrible inconvenience of holding his mail coat up with one hand as he made love to her was worth it.

She was worth it.

Everything about her was worth his life and more.

Beneath him, Sophina was still twitching, still weeping softly with continuing releases as Lucien gently thrust into her. He wanted to stay that way the rest of his life, buried in her sweet body, feeling her flesh react to his. He'd never experienced anything so satisfying. But along with that sweet thought was another harsher thought; reality was crashing. He could hear voices in the bailey and knew he'd been over-long. He had let his time with Sophina extend well beyond what was reasonable. Someone would come looking for him sooner or later and he certainly didn't want to be caught with a woman impaled on his manhood. As much as he was loath to, he had to get moving.

"I am so sorry," he whispered. "I should not have… but never have I known anything so glorious. My lady, would that I could take the time for… *this*. I should have taken the time. But…."

Sophina put her fingers to his lips. "Stop talking," she murmured, grinning. "You have men to attend to and I must go to the kitchens. But I am not sorry in the least that we have been delayed."

He returned her smile, rather slyly. "I look forward to revisiting this moment when I am not rushed," he said. "In fact, I should go chase the incoming army away right this very minute. They must understand that I have more important things to attend to."

Sophina laughed softly and he shifted, attempting to withdraw from her body. But the mere stimulation from his movement caused her to climax again and he felt her body throbbing around his semi-flaccid member, feeding his lust. He swooped on her, his lips suckling hers, grinding his hips against her Venus mound to soak up every last quiver from her body.

Gasping as the tremors died away, Sophina fell back on the table, watching Lucien as he pulled himself from her body entirely and pulled up his breeches. He tied them off, letting his mail coat settle down again, but when he looked up and saw Sophina laying there on her back, her legs still spread, he growled.

"Get up," he told her, feigning sternness. "Get up and go about your duties. You are like a siren, luring me to my doom. I would rather bed you a thousand times on this table than tend to duties that cannot wait. You will be the ruin of me."

Sophina sat up, smiling at him because he had winked at her. He'd meant everything he'd said as a compliment and she knew it. With his help, she slid off the table, pulling the robe around her body again and securing the sash. He was trying to straighten his coat and scabbard, helping her in the meanwhile, smoothing at her robe but he ended up grabbing her buttocks, instead. She laughed softly and moved away from him.

"You have more pressing things to attend to," she reminded him, moving for the door. "I will be here in the keep and I will ensure that no one leaves or comes in unless I have your approval."

He was following her out of the solar, so much lust in his eyes that he was certain every man who saw him from this point forward would know exactly what was on his mind. He didn't much care, to be truthful.

He was officially smitten.

Lucien and Sophina parted ways at the keep entry, him heading for the gatehouse and her for the kitchens. But their parting was not without tender glances and a bold wink on his behalf, for now, things had changed between them. It was no longer a mutual attraction and a marriage proposal.

It was stronger even than that.

CHAPTER THIRTEEN

LUCIEN COULDN'T BELIEVE his ears. An hour and several minutes after the incoming army had been sighted before dawn, approaching Spelthorne across the pre-dawn fields like a tide of ants, Jorrin de Bretagne, garrison commander at Sherborne Castle, was standing at Lucien's portcullis. Now, the matter of Henry's banners was explained since Sherborne was a crown garrison, but the words spouting forth from de Bretagne's lips were outrageous at best. It was a struggle for Lucien not to charge the man.

"He told you *what*?" he demanded.

De Bretagne sighed heavily. "St. Michal du Ponte came to Sherborne yesterday to inform me that you had ambushed the escort bringing his betrothed to Gillingham Castle," he repeated what he'd already told Lucien most reluctantly. Finally, he shook his head as if embarrassed. "He was lying, wasn't he?"

Lucien was filled with rage. "Of course he is lying," he snarled. "Did that bastard come with you?"

De Bretagne nodded. "He did," he replied. "He has asked for my mediation in this matter. He is convinced you ambushed the escort and stole his betrothed. Is the woman here, de Russe?"

Lucien could have lied at that moment. He could have lied and told de Bretagne that Sophina wasn't under his roof, but he couldn't bring himself to do it, at least not to de Bretagne. Lucien's credibility was on the line and he wasn't about to destroy what thirty years of honesty had created. He just couldn't do it.

"Aye," he said. "But you should hear my side of the story – the truthful side – before you make any determinations."

"I am listening."

Lucien cocked an eyebrow. "I was riding south yesterday when I saw the ambush take place on du Ponte's party," he said. "There was a carriage in the water and I could hear screaming, so I swam to the carriage and saved a lady and her daughter when du Ponte's men ran off and abandoned them. I brought the women back here. They were quite shaken, understandably."

De Bretagne nodded in understanding. "Did the lady tell you that she was destined for Gillingham Castle?"

"She did."

"Yet you did not send word to du Ponte that you had rescued his intended and that she was safe?"

Lucien shook his head. "I am entertaining the Earl of Holderness at the moment," he said, deliberately avoiding a direct answer. "But du Ponte's intended is in good health, as is her daughter. They are in the keep."

De Bretagne didn't seem to notice that his question hadn't really been answered but the reply that Lucien gave him seemed to satisfy him. He didn't press. Still, there was another question that needed an answer.

"Du Ponte and his men returned to the scene of the ambush yester-day at some point and saw your men scavenging the carriage and the goods that it carried," he said. "Is that true?"

Lucien rolled his eyes. He was very close to the end of his patience with du Ponte and his idiocy. "We were salvaging the ladies' trunks," he said. "We had to pull the carriage from the lake in order to get their possessions. Du Ponte's men attacked my men for no reason and when my knight tried to explain why he was there, du Ponte would not listen. He tried to kill my men."

De Bretagne scratched his head to the puzzling situation. "He said you were scavenging."

Lucien simply looked at the man as if he had lost his mind. "Would I be the type to not only ambush an escort, but loot their goods?"

"Never."

"Clearly, you must believe otherwise," Lucien said. "Your mere presence here suggests you must have some inkling of doubt in my honor."

De Bretagne shook his head firmly. "Nay, Lucien, that is not true," he said. "I have complete faith in your honor. But du Ponte has a document that he claims is from the lady's father and he is here to remove her. He believes you stole her. I do not need to remind you that du Ponte is a relative of Henry's queen and if he wanted to make trouble for you, he could. So my presence here is to be a neutral party to mediate this situation and keep this fool from running off to Joan and telling her that Henry's Iron Knight has stolen from him."

Lucien could see his point. There was truth in what he said. Du Ponte was, indeed, related to the queen and he could cause some problems for Lucien if he wanted to. But more than that, Lucien was fixated on the fact that du Ponte had evidently brought documentation of his rights to the lady with him. Lucien could contest the documentation, of course, and refuse to turn over the lady, but then that would reveal to all, including Holderness, that he intended to marry Lady Sophina. His refusal to turn her over to du Ponte was personal.

With that thought, he was coming to feel the least bit uneasy. This had to be settled now and settled without a shadow of a doubt as only The Iron Knight could do it. Knowing what he had to do, he took a step back from the portcullis and ordered it lifted before returning to de Bretagne.

"Bring du Ponte in here," he grumbled. "Only you and he. Leave your men outside."

De Bretagne nodded, turning around and heading for his army, collected about a quarter of a mile away. Lucien couldn't have watched the man go; he had turned towards the great hall, snapping orders as he went, pulling de Royans and Pembury with him and leaving Laurent on the wall. Once he entered the great hall to see Holderness sitting at a table with a full pitcher of wine in front of him, he told the man to return to his quarters. He didn't want Holderness hearing what was about to be discussed.

Lucien, Colton, and Gabriel settled down at one end of a long feasting table and began to quietly discuss the reasons for Sherborne's appearance. Lucien knew he had to be honest with them and quickly told them his reasons behind his intention to refuse to return Lady de Gournay to du Ponte.

To their credit, neither Colton nor Gabriel flinched at the news, although it was surprising considering they'd never known Lucien to show interest in any woman following the death of his wife. But the man was human and Lady de Gournay was quite beautiful, so when the surprise settled, they didn't blame him in the least. Moreover, they knew of du Ponte's reputation, too. He did not deserve so fine a lady. Therefore, when de Bretagne and du Ponte were finally escorted into the hall by Laurent, who left them there to return to his post on the wall, Lucien and his knights were ready to debate what was to come. Or, so they thought.

What they didn't know was that Holderness, refusing to be ordered around by a mere knight, had not returned to his quarters at all.

He was in the alcove near the servant's door, ready to listen to ever word said.

☓

"You DO REALIZE that you are insulting Lord Tytherington by suggesting he ambushed your escort and pilfered the contents?" de Bretagne asked as he sat at the very end of the feasting table, looking at du Ponte. "He is a man of honor and would never do such a thing. You have heard his reasons as to why he was dragging the carriage from the lake. Why do you not believe him?"

Du Ponte was seated across from Lucien and his two big knights, who were glaring at him as if one word from Lucien and they would leap across the table and snap his neck. He felt cornered and threatened, unable to bring either of his knights into Spelthorne for his meeting with de Bretagne and de Russe. Now, he sat alone, feeling as if his life was worth very little in the great hall of Spelthorne. However, he had one thing that gave him the power above all else – the vellum upon which the marriage offer to Lady de Gournay was written. He held it in his hand, tightly, waiting for the correct moment to present it.

"Because his men were seen at the ambush and my men will attest to that," he lied. "Then, when we returned to collect the carriage and save the women, his men were pulling the carriage from the pond and bringing all of the trunks onto the shore. Why else would he be doing that if he wasn't trying to steal it all?"

Lucien wouldn't keep silent as his honor was called into doubt. "I have told you, repeatedly, that I came upon the ambush during the course of the attack," he said, his jaw ticking. "I pulled the women from the carriage to save their lives, which is more than your men did. They abandoned those women like cowards and I had no choice but to bring them back here. I sent my men to retrieve their belongings and that is what you saw when you returned to the lake. Are you truly such an idiot that you think I would resort to the same highway robbery you have been a party to? Don't make me laugh."

Du Ponte turned red around the ears, grievously insulted even if it was true. "How dare you slander me!" he said, banging a fist against the tabletop. "I demand an apology immediately!"

Colton couldn't take anymore; he was a hot-blooded man, and young, and he sailed across the table, wrapping his hands around du Ponte's neck as Gabriel and Lucien reached out to grab him. Gabriel had him around the waist as Lucien slid onto the tabletop and removed Colton's hands from around du Ponte's neck.

"At ease, Colton," Lucien said steadily as he pulled the young knight back and away from the table. "I'll no let you throttle him; not yet, anyway."

Du Ponte, who had nearly fallen to the floor with Colton's outburst, stood up from his seat, rubbing his neck and glaring at Lucien.

"Are your knights so poorly behaved, de Russe?" he barked. "I demand my own knights be allowed to protect me while this, – this *interrogation* goes on!"

De Bretagne was on his feet. He very much sided with Lucien but he was here to keep order and, it appeared, for good reason. There was a good deal of animosity and lies being flung about. He crooked a finger at Lucien as Gabriel kept Colton at bay.

"A word, my lord?" he asked.

Lucien came close, not particularly eager to hear what de Bretagne had to say. "What is it?"

De Bretagne spoke quietly. "We can do one of two things," he muttered. "I can let your men have free rein on du Ponte and kill him, and we can say it was an accident, or I can let his brutes in just so he will shut his damn mouth. I've had to listen to that bastard spout off since yesterday and I very much want to do what your knight just did, but if it gets back to Henry...."

Lucien could see there was some humor mixed in with the serious suggestion. "Killing him is my first choice, but I suppose that would raise too many questions."

De Bretagne nodded reluctantly. "It would. And you and I are charged with keeping the peace in this area."

"That is very true."

De Bretagne cast a long look at du Ponte. "Had I come here alone, with only him, I would be happy to bury the body for you, but as it is, we have many witnesses that have seen him enter your great hall. His death, while it would not be questioned, might reflect badly on you, my lord. Men would talk."

Lucien appreciated the sage advice. He didn't particularly care if it reflected badly on him or not because his primary concern was Sophina. If he had to kill a man to keep her safe, he would do so without hesitation. She hadn't really come up yet, so far, but he knew she would. It was only a matter of time.

But the truth of the matter was that du Ponte's death would bring up trouble Lucien didn't particularly want. He wanted to live with Sophina in peace and if it was known that du Ponte died "accidentally" right before he married the man's intended, then it could create something of a bad situation for them both. He didn't want du Ponte's death to be her burden. Still....

"I will send de Royans to bring his men in," Lucien said. "Meanwhile, come with me. I want you to hear something."

De Bretagne followed Lucien back to the table. He was interested in what the man had to say. As Lucien muttered a few words to the still-angry Colton and the young knight walked away, Lucien then turned his venom loose on du Ponte.

"Now, du Ponte, you are going to listen to me because I have had an earful of your slander and lies," he said, jabbing a finger in the man's face when he opened his mouth to protest. "Shut your stupid mouth and listen to me. Are you listening? Good. Now, this is the situation as I see it – because everyone knows you are linked to the outlaws in this area and they further know of your unscrupulous reputation, it is my opinion that you arranged the ambush on your own carriage for the purpose of murdering your intended. When you saw my men trying to salvage the carriage, you conveniently pinned it all on me."

Du Ponte's mouth flew open. "You *slander* me!" he hissed. "You are mad, de Russe, *mad!*"

"Then deny it. To my face, deny it."

"Of course I deny it!' du Ponte was so agitated that he nearly spit in Lucien's face as spittle flew from his lips. "Why would I do such a terrible thing?"

Oddly enough, the more agitated du Ponte became, the cooler Lucien became. "To collect the dowry," he said simply. "You could tell Andover that his daughter was killed by outlaws and you would still be entitled to her money without the matrimonial entailments. There is simply no other explanation for the ambush because it is *you* who controls the outlaws in the woods west of Tisbury and everyone knows it. De Bretagne, have you heard such things about du Ponte?"

De Bretagne was looking at du Ponte, now coming to understand more to the story than what du Ponte had told him. Of course, what Lucien said made perfect sense. Du Ponte was rumored to control several bands of outlaws in the area but no one had been able to definitively pin it on him. Aye, what Lucien said made perfect sense, indeed.

"I have," he said steadily. "It seems that whenever we find someone who is willing to testify against him, they mysteriously vanish. I wonder how many murders are on your conscience, du Ponte."

Eyes wide, du Ponte's entire body stiffened with fury. "That is outrageous!" he sputtered. "You have no basis to make such accusations!"

Lucien spoke without hesitation. "Untrue," he said. "We have had witnesses attest to seeing your men mingled with the outlaws west of Tisbury and also with a gang that is based around Shaftesbury. But those witnesses have vanished. Based on this knowledge, I say that it is *you* who ambushed your own carriage. Moreover, if you think, for one moment, that I am going to return Lady de Gournay and her daughter to you, then you are a fool."

Du Ponte was enraged. "Then you cannot prove anything!" he said. With jerky movements, he pulled forth a rolled piece of vellum, tied off with hemp. He was so angry that his hands were shaking as he pulled off the string and unrolled the vellum. "This is a missive from Lord Andover, Lady de Gournay's father. He has offered the lady's hand to me and I have accepted. If you refuse to give her to me, then you have abducted my property and I can have you charged with theft. This is a legally binding contract between me and Lady de Gournay's father!"

So the contract had been brought into play, the crux of the conversation at this point. Lucien, however, was unmoved. Nothing in the world was going to coerce him into turning Sophina over to du Ponte.

"It could be a forgery," he said evenly. "You could have written that yourself for all I know."

If they didn't think it was possible for du Ponte to grow any angrier, they were wrong. He slammed the missive onto the table. "You dare go against the laws of this country?" he snarled. "You – a man who has sworn to uphold them?"

Lucien crossed his big arms. "I did not say I was going to go against the laws of England," he said. "I simply said that your missive could be a forgery. You are not beyond such tactics."

De Bretagne picked up the missive and looked at it. "It is signed by Lord Andover," he said casually. "It also contains a seal. Lord Tytherington, you told me at the gatehouse that the lady confirmed she was destined for Gillingham Castle. This would seem to confirm that du Ponte is telling the truth. You can certainly bring the lady here to confirm this is her father's signature if you truly believe it to be a forgery."

Lucien's heart sank. He knew de Bretagne was only pointing out the truth, trying to be fair in both cases. He didn't know that Lucien was deeply attracted to Lady de Gournay and wished to marry her. Nay, he didn't know any of that but, very quickly, he was going to catch on. There was no earthly reason for Lucien to keep the woman here when her intended was demanding she be returned to him. Very quickly, this was going to go against him if he didn't say something.

Confess.

Say something!

"It is not necessary to produce the lady," he said. "I believe I am satisfied."

Du Ponte smacked the vellum triumphantly. "Then you *will* produce my intended," he said. "And my carriage – I want my carriage returned to me, also."

Lucien glanced at Gabriel, who had so far been standing strong and silent behind him. "Tell him of his carriage," Lucien muttered.

Addressed, Gabriel took a step forward. "Your carriage is back at the lake, my lord," he said formally. "We recovered the baggage and left the vehicle."

Du Ponte appeared surprised by the news. "You left it there?"

"There was no reason to bring it back to Spelthorne, my lord."

Truth be told, du Ponte was astonished by the news. His carriage had been more important than the return of the lady. As he'd planned, the entire fuss about the woman had been a cover to get that fine carriage back. He thought he'd been fairly clever about introducing the carriage into the conversation without making him seem very petty, but now that he was told it was still back at the lake it was all he could do to keep from running out of the door and ordering his men to flee south to claim the carriage. In fact, someone else could have claimed it by now and his astonishment at the news began to transition into agitation again.

"So you left it there but brought the woman and her baggage to Spelthorne?" he asked. "That makes no sense. Now you've left the carriage for someone else to take it!"

Gabriel felt as though the words were directed at him, at least about the carriage. He didn't have the luxury of showing his distaste with du Ponte like Lucien and de Bretagne did. Of a lesser rank, he had to maintain the illusion of respect.

"My lord, I had seven wounded men as a result of your attack by the lake," he said. "It was more important to me to get them home than drag along a carriage that was of no concern to me. I was leading the salvage contingent and I tried to call to you when your men attacked, but you did not hear me. You never made any attempt to find out who we were or what we were doing there. You simply sent your men against us with swords drawn, forcing us to defend ourselves. Hauling that carriage back to Spelthorne was the least of my worries after that."

Du Ponte could hear a rebuke in that polite statement. His eyes narrowed. "You made no attempt to contact me."

"I did, my lord. Several times."

Du Ponte could most definitely hear the rebuke, then. He refrained from responding to the knight, as the man was beneath him, and, instead, turned to Lucien again.

"I will go and retrieve my carriage," he seethed. "If it is missing, then I hold you responsible. Right now, however, I want what I have come for. You will give me Lady de Gournay."

Lucien couldn't help but notice the entire time he spoke of Sophina, he'd never once mentioned Emmaline. Lucien was coming to wonder if du Ponte even realized the woman had a daughter.

But it didn't matter in the grand scheme of things. Lucien already had his answer ready and waiting. It was time to take a stand against this unsavory bully of a man and he knew how to do it without causing a battle. At least, he thought he did. He could only pray that de Bretagne would support his stance of what he was about to do.

Confess.

"How much will it take to buy the contract?" he asked.

Du Ponte wasn't sure he heard correctly. "Buy it?" he repeated, irritable. "What are you talking about, de Russe?"

"Exactly what I said. I want to buy the marriage contract with Lady de Gournay. How much will you take for it?"

Du Ponte stared at him; quite honestly, so did de Bretagne. "You want to buy the contract?" du Ponte finally said.

Lucien nodded. "I will give you seven thousand *denier* and three thousand *florins*," he said. "That is a great deal of money, far more than the value of her dowry, I am certain. Will you take it?"

Du Ponte's agitation was starting to fade as the surprise of Lucien's proposal settled in. He was genuinely perplexed. "But why should you buy it?"

"Because I want to marry her."

Du Ponte's eyebrows lifted in shock. Lucien wasn't looking at de Bretagne. If he had been, he would have seen the man's jaw drop. Even Gabriel, standing behind Lucien, looked at his lord with some surprise before quickly wiping it off of his face. All of them were stunned to hear Lucien's reply but no one was able to speak before, from the shadows, Holderness appeared.

"You cannot marry her!" The earl emerged from the alcove where he had been listening to the entire conversation. "You are pledged to my daughter and you cannot marry another! Damn you, de Russe! I knew you had brought that woman here for a reason. Now I know! You want to shame my daughter and marry this man's betrothed!"

Lucien had been in control of the conversation until Holderness purged himself from the alcove near the hearth. When he heard the man shouting, there was nothing he could do to prevent him from not only speaking, but the others from hearing. He was startled to realize that Holderness had disobeyed him and, quite soon, furious. Moving around the table, he went to head off Holderness from getting any closer to du Ponte or de Bretagne.

"What I do is none of your affair," he snapped, reaching out to grab the earl by the arm in a complete breach of etiquette. As a man of lesser rank, he had no right to touch the earl. "I told you yesterday there would be no betrothal. I told you yesterday I would not be related to the likes of you. Now, get out of this room before I do something you will wholly regret."

For the first time since his arrival to Spelthorne, and through all of the arguing and insults he'd dealt Lucien, Holderness finally felt some fear of the man. He was finally coming to realize that perhaps he shouldn't have spoken as he did because the expression on Lucien's face suggested utter murder.

His murder.

But, true to his nature, he couldn't stay still.

"Is that why you refused the betrothal?" he demanded. "Because you lust after this man's intended?"

"Lust after her?" du Ponte had heard him. He was coming towards Lucien and the earl, his face alight with the realization. "So this is why you have refused to bring my intended to me, de Russe? Because you want her for yourself."

Lucien was caught. Everything they said was true. But he would not relinquish the control in this situation, not even if it cost him everything. And it quite possibly would. He knew how to get to the heart of men, at least the heart of these men. He yanked Holderness off to the side, getting in the man's face.

"I will pay you to agree to dissolve the betrothal," he hissed. "Keep your mouth shut and get out of here, and I will make it well worth your while. Do you understand me?"

Holderness could see, in that brief instance, what he had wanted from Lucien all along – his financial backing. The de Saix family had been bereft for years now, hiding their poverty behind their good name. That had been the driving reason behind the marriage between his daughter and de Russe, to get his hands on the de Russe wealth. That's why he'd fought so hard against Lucien's desire to break the betrothal. That, and the fact that his daughter was newly pregnant.

That was the little secret she had been hiding. Holderness had been determined for the marriage to take place immediately so that de Russe would claim the bastard as his own, but now, the situation had changed a bit. Now, the earl had the opportunity for wealth in a most unexpected way. Wealth for himself and wealth for his daughter, who would be unmarriageable once her pregnancy became public knowledge. Holderness might even be able to get more money out of Lucien if he was to threaten to tell everyone that he forced himself on Juno and when she became pregnant, he abandoned her. Most assuredly, they were thoughts to consider. Holderness was never one to let an opportunity for money pass him by. Firmly, he pulled himself out of Lucien's grip.

"You will find me when this is over," he said. "You *will* make this well worth my while or I will not relinquish my suit, not in any way. Is this clear?"

Lucien hated the man. He really did. Petty, vicious bastard. "Get out of here," he said, his voice low. "Be prepared to negotiate when I find you."

That was good enough for Holderness. Swiftly, he moved to clear the hall but du Ponte wasn't going to let the man go so easily. He started to follow him but Lucien put himself between the earl and du Ponte. But du Ponte didn't much care. He was starting to see the reality of the situation with Lucien and his intended and he saw a remarkable opportunity to control The Iron Knight.

This knight, one of Henry's most respectable and seasoned men, wasn't going to be so respectable when du Ponte was finished with him.

"Now, de Russe," du Ponte said, no longer the agitated fool. "You and I are going to have a long discussion about your lust for my intended or the king and the church will hear about your misbehavior. They won't like it very much, considering that you are also betrothed to another woman. Shocking, indeed."

CHAPTER FOURTEEN

T HE KEEP WAS locked up tightly. The shutters were in place and food stores had been neatly tucked into the solar off of the entry. Emmaline, Juno, and Aricia had been put to work and they were very good workers, helping Sophina with the inventory and organizing it into groups – things that would spoil quickly and things that wouldn't. The process was very businesslike, with no apprehension involved thanks to Sophina's leadership. Moreover, it gave the younger women something to do while Sophina pretended not to worry about what was happening outside of the keep.

Because the shutters were closed, they couldn't see the bailey or what was happening beyond. More than once, Sophina paused in her tasks, her attention turning towards the entry to the keep, now bolted and braced. It was the last place she had seen Lucien and in the solar where the young women were organizing things, her gaze kept drifting to the heavy oak table where Lucien had taken her. It made her feel flushed simply to look at it, her heart fluttering against her ribs at the memories of his touch. It was difficult to keep the smile from her face so she tried not to think about it, focusing, instead, on the tasks at hand. But, Sweet Mary, it was difficult.

One of the other results from Sophina's trip to the kitchens was the fact that she had been able to reclaim her clothing from the washer-woman, who had spent the previous evening scrubbing everything out and putting them out to dry.

When Sophina had entered the kitchen yards, she had seen her clothing, as well as Emmaline's, strung up on hemp ropes, drying in the sun. They were clean and didn't smell of the swampy lake, so she had collected the items that were completely dry and took them back to the keep. The result was that she was in her own clothing now and so was Emmaline. Dressed in a durable broadcloth dress with a leather girdle and broadcloth apron, she was much more comfortable than she was in Juno's tight clothing.

And it was dirty work, too, moving stores into the solar and locking up the keep. Some of the shutters that covered the ventilation windows appeared to have not been closed, or cleaned, in years, so there was a great deal of dust on them. There were even spiders. One fell on Emmaline's arm at some point and the girl screamed as if Lucifer had just appeared and demanded her soul. That had made Juno and Aricia laugh uproariously. Even Sophina had grinned at her dramatic daughter; it *had* been rather humorous.

As the morning deepened and the stores were arranged, thoughts moved to breaking their fast. The younger women were quite hungry. There was fresh bread, wrapped up in sacks, and there were also dissected wheels of white cheese, cut into sections so they wouldn't be so heavy to carry.

Sophina had the young women bring forth the bread and cheese as well as jars of pickled fruits and fresh apples. They spent some time tearing the bread apart and cutting the apples and the cheese. Sophina found a big spoon in all of the things she had brought from the kitchens and spooned the spiced, pickled pears and some cherries into two small wooden bowls. They were quite tart, but quite good. As the three young women began to delve into the food, Sophina's thoughts inevitably turned to the young girl on the floor above.

She'd not heard a peep out of Susanna since the spanking yesterday. Odd, considering how much the girl had screamed up to and including that spanking. Spying a tray over on another table in the solar, a table littered with maps and other items, Sophina removed a pitcher of stale wine and three dirty cups from the tray and loaded it up with bread and cheese and small apples. The girls, stuffing their faces, noticed what she was doing.

"Where are you going with that, Mama?" Emmaline asked, her mouth full.

Sophina took one of the two bowls of pickled fruits and put it on the tray as well, balancing it out with the other items on the tray. "I am taking this to Lady Susanna," she said. "She must be famished."

Emmaline swallowed the bite in her mouth, frowning. "You are being kind to a girl who threw things at you."

Sophina cocked an eyebrow at her ungracious child. "And I am supposed to let her starve because of it?" she said. "Now, that *would* be very unkind, wouldn't it?"

"But she was very naughty. She should be punished."

"I *did* punish her. Now I am to let her starve, too?"

Emmaline didn't have an answer for her mother, whom she thought was being much too kind to a nasty little girl. She went back to her food but, sitting next to Emmaline, Aricia stood up from her seat.

"I will go with you," she said. "May I help?"

Sophina nodded. "That would be appreciated, my lady."

As Emmaline and Juno turned back to their food, Aricia accompanied Sophina from the chamber. Aricia held the heavy door open for her and then closed it again once she passed through. Together, they moved up the narrow spiral stairs.

"I did not have the opportunity to tell you that your scarf is lovely today," Sophina said. "My daughter told me that you personally embroider them."

Aricia was clad in an unbleached linen dress, very simple, with a yellow scarf over her head, across her face, and draped down over her shoulders. She nodded to Sophina's statement.

"I do, my lady," she said. "I have always liked to sew and create things. My mother was an excellent seamstress and she taught me her skills."

Sophina was moving slowly up the stairs, afraid of tripping on the slippery stones. "You are very talented," she said. "And I have not yet had the chance to mention to you that when I was in the kitchens this morning, I managed to find both honey and a small sack of cinnamon. I shall mix a potion for you after we are finished eating and you can try it upon your skin."

Aricia was very interested. "Thank you, my lady, I am very grateful," she said eagerly. "And you will show me how to do it?"

"Aye."

"You also mentioned something about making vinegar from apples? Will you show me how to do that, too?"

Sophina nodded as they reached the top of the stairs. "It is quite simple, truly," she said. "You may take apple peels and cores, mix them with some honey and warm water, and let all of it sit for several weeks and it will make vinegar. You may use that to wash your skin. I believe it will help a great deal."

Aricia was brimming with the great and wonderful things she was going to do, under Sophina's instruction, to help her skin condition. She hadn't felt so much hope in a very long time. As she followed Sophina to the door of the *mal enfant*, she put a hand on Sophina's arm, gently begging the woman to pause.

"Wait," Aricia said softly just as they reached the oak panel. "I… I would like to say something before you knock on the door."

Sophina turned to her attentively. "Of course."

Now that Aricia had Sophina's attention, she suddenly seemed uneasy. "I… I just want to say that you have been extremely kind to me. I do not have any friends, save my cousin, and you and your daughter have been very… kind. So very kind. I do not know if I can ever thank you enough for the friendship you have shown me but I wanted you to know that you have my undying gratitude."

Sophina smiled at the awkward young woman. "It is our pleasure," she said. "I am glad Emmaline has become your friend. She is a good girl. I hope she stays your friend for years to come."

Aricia nodded, still seemingly uncertain, as if she had more to say but couldn't quite speak of it. She averted her gaze even though her hand was still on Sophina's arm. Firm, long fingers with soft, pale hair on the knuckles. *A man's hand.*

"I want to explain something to you, my lady," she said, so softly that Sophina barely heard her. "Yesterday, when you examined my skin, you saw... my face, my neck. You saw... I know what you saw. I was born as you see. I have been wearing clothing such as this for as long as I can remember. I do not want to be what I am... only what I was meant to be. My mother and grandmother understood that. I just wanted you to know that I have always been this way. I... I cannot explain it more than that, my lady, but you have my thanks for not turning away in disgust or telling anyone what you saw. I am... grateful."

Sophina knew what she was trying to say; it was clearly painful for her to speak of it, struggling over her words as she did. No doubt, her desire to dress as a woman was strange. According to the teachings of the church, it could also be considered heresy in violation of God's moral code. Men were men, women were women, and the church frowned upon the manner in which Aricia was living her life.

Nonetheless, Sophina's opinion remained the same – this gentle creature lived the life she chose to live and it wasn't Sophina's place to judge. That was up to God. Therefore, she sought to put Aricia at ease.

"I saw a young woman with angry red skin that I hope to help," she said simply. "That is all I saw."

Aricia's eyes widened. "You... but you saw...."

"I know what I saw. And I know how kind you have been to my daughter. That is all I truly know."

Aricia stared at her a moment, her eyes growing moist. It was apparent that she hadn't expected such a reaction. "I... I sought to clarify because I did not want you to think I was trying to lie to you or pretend I was something I am not," she said. "I was born Aric. But Aric died when I was a baby and I have ever been called Aricia. My mother… my mother wanted a girl-child when I was born. I have never known anything else but dressing and living as a girl."

Sophina's smile faded. "Then your mother made you who you are?"

Aricia shook her head. "Nay," she said. "Not in the sense that she forced me. But she dressed me in beautiful things and I loved it. I have always loved it. This is who I am."

Sophina didn't particularly understand what Aricia said, but she accepted it. "If you are happy, that is all that matters."

Aricia sighed heavily, as if a great weight had been lifted from her slender shoulders. "I am happy where I am," she said. "I am happy with Juno. I am her spinster cousin and that is all anyone need know."

Sophina's smile returned, a gentle gesture. "Then I am happy for you," she said. "But… Juno's father. Does he know the truth?"

Aricia shook her head. "Nay," she said. "He never will. I met him for the first time when I was seven years of age, so he has always known me as a female. He will never know the truth. He is a difficult and harsh man. I fear he would not be quite so accepting."

Sophina felt pity for gentle Aricia and the life she led. Even if she said she was happy, still, there could be complications if her secret was revealed. It must have been difficult to live that way.

"You are the bravest woman I know," Sophina said, "and I wish you nothing but joy. Now, shall we feed this terrible child before my arms fall off? The tray is heavy."

Aricia giggled and knocked on the panel. Both women stood back, away from the door, as if fearful of what would come flying through it. But there was no response after the first knock so Aricia knocked again. She even took the tray from Sophina to relieve her of the burden. Just as Sophina handed over the tray, the door creaked open.

It was just a crack, really, with a black eye peering through it. Sophina recognized Lady Susanna's old nurse.

"My lady," Sophina greeted politely. "An army has been sighted and Sir Lucien has asked me to lock up the keep and take charge of the occupants. I have brought a meal for you and Lady Susanna. May I deliver it?"

The old woman didn't say a word. She simply stood back, opening the door wide so Sophina and Aricia could enter. Holding out a hand to Aricia, begging the woman to remain where she was, Sophina hesitantly stepped through the doorway, preparing for pewter cups to come flying out at her. The first thing she saw was Susanna, sitting in one of the small chairs in the corner of the room that held all of her playthings. The pewter set was in front of her, on the table, but she didn't make any move to pick anything up, at least not yet. Still, she didn't look at Sophina; she had a poppet in her lap and that was all she was looking at.

"Good morn, Lady Susanna," Sophina said evenly. "I have brought your morning meal. Would you like to have it placed on the table before you?"

Susanna didn't look up. "Go away," she said glumly. "I am not hungry."

Sophina could see that nothing had changed since last night. "You might not be now but you will be at some point," she said. "I will leave the tray here and you may eat at your leisure."

With that, she motioned Aricia in, who slipped in, trying not to gape at the opulence of the chamber. Sophina pointed to a small table over near the hearth and Aricia moved to it, swiftly, with Sophina behind her. Together, they removed the items from the tray and set them down on the very pretty painted table. In fact, Aricia was having difficulty absorbing the beauty of everything in the room; it was the most beautiful room she had ever seen.

Sophina silently motioned towards the door and Aricia nodded, but she didn't follow when Sophina moved towards it. In fact, Sophina was all the way to the panel when she realized that Aricia wasn't with her. She turned to see that the young woman was looking at several small paintings near the hearth and a small easel that had a half-finished painting on it. As Sophina opened her mouth to gain Aricia's attention. Susanna spoke.

"Where is my father?" she asked.

Sophina turned her attention to the girl. "An army is approaching Spelthorne and this requires your father's attention," she said steadily. Then, she looked around the pretty chamber. "In fact, we must close your shutters for safety's sake. If the castle is breached, we do not want to make it easy for the enemy to gain access to the keep."

She moved away from the door again, indicating to Aricia to close the shutters nearest to her, which she did. As Sophina closed the second set of shutters with some effort, Susanna spoke.

"Do you mean that there is going to be a battle?" she asked.

Sophina settled the bar across the shutters. "I hope not," she said. "But, to be safe, your father has asked that the women stay in the keep."

Susanna finally looked up from her poppet, her dark eyes following Sophina. "He has gone to war before," she said. "He has stayed away for years."

"This is not going to war. This is a threat to Spelthorne."

Susanna's baleful gaze lingered on Sophina before returning to her poppet. It was clear that all was not forgiven from yesterday. "Am I still going to the nuns?"

Sophina brushed the dust off her hands from the shutters and moved in the direction of the door once more. "That is up to you," she said. "If you promise to behave yourself, then I see no reason to send you. However, if you have no intention of being pleasant, then I am sure Cranborne is your next destination."

Susanna didn't say anything for a moment and Sophina assumed the girl was finished. Just as she reached out to open the door, Susanna spoke again.

"You hate me," she hissed. "My father hates me and you hate me, too. Well, I hate you, too! You are a terrible person!"

Sophina turned to the child, calmly. "I do not hate you," she said. "Why would I?"

Susanna was beginning to grow angry. She tugged at the hemp hair of her poppet. "You *beat* me!"

"I spanked you."

"You took your hand and you… you beat me!"

"You threw pewter cups at me. Did you think I would not punish you for it?"

"You have no right to punish me!"

"Your father gave me permission to punish you."

Susanna was verging on tears, now tearing her poppet to shreds. "My father hates me!"

Sophina sighed faintly. She could hear such hurt in Susanna's voice. But before she could move to the girl to speak with her, Aricia entered the conversation.

"Nay, he does not," she said, moving in Susanna's direction. "My name is Aricia and I came here yesterday. I heard you screaming. My cousin and I have come to Spelthorne. I can tell you for a fact that your father does not hate you. Do you know how I know that?"

Susanna had at least stopped tearing at her poppet. She looked at Aricia, eyeing the scarf-clad woman warily.

"Where did you come from?" she asked.

Aricia gazed down at the young girl. "France," she said. "Do you know where that is?"

Susanna shrugged; she didn't really but didn't want to admit it. She wasn't keen on admitting she didn't know everything. "Near to us," she said arrogantly. "It is near England. Why did you not come to me yesterday when I called to you? I wanted you to come and entertain me."

Aricia moved closer. "Because we had only just arrived and it had been a very long journey," she said. "But I am here now. Do you want me to tell you how I know your father loves you? Because my father did not love me. He told me so. Has your father ever told you that he hated you?"

Susanna looked at Aricia with uncertainty. "He tells me he does not hate me but I know he is lying."

"How do you know that?"

"Because I do!"

Aricia shook her head. Because Susanna was seated, Aricia went down on her knees a few feet from the girl, looking at her quite seriously.

"He is not lying," she said. "Do you know how I know that? Because you have a beautiful room. You have beautiful toys and you have everything you could possibly want. You have a fine bed and fine food to eat. If your father hated you, he would not give you these beautiful things. He would beat you. Has your father done that?"

Now, Susanna was genuinely stumped at the question. She was also genuinely interested in what Aricia was saying in spite of herself. Something was clicking in her mind, something that forced her to listen. After a moment, she shook her head.

"He has not."

Aricia nodded with confidence. "I did not think so," she said. "If he hated you, he would beat you. He would tell you he was ashamed of you and wished that you had never been born. He would tell you that he wished you would die. He would tell you that you were a disgrace to your family and an offense to good and moral people. Has he ever said any of those things to you?"

Susanna's brow furrowed. "Nay," she said. "He would be a terrible man for saying such things."

Aricia nodded, the light of recollection in her eyes. "Aye, he would," she agreed softly. "That is how I know your father does not hate you. He loves you. You have everything you could possibly need or want. You are very, very fortunate because, you see, my father has said those things to me. He told me he hated me, so I know what it means to have a father who hates you."

Susanna stared at Aricia. It was apparent that she had no idea what to say. She averted her gaze a moment, looking at her destroyed poppet, her toys, before finally returning her focus to Aricia. For the first time in her life, she had met up with someone who made some sense to her. Adults couldn't get through to her but a soft-spoken young woman evidently could. Those softly spoken words meant something, spoken to her in a way she could understand.

"Why does your father hate you?" she finally asked.

Aricia reached up and unfastened the yellow scarf covering the lower portion of her face. Discreetly, she revealed her terrible skin for just a brief moment to Susanna before covering herself up again.

"Because he hated the sight of me," she said softly. "I am ugly; so very ugly. My father would tell me that every day. But you... you are beautiful. You are loved. You are so very fortunate and you do not even know it."

Susanna caught sight of the red, bumpy skin before Aricia covered it up quickly. She'd never seen such a thing before and she was naturally curious. "What happened to your face?"

Aricia finished securing the scarf. "My skin has eruptions," she said. "My father said they were ugly, and they are. He left my mother some time ago and we've not seen him since, but I am at peace with that. He was a very bad man. I do not care if I ever see him again. But your father... you must not think unkindly of him, for he does not hate you. He shows you his love in this beautiful room and all of the possessions you have. Even if he does not tell you he loves you, he shows you. If he hated you, you would not have all of these wonderful things. You must remember that."

Susanna was left to ponder a great deal. It was quite a burden for a young girl, but she was very smart. She processed it quickly. In the dark and bitter clouds that filled her mind every hour of every day, somewhere behind them, a ray of hope began because in that woman with the yellow scarf over her face, she saw something of a kindred spirit. The woman had flaws just like she did.

Somewhere, a seed of understanding sprouted.

"You have red skin," she said. "But I... I cannot walk very well. I have never been able to."

Aricia nodded. "I heard that about you," she said. "Are those your paintings over by the hearth?"

Susanna nodded. "Aye."

"They are very good," Aricia said. "Will you show them to me?"

Susanna nodded and tried to stand up, but without her canes, it was difficult. "I cannot walk without my canes," she said, turning to look at Sophina. "She took them away from me."

Aricia wouldn't let the girl dwell on her anger towards Sophina. She reached out and took Susanna by the elbow. "You do not need them," she said. "I will help you walk. Come and show me your paintings. I want to know how you made such beautiful pictures."

Susanna didn't recoil. She actually permitted Aricia to help her take a few steps, in the direction of the paintings. She was calm and she wasn't screaming; it was something of a miracle. Together, Susanna and Aricia moved, very slowly, across the wooden floor.

Meanwhile, Sophina was watching with tears in her eyes. So much of Aricia's life had come clear in that quiet conversation to Susanna and it hurt Sophina's heart to know that Aricia's father had treated her so poorly. Aricia had said that she only lived with her mother and grandmother; now, Sophina knew why. The man had spouted his hatred upon this gentle creature and abandoned her.

Sweet Mary, what a horrible thing to have had happen. Sophina was also quite certain that the father had more of a reason to abandon Aricia than simply her skin. As her father, he knew she had been born male. That must have been why he had told her he was ashamed of her and wish she had never been born. But Aricia had weathered it; her heart had been stronger than her father's hatred.

She was a remarkable woman, indeed.

"Aricia?" Sophina called out softly. "I will be down in the solar if you require me."

Aricia waved her off. "I will be fine," she said. "Lady Susanna is going to show me how to paint."

With a smile on her lips, Sophina left the chamber. She wouldn't have believed it had she not seen it with her own eyes.

Thoughts lingering on Aricia and Susanna, Sophina took the narrow stairs down to the ground level. She could hear Emmaline and Juno in conversation in the solar and as she made her way towards it, with quite a story to tell the pair, she heard banging on the entry door.

Curious, she made her way over to the panel and opened the small peep hole that was about level with the top of her head. It was a very small section of the door, cut-out so those inside could see who was on the other side, but she couldn't see much other than the top of a bushy gray head.

"Who is it?" she asked.

"De Saix," Holderness said. "Let me in!"

Sophina hesitated. Lucien had told her not to let anyone inside unless he gave her permission. "I am sorry, my lord," she said. "Sir Lucien gave me instructions not to let anyone in."

"It is Sir Lucien I have come to tell you of!"

He's injured! That was Sophina's first thought. In a rush, she lifted the big wooden bar that secured the door horizontally, from one side to the other, before unbolting the small iron bolt that held the door securely shut. Just as she was pulling the panel open, Holderness was shoving at it from the other side. He nearly shoved her over.

"Where is my daughter?" he demanded.

Fearful, Sophina pointed to the small solar. When Holderness dashed for the chamber, she followed on his heels. As he rushed into the room, he startled Juno and Emmaline, who gasped at his sudden appearance. Juno was on her feet.

"Papa!" she gasped. "Why are you here? What has happened?"

Holderness was beside himself. He grasped his daughter by the wrist. "De Russe has shown an aversion to marrying you and now I know why," he said, turning to Sophina. "It is Lady de Gournay he wishes to marry, but Lady de Gournay's betrothed is here and demanding that de Russe relinquish her."

Juno's eyes widened at Sophina. Even Emmaline looked at her mother with surprise. But Sophina didn't look at either girl – she was frozen for a moment, unable to speak because Holderness had revealed a very horrible piece of information that had her reeling with shock.

Lady de Gournay's betrothed is here!

"Is *that* who brought the army here?" she asked Holderness, incredulous. "St. Michael du Ponte brought his army here?"

"Ah!" Holderness pointed a finger at her accusingly. "Then you admit he is your betrothed!"

Sophina was more concerned for Lucien and the apparent arrival of du Ponte than she was for Juno at the moment. She simply couldn't help it. She certainly hadn't expected du Ponte to come to Spelthorne because, in her mind, there was no way he could have known she was here unless one of his men recognized Lucien when he saved her and Emmaline from the sinking carriage. But if that was the case, why did du Ponte simply not come alone? Why bring an entire army?

It was deeply puzzling, and concerning, and Holderness' condemning attitude was only serving to feed her anxiety. She didn't appreciate the fact that he was practically screaming accusations at her.

"My father approached St. Michael du Ponte with a potential marriage," she said evenly. "I was on my way to Gillingham Castle to meet with Sir St. Michael when we were set upon by bandits and saved by Sir Lucien."

Holderness wasn't finished condemning her. "And you seduced de Russe!" he said. "You stole him from my daughter!"

Emmaline leapt to her feet. "That is not true," she said hotly. "He was kind to us and she helped him!"

Sophina put her hand on her excitable daughter. "Sit down, sweetheart," she said softly, firmly. "We know that what he says is not the truth."

"Not the truth?" Holderness said, unconvinced. "Do you know what de Russe just did? He offered to buy du Ponte's contract. He is trying to buy himself one bride and bribe himself out of another. Aye, you heard me correctly – he wants to *pay* me to dissolve the contract between him and my daughter and I will tell you now that it will cost de Russe every last pence he has to do it. If he wants to marry you, then I will take everything from him before I break the contract."

"Nay, Papa!" Juno finally found her tongue. "For the Love of Christ, you will not take his money, do you hear? You will not do this at all! I have watched you bully and gloat and push people around, but I will not stand by and watch you do it anymore. If Sir Lucien wants to marry Lady de Gournay so badly that he is willing to pay for it, that should speak great testimony to his wants and needs, which do not include me. I am glad, do you hear? I am glad!"

Holderness turned on his daughter. "Shut your mouth," he hissed. "It is because of you that this marriage must happen immediately. You have forced my hand."

Juno yanked her arm from her father's grasp. "It is because of *you*," she fired back. "You and your petty arrogance. No one but a great husband would do for me when the truth is that the only husband I want is in Warwickshire. He is a simple knight and the father of my child, but that is not good enough for you. Nay! You must have a prestigious husband for me, forcing me into marriage with Sir Lucien so he will believe the child I carry is his own. You are despicable and horrible to be so deceitful!"

Holderness turned white, hearing Sophina gasp behind him. Suddenly, the situation had turned on him as the truth was revealed from his daughter's lips. Anger such as he had never known flooded him, shame beyond compare. Now, everyone would know what had happened, something he was trying very desperately to salvage. But now, there would be no salvation. Now, the truth was out.

"You foolish wench," he said to his daughter, his lips trembling. "You foolish, lowly girl. If you'd only kept your legs closed, this would not have happened. You have ruined us."

"And if you'd only listened to me for once in your life, we would not find ourselves in this position!"

"Ungrateful chit!"

Juno grunted in frustration and turned away, bursting into quiet tears. Emmaline rushed to her friend's side, putting her arms around her quite protectively as she glared daggers at Holderness, who showed no emotion whatsoever to tears from his daughter or the hateful stares from a young woman. When he finally turned around to face Sophina, she was staring at him with a hand over her mouth. Her dismay was evident.

"I supposed you are going to run to de Russe and tell him everything you just heard," he muttered. "My foolish daughter just made it easy for you to claim him. Now you know. Well? What are you waiting for?'

Truthfully, Sophina was still in shock. Juno was pregnant by another man and Holderness wasn't going to tell Lucien about it. Now, the man's aggressiveness in pushing the marriage between his daughter and Lucien was starting to make some sense. Juno was pregnant and Holderness wanted Lucien to believe he was the father. It was beyond vile; it was reprehensible. Holderness would have his wants and didn't care who he hurt or tramped on in the process.

Lowering her hand, Sophina walked a wide berth around Holderness to where Juno and Emmaline were standing.

"Go up to your chamber," she said softly, turning Juno and Emmaline for the door. "Go up there and bolt it. You will not open it for anyone but me or Lucien or Lucien's knights. Is that clear?"

Emmaline nodded, pulling the sobbing Juno out the door with her, helping the young woman up the stairs. Sophina followed them from the room, standing at the bottom of the stairs until the two young women disappeared from sight.

Once they were gone, she couldn't even bring herself to look at Holderness. He was the lowest form of life as far as she was concerned. He was trying to control everyone and everything around him without care or consequence. He was, in fact, much like her father. Aye, she knew men like that. She knew what lengths they would go to in order to gain their wants. But Holderness wouldn't gain his wants this time. Without another word, she turned on her heel and quit the keep.

What she didn't count on was Holderness pursuing her with a dagger.

CHAPTER FIFTEEN

L AURENT AND COLTON were escorting du Pontes two knights, de Fey and l'Evereux, through the gatehouse when they both saw Lady de Gournay exiting the keep. The morning was brightening up, the sky above a clear and deep shade of blue, and the vision of Lady de Gournay coming from the keep was without obstruction.

In fact, Laurent and Colton eyed the woman, for she cut a fine figure as she walked. Clad in brown broadcloth with a leather girdle cinching up her small waist, she was quite lovely and a bit of sweetness upon their eyes. Colton knew that Lucien thought the same thing although Laurent hadn't been around enough to see how Lucien was eyeing Lady de Gournay. Nor had Laurent heard Lucien confess that he intended to marry the woman. It made for some interesting dynamics considering Lucien's betrothed was in residence, the pale but lovely Lady Juno. Aye, odd dynamics and actions were afoot these days at Spelthorne.

As they were eyeing the lovely woman, they saw Holderness exit the keep, too, moving quite swiftly after Lady de Gournay. The man was moving in a bizarre manner, in fact, it appeared that he was staggering. He was grabbing at something in his robes, something neither Laurent nor Colton could see, but soon enough, they saw that he had a dagger in his hand. His pursuit of Lady de Gournay increased. Colton was the first one to speak.

"What is your father doing?" he asked Laurent. "What is he going to do with that dagger?"

Laurent was watching with concern. He knew his father could be rash and aggressive at times, but following a woman with a dagger in his hand was never a good sign. Knowing his father, the man was capable of anything, especially in light of recent events involving Lucien and his reluctance to marry Juno. Therefore, Laurent didn't even answer Colton. He simply took off at a dead run towards his father. Startled, Colton did, too, yelling at du Ponte's knights as he went.

"Into the hall!" he bellowed. "Go!"

Colton didn't spare the attention to see if they obeyed him. He simply kept running after Laurent because the man's father had a big dagger in his hand as he went in pursuit of Lady de Gournay. Something terrible was about to occur and they had to stop it. But Colton was a faster runner than Laurent and was on the man's heels by the time they reached Holderness, who saw them coming. He tried to run at Lady de Gournay in a sprint, dagger lifted, but Laurent managed to put himself between his father and the lady. The dagger came down into Laurent's shoulder.

Sophina, who had no idea that Holderness was behind her until the running knights drew close, screamed as Laurent and Colton tackled Holderness, all three of them hurling to the ground in a violent crash of flesh. Terrified, she jumped back just as de Fey and l'Evereux also came running up, watching Laurent roll off of his father with a dagger in his clavicle. That left Colton wrestling with the earl on the ground, trying to subdue the man.

Instinct took over and Sophina ran to Laurent with the hilt sticking out of his shoulder. "My God!" she gasped. "Sir Laurent! Let me get a look at this – let me see what damage the blade has done."

Laurent was grunting with pain. The blade had rendered his left arm fairly useless. He pushed himself up, grabbing Sophina by the arm and trying to usher her away from the brawl as de Fey and l'Evereux jumped in. Holderness was howling, screaming to be released, but

Colton had the man fast by the arms as l'Evereux grabbed the man by the legs, trapping him. More men began coming, lured by the screams.

"Move away, my lady," Laurent said, staggering up to his feet, still holding her arm. "Quickly, move away. My father is far gone into madness."

Sophina let the big knight move her away but she was thoroughly puzzled and very frightened. "But why?" she asked. "Why did he stab you?"

Laurent was moving her in the direction of the hall. Men were shouting now, some of them running over to the skirmish where the three knights now had Holderness pinned and subdued. But the man was still screaming his head off.

"It was an accident," he said, sweat on his upper lip from the pain. "He was going after you, my lady. We stopped him."

Sophina looked at the knight, horrorstruck. "Me?" she repeated. "But… why…?"

"That is what I would like to know," Laurent said, pulling her to a halt well away from the pile of men. "Did you have a conversation with him recently? What did you say to him that he would come after you with a dagger?"

Sophina's gaze trailed to the earl, now on the ground as Colton and another knight tied him up with rope that one of the de Russe soldiers had brought. Her mouth was hanging open, shocked, as she tried to grasp what had just happened.

"We just spoke in the keep," she said hesitantly. "He said that Lucien does not wish to marry your sister and tried to buy out the marital contract. Your father called it a bribe. He… he accused me of seducing Lucien. But your sister… Sweet Mary, your lovely sister said that your father was only forcing her to marry Lucien so that Lucien would believe he was the father of your sister's child."

Laurent understood a good deal in that stammered explanation. He looked at Sophina for a moment, astonishment on his face, before turning his attention to his father. Colton had just finished tying his hands behind his back and Holderness lay there and screamed.

"Good God," Laurent finally hissed, rolling his eyes as if coming to understand the gist of a very bad situation. "She said it. She really said it."

"Who?"

Laurent glanced at Sophina. "My sister," he muttered, putting a hand to the hilt of the dagger still sticking out of his shoulder as if to somehow ease the pain. "My lady... I am so very sorry. Sorry my father tried to...."

He was cut off as Lucien suddenly appeared with de Bretagne and du Ponte behind him. They'd come hurtling out of the great hall after being alerted by one of Lucien's soldiers, now seeing a gang of men in the area between the hall and the keep with Holderness on the bottom of it, restrained. Colton and du Ponte's two men were standing over him. Lucien's expression was twisted with concern and bewilderment.

"What in the hell goes on here?" he demanded. Then, he noticed Laurent standing there with a dagger in his shoulder. His concern grew. "Who did that?"

Sophina was so relieved to see Lucien that she was nearly in tears. "His father did," she said, struggling not to cry. "He was trying to stab me but Laurent saved me. His father stabbed him, instead."

Lucien's face lost some of its color at that moment. He looked at Sophina and, seeing how upset she was, couldn't restrain himself from going to her. But he didn't pull her into his arms, as much as he wanted to. He stopped short of touching her. But he stood very close to her, looking her over just to make sure she was unharmed.

"What happened?" he asked again. "Why did Holderness try to kill you?"

To have Lucien so close made Sophina feel very weak. God, she wanted to feel his arms around her. She wanted his comfort. She put up a hand, resting it on his chest. She simply had to touch him.

"He said terrible things, Lucien," she whispered tightly. "He said that you were trying to buy my contract with du Ponte. He said you tried to buy his contract with Juno, paying him so that you would not have to marry her. He said he would take every pence from you before he would agree."

Lucien still wasn't clear on why Holderness had tried to kill her. "I did offer," he said without hesitation. "I said exactly that. I offered to buy du Ponte's contract and I further offered to pay Holderness if he would dissolve my betrothal with his daughter."

Sophina wiped at her eyes because the tears were forming. "Lucien, Juno is pregnant," she said quietly. She didn't want anyone else to overhear. "That is why Holderness was trying to force you to marry the girl, so that you would think the child was yours. I suppose… I suppose Holderness knew I was going to tell you the truth so mayhap he was trying to silence me."

Lucien's eyes widened and his jaw dropped. "She is with child?"

"Aye."

Lucien stared at her, utterly shocked. "But… how…?" he stammered. "How long have you known?"

Sophina gazed up at him with her big, bottomless eyes. "I was just told," she said. "When the earl said those terrible things to me, Lady Juno confessed the true reason behind him pushing the marriage between you and her. He was trying to force the marriage quickly so you would not know Lady Juno was pregnant when you married her."

Lucien felt as if he had been struck. Immediately, his accusing gaze flew to Holderness as the man now sat up, hands tied, on the ground of the bailey. But, just as swiftly, his gaze moved to Laurent, standing pale and injured. The realization of what the House of de Saix had tried to put over on him had him reeling. Even if he didn't really know the earl, by virtue of the man's station, he'd had no reason to mistrust him. Until now.

But Laurent… Lucien had fought with Laurent many a time. He trusted the man or, at least, he had. Now, he struggled not to become enraged as a very terrible secret came to light.

"Did you know?" he asked Laurent. "About your sister's condition – Laurent, did you know?"

Laurent swallowed hard. "Aye, my lord," he said, defeat in his voice. "I knew. But it was my father's arrangement with you. He told me not to interfere. He threatened me, in fact."

Lucien felt as if he'd been betrayed. "And you were not going to tell me?"

Laurent sighed heavily. "And go against my father?" he asked, trying to defend himself. "I am his heir, Lucien. He can easily cut me out and you know it. Everything I have depends on him. Would I have told you about my sister and risked my inheritance? It would have been the right thing to do, that is true, but it is an action that would have more than likely left me penniless. Was that worth telling you? Ask yourself that question. Could you have made that choice? You would have married my sister, she would have given birth to the child, and you would not have been the wiser. And it was a secret I would have taken to my grave with me. I am sorry, but that is the truth. I understand if you cannot forgive me for thinking of myself over you, Lucien, but my failing is that I considered my plight over yours."

Lucien felt many different emotions at that point. He was disappointed with Laurent's stance but, in a way, he understood it. He really did. Telling him what he knew about his father's dirty dealings wasn't worth the cost of the Holderness earldom. Nay, Lucien couldn't really fault him that. Risking his entire legacy over a matter that, had it gone as it was supposed to, would have had Lucien believing that the child his young wife bore was his. Lucien certainly wouldn't have suspected otherwise.

Still, he was disappointed. Disappointed and angry. Without much more to say on the subject, at least to Laurent, he turned to Sophina.

"Would you please take Laurent into the keep and tend his injury?" he asked quietly. "I have other pressing matters to attend to."

That was an understatement. The situation with du Ponte and the arrival of an army had been chaotic enough without Holderness attempting murder. Sophina studied Lucien's face, trying to determine what he was going to do and how he was reacting to all of this. She was concerned for him.

"Laurent saved my life," she reminded him quietly. "Remember that before passing judgment on him."

Lucien looked at her, into that spectacular face he was coming to depend on. *To love.* Aye, he loved her. He knew he did. It was a thought, so warm and subtle, that he wasn't surprised when it occurred to him. It was as if he had loved her all along. Was it possible, at his age, to love someone without even knowing them for a day?

He was a fool for thinking that it was, indeed, possible because it had happened to him. Something about Sophina connected to something deep inside of him, as if they were of one mind and one soul, thinking similar thoughts, understanding each other because of the things in life they had experienced. All he had to do was look at her and know she was true and noble. All he had to do was look at her and feel complete, once again.

With her, The Iron Knight wasn't so empty, after all.

"I cannot judge a man who does what he must do in order to survive," he finally said. "And for saving your life, he will always have my gratitude."

Sophina was relieved, for Laurent's sake. "What will you do with Holderness, then?"

Lucien didn't look at her. His focus moved to Colton, standing over Holderness several feet away. "De Royans!" he shouted. "Put him in the vault!"

Colton nodded, hauling Holderness to his feet as the man bellowed his displeasure. As Colton pulled the man away, towards the gatehouse where the vault was located, Sophina couldn't even look at him. Instead, she took a closer look at Laurent's wound and realized it wasn't too terribly deep. Messy, but not deep. Still, she needed to remove the dagger, a dagger that just as easily could have been planted in her back had it not been for Laurent.

"Come with me," she said to Laurent, taking his elbow to help him along. "Let me tend your wound."

Laurent went without prompting. He, too, was eager to get the knife out of his shoulder and put this terrible incident behind him. He still couldn't believe his father so blatantly tried to murder someone, but given how badly his father wanted Juno to marry de Russe, in hindsight, he wasn't so surprised after all. Just as he started to move with Sophina at his side, a voice rang out nearby.

"So this is Lady de Gournay," a man said. "De Russe, now I see why you're willing to surrender your fortune for her. She is exquisite, indeed."

Walking next to Laurent, Sophina froze, turning to see a man she didn't know standing a few feet away from Lucien. He was tall, and dark, and not unhandsome. His French accent was heavy. He was looking at her quite lasciviously and it didn't take a great intellect to deduce who he was. *Du Ponte*. It could be no one else. No use in running away; he had sighted her. Therefore, she faced him without fear.

"I am Lady de Gournay," she said coldly. "And you are St. Michael du Ponte?"

Du Ponte bowed gallantly. "At your service, my lady," he said. "It is a pity the carriage did not make it to Gillingham. We should not find ourselves here, disrupting de Russe's life. I trust you were not injured in the ambush?"

Sophina found his concern offensive. "That was yesterday," she said. "Had your men not run like cowards, they could have told you that I nearly drowned and my daughter along with me. Had it not been for Sir Lucien, we would have perished."

The smirking smile on du Ponte's lips faded. He didn't like insolent women. "I would not insult my men if I were you, my lady," he said, a veiled threat. "They are fine warriors. And you will let another tend to that knight. You and I have much to discuss."

Sophina shook her head. "We have nothing to discuss, my lord," she said. "Sir Lucien has made you an offer for our marriage contract.

Know that it is my wish to be married to Sir Lucien, so any business you have to discuss will be with him. Good morn, my lord."

She turned away, continuing her walk with Laurent, but du Ponte wasn't finished with her. "You will not turn your back to me," he said, hazard in his tone. "As long as I hold your father's offer, you are essentially my property and you will obey me. Do you understand?"

Sophina kept walking without answering him, which utterly inflamed du Ponte. "Come with me now or I will force you!"

That brought Lucien to du Ponte's side. An enormous hand shot out, grabbing du Ponte around the neck as de Bretagne and Pembury, who had been standing off to the side observing the unruly situation, rushed to prevent a fight. De Bretagne pulled Lucien away as Pembury, a mountain of a man, yanked du Ponte clear of Lucien's murderous grip. Du Ponte, infuriated at being grabbed and manhandled, shoved Pembury away by the face and broke the man's grip on him.

"That woman is my property, de Russe," he shouted. "You have no right to interfere in my business!"

Before Lucien could fire off a reply, de Bretagne got in his face. "He is right," he hissed. "The woman belongs to him no matter how much you want her. If he demands I enforce the contract, I must rule in his favor."

Lucien looked at the man, stricken with disbelief that de Bretagne should side against him. It didn't matter that he was pointing out the obvious; Lucien didn't care about that at all. "I will *not* turn her over to him," he muttered. "He cannot have her."

De Bretagne sighed heavily. "Lucien...."

"*Never.* You will have to kill me in order to take her from me. Is that in any way unclear?"

De Bretagne looked at him, his expression tense and torn. "Are you telling me that I shall have to take her by force?"

"That is exactly what I am telling you."

De Bretagne stared at him a moment longer before releasing him. There was exasperation to his movements, caught in the middle of something he was most reluctant to be part of. With a harsh sigh, one of extreme frustration, he turned to du Ponte.

"Get in the great hall," he commanded. "You'll not spout threats out here for all to hear. Get into that hall and we shall come to a satisfactory conclusion of this situation or I swear I will take my men and ride from here, and you shall have no further help from me."

Du Ponte was incensed. "I am within my rights!"

"Get into the hall and prepare to negotiate or I leave this minute."

"And I shall tell Henry!"

"And I shall tell Henry what I know of your suspect dealings with outlaws in the area. De Russe will support my claims. We shall see who comes out on top of that particular battle."

Du Ponte's face turned red but he shut his mouth. He knew it could mean great trouble for him if de Bretagne carried through on that particular threat. With a baleful glance at Lucien, he turned and marched for the great hall. De Bretagne watched him go all the way in before turning to Lucien.

"Now," he said seriously. "I have no desire to do battle with you, Lucien, but in the matter of supporting a legitimate contract, I have no choice. You know this. So it is my suggestion that you go in there and make your offer to du Ponte so sweet that there is no possibility he will refuse. Is *that* in any way unclear?"

Lucien almost grinned when he heard de Bretagne use his own words against him. But he couldn't quite manage it; this wasn't a grinning situation. This was damn serious. Turning for the hall, he preceded de Bretagne into the structure.

Sophina had been watching the entire thing. She'd seen the scuffle between Lucien and du Ponte. When Pembury and another knight had separated them, she watched with concern as first du Ponte and then Lucien retreated back into the hall.

She knew their impending discussion was to be about her and she wanted to hear what was said. She wanted to know just how much Lucien was prepared to lose in order to gain her and she wasn't entirely sure she should let him. Not that she wanted to be married to du Ponte, for she clearly didn't, but having Lucien give away his fortune because of her... she wasn't sure she could stomach that. It just didn't seem right for the man to become a pauper simply to gain a woman he'd known all of a day.

No matter how much she loved him.

Aye, she loved him. She couldn't remember when she hadn't. But she still couldn't let him sacrifice everything he'd worked so hard for just for her. She had to be part of that discussion. Seeing that Gabriel was still nearby, clearing out the men who had come to break up the fight, she called out to him.

"Pembury?" she said. "Come and tend to Sir Laurent."

Gabriel obeyed. He moved to Laurent's side, eyeing the protruding dagger with concern, but he was rather confused by the request. Sophina pointed to the keep.

"Take him into the solar," she said. "My daughter is in our chamber on the third level. You will ask her for needle and thread. She will be able to help you."

Gabriel was still confused. "Where are you going, Lady de Gournay?"

Sophina began walking towards the keep. "To see what is transpiring inside," she said. "Do as I say, now."

Gabriel wouldn't dream of disobeying a lady's request but the truth was that he didn't think she should be in the hall. He, in fact, had been in the hall since the beginning of du Ponte's visit and it hadn't been pleasant. He was about to say something to that effect but Sophina was walking away from him, quickly heading towards the hall. Gabriel hoped that Lucien wouldn't become angry with him for not preventing her, but Laurent needed help and that was his priority at the moment. A man with a dagger in him took precedence over a determined lady.

So he turned away, walking with Laurent towards the hall, until a scream stopped him. He and Laurent turned sharply to see a very unwelcome sight – two big knights, du Ponte knights, had hold of Sophina and were dragging her towards the hall.

Releasing Laurent, Gabriel broke into a dead run after them.

CHAPTER SIXTEEN

"I S THAT DU Ponte's lady?" l'Evereux hissed.

De Fey looked at him strangely. "You were there," he said. "You *saw* the woman."

L'Evereux shrugged. "I did not look at her closely," he said. "She had red hair but it was pulled back upon her head. I do not recognize this woman at all."

De Fey rolled his eyes. "That is the problem with you," he hissed. "You are as stupid as a post. Of course that is the woman we were bringing to Gillingham. Even if you did not recognize her, you just heard du Ponte speak to her. *That's* the woman we have come to retrieve."

In the wake of Holderness' attempted murder attack, de Fey and l'Evereux had been left without a guard. Colton and Laurent had run off to protect a lady from a murderous ambush and the two du Ponte knights had rushed to help. At first, de Fey and l'Evereux had aided with the submission of Holderness but when more of de Russe's men rushed in, they'd been pushed aside.

Now, they were standing on the outskirts, watching everything and also hearing everything. They'd heard du Ponte when he'd caught a glimpse of Lady de Gournay for the first time and they'd further heard when de Russe had refused to relinquish the woman.

Now, du Ponte and de Russe were inside the hall, no doubt arguing over custody of the lady. Most of de Russe's men were gone, leaving Lady de Gournay with only two knights as protection, one of which was injured. L'Evereux, as dense as he was, still knew a good opportunity when he saw one. He turned to de Fey.

"Why not take her now?" he questioned. "You heard what du Ponte said – he wanted her and de Russe would not relinquish her. If we take her, then de Russe will have no choice."

De Fey's gaze tracked the woman as she was in conversation with two other knights, including one who had a knife sticking out of his shoulder. He wasn't exactly sure how to get to the woman considering she was at the side of two armed men, but his dilemma was solved when she abruptly broke away from them and headed for the great hall.

"Look at her," he muttered. "She is without an escort now. When she gets far enough away from those two knights, we will confiscate her and take her to du Ponte."

L'Evereux nodded. "We can reclaim what the ambush took from us," he said, pulling out a nasty looking dagger from his breeches, a weapon that the gatehouse guards had missed when confiscating his arsenal. "Du Ponte cannot be angry with us any longer. What we lost, we will regain."

De Fey nodded, ever so slowly. "Move in her direction," he said casually, "but make no sudden movement. If we do not take custody before de Russe's men can get to her, our lives are forfeit. They'll kill us."

"How do you know that?"

De Fey looked at him like he was the most idiotic man on the planet. "Did you hear de Russe argue for her?" he hissed. "God's Balls, you fool! She means something to the man!"

L'Evereux had heard the arguments between de Russe and du Ponte but the fact that the woman meant something to de Russe still didn't register with him. At least, not on a personal level. "He wants her to warm his bed," he said. "What else is a woman good for?"

De Fey didn't respond; l'Evereux was a hopeless idiot so he didn't bother to explain. He had noticed how passionate de Russe had been in the conflict with du Ponte, so he understood that there was something more there, something more than just simple possession. A man who was passionate about a woman would do anything to keep her.

So de Fey started walking, very casually, heading towards the hall because that seemed to be the direction Lady de Gournay was moving in. He could even see her features as their paths drew near to one another. Her brow was furrowed in thought and it was clear that she wasn't paying attention to her surroundings. Her mind was miles away, perhaps pondering the recent attempt on her life or even the argument between du Ponte and de Russe.

Whatever the case, she was heading for the hall and she didn't notice that de Fey and l'Evereux were heading for the hall, as well. Their paths were about to cross about twenty feet from the main entry to the hall. By the time she realized the du Ponte knights were near her, it was too late.

De Fey reached out a big hand and grabbed Sophina, snatching her by the wrist and nearly pulling her arm off in the process. Sophina let out a scream but l'Evereux was quickly at her other side, his nasty-looking dirk poking her in the ribs.

"Silence, my lady," de Fey said steadily. "You will come with us."

Sophina, startled and terrified that she seemed to have been taken prisoner in Lucien's bailey, tried to pull away. "Let me go," she demanded. "Let me go, I say! Release me!"

L'Evereux jabbed her with the tip of the dirk and she yelped, for the poke broke through her garment and scratched her tender skin. "Ouch!" she gasped, trying to pull away from the dagger. "Stop! Let me go!"

De Fey shifted his grip from her wrist to her arm and Sophina yelped as his fingers bit in to her tender flesh. "Listen to me well, lady," he hissed in her ear. "I will not let you go. You are du Ponte's property and now we shall return to Gillingham. If you fight, my comrade on your other side will make sure you experience a good deal of pain. You will bleed to death before de Russe can save you. Do you comprehend?"

Cold fear rushed through Sophina as she realized that was not some inane temporary plan. She looked up at de Fey, terror and recognition filling her features.

"You," she breathed. "You came to Thruxton Castle. You were at the head of du Ponte's escort."

De Fey nodded. "Indeed, I was," he said. "You should not have run away from the carriage."

Sophina was outraged at his suggestion. "You and your men fled," she said hotly. "Sir Lucien saved me and my daughter. I did not 'flee'. Had I remained at the carriage, God only knows what would have happened to me and my child."

De Fey prepared to reply but movement out of the corner of his eye caught his attention. He turned swiftly to see one of de Russe's knights bearing down on them and he quickly turned so that Sophina was in front of him, like a shield. Even though l'Evereux had a dagger pointed at her, de Fey threw his arm around her neck. The message was clear.

Come closer and she dies.

"Go no further," he commanded the knight. "One more step and I shall snap her neck."

Gabriel came to a halt, struggling not to show the concern he felt to see Lady de Gournay in the grip of a du Ponte knight. His heart sank; *damnation!* Had he been so ignorant of the movement of du Ponte's men that he permitted the woman to come to harm? Slowly, he raised his hands to show that he was not armed.

"I will not come any closer," he said. "Why are you doing this?"

De Fey's gaze lingered on the very tall knight for a moment, contemplating his answer, before turning to l'Evereux.

"Cover my back," he muttered. "Make sure no one comes up behind me."

L'Evereux did as he was told. He moved to stand behind de Fey, his back to de Fey's to protect the man's rear. Meanwhile, de Fey returned his attention to Gabriel.

"Go inside and get de Russe," he said. "Bring both him and du
Ponte out here. Do it now."

Gabriel didn't like to be pushed around. He hated for someone to
have the upper hand on him. His bright blue eyes glared at de Fey.

"Are you sure you want to do this?" he asked.

De Fey wouldn't be sucked into a conversation with him. "Do as I
say. Go get your master."

Gabriel sighed faintly. "You have no idea the fierceness of the wrath
you are about to incur."

"I will not tell you again."

Gabriel didn't want to push him, not when he held the lady's neck
in such a precarious position. With a lingering look at de Fey, as if to
emphasize to the man how very much trouble he was about to face, he
turned away and headed to the great hall.

Sophina, meanwhile, didn't say a word. She remembered these
men, as they had been part of her escort to Gillingham, but neither one
of them had hardly said a word to her the entire trip. She didn't even
know their names. When their escort had been ambushed, the pair, and
the other du Ponte soldiers, had simply run off. Whoever these men
were, they were unscrupulous and cowardly, but she wouldn't tell them
that with a big arm across her neck. She didn't want to have her neck
snapped in a fit of rage. She had a great deal to live for.

She very much wanted to see her daughter grow up and marry and
have children of her own. She very much wanted to become Lady de
Russe and spend her life coming to know a remarkable man. Perhaps
there would even be children for them in the future. She'd never really
thought about having more children but she would be more than happy
to provide Lucien with a son or two. What a lovely family that would
be.

Thinking thoughts of Lucien and their future together kept her
calm with a man threatening to snap her neck, but when Lucien
suddenly emerged from the great hall, his features edged with disbelief,
she could feel her composure slipping. She didn't like that look of

desperation in his eye.

Before Lucien could speak, du Ponte spilled out behind him. The man's voice rose in glee, blotting out everything else.

"Ah!" du Ponte said. "I see we no longer have an issue to discuss, de Russe. My men have claimed what is rightfully mine."

Lucien was struggling not to rush du Ponte. He was fairly sure he could get to the man and twist his head off but he wasn't entirely sure he could do it before du Ponte's men broke Sophina's neck. Wild, murderous thoughts like that raced through his mind but he forced them away, killing them. He couldn't risk Sophina just to satisfy his rage. Therefore, he simply stared at the man holding Sophina without making eye contact with her; to do so would surely destroy his composure.

"This is how you repay my hospitality?" he asked. "By taking one of my guests hostage?"

Du Ponte wouldn't let de Fey answer. He made sure to put himself between de Fey and Lucien. He wasn't entirely certain that de Russe wouldn't try to physically wrest the woman from his knight. Therefore, he put himself in between Lucien and his knights and began ushering his men in the direction of the gatehouse.

"I have what I came for, de Russe," he said, his manner quite glib. He threw up his hands, grinning. "I will take what rightfully belongs to me and I shall leave. I am sorry to have troubled you."

Lucien was following, flanked by de Bretagne. He was trying so very hard not to show any weakness, any fury, but inside he was spilling over. He was frightened and he was furious, so much so that his hands were shaking. Having never faced a situation like this before, personally, it was very difficult for him to control himself.

"So you walk out during the course of a bargain?" he asked, realizing his voice was trembling. "I offered you a great deal of money for your marriage contract, du Ponte. Are you telling me that you do not need the money?"

Du Ponte's smirk faded somewhat. It was true that de Russe had offered him a more than fair price for Lady de Gournay and it was further true that du Ponte wanted the money. To be honest, he probably wanted the money more but he simply couldn't resist having the upper hand on de Russe. He had something that de Russe very badly wanted; this man, lauded by the king, a man that soldiers and nobles alike called The Iron Knight for his durability in battle. Du Ponte knew there was never any way he could possibly best de Russe in battle.

The only way he could do it was to take what the man wanted.

De Russe had tried to gain the upper hand with him, the righteous bastard, which was what made this particular incident so sweet – de Russe had been trying for a very long time to bring du Ponte to justice, to tie him to the outlaws in the area, knowing that du Ponte had a connection with them. The man had tried to ruin his livelihood. That being the case, du Ponte was going to punish him now. Punish him for every bit of slander he'd ever spoken against him.

Now, de Russe was going to pay.

"*You* made the offer," de Ponte said. "I never accepted. I never hinted that I would accept. I told you that I wanted my property returned and here she is, now safe with my own men. I do not know how she came into their possession and I do not care, but I do know this – if you do not let us pass from Spelthorne unmolested, I can promise you that the lady will not live to see the sun set. Is that what you wish?"

Lucien wasn't sure if du Ponte was bluffing but he couldn't take the chance. He also couldn't let the man leave his castle. If he did, he was afraid he would never see Sophina again. Already, it was killing him to watch that brute of a knight drag her across the bailey as she struggled against the arm across her neck. As he watched her in the fight for her life, he realized he was going to have to make the most difficult decision of his life. He could try to free her, but he might not be able to before du Ponte's man killed her.

It was that very thought that was tearing him apart.

"Nay," he said steadily. "But hear me now; let her go and I will give you everything I own – my coinage, my horses, my property – everything. The dukedom of Exeter will be mine upon my father's death and I will even provide you with ten thousand *deniers* annually from that until your death. I can make you a very rich man, du Ponte. All I ask is that you give me the lady, unharmed."

Du Ponte liked the sound of that. He truly did. To have all that de Russe owned plus ten thousand a year? That was an astonishing amount of wealth. It was enough for him to actually consider it. He knew that de Russe was a man of his word; men like him were insipid in their belief in honor. He knew, no matter if it cost him everything, that de Russe would stick to the bargain.

"Very well," he said. "I will consider it. I am going to take the lady with me back to Gillingham and you may bring all of your wealth, your horses, and everything you own to Gillingham as well. Only when I have everything of yours will I even consider turning the lady over to you. Until then, she stays with me."

They were nearing the gatehouse now as Lucien's entire army turned out to see du Ponte and his two knights dragging Lady de Gournay to the gatehouse. They were pulling her awkwardly so it was difficult for her keep her footing. She gripped the arm around her neck so she would not accidentally kill herself by tripping. It was a rather harrowing scene with de Russe following closely, a desperate look on his face.

The Iron Knight wasn't one to show emotion. He never had been. He had weathered whatever God and men had thrown at him and he'd always come through. But at this moment, he was showing his humanity in all things. One small lady had managed to do that to him. It was a sorrowful thing to watch.

"Wait," Lucien said as they moved through the gatehouse. "Please… just wait. Do not take her. Stay here and, by morning, I will have everything that I promised for you to take with you back to Gillingham. I swear it, du Ponte. Just… do not leave with her. Stay here and no one will harm you."

"Nay, Lucien!" Sophina finally found her voice. She couldn't stand to hear what du Ponte was doing to Lucien. She simply couldn't let the man give up everything for her. "Do not give him anything! Please! There must be another way. You must keep your wealth!"

De Fey gave her a squeeze to silence her and she yelped. Lucien nearly came apart. He could feel a hand on him, begging him not to charge. It was de Bretagne but he didn't turn to look; all he knew was that someone, someone who cared, was trying to prevent him from doing something foolish.

God, he very much wanted to do something foolish.

He wanted to kill.

They were entering the undercarriage of the gatehouse when suddenly, a body came flying out of the guard's room, plowing into l'Evereux and taking the man down. De Fey lurched, trying to keep Sophina in his grip as Colton, massive dagger in hand, planted the blade squarely in l'Evereux's chest.

Sophina screamed; du Ponte screamed. Even Lucien bellowed, telling Colton to cease, terrified that de Fey was going to snap Sophina's neck on the spot. But Colton, faster and more agile than any man alive, leapt up and rammed the same dagger into de Fey's thigh. The man howled and released his grip on Sophina, but du Ponte was closer to her than Lucien was. As de Fey staggered and fell, an enormous blade in his leg, du Ponte grabbed Sophina by the hair and pulled her up against him, his hand to her throat.

"Cease!" he roared. "One more move and I will kill her! Do you hear me? *One more move and she dies!*"

Lucien threw up his hands. "Colton!" he bellowed. "Stop!"

Colton was in battle mode. He had just ripped the blade from de Fey's leg and kicked the man to the ground when Lucien screamed at him. He was fully prepared to use the blade on du Ponte. In fact, he had the dagger in his hand and was making stabbing motions in du Ponte's direction. But Lucien's panicked cry had him hesitating, going against his natural battle instinct. He was going to kill du Ponte. That was his goal. But when he saw the way the man was holding Sophina's neck, he could see that it would only be by sheer luck for him to kill du Ponte before he killed Sophina.

He was sure he would be fast enough to complete the job in order to save her.

"Drop the dagger, Colton," Lucien half-commanded, half-begged. "Please… drop it."

Colton couldn't seem to do it. He had a difficult time lowering his hand but dropping the blade was another matter. "Lucien…," he hissed.

"Drop it. *Please.*"

Colton grunted, unhappy and still very much in battle mode. He'd been emerging from the vault, having just left a screaming Holderness, when he saw what was happening in the bailey. He saw du Ponte's men dragging Sophina across the dirt, holding her captive, and he had been positive that if he took the knights out, Lucien would handle du Ponte. But it hadn't worked that way. Now, there was one dead knight, one wounded knight, and du Ponte still had the lady. Gloriously frustrated, Colton growled and threw the knife away, out into the bailey.

"Colton," Lucien said hoarsely. "Come away from there. Get back behind me."

Colton was furious and agitated. He kicked l'Evereux, who was clearly dead, and punched de Fey in the head as he staggered out of the gatehouse to be grabbed by Gabriel. Pembury, having seen the entire shocking incident, held on to Colton, fearful the man would go on another rampage and everyone would die. Colton was the best young knight in England, without a doubt, but he hadn't learned yet to control his temper. He was impetuous, angry, and very strong, which could be a deadly combination under the proper conditions.

Lucien watched Gabriel corral Colton, deeply impressed with the young knight's actions but knowing du Ponte wouldn't see it that way. He returned his attention to du Ponte, holding up his hands in a gesture of supplication.

"I will come to Gillingham tomorrow morning with everything I own," he said steadily. "I want the lady returned to me *unharmed*. That is the bargain."

Du Ponte was furious with what had happened to his knights. He looked at l'Evereux, bleeding out on the dirt of the gatehouse, and then to de Fey, who had a massive knife wound in his leg. Then his focus turned to Lucien.

"I told you what would happen if we were set upon," he said, his voice trembling with anger. "Did you not believe me?"

Lucien could see that this was about to go very badly and he forced himself not to sound like he was pleading as he spoke. He had to find that knight within him, detached from what was happening, and draw upon him.

He had to find that iron knight again.

"If you harm her, I can promise you that you will not leave Spelthorne alive," he said. "My men will capture you and I will make sure that your death is as painful and drawn-out as possible. I will strangle you until you are close to death, upon which time I will revive you and make sure you are alert when I cut off your manhood. I will then proceed to stuff it down your throat as I take the same dagger and slit your belly from chin to pelvis. Are you listening, du Ponte? Because after that, if you are still alive, you shall smell your entrails as I burn them. I will make you wish you were dead over and over again. If you harm one hair on Lady de Gournay's head, you will know the true meaning of pain."

Du Ponte could see by Lucien's expression that he meant every word. But he was power-drunk with the control he had over de Russe at the moment by holding close to Lady de Gournay, power-drunk enough to consider actually hurting the woman. But he was starting to sober up as he realized that Lucien would be very capable of quartering him most painfully. He had no desire to feast upon his manhood and smell his innards burning. Still, he could not relinquish the lady, not now. Even if he let her go at this moment, he was quite certain de Russe would throw him in the vault and never let him out. Therefore, for his own sake, he needed the woman to make sure he left Spelthorne alive. With l'Evereux dead and de Fey wounded, that was his only hope.

"Then bring everything to me tomorrow at Gillingham," he said as he began backing out of the gatehouse again. "I will be waiting."

"Wait."

It was de Bretagne. He had remained silent until this point, watching and waiting to see how it developed, but he found that he could remain silent no longer. He had to intervene because none of this was going well, for anyone. His conversation was directed at du Ponte.

"I will ride with you back to Gillingham to ensure the lady's safety," he said evenly. "Not to say that I do not trust you, but I do not. Although the lady is your property, obviously, there is some contention here. De Russe wants her and he has made you a very fair offer for her, giving you enough wealth that you can live most comfortably for the rest of your life. That makes the lady a prized commodity and a point of contention."

Du Ponte liked de Bretagne about as much as he liked Lucien; they were both self-righteous bastards. "Nay," he said flatly. "You will not ride escort. I do not trust you. I believe you will try to wrest the lady from me."

De Bretagne's jaw hardened. "I send a report every month to the king," he said. "As his garrison commander, it is my duty to inform him of issues pertaining to the laws of England. Right now, your mention in this report will be minimal, even with all of the chaos you have caused. But if you so much as put a scratch on that woman, I will make sure Henry knows every dastardly deed you've committed. I will make sure he understands your unworthiness for the Gillingham fiefdom and, believe me, if Henry chooses to take it away from you, there is naught your Aunt Joan can do about it. Therefore, I *am* riding escort with you and there isn't a damned thing you can do about it."

With that, he turned to Lucien and pulled the man aside. Lucien was reluctant to take his eyes off of Sophina so he moved stiffly, resistant. De Bretagne grabbed him around the head, pulling Lucien's ear down to his lips.

"Listen to me," he whispered. "I will ensure Lady de Gournay is not harmed but you must mount an ambush the likes of which we have never seen. It will only take us a few hours to get to Gillingham and there are many patches of trees where you can successfully plan an attack. But do it in clothes that outlaws would wear, Lucien. Do not wear de Russe tunics or fly the Tytherington banner. You must become stealth personified. Do you comprehend me?"

Lucien was very interested in what he was saying; *dress as the outlaws do*. Aye, Lucien understood what de Bretagne was telling him. He felt stupid that he hadn't thought of it himself, but when emotions were involved, it was difficult to think clearly.

An ambush!

"I do," he said. "Brilliant thinking, Jorrin."

De Bretagne smiled thinly. "We will beat du Ponte at his own game. Too many times, he has been the attacker. Too many times has he sent men out, or paid men, to ambush travelers on the road and too many times we could not prove it. Now it is time for his comeuppance. *He shall become the victim this time.* Are you up to this?"

He meant Lucien's old injury and mediocre health. He knew of it, as most of Henry's fighting men did. Since Bramham, it had been no great secret. But Lucien was more than up to the challenge.

The stakes, for him, had never been so high.

"You needn't worry about me," he said. "I will execute the operation perfectly when the time comes."

De Bretagne believed him. "Leave no witnesses," he said. "You will make sure that everyone in du Ponte's party is killed."

"How many did he bring with him?"

"Thirty soldiers. And you will recognize them all because they will be riding around him. I will keep my men at a distance."

Lucien nodded, finally feeling the distinct notes of hope and relief. But it was more than assurance that the situation would be resolved, with finality, in his favor.

It was vengeance.

"Make sure you pull your men out of the way when I attack," he mumbled. "I will not have time to pick and choose my targets."

De Bretagne looked surprise. "Out of the way? Absolutely not. I intend to help."

Lucien looked at de Bretagne, sharply, only to see the man fighting off a smile. Lucien, too, fought off a smile. "No survivors," he muttered.

"No survivors."

"Du Ponte is *mine*."

"Without question."

With that, Lucien turned away from de Bretagne, moving back to where he had been standing, watching Sophina as du Ponte held her. She was gazing at him, wide-eyed with fear, silently pleading for his help. All he could do was look at her, his fragile heart ripped to shreds by what had happened. But now, there was hope. God, his mind and soul and body were soaring with it.

Now, there was a chance.

"What were you two whispering about?" du Ponte demanded. "What did you tell him, de Bretagne?"

"To remain calm," de Bretagne said without hesitation. "I told him to remain calm and that I would make sure the lady came to no harm."

Du Ponte snorted as if he didn't believe it and looked to Lucien. "I will see you tomorrow," he said. "You had better bring enough wealth to satisfy me."

"And you had better make sure Lady de Gournay is unharmed and untouched in any fashion."

Du Ponte actually had the nerve to grin. Since he had Sophina around the neck, it was a simple thing to lick her on the cheek as she squirmed with disgust.

"Lucien!" Sophina squealed. "Do not do anything! Please stay where you are!"

Lucien could hear the panic in her voice, panic that Lucien would try to charge when he saw du Ponte's disgusting actions. But Lucien remained firm no matter how much it was killing him to do so.

"I won't do anything," he assured her. "Be calm. All will be well."

Sophina was struggling against du Ponte. "Emmaline," she gasped as he tried to lick her again. "My daughter...."

"She will be safe here with me. Have no fear, sweetheart."

Sweetheart. That seemed to calm Sophina a great deal, enough so that she relaxed and du Ponte was able to get in another lick. It was a taunt, trying to force Lucien into doing something stupid, but Lucien remained where he was. He didn't say a word. But inside, he was planning du Ponte's death down to the last breath. The man was going to die as painfully as possible.

Lucien would make sure of it.

De Bretagne went with du Ponte as he dragged the lady from the gatehouse. Lucien stood there and watched the entire thing. He didn't say a word, fearful that if he said one thing to her, it would break the dam and everything he was feeling would come spilling out. He couldn't show that lack of control in front of du Ponte. So he watched as du Ponte and Sophina cleared the gatehouse, his heart breaking into a million pieces. It was hope, however, that restored that shattered heart.

Hope in what needed to be done.

"You let him take her, Lucien." Colton was standing beside him now, watching the sickening event. "In God's name, why did you allow it? You will never get her back now."

Lucien drew in a deep, steadying breath. "Aye, I will," he said, turning to Colton and Gabriel. "De Bretagne and I have a plan."

"A plan?"

Lucien nodded, a deadly gleam in his eyes. "Aye," he said. "Listen closely, lads."

They did.

CHAPTER SEVENTEEN

S OPHINA RECOGNIZED THE lake.

Other than the fact it was the bucolic body of water where she and Emmaline very nearly lost their lives, she would have recognized it anyway because the carriage was still there, half-out of the water. As their party passed by, du Ponte sent his men to pull the carriage out of the water completely.

Du Ponte seemed quite excited about the carriage, admonishing his men to be careful with it as they hauled it up to the road. He finally went to inspect it, pulling Sophina off of the horse they had been riding on, together, and forcing her to accompany him as he looked the carriage over. He had her by the wrist, unwilling to let her go with de Bretagne and five hundred men trailing behind him. He was convinced that de Bretagne would take her away from him given the chance. Therefore, he towed her around like a barge as he inspected the carriage. Sophina dragged her feet the entire time.

The carriage, other than being partially waterlogged, seemed to be okay. But without horses to pull it, du Ponte appointed some of his soldiers to be the wagon team. Therefore, travel was slow once they resumed their trip to Gillingham, with ten weary soldiers lugging a very heavy, fortified carriage along the dusty, bumpy road.

Sophina ended up seated in front of du Ponte again as they continued down the road. He held on to her firmly with one hand and, at one point when she'd moved as if trying to slide off the saddle, he'd grabbed her firmly by the hair. That seemed to be his control point with her, yanking on her hair to keep her in check. He'd done it more than once. Sophina was tired of getting her hair pulled every time she moved.

Oddly enough, there had been no conversation between them. Not one word. Du Ponte spent his time humming or yelling at his men, but he'd ignored Sophina for the most part. Once they'd collected the carriage, he seemed far more concerned for that soggy vehicle than for her. He spoke to one of his men about cleaning it up once they reached Gillingham. Something else was strange in that he'd not mentioned the men he'd left behind, the dead knight and the wounded knight. Sophina was coming to realize that St. Michael du Ponte was a strange and petty man in general, much as Holderness had so crudely described to her.

In truth, he'd been right.

Sophina couldn't even think about what was going to happen once they reached Gillingham Castle. She didn't want to. She kept her fear in check by thinking of her daughter, safely tucked away in the keep of Spelthorne, and in thinking of Lucien. He'd told her that all would be well but he'd meant that he would produce every last bit of property and coinage he owned for her freedom. Tears stung her eyes as she thought of the man giving up everything for her. It simply wasn't right. Surely, there had to be another way.

How was it right for a man who had worked all of his life, as Lucien had, to give up everything at the spur of the moment? They'd known each other so short a time. She'd lamented that fact before. But would she have been hurt if Lucien hadn't offered to give up everything he owned for her? Of course she would have been. She would have been devastated. But it would have been a more sensible decision on Lucien's part. They weren't young lovers, without the experience and wisdom that a long life can bring. They were older and, presumably, more reasonable people. Lucien was in his fortieth year and she was just a few years younger. They were certainly old enough to know that giving away everything one had worked for could quite possibly ruin one for the rest of his or her life.

The rest of Lucien's life.

… would he come to resent her in years to come for having given up everything he'd worked so hard for, just for her?

She wondered.

Lost in thought, Sophina didn't stop to notice that they were well past the lake that had almost claimed her life and heading into a thicker grove of trees. The moisture in the air was heavy, dragging at the branches on the trees, pulling them down. The air was heavy to breathe as well, thick in the lungs. Moist heat cloaked them.

Had Sophina been paying attention to her surroundings, she would have noticed that the birds had stopped singing. In fact, it was as if they'd vanished altogether, for nothing was moving in the branches overhead. Even if Sophina hadn't noticed, the men had. They kept looking around, wondering why everything seemed to still. Behind her, du Ponte spoke.

"Tell the men pulling the carriage to pick up the pace," he said to one of the men riding beside them. "I would be home well before sup."

The soldier spurred his horse forward, towards the men who were lugging the weighty carriage. Du Ponte's horse jumped when the soldier rode forward and Sophina slipped a bit on the saddle, gripping it so she wouldn't fall off. Her movement, however, caused du Ponte to grab her by the hair again. In irritation, she slapped at his hand.

"I am not trying to jump off or escape," she said. "You will cease grabbing my hair every time I move. It is growing tiresome."

Du Ponte didn't let go. "Shut your lips," he said. "You will speak when you are spoken to."

"And you will stop treating me like a prisoner."

"You belong to me and I can treat you however I wish."

Sophina sighed heavily, with great hatred for the man whose fingers were currently buried in her locks. He was a nasty bastard. Still, she shut her mouth because she didn't want to be hit or, worse, thrown from the horse in a fit of anger. He'd already threatened to kill her and without Lucien around, she had no way of knowing what he'd really do.

But she took some comfort in the fact that the knight who had seemed to be on Lucien's side throughout the circumstances at Spelthorne was riding behind them, keeping his rather large army several paces back. Sophina didn't even know who he was or where he'd come from, but he had been in charge of the army that had also escorted du Ponte to Spelthorne. So much of this situation was confusing to her and she was understandably curious. Ignoring du Ponte's command to say silent, she spoke quietly.

"Who is the man riding behind us?" she asked. "Is he your ally?"

He didn't reply for a moment but she could feel him move around, perhaps turning to look at the army to his rear. Surprisingly, he didn't snap at her for speaking.

"That is Jorrin de Bretagne," he said, sounding disinterested. "He is the garrison commander at Sherborne Castle."

Sherborne Castle? Sophina was still confused. She thought she might have heard of Sherborne but she couldn't be sure. But why in the world was the Sherborne garrison escorting du Ponte? So many questions with answers she did not know or had not been privy to. She knew du Ponte probably wouldn't answer any more of her questions so she didn't ask. She really didn't want to talk to him, anyway. All she wanted to do was go back to Spelthorne.

Longing to return to Lucien was her last coherent thought before hell erupted all around her.

CB

WITHIN A HALF-HOUR of du Ponte and de Bretagne's departure, de Russe and two hundred of his most seasoned men were suiting up in peasant clothing and preparing to take the road south. It really wasn't peasant clothing as it was whatever they could find that would make them look as if they weren't part of a military garrison. Concealment was the word and they understood it. So was speed. They dressed quickly, preparing for their mission.

Lucien had explained it to Colton and Gabriel, who in turn hand-selected the men they wanted to accompany them and explained the gist of their task. Most of the men had seen what had happened in the bailey of Spelthorne or had at least heard of it, from Holderness' attack on Lady de Gournay to St. Michael du Ponte dragging the woman from the fortress. The men were quite eager to help Lucien regain the lady and enact a bit of revenge against du Ponte.

More than that, they were eager to follow The Iron Knight into action, once more. Some of the older men thought they'd never see this moment again. When Lucien surrendered his spurs two years ago, they were certain it had been the end of the man. Therefore, less than an hour after du Ponte and de Bretagne's departure, two hundred seasoned men were dressed and ready to depart, ready to follow their adored liege into battle again.

Lucien inspected them personally. He, too, was dressed in a disguise, in clothing he had borrowed from the smithy of Spelthorne because the man was bigger than Lucien was. In woolen breeches and tunic, with a big leather coat on, one that the smithy used against sparks and spraying fire, he cut quite an interesting and mysterious-looking figure.

But his long hair still made him recognizable and Lucien knew he would have to do something with it, lest he be clearly known to all. Other than run a comb through his hair on occasion, or have the surgeon cut off the bottom of it when it grew past his shoulders, he didn't give much thought to the curling dark locks with graying temples. Therefore, he had to seek an expert in this matter to help him.

He sought out the women.

Emmaline and Juno were in the small chamber that Emmaline shared with her mother. Both young women were very surprised to see Lucien and when he explained recent events and why he had come, both women were in tears. Juno was upset over her father's actions and Emmaline was afraid for her mother. It was quite overwhelming for them both but Lucien sought to comfort Emmaline. He told her that they were off to ambush du Ponte's escort so they could get her mother back, which only seem to frighten her more. Weapons and the thought of an ambush scared her, but Lucien assured the young woman he would bring her mother back. But he explained he also needed her help. He had an attack to attend and couldn't go into it looking like Lucien de Russe.

His strange request gave the young women something to focus on. Using a ribbon, because they had nothing else, Emmaline tied his hair off. Juno, understanding the severity of the situation and realizing that Lucien was trying to conceal his identity somehow, went across to her chamber and came back with one of the scarves that Aricia wore so often. This one was a very dark blue scarf and Lucien had allowed her to wrap it around his head, neck, and, partially, his face. She had become something of an expert in helping Aricia do the same thing and Lucien was pleased with the results. Now, no one would be able to recognize him. Thanking the pair and assuring them yet again that all would be well, he fled the keep.

Colton, dressed like a farmer, and Gabriel, looking as if he'd stolen his clothing from a beggar, were waiting in the bailey with all of the men mounted. No one looked as they should. They looked like a gang of homeless poor. It was a very large group for an ambush, especially one they wanted to conduct in stealth, but Lucien wasn't about to take any chances. He wanted to overwhelm du Ponte and not leave any traces. His men understood that.

"Now," he said to Colton and Gabriel as Colton handed him the reins to Storm, "I am going to assume they are taking the road to Semley, which will take them to the main road that leads down through Shaftesbury. They will go through Shaftesbury and then continue northwest to Gillingham. They have an hour's start on us which means they should be at least to Semley by now."

Both Colton and Gabriel looked up, checking the position of the sun. "If they moved at a normal pace, I would agree with you," Colton said. "But if they've moved faster, they're probably already nearing

Shaftesbury."

"I am not entirely certain they will be traveling that fast."

"If du Ponte wants to return home quickly, then I would not be surprised."

"What do you suggest, then?"

Colton had a very sharp mind and he always, without fail, had a plan in mind. He was a man of action. "On the road leading from Semley to Shaftesbury, there is a dense stretch of wood called The Montcombe," he said. "'Tis a royal hunting forest."

"I know it."

"There are two roads out of Semley," Colton explained. "A bigger, more traveled road that turns west and leads to the main road south into Shaftesbury, and then a small road that cuts south out of the town. If we ride swiftly and take the smaller road that leads south, the road cuts through The Montcombe and intercepts the larger road. We can wait for them there."

Lucien nodded, satisfied. "An excellent plan," he said. "However, I suggest we send out two of our fastest riders to scout where, exactly, du Ponte and de Bretagne are. If they have already made it to Shaftesbury, then we must know."

"I have already sent out scouts," Colton said. "They have been following de Bretagne since he left. We should know something shortly."

Lucien looked at Colton, a faint smile coming to his lips. "You think of everything."

"I try to."

Pleased, Lucien patted the young knight's shoulder before turning for Storm, who was already worked up with so many horses around him. The horse smelled a fight. Lucien slapped the big silver beast on the neck.

"Are you ready for this, old friend?" he asked. "You and I have seen a good deal of action together but it has been a long time, for both of us."

Colton and Gabriel, who had already mounted their steeds,

watched Lucien as he climbed up into the saddle with slower move-ments that weren't like him. The Lucien before Bramham would literally leap into the saddle. The Lucien after Bramham moved like an old man sometimes. The fact that this would be the first action Lucien had seen since his near-fatal injury wasn't lost on either knight. They were concerned for him but didn't want to show it. He wouldn't have taken it well.

Still, Colton couldn't help it. He didn't like seeing Lucien grunt and groan simply to get into the saddle.

"Are you well enough to do this, Lucien?" he asked, his voice quiet so the others couldn't hear. "If you do not feel strong enough, Gabriel and I will retrieve Lady de Gournay for you. You needn't worry."

Lucien looked at the strong young knight. He was pure of heart and intention. Lucien knew he hadn't asked to make him feel less like a man but simply out of concern. Colton was so much more a son to him than his own was. He smiled faintly.

"You would deprive me of the smell of battle for the first time in two years?" he teased, watching Colton grin. "I am deeply hurt."

Colton shook his head. "I would not dream of depriving you of that which you love," he said. "But... well... you may prefer to go and deal with Holderness while we retrieve the lady. The earl is in the vault screaming as if we have wronged him somehow."

Lucien's smile faded. "I will deal with him at the appropriate time," he said. "Where is Laurent, by the way?"

Colton threw a thumb in the direction of the keep. "Asleep," he said. "Those three young women in the keep sewed beautiful red stitches in his shoulder and he is asleep with some fuzzy beast next to him, a pet of Lady Emmaline's. They are all watching over him as if afraid he is going to stop breathing at any minute. It is really quite humorous."

Lucien started to chuckle. "Red thread?" he said. "And he let them?"

"He had no choice. It was the finest thread they had for stitching, although Lady Juno fainted at the first stitch. Evidently, she has never sewn a man's flesh before, so Emmaline had to step in and finish the job."

Lucien cast a long look at Colton. "Emmaline, is it?" he said. "That is rather informal address."

Colton cleared his throat, embarrassed. He looked away, clearly caught off guard by the gentle reproach because he, too, realized he had been quite informal. Emmaline had given him permission to call her by her given name and, rather wanting to use it, he had. But now Lucien knew that he had and he was mortified at the slip. He didn't want Lucien to suspect that he found Emmaline somewhat... pleasing. The lass was strangely growing on him.

"I apologize if I have offended you," he said.

"Me? You did not offend me in the least. I simply commented that you are rather informal in the manner in which you address Lady de Gournay's daughter. Lovely girl, by the way."

Colton was starting to turn red around the ears. "We had better depart," he said, completely changing the subject as he turned to Gabriel and lifted an arm. "We ride!"

Gabriel, in turn, bellowed orders to the men and the entire contingent began to move out. Lucien was at the head while Colton spurred his frisky charger back to the rear of the group, no doubt to avoid any further comments or questions about Emmaline. Lucien found himself grinning as the contingent thundered from the gatehouse. What was it he had said to Sophina? *Colton is far too young for whatever Emmaline has planned for him.*

Perhaps he had been wrong.

Thoughts of young romance aside, he found himself looking forward with anticipation to the fight ahead. The ride south wasn't a difficult one and the day was mild with scattered clouds across the deep blue sky. The roads were passable, well-traveled even, and Lucien and his men cantered past more than just a few people who were either heading into or away from Tisbury. This was the road to Tisbury, after all, the very same road where, yesterday, Lucien had walked with

Sophina and Emmaline. It was a road that he'd never had any particular fondness of until now.

Now, it was where he became acquainted with Sophina.

I am coming, sweetheart, he thought, as if she could read his thoughts wherever she was. *Hold fast... I am coming.*

It wasn't long before Tisbury appeared on the southeast horizon, the steeple from the church of St. John the Baptist reaching above the countryside. It was the church Lucien would marry Sophina in as soon as they returned to Spelthorne. He wasn't going to spend one more day without the woman by his side. As for du Ponte, he'd signed his death warrant the minute he'd gotten his hands on Sophina. Thanks to Colton, du Ponte's knights had already paid a stiff price with one dead and one in the vault, but now it was a matter of dealing with du Ponte himself.

His time was coming.

The group moved quickly past Tisbury. Once past the town, they came across the two scouts that Colton had sent out only to be informed that de Bretagne's group hadn't moved as quickly as anticipated. They were nearly to the road that led to Shaftesbury which meant it was quite possible they had their own scouts out and could see Lucien's group. With that knowledge, Lucien sent the scouts back out to make contact with de Bretagne and let the man know they were going to be waiting for them in The Montcombe.

Taking to the meadows and cutting across the great expanse of warm summer grass, Lucien and his men buried themselves in the outskirts of The Montcombe, their travel slower now that they were off the road and moving through the dense trees. It was Lucien's goal to get his men into position and settled before du Ponte's group made it to the road that led to Shaftesbury.

On a smaller road, they could destroy du Ponte and all of his men without the threat of witnesses hanging over their heads, as would happen if they were to conduct their ambush on a better-traveled road. It was strategy now, and stealth, and between Lucien and Colton and

Gabriel, they got the men spread out on both sides of the road, setting the trap for du Ponte. Once everyone was hidden in the overgrowth, fed with anticipation, all they had to do was wait.

It was less than an hour before du Ponte's party was sighted coming down the road. Lucien and Colton were together, towards the edge of the road and down in a ditch, and their eyes were about level with the road itself. They could both see and hear the marching feet of du Ponte's men but they could also see something else – a damaged carriage that several of du Ponte's men were hauling down the road. One of the axles was bent, so it wobbled unsteadily, and Lucien recognized the carriage right away as being the one he'd rescued Sophina and Emmaline from.

De Bretagne and his troops were well back from du Ponte's party, a well-planned tactic on de Bretagne's part. Not knowing where, or when, Lucien would attack, it was wise for him to stay well back from du Ponte's group. In fact, Lucien and Colton could barely see de Bretagne and his men far down the road but it was clear from the distant sound of men and horses, feet and hooves against the hard earth, that they were bringing up du Ponte's rear.

This is what he was born and bred for. Lucien was more at home in a battle situation than he was most anywhere else. His heart was thumping steadily against his ribs, his breathing deep and even as the party approached. He was filled with anticipation, straining to catch a glimpse of Sophina without giving himself away, but all he could see were feet and men and the wobbling wheels of the carriage. When they drew closer, he and Colton ducked back into the undergrowth away from the road. They watched, through branches and leaves, as du Ponte's party began to pass in front of them.

The men pulling the wagon were struggling with it. They could hardly pull it in a straight line because of the bent axle. Directly behind the wagon were some mounted men, including du Ponte with Sophina sitting in front of him in the saddle. He still had the woman by the hair and Lucien's blood began to boil.

Colton, still next to Lucien, must have sensed the man's mood because he glanced at him uneasily, fearful of what he was about to do. He could almost smell the fury. As du Ponte and Sophina plodded down the road behind the crippled wagon, Lucien turned to Colton.

"I will take your crossbow and head down the road," Lucien whispered in the man's ear. "I will take out du Ponte. Your objective will be to take Lady de Gournay to safety. Is that clear?"

Colton nodded, carefully handing over the crossbow he held in one hand. It was locked and loaded, with a hair-trigger, so he handed it to Lucien very carefully.

After that, Lucien shadowed du Ponte and Sophina as they moved slowly down the road. He was far enough back in the trees that he wasn't making much sound and Colton moved with him, closer to the road, keeping his eye on Lady de Gournay. He had no idea when that arrow was going to fly into du Ponte but he wanted to be ready. Anticipation, and the smell of the hunt, filled him.

Now, when his dagger came out, there would be no one to pull him off this time.

When the carriage lurched to a halt, unable to move forward any further until they did something about the wobbly wheels, du Ponte was forced to come to a halt as well. That was when Lucien swiftly moved forward, closer to the road. He had to find an area that was free of branches and leaves but by the time he did, du Ponte's horse had shifted and the man's entire back was turned to him.

It was the perfect target. Lucien lifted the crossbow and braced himself against a tree, aiming for a target just over du Ponte's head. His experience told him that the distance and lack of wind would bring the arrow to bear squarely in the man's back. His only fear was that it would have too much velocity and go all the way through him, hitting Sophina on the other side. There was no guarantee that it wouldn't.

That thought made him hold off, waiting until du Ponte's horse shifted again so that he had more of a profile to shoot at. It was more difficult, to be sure, but it was safer. Sweat beaded on his upper lip as he watched, waited. The men trying to fix the wagon seemed to have repaired one of the wheels so, at that point, there was no more time. He had to move. When du Ponte's horse shifted again and swung around, he could see Sophina full-on, like a human shield in front of du Ponte. Therefore, Lucien aimed at the man's head. It was the only thing he could get a decent shot at. Finger on the trigger, Lucien held it steady as he slowly squeezed.

Once that arrow flew, Colton and Gabriel, across the road, gave the signal to attack and chaos reigned.

CHAPTER EIGHTEEN

S OPHINA HEARD THE arrow for a brief second before something sailed past her head, hitting du Ponte on the saddle behind her. He grunted, gurgled, and the hand in her hair tightened. She screamed as he tumbled off the horse and took her with him.

Fortunately for Sophina, she had fallen on top of him so he had broken her fall somewhat, but the trees around them were coming alive with men, all of them whooping and yelling, filling the air with panic. The noise startled the horses and du Ponte's horse was dancing about nervously, its hooves far too close to Sophina's head for her liking. She didn't even look at du Ponte. She didn't care if he was alive or dead. He had her hair still wrapped in his fingers and she began swinging her arms, beating at him, yanking at his hand in an attempt to force him to let her go. He simply held on tighter.

Infuriated and terrified, she managed to roll off of him and onto her side, turning to see that the arrow had hit in him right above the mouth, of all places. It had carved into the small area between his upper lip and his nose, and his eyes were open and watching her as she struggled to pull away from him. He was trying to sit up, too, but Sophina gripped the hilt of the arrow and shoved at it, causing du Ponte excruciating pain. But she didn't care. The man wouldn't let her go and the road was awash with men with swords and horses ready to kick her in the head. Panicked, she shoved on the arrow again and he responded by letting her hair go and slapping her all in the same motion.

Cheek stinging, Sophina lurched to her feet, finally free of his grasp. With fighting men all around her, she had no idea where to run to safety. Du Ponte made a grab for her ankle and she kicked him, hitting him in the shoulder as he tried to yell, tried to curse her. Ignoring his cries, she began to run, pushing through the excited horses, trying to reach the other side of the road where there seemed to be some hint of freedom. She hoped to make a break for it and run through the trees, running away from the fighting and from du Ponte.

Run back to Lucien!

But Sophina's hopes were cruelly dashed when she was grabbed from behind. Someone had her, someone with massive arms and a powerful body. She was slung up over the man's shoulder and carried off of the road before she realized it, bouncing about on his shoulder as he ran. Terrified, she tried to fight and kick, but the man held her fast. He was far too strong for her to resist. Once they had run off the road, however, and into the trees, the man set her down. As she stumbled back, fists balled and ready to fight, she immediately recognized Colton.

"Colton!" she gasped, nearly collapsing with relief. "Sweet Mary... it's *you!*"

"It is, my lady."

"But... but what is this? What is happening?"

Colton could see how terrified she was and sought to quickly explain his presence. "Lucien staged an ambush to save you," he said simply. "Are you well, my lady? Did du Ponte hurt you?"

Sophina put her hand on her chest, trying to catch her breath. She was astonished and shocked, but the relief that swamped her was overwhelming. In fact, tears sprang to her eyes when she realized that Lucien had come to save her.

Sweet Mary... was it really true?

"I am not hurt," she said, breathless. "But... I was for certain that Lucien was going to give away everything he owned to du Ponte to gain my freedom. I cannot tell you how relieved I am to hear that he has come to fight for me, instead. It may seem strange to be thankful for that, but I am. I did not want him to lose everything because of me."

Colton shook his head. "I do not believe he ever intended to give du Ponte everything he had," he said, turning to catch a glimpse of what was happening on the road. It was a roiling mess of men from what he could see. "Du Ponte was too greedy for his own good, my lady. Lucien might have given him a few hundred coins simply to purchase the contract and du Ponte should have taken it. But once the man put his hands on you, his death was assured. Lucien was determined to punish him."

Lucien. The sound of his name brought tears and she was desperate to see him. "Where is Lucien?" she begged.

Colton pointed out to the road, to the exact spot where she had fallen off the horse with du Ponte. "Look," he said simply.

Sophina did and, suddenly, she could see Lucien through the mess of men as he stood over du Ponte, who was in a bad way with a big arrow protruding from his face. Du Ponte had rolled over onto his hands and knees, blood pouring from his face and dribbling onto the road. It was a smart position, to be truthful, because any other position would have seen him drown in his own blood. This way, at least, he could breathe, but there was nowhere for him to go, nowhere he could hide.

Death was coming for him.

The Iron Knight was coming for him.

UNAWARE THAT SOPHINA and Colton were watching him from the trees, Lucien stood over du Ponte as the man tried to get away from him in an exceptionally futile gesture. For Lucien, however, there was the satisfaction of the moment – satisfaction that Sophina was safe because he'd seen Colton run off with her and satisfaction that, finally, he would be able to punish du Ponte for the grief he'd put them all through. Those were the only things on his mind at the moment. He watched as du Ponte now tried to struggle to his feet.

"It is unfortunate that my arrow did not kill you immediately," Lucien spoke frankly. "Now you will have to suffer and die a horrendous death. Such is the punishment for taking Lady de Gournay captive. You should have left her with me as I'd asked."

Du Ponte was on his feet now, the horrible arrow protruding from his face, blood running everywhere. As Lucien watched the man grapple clumsily for the broadsword at his side, he caught sight of de Bretagne. In fact, all around him, his men and de Bretagne's men were subduing and killing du Ponte's escort. It wasn't much of a fight to be truthful, but still, he felt at home in the middle of it, calm and at peace as much as he could be. This was where he belonged.

Battle was in his blood.

"Did you do that?" de Bretagne asked as he walked up beside Lucien. He was pointing at du Ponte's face. "Excellent aim, whoever fired the shot."

Lucien was looking at du Ponte, now standing there with his broadsword wielded offensively. "It was me," he said. "A pity it didn't kill him. Now I see that I must finish the task."

De Bretagne simply backed out of the way as du Ponte, moving extremely awkwardly with the spine of an arrow jutting from his face, struck at Lucien with his elaborate broadsword. Lucien merely moved aside and the weight of du Ponte's broadsword caused him to fall to his knees. By the time he pushed himself up again, Lucien was standing behind him with his own broadsword in-hand.

The massive weapon had seen many campaigns with its master, now once again called into service. Lucien called out to de Bretagne, who was still standing off to the side.

"Hold him there," he said, indicating du Ponte. "I want him to see this."

De Bretagne simply moved to du Ponte's side to make sure the man didn't move. Du Ponte leveled his weapon at de Bretagne, who simply slapped it away. Du Ponte wasn't in any condition to fight anyone. Lucien, however, was and de Bretagne seriously wondered what the man was going to do.

He soon found out.

The Iron Knight began to go after every du Ponte man that wasn't already down or killed. Those who were still on their feet were met with bone-crushing blows from a mountain of a man with his face and head covered in fabric, bearing no armor, fighting with a custom-made broadsword that was as tall as a woman. It wasn't exactly a longsword, but more of a broadsword, heavy and sharp, that had been elongated and fortified. It was the weapon of a master swordsman.

Two, three men fell to the massive blade as Lucien plowed through a group of fighting men, pushing aside his own men and killing their opponents. The more he moved, the faster and more powerful he became. No man was a match for him as he felled more men, kicking aside the dead and the wounded, going after those who were still standing.

It was truly a sight to behold, this man whom Henry had relied on for so long, a man who knew how to fight better than most people knew how to breathe. Those skills, nearly silenced at Bramham, were making a powerful resurgence as Lucien gored men, slit throats, and then went in for the kill stroke once they were down. Man after man, fool after fool, fell beneath his powerful blade.

In truth, Lucien's men had stopped fighting their opponents. They were simply herding them in Lucien's direction and The Iron Knight made short work of them. It was as if two years of inactivity, and of depression and illness, were finally finding a release. *An ending.* Now, Lucien was a man again, able to bear a weapon again, and fighting for something more valuable to him than anything the king ever had to offer. He was fighting for his self-respect, which du Ponte had tried to take away from him. More than that, du Ponte had tried to take away the one thing that had given Lucien life again.

Sophina.

Aye, this was all for her as much as it was for him. Lucien could feel his confidence returning, the faith that he was still as good as he ever was no matter what had happened at Bramham. Truth was, he'd let himself believe that everything he was, everything he had ever achieved, had ended when that arrow had pierced his back. But that wasn't the truth at all.

What that arrow took, time – and Sophina – had brought back.

It wasn't the end at all, but the beginning.

It was a rebirth.

The very last du Ponte man tried to run but de Russe men trapped him and shoved him back in Lucien's direction. The du Ponte soldier had a sword but it wasn't any match for Lucien and, within three strokes, the man was dead on the ground, bleeding out. By this time, Colton and Sophina had emerged from the woods, watching Lucien tear through most of du Ponte's legion. Those who weren't already dead would have the honor of being put in their grave by the man known as The Iron Knight.

In truth, it had been gloriously impressive to watch. Lucien may have been in his fortieth year but he moved with the grace and agility and power of a man much younger. There was no age when it came to talent. Lucien's talent, in fact, was ageless. The old wound, the Bram-ham wound, had hardly acted up at all. It was true that Lucien felt a little winded, but he also felt overwhelmingly satisfied and vindicated. When the last du Ponte man fell, he made sure the man was dead before turning to du Ponte.

There was something in his eyes that suggested complete and utter victory as he gazed at the man who had tried to destroy him. The smoky-brown eyes glittered with the reclamation he felt. Reaching up, he removed the scarf from around his head where it hadn't already pulled away in the course of his fighting, revealing himself in full. Now, he wanted du Ponte to look into the face of the man who had bested him.

"Now," he said, winded from his rampage. "You have watched your men fall to me. They fell like women, all of them, and you will be next. But before I end your life like I have done these others, I wanted you to know that you and everything you have ever stood for are finally at an end. You have gone on these years believing you were smarter than anyone else and more clever, but the truth is that you are a foolish whelp whose only connection to the nobility comes through your aunt. You are a worthless excuse of a man. And your gravest mistake was in demanding that I return Lady de Gournay. Your greed and arrogance will be the death of you."

Du Ponte was verging on unconsciousness because of the blood loss. He was holding on to the hilt of the arrow protruding from his face, trying to take some of the pressure off. But the truth was that there was no relief to be had. He was about to die and he knew it, but he still couldn't believe it. His proud heart refused to surrender so easily.

"Over a *woman*?" he asked, although he was barely understandable with the destruction of his upper palate and nasal cavity. "You did this over a woman?"

Lucien handed his sword over to de Bretagne before walking up to du Ponte, getting in the man's face. Du Ponte was still holding his sword and Lucien grabbed it, tossing it far away into the grass beside the road. When du Ponte tried to turn in an attempt to go and reclaim it, Lucien grabbed him by the neck and forced the man to look at him.

"This is not just any woman," he hissed into du Ponte's fearful eyes. "This is the woman I love. She belongs to me, and no other, and your death and the deaths of your men are a direct result of you being foolish enough to try and take her away from me. No man will touch the woman I love and get away with it. Do you comprehend me?"

Du Ponte didn't want to agree with him; he didn't want to in the least, but his knees were growing weak. He was having a difficult time standing. He hoped that if he merely gave in and supplicated that it would be enough for de Russe. Men like him were foolish in their mercy. Perhaps de Russe would show him some of that mercy if he was contrite enough.

"Aye," he muttered, spittle and blood dribbling. "I should have taken your offer."

Lucien's eyes narrowed. "But you did not," he replied. "Much is your misfortune. Let my eyes, full of hatred, be the last ones you ever see in this life. So goes the depth of my vengeance."

Du Ponte realized there would be no mercy for him and his eyes widened, terror in their depths. He still couldn't believe Lucien's motivation for all of this and it was a question that bore repeating.

"Over a *woman*?"

Lucien had him by the neck. Reaching up, he grasped the hilt of the arrow and rammed it, full-force, up and back into du Ponte's head, all the way through his brain until it hit the back of his skull. Du Ponte's eyes were wide with shock and agony as he fell back to the dusty road, an arrow through his brain.

Lucien watched him fall, his entire body twitching with rage. Then, he bent over him, wondering if the man could still hear his voice.

God, he hoped so.

"Aye, you foolish bastard," he hissed. "Over *my* woman."

Du Ponte breathed his last.

CHAPTER NINETEEN

Spelthorne Castle
Two Days Later

"**H**OW DOES IT feel to be married again?"

It was after sunset and the great hall of Spelthorne was aglow with candles and torches, illuminating the cavernous room and the feast spread within it. De Bretagne asked the question and Lucien simply grinned in reply, but not just any grin. It was an ear-to-ear grin, as if everything joyful and wonderful was bubbling up from his soul, begging for release. He laughed softly, laughing even more when de Bretagne started to chuckle.

"To tell you the truth, I do not know," Lucien said. "I have hardly seen my wife except for the ceremony today at St. John the Baptist because she had been running around like a madwoman in preparation for this wedding feast. Yesterday, it was planning out the meal as well as the wedding and today, it has been the wedding and managing the meal. I think I am going to have to capture her and carry her away to have any time alone with her."

De Bretagne smirked. "You very well may have to," he said, watching Lady de Russe over by the hearth, instructing a pair of servants. "The woman has eyes for everyone but you."

Lucien couldn't take his eyes off of her. "She simply wants everything to run smoothly," he said. "She is the best chatelaine I have ever seen. But I have come to discover something."

"What is that?"

"She is an exacting taskmaster and she scares me to death."

De Bretagne snorted into his cup, turning away from Lucien as he was lured by some of his men over into a game of dice. Alone, Lucien kept his eyes on Sophina as he wandered casually in her direction. He was starting to think he needed to take his own advice and sweep her from this room because at the pace she was going, she wouldn't run down until the sun came up. That was unacceptable for a man on his wedding night. But before he could reach her, he ended up face to face with Laurent.

Lucien had seen Laurent briefly upon his return after rescuing Sophina but they hadn't been given much opportunity to talk about any number of pressing things between them, most obviously about what would become of his father. It wasn't that Lucien had been avoiding him; it was more that he hadn't been entirely sure what to say and he'd had a number of other things to attend to. But a long talk with Sophina the night before had helped him think clearly about the situation. He was coming to think that she was a great voice of reason and he valued her advice. Therefore, he was moderately prepared when faced with Laurent. Moreover, he had some good news for the man.

And his sister.

"You are looking well enough tonight, Laurent," Lucien said evenly, looking the room over and spying Juno over at the far table with Emmaline, Aricia, and surprisingly, Susanna. "I realize I have been quite busy since you received your injury, but I was wondering if I might have a word with you and your sister. I must thank her for not contesting my marriage to Lady de Russe. She has been most gracious about the entire thing."

Laurent nodded, looking over at his sister, who seemed happy and rosy-cheeked as she chatted with Emmaline and Aricia. "She has a reason to be," he said quietly. "You are most gracious not to tell Henry what my father was planning. Lucien, I cannot tell you how sorry I am for everything that happened. My father… he is not a wicked man, merely ambitious. *Very* ambitious. Having his wishes fulfilled was all he could think of no matter who was hurt in the process."

Lucien nodded faintly. "He hurt *you*," he muttered, indicating the man's bandaged shoulder. "I will thank you yet again for what you did. Had you not intervened, the situation with Lady de Russe could have been quite different. You have my undying gratitude for your heroism."

Laurent smiled modestly. "It was my pleasure, truly," he said. "It was the least I could do."

"Even with a dagger wound?"

"Even with that."

Lucien returned his smile. "You are a decent man, Laurent," he said. "My wife holds your sister in high esteem. As I said, I was hoping to have a private word with the two of you at some point this evening. There is something we must discuss."

Laurent thought he knew what it was. "Of course," he said, sighing sadly. "We were both wondering what you intend to do with our father. Since he tried to kill Lady de Russe, you are well within your rights to keep him locked up in the vault for the rest of his life. I would not blame you."

Lucien knew what his rights were but he was also sympathetic to the two children of an unscrupulous man. "You are a much better choice to rule than your father, Laurent," he said quietly. "As your father's heir, it would be within your right to assume control of the earldom with your father incarcerated. But I intend to discuss the situation with Henry to see what he wishes to do. I fear this is a decision I cannot make alone. In any case, that was not what I wished to discuss with your sister. In fact… in fact, mayhap you can simply tell her for me."

Laurent nodded. "I would be happy to deliver a message."

Lucien happened to glance at his wife a moment before returning his attention to Laurent. "At the request of Lady de Russe, I asked Colton to discover what he knew about the father of your sister's child."

Laurent cocked his head curiously. "Colton did speak to me yester-day about it, in fact," he said. "He knows the knight. His name is Reid de Titouan and he is not simply the father of her child; they love each other deeply. I do not want you to think my sister is an immoral woman, for she is not. Reid and my sister are very much in love."

Lucien shook his head. "I never thought her to be immoral," he said. "God only knows what I was willing to do for the love of a woman, so I understand what that emotion will drive one to do. In any case, Lady de Russe was determined to find out who he was and where your sister's lover was located and Colton was able to find out. Yesterday, I sent a rider to Wellesbourne Castle to summon Sir Reid. If the trip went as planned, he should be arriving at Spelthorne by tomorrow."

Laurent's eyes widened. "You... you *sent* for him?"

Lucien nodded. "Lady de Russe did," he clarified, a glimmer of mirth in his eye. "I was only doing her bidding."

Laurent was genuinely speechless. "My God," he exclaimed after a moment, struggling with the words. "I... I simply cannot believe you would do such a thing."

"Why not?"

Laurent shrugged, still struggling with his surprise. "Lucien, my father tried to cheat you by marrying you to my pregnant sister," he insisted softly. "That's exactly what he tried to do. That you would be generous enough to reunite my sister with the man she loves goes beyond mere compassion and benevolence. I... I simply do not know how to thank you."

Lucien could see that the man was genuinely touched. "You and your sister are good people who were being manipulated by a man who has lost his moral direction," he said. "I am not angry with either one of you. Everything will work out as it should and we will move on with our lives. There is no use in dwelling on grudges or past anger. It will kill a man as surely as a sword will."

Laurent nodded, smiling at Lucien in a way not often seen. It was gratitude, it was humbleness. Laurent knew that, given the situation, it could have gone very different for him and his father and his sister. But instead of taking them to task and ruining reputations and livelihoods, Lucien had been most magnanimous in his outlook. Only a man with great wisdom was capable of such things.

"I will go and tell my sister what you have told me," Laurent finally said. "If you see her weeping hysterically, do not be troubled. It will be tears of joy."

Lucien's lips twitched with a smile as Laurent begged his leave and headed to the table where the women were. He was watching them, in fact, when Sophina snuck up beside him. He didn't even see her until she looped her hands into the crook of his elbow. Gazing down at her, he smiled into her lovely face.

"So you think to give me some of your time, do you?" he said. "I am honored, Lady de Russe."

Sophina laughed softly. "I have been very busy ensuring that my husband is pleased with his wedding feast," she said. "Has it met with his expectations?"

Lucien nodded, kissing her on the forehead. "It has," he said. "As have you."

Sophina smiled prettily for him, coyly batting her eyelashes until he laughed. She laughed, too, a joyful sound. Finally, for them both, there was joy to be had in every moment, relishing their time together as they never had before. It was their life together, now, and they intended to enjoy every minute of it.

"I saw you speaking with Laurent," she said as the giggles died away. "Did you tell him what we have done for Juno?"

Lucien nodded. "I did," he said. "He was most grateful. That was a remarkable suggestion, my lady. You are most generous and kind."

Sophina shrugged, leaning her cheek against his big bicep as she gazed at the table with Juno and Emmaline and Aricia and Susanna, now joined by Laurent. "I understand what it is to be apart from the man you love," she said softly. "Juno is so very young and kind and vulnerable. She has spent her life being manipulated by her father. It is time for her to know some happiness."

Lucien's gaze was lingering on the table as well. "Holderness will not be an issue," he said. "That man will never know freedom again for what he tried to do to you. He is very lucky that I did not punish him as I punished du Ponte."

Sophina put her fingers to her lips in a hushing motion. "Shhhh," she said. "We promised never to speak his name again."

He nodded, contrite. "My apologies," he said. "You are correct."

Her smile returned. "I usually am."

He laughed softly now. "Am I going to have to listen to this for the rest of my life? How correct you always are?"

She giggled because he was. "Of course," she said. "What did you expect?"

He continued laughing as he put his arms around her, pulling her close and kissing the top of her head. "I am a willing servant, my lady," he said. His gaze ended up on the young women again and, in particular, his daughter. It reminded him of just how quiet she had been for the past two days. "Speaking of willing, my daughter has been most obedient for the duration of this meal. She was even obedient during the wedding mass. What miraculous spell have you cast over her that she is not screaming and trying to hit people?"

Sophina shook her head. "Not me," she said. "Lady Aricia. She has worked wonders with Susanna in ways I would never be able to. Susanna has found a kindred spirit in her, I think. They have become fast friends."

Lucien's eyebrows lifted. "Truly?" he said, astonished. "Why have I not been told of this?"

"Because it has really only just happened. Moreover, you have had other things on your mind – murderous earls, reuniting lovers. Those kind of things. Aricia has helped Susanna very much in the short time they have been friends."

Lucien could hardly believe it. "Then I must thank her."

Sophina looked up at him. "I was thinking of something more than that," she said, a calculated statement. She had been thinking of a way to broach the subject of Aricia and Susanna for two days and this was the perfect opportunity. "I believe it would be an excellent idea to keep Aricia here as Susanna's companion. If she has done so much with Susanna in just a few days, imagine what she can do with her for a lifetime. Mayhap we can offer her a small stipend to live here and be Susanna's companion, and she can become part of our household. I like Aricia very much, Lucien. I think... I think I want her to belong here, with us."

Lucien liked the idea a great deal. Anyone who could help his daughter learn to behave was someone he was more than happy to have around.

"If you believe it to be a good idea, then I trust you," he said. "Do what you must in order to convince her to remain with us. She will be a welcome addition."

Sophina was happy to have his approval but it also brought up another thought – the subject of Aricia's true sex. She didn't think that Lucien would have an aversion to it, but it would not be fair not to tell him. If Aricia was going to be so close to Susanna, it was only right that Lucien, as the child's father, know everything and Sophina realized, in good conscience, that she could not willfully withhold such information. Therefore, she wrapped her arms around his waist and looked up at him. She wanted to look him in the eye for what she was about to tell him.

"There is something else you must know about Lady Aricia," she said, lowering her voice. "Before I tell you, let me say that I have spent some time with her, as has Emmaline, and we have found her to be warm and genuine and kind. She is very talented and the way she has dealt with your daughter has been nothing short of miraculous. You see, she understands what it is to be different from other people. She knows what it is like to be shunned. Although Susanna has never been shunned, in her young mind, she believes that people have been cruel to her at times. Aricia was able to explain to Susanna just how wrong she was in a way that Susanna understood."

Lucien was listening carefully. "Susanna is convinced I hate her," he said quietly. "Given our relationship, I suppose she has every right to believe that. It has been difficult to convince her otherwise."

Sophina nodded. "I know," she said. "I have heard her say it. So has Aricia. But Aricia... her father truly hated her. He said awful things to her, Lucien, just terrible things that a father should never say to a child. Aricia is such a good and gentle creature, but her father did not see her that way. He saw her as an abomination and a vile affront to moral men."

Lucien's eyebrows furrowed. "Why would he think that?"

Sophina's expression was soft. "Because Aricia was not born a girl," she said softly. "She was born male, but she has dressed and lived as a girl since she was an infant. Her mother understood this where her father did not. Aricia is not an abomination of nature, but a girl trapped inside of a boy's body. She lives as a girl and always will. Juno knows this but her father did not. I do not know if Laurent is aware. But believe me when I tell you that Aricia is as kind and good a person as I have ever seen. She will make a wonderful companion for Susanna and Susanna already adores her. Nothing strange or unseemly will happen; Aricia is trustworthy. I would stake my life on it. But because I have recommended she be your daughter's companion, I think it only fair that you know that she was not born a girl. I pray you are not angry with me for telling you this."

Lucien was looking at her quite seriously by the time she was finished. He had to admit, he was shocked by the news. Inevitably, his gaze moved to the table with the women, specifically looking to Susanna and the young woman beside her. *A young man*, he thought. Even as he looked at her, there was disbelief because she didn't look like a man at all. As he continued to watch, Susanna whispered something in Aricia's ear and, when Aricia nodded, Susanna burst out laughing. He'd never seen his daughter laugh like that, not ever. He was astonished. It was a moment before he could answer Sophina.

"I know you would not allow anyone to harm my daughter," he said hesitantly. "I believe you when you say Aricia is trustworthy. But... a male?"

"Aye."

"Does... does Susanna know?"

Sophina looked over to the table as well, watching the interaction between Susanna and Aricia. "I do not believe so," she said. "There is no point in telling her. She has found a friend and that is all she knows. She is happy."

Lucien couldn't deny that. The evidence was there. "Aye," he admitted. "She seems to be. I have never seen her so happy."

Sophina turned to look at him. "Then Aricia can stay?"

Lucien's gaze lingered on his laughing daughter a moment longer before turning to his wife. "Aye," he said softly. "She can stay. I suppose it does not matter if she was born a male or a female. If her heart is good, that is all I care about. If she can make my daughter happy, then she has my gratitude."

Sophina smiled, reaching up to sweetly touch his cheek. "You are as generous as you are wise," she said. "Aricia's secret will be our own. I believe she will make a fine addition to our household. And I also believe she might help you in your relationship with Susanna. She has been speaking to Susanna on what it means to have a father who cares and I believe Susanna is listening to her. Mayhap she will help you both heal, someday."

Lucien couldn't dare to hope but he was willing to try. If Sophina thought that Lady Aricia could help mend what had been damaged by helping Susanna grow and learn and understand what it meant to be a kind young woman, then Lucien was willing to let that process take place. Perhaps there was yet time to make Laurabel proud of the daughter he had raised. And perhaps he, too, could be the father he had always wanted to be. No more guilt, no more running.

Perhaps, someday, he would have a daughter who loved him.

So he stood there and hugged his wife, thanking God yet again for the day He brought her into his life. It had been less than a week but in those few days, his life had changed forever. It was difficult to comprehend all of it, just how much things had changed, but he would have a lot of time to ponder that in the future. He was looking forward to it perhaps more than he'd looked forward to anything else in his entire life.

As Lucien's thoughts turned to the coming night and the first night he would spend with his new wife, he happened to see Colton approaching the table where the women were. He and Gabriel had been over in the corner with the de Bretagne men, rolling dice, and while Gabriel remained crouched down on the floor, gambling with the others, Colton was sauntering casually towards the table that, not strangely, contained Emmaline. Lucien continued to watch as Colton stood behind Emmaline as she chatted with Juno and Laurent but when she happened to catch a glimpse of Colton, she invited him to sit. He did, quite eagerly, beside her.

"God's Bones," Lucien grunted. "I told you to keep your daughter away from Colton. See how she lures him!"

Sophina turned to see what had him scowling and she laughed softly. "You blame her?" she said. "Blame him. He buzzes around her like bees to honey."

Lucien frowned. "Impossible," he scoffed. "Colton de Royans is above buzzing. She is bewitching him somehow with her beauty and sweet disposition. How can he resist such things?"

Sophina shook her head. "He cannot," she said flatly. Then, she eyed him. "I know we have jested about this subject before, but mayhap we should speak on it seriously. When Emmaline's father died, he left very little by way of finances, which is why we had to live with my father. I have managed to save a small dowry for Emmaline, but certainly not what Colton might be looking for. If he chooses to seriously pursue her, then he should know she is not wealthy."

Lucien waved her off. "Colton is heir to a very wealthy barony," he said. "He would not be interested in her for her money. He is a smart lad. I am guessing he knows she more than likely does not have much of a dowry. That is of no concern to him. Moreover, now that Emmaline is my daughter, I will supply her dowry. Trust me when I tell you that she will have more than enough behind her to attract any husband in England."

Sophina had to grin. "When I brought up her lack of a fortune, I did not mean you should supply it," she said. "That was not my intent."

"I know."

"And I would much rather have her marry for love than marry someone who simply wants her fortune. I only wish for her to be happy above all."

Lucien couldn't disagree. Looking around the room, at the smiling faces and the laughter, he couldn't ever recall being happier above all. A life that had been so full of battles and duty for the king, a life that had, until a few days ago, been one of loneliness and hopelessness.

Marrying for love? He couldn't imagine anything greater. It was love that had saved him, love that had given him faith again. Love was more powerful than kings and countries as far as he was concerned and as he looked at Emmaline, laughing with Colton, he could only wish them both the very best of love, and of devotion, and of hope. Perhaps kings ruled the world but in matters of the heart, love was the most powerful thing on earth.

"She will," he murmured, holding Sophina close. "She is a dreamer, that one. Look at her face. When she looks at Colton, she sees everything she could possibly want in him."

"Including love?"

"Including love."

"I thought you said he was too young for such things."

Lucien sighed faintly. "I was wrong," he admitted. "One is never too young or too old for love."

Sophina's gaze upon him was an adoring one. "I do love you, you know."

He looked down at her, this spectacular woman with whom all

things, for him, were possible. Four days ago, he was resigned to a hopeless existence, but now, all he could feel was eagerness towards the future.

"I know," he said, bending over to kiss her. "As I love you."

"Forever?"

"Until the end of time."

The man of iron, with a soul of courage, finally managed to heal his fractured heart.

EPILOGUE

Year of our Lord 1411 A.D.
Month of July

"PLEASE LET ME pin the ribbons on!" Susanna begged. "They would be so pretty in your hair!"

It was hard to resist her when she'd worked so hard on fashioning the bows. In her massive and lavish bower, which she now shared with Aricia and Emmaline, the girls were preparing for a very big day ahead, the biggest day Spelthorne had seen in a year.

"They would look quite pretty," Aricia said to Emmaline. She was no longer wearing the scarves over her face, as the potions Sophina had made for her had greatly helped her tender skin and the transformation had been quite astonishing. She grinned at Emmaline, holding up one of the bows. "Let us fashion them in your hair."

Dressed in a gown of pink silk that Aricia had made for her, Emmaline looked like a queen. But that was befitting considering it was her wedding day. In just a very few hours, she and Colton would stand before the entry to the church in Tisbury and say their vows. Emmaline could hardly believe this day had come and, to be truthful, she was a little flighty because of it. It had taken both Aricia and her mother, on this day, to keep the woman sane and calm.

"Come," Aricia said. "Sit down. We will fix your hair."

Emmaline sat carefully on a stool, careful not to muss her spectacular gown. With a long, trailing skirt and long, trailing sleeves, the bodice had been embroidered with flowers and birds by Aricia in some of the finest example of sewing Emmaline had ever seen. Aricia had even sewn most of Emmaline's trousseau, now filled with more beautiful surcoats and shifts.

In all, it was quite an elaborate production for Emmaline to begin her new life as Lady de Royans and, having turned seventeen years of age last month, Emmaline was more than ready to embark on her new life. The joy of a future with the man she loved was all she could think of. Surely nothing could be finer.

But her hair style on this day was her crowning glory. Aricia had combed and braided and pinned it on top of her head, with a single thick braid emerging from the top of the very elaborate style, draping over Emmaline's right shoulder with a curl at the end of it. It was to this elaborate hairstyle that Susanna pinned her pink bows and, under Aricia's guidance, Emmaline soon had four beautiful bows pinned to the upswept style. It made for a truly stunning creation.

As Aricia and Susanna were fixing the last of the bows, the chamber door opened and Sophina entered. Enormously pregnant, she was still moving swiftly, busily, and behind her came a pair of servants bearing trays of food. Emmaline took one look at the food and waved her mother off.

"Nay," she told her mother flatly. "I cannot eat. I will vomit!"

Sophina was trying not to grin at her dramatic daughter. "You will not vomit," she said. "And you must eat something, Em. You will become ill if you do not. I'll not have you fainting dead away while you take your vows tonight."

Emmaline stood up from the stool, her lovely dress trailing out behind her. "I will not faint," she said irritably. Then, her manner changed swiftly to that of an eager bride. "Where is Colton? Have you seen him?"

Sophina nodded as she poured her daughter a measure of wine to calm her down. "I have," she said. "He is in the hall awaiting the arrival of his parents. He has eaten and so should you."

"Is he excited?"

"More than you are."

That brought a smile to Emmaline's lips and she accepted the cup her mother was extending to her. Taking a big gulp, she put her hand on her mother's belly because that was something she had been doing since the day her mother informed her that she was with child. Emmaline liked to put her hands on the woman's belly and speak to the baby, making a nuisance of herself at times. On this day, she put both hands on her mother's massive stomach and kissed it.

"Good day to you, my sweet babe," she said. "I am so very happy you will be at my wedding today."

As Sophina watched her daughter, the smile faded from her lips. She didn't want to tell her that she'd been having odd pains since late the night before, cramping that was in her lower back and down her thighs. She hadn't even mentioned it to Lucien for fear the man would fall into fits, as he was extraordinarily protective and concerned about his pregnant wife. Considering what had happened to his last wife, she didn't blame him. But she couldn't take a step without him ensuring her way was clear and was, therefore, afraid to tell him about the pains she'd been having for fear he'd force her into bed so that she would not be able to attend her daughter's wedding. And nothing short of hard labor was going to prevent that.

"He shall be there," Sophina said, patting her stomach. "We would not miss it."

Emmaline went back to drinking her wine and Sophina forced the young woman to eat some bread and cheese along with it. The last thing they needed was a tipsy, nervous bride. As Aricia went to help Susanna with the dress she was going to wear for the wedding, there was a soft knock at the door. One of the servants went to answer it.

Lucien was standing at the door when it was opened. Dressed in leather breeches and a finely embroidered dark tunic, he looked incredibly handsome. He smiled at the women in the room but did not attempt to enter.

"May I come in?" he asked. "I do not wish to disturb the bride."

Emmaline crossed the room towards him, wine in hand and re-splendent in her pink silk gown and elaborate hair. "You are not disturbing me," she said, greeting him with a kiss and pulling him into the room. Then, she stood back. "Well? What do you think of my gown? Do you like it?"

Lucien looked at her, all pink and perfect and beautiful. "My God," he said softly. "You are a magnificent creature. I do believe I may shed a tear."

Emmaline laughed, twirling about in the garment so he could see the whole thing. "Isn't it beautiful?" she said. "Aricia made it. I think it is the most beautiful dress I have ever seen."

Lucien nodded. "And I completely agree," he said. "Colton is a most fortunate man."

Emmaline stopped twirling. "How is he?" she asked anxiously. "He is not nervous, is he?"

Lucien fought off a grin. "He is not," he said. "But he is eager to be wed. And he is eager for his parents to meet you. They have arrived, in fact, and I have brought them with me. May I bring them in?"

Emmaline's eyes widened. "They are here?"

"Aye."

"But surely Colton wishes to introduce us!"

Lucien nodded. "He does, but Baron Cononley refuses to wait. He wants to meet you now and Colton says he is not permitted to see you before the wedding, so we have a dilemma."

Emmaline pursed her lips, torn. "Well," she said reluctantly, "I told him he was not permitted to see me before the ceremony. I want my dress to be a surprise. Mama, what do you think? Should I allow him to introduce me to his parents now?"

Sitting on Emmaline's bed because her legs were starting to serious-ly ache, Sophina simply grinned as Oswald played in what was left of her lap.

"That is your choice, sweetheart."

"But I do not know what to do now!"

"Then mayhap you should let Lucien introduce you to Colton's father since he is already here. It would be rude to turn him away."

That made sense to her, so Emmaline turned to Lucien with a nod. "Very well," she said hesitantly. "I would like to meet the baron and his wife."

With a smile, Lucien turned for the door. He went out to the landing and disappeared down the stairs to the floor below. When he returned, it was with two people – they could all hear the voices out on the landing. Emmaline went to the door, positioning herself in front of it as she nervously prepared to meet her future husband's parents.

Lucien came through the door first followed by a man and a woman. The woman was dressed in green brocade, an absolutely lovely woman who was, perhaps, Lucien's age, with green eyes and honey-blonde hair. She was followed by an enormous man with shoulders so wide that he nearly went from once side of the doorframe to the other.

The moment Emmaline looked at him, however, she knew it was Colton's father because they looked exactly alike – square jaw, dimpled chin, and the shape of the nose was the same. The resemblance was uncanny. She smiled timidly at the couple as they fixed on her.

"Lord and Lady Cononley," Lucien said, indicating Emmaline. "I am proud to introduce you to my daughter, Lady Emmaline de Gournay. Emmaline, be honored to meet Colton's parents, Weston de Royans and his wife, Amalie."

Lady Cononley was the first one to move forward, reaching out to take Emmaline by the hands. "My lady," she said softly, her voice sweet and rich. "We have eagerly awaited this moment for months, ever since Colton told us he had asked for your hand in marriage. I am so very pleased to meet you."

She kissed Emmaline on the cheek and Emmaline smiled bashfully. "It is an honor to finally meet you as well, my lady," she said, quickly looking to Lord Cononley. "Both of you. I have heard so much about you from Colton that I feel as if I already know you."

Lord Cononley came forward, looking Emmaline over, scrutinizing everything about her. An intimidating man and a fierce warrior much like his son, he wanted to get a good look at the young lady who had stolen his beloved Colton's heart. He had waited a long time for this moment and he was the first one to admit that he had created all sorts of terrible scenarios in his mind. Of course, no woman was good enough for his son but in gazing at the lovely Emmaline, he realized that he was not displeased. Perhaps she would, indeed, do.

"My lady," he greeted formally. "As my wife said, we have been eagerly awaiting this moment. When Colton wrote to us to tell us when the wedding would be, we wasted no time in coming to Wiltshire. I will admit that I wanted to see you before I would permit any nuptials to take place."

Emmaline's face fell. "You... you wanted to...?"

Lady Cononley saved the moment. "My husband is very protective over his children, my lady," she said. "Please do not misunderstand. It is simply that my husband is very attached to his children and most especially to Colton, as his first-born son. He wanted to see for himself the woman that Colton speaks so fondly of. As a parent, it is always difficult to realize that your children are growing up and will soon have children of their own."

Emmaline looked, wide-eyed, between Lady Cononley and her husband. She still wasn't sure if that meant Colton's father would permit the marriage. Now, she was frightened.

"If you have any questions of me I would be happy to answer them," she said, struggling not to tear up. "My mother has taught me a great deal on how to run a house and hold. I can manage money, I can manage kitchen stores, I can...."

Lady Cononley cut her off, putting her hands on Emmaline's shoulders. "You are young and beautiful and Colton adores you," she said. "I can see that you are also well spoken and polite. That is all I need to know. I am sure you will make my son very happy."

She kissed Emmaline on the cheek again but there was still the matter of Lord Cononley. He was looking at Emmaline seriously. He seemed to still be trying to figure out how he felt about all of this. After a moment, he lowered his gaze.

"I have six children, my lady," he said. "My eldest, Aubria, was recently married. Colton is two years younger and now I find myself attending his wedding. When my children were young, I will admit that I spent too much time with them. Far too much time. I was attentive to the point of hovering. Has Colton told you any of this?"

Emmaline nodded, still uncertain of the man and his motives. "Aye, my lord," she said. "He said that you insist on hugging him constantly."

Lord Cononley nodded. "I do," he admitted. "I hug all of my children. I adore them all. Aubria, Colton, Torston, Kingston, Elizabeth, and Seton. My youngest, Seton, has come to the age in life where he fights me off when I try to hug him. He does not want to be embarrassed. But my point is this – it is difficult for me to let my children grow up. Colton is my heart. Now, I give him to you so that he will become your heart as well. All I ask is that you be a good wife to him, my lady. Love him unconditionally. He is a good man and deserves that."

Emmaline was starting to understand Lord Cononley a little now. He was obviously quite emotional about his children and quite concerned. He wanted to make sure his beloved Colton was marrying someone who would care for him as he did. Truth be told, she felt somewhat relieved now that she understood his reasons.

"If it comforts you, know that I love him already," she said. "Colton and I understand one another. We will be good for each other, I promise. I will not disappoint you."

Lord Cononley grunted, wiping at his nose, trying to pretend he wasn't as emotional as he was. "I am sure you will not," he said. "Did he tell you that every de Royans' male has a name that ends in 'ton'?"

"He did."

"You must name all of your sons in that tradition. Every de Royans wife must understand that."

"I will, I promise."

Lord Cononley lifted his head to look at her and, seeing the impish grin on her face, winked at her. They had an understanding now and he had said what he needed to say. He was satisfied. He turned to his wife.

"There," he said. "She is properly conditioned. She may marry our son now."

As Lady Cononley laughed, Lord Cononley suddenly turned to Emmaline and put his arms around her, squeezing her so hard that her back cracked. It was one of his legendary hugs that left Emmaline laughing as he pulled away, embarrassed for the display of emotion. Lady Cononley grasped her husband's elbow, pulling him towards the door.

"Thank you for receiving us, Lady Emmaline," she said. "We will see you in a short while at the church."

Emmaline nodded, watching the pair go, her heart warm from the encounter. They seemed like lovely people. Once they vacated the room, she turned to look at Lucien, who was grinning at her knowingly.

"I think you impressed them," he said.

She shrugged. "I hope so."

Lucien's smile lingered. "I am proud of the way you handled yourself with them," he said. "You will make Colton a very fine wife and they are eased. Now, on to business – I will return for you when the carriage is brought around. They are preparing it now, so make sure you are ready to leave."

Emmaline nodded eagerly. "I will."

As Emmaline turned for Aricia and Susanna, to make sure that all of them would be prepared to depart soon, Lucien turned for the door but a soft hail from his wife stopped him.

"Wait," Sophina said, pushing the frolicking Oswald aside and laboriously rising from the bed. "I will walk with you."

Lucien held out a hand to her as she waddled in his direction, which was unlike her. Her entire pregnancy, she had been energetic and spry.

She was walking strangely now and he didn't like it. He took her hand when she came close.

"What is wrong?" he asked. "Are you feeling well?"

Sophina nodded, putting a finger to her lips to silence his questions. He had no idea why until they quit the room and shut the door. Then, she bent over, still holding on to his hand, and nearly broke his bones.

"Sweetheart," Lucien bent over with her, trying to look her in the face. "What is wrong? Are you ill?"

Sophina drew in several long, deep breaths, blowing them out loudly before she tried to stand straight.

"Nay," she said. "Not ill. But I do believe our son is demanding to make his appearance into the world."

Lucien felt as if he'd been struck. All of his breath left him. "*Now?*"

She chuckled ironically. "I wish it were not so but one cannot time these things," she said. "Now, listen to me. I do not want to spoil Emmaline and Colton's day, but I am afraid I will not be able to make the mass. You must send for the midwife in Tisbury right away. Do not delay. I will go to our chamber now and wait for her. But do not tell Emmaline yet, do you hear? I do not want her to worry."

Lucien was struggling to keep his control with the rapid shift of events. Frankly, he didn't care about worrying Emmaline or not; *he* was worried enough for both of them. "I will help you to bed," he said.

He started to pull her across the landing to their chamber on the other side but Sophina shook her head. "Nay," she said. "You must send word now. I do not think this child will wait and I do not wish to deliver him myself."

Lucien's control took a hit. "It will happen that quickly?" he asked apprehensively. "Are you just now feeling pains? Surely there will be time."

Sophina continued shaking her head. "I felt the pains start last night but I thought it would be a day or two," she said. "I thought there would be time for Emmaline's wedding before the child came but I was wrong."

Lucien couldn't help it; he felt genuine panic but he managed to hold himself together, at least long enough to get Sophina into their chamber and help her remove her surcoat. The shift was on beneath. She left that on and climbed into bed with his assistance. When he was sure she wasn't going to explode that very moment, he bolted from the chamber.

His son was coming and would not wait.

The first thing he did was do exactly what Sophina didn't want him to do. He ran into the chamber where Emmaline and Aricia and Susanna were and told the women to rush to Sophina's side because the baby's arrival was imminent. While the girls fled into the master's chambers where Lucien could hear Sophina lament the fact that her husband had opened his big mouth, he rushed down the stairs and into the bailey where Lord and Lady Cononley were just crossing over to the great hall. He managed to catch up with them and, as calmly as he could, asked Lady Cononley if she would sit with Sophina until the midwife arrived.

Having birthed six children of her own, Lady Cononley was more than willing to help tend Lady de Russe and made her way back to the keep while Lucien and Lord Cononley continued on to the gatehouse where Lucien had Gabriel send a messenger to collect the midwife. By that point, the news of the impending birth spread like wildfire throughout Spelthorne and the decision was quickly made to postpone Colton and Emmaline's wedding.

In truth, Colton and Lord Cononley had made that decision because Lucien's mind was incapable of making such choices at the moment. Even though they kept him in the hall, plying him with wine and trying to keep his attention off of his laboring wife, nothing seemed to work. Lucien would not be distracted from what was going on in his bedchamber.

The moment he had been dreading had finally arrived.

The wait for the midwife seemed like days when, in fact, it was less than two hours. With the trusted midwife and Lady Cononley attending Sophina, she was in very good hands but Lucien's mind still would not be eased. He was a mess. The last time a wife had birthed his child, it had resulted in her death and he wasn't prepared for that to happen again. He prayed, they all prayed, for Sophina and the child to emerge healthy. The long afternoon wait turned into a long evening wait.

On a night that should have been filled with the music and happiness of a wedding feast, the mood of the entire castle was both somber and anxious. Lucien sat in the hall with Colton and his father, as well as Gabriel and a few other senior men, all of them waiting for word from the keep.

Eventually, Aricia and Susanna came to join the group but Emmaline had chosen to remain with her mother. Lucien had peppered Aricia and Susanna with questions about Sophina but they didn't know much. All they could tell him was that the midwife and Lady de Royans were making Lady de Russe comfortable, which didn't make him feel any better. It only made him feel worse.

The night dragged on. The beautiful wedding meal that had been in the process for days was served because most of the food had already been prepared, lovingly supervised by Sophina. So they ate roasted peacock and roasted swan, boiled beef, boiled vegetables, different types of bread, including bread that had been baked in the shape of ducks. All of this was finished with a great marzipan subtlety shaped like a castle complete with little banners flying from the turrets.

Lucien hadn't eaten anything, but he encouraged the others to. He watched as Colton and Susanna and Aricia cut into the castle subtlety and dished out big slabs of it. He mostly sat alone while everyone else quietly enjoyed the meal around him, but as the evening dragged on and still no child, Lord Cononley moved in to sit next to him.

Weston had been watching Lucien all evening, concerned about him just like everyone else was. He was, perhaps, the only one qualified to truly be concerned given how many children he had and how many times he had suffered through the same wait that Lucien was suffering through. He understood the worry. Moreover, he had known Lucien for many years and they were friends. There weren't many secrets between them, including the fear of a woman in childbirth.

"Your wine is excellent," Weston said. "Wherever did you purchase it?"

Lucien turned to the man, not particularly feeling social. "It is Spanish," he said. "I had it for the first time several years ago at Kenilworth Castle and it has been my favorite ever since. There is a broker in Southampton who ships it to me. I will give you his name if you like."

Weston held up the cup in a salute of gratitude. "I would appreciate it," he said. "My wife will like it a great deal."

The mention of a wife caused Lucien to sink back into his depression. His entire countenance changed. Weston saw the change and set his cup down.

"I know your worry on this night, old friend," he said quietly. "I have had six children of my own so this wait we are sentenced to is something I am familiar with."

Lucien sighed faintly. "I hate it," he muttered. "The last time I was forced to wait like this, I lost her. I lost her before I could tell her that I loved her, West. She died and my voice was not the last one she heard in this life. Do you know that is something I have never forgiven myself for?"

Weston put his hand on Lucien's shoulder in a show of sympathy. "I know," he said. "And I understand. But worry will not do any good. Your wife is in God's hands now and all you can do is pray. I have been praying with you all day, you know that."

"I know."

"God is merciful. He would not have brought you another woman to love if He planned to take her away so soon."

Lucien hadn't thought of it that way. Strangely enough, it gave him comfort. He nodded his head in silent thanks for Weston's words and Weston patted him on the shoulder one last time before making his way back to Colton, who was still dishing out the subtlety and, unfortunately, making a mess of it. Meanwhile, Susanna made her way over to her father, walking stiffly and awkwardly, but walking unaided just the same. She had been walking unaided for several months now thanks to Aricia, who had worked with her to help her become independent of the canes that Sophina would no longer allow her to have. Lucien looked up and saw his daughter approaching, holding up his hand for her which she grasped tightly. He helped her to sit.

"Papa, will you not eat?" she asked. "There is so much food and you have not eaten."

Lucien forced a smile. "Mayhap I will, soon," he said. "I am not very hungry right now."

Susanna studied him. For all of her youth, she had grown up quite a bit in the last year thanks to Aricia's guidance and the nurturing from her new stepmother. All of that anger and bitterness she had harbored for so long had been dissolved for the most part. She'd come to understand that her father had done the best he could with her given the circumstances. There was more growing to do for her, but she'd made progress. Therefore, there was a good deal of peace between Susanna and her father these days.

"Sophina will be well," she said after a moment. "I know she will. I cannot wait to meet my new brother. Do you think he will look like you?"

Lucien's smile turned genuine. "That is difficult to say," he replied. "Only God knows for sure who a child will look like."

"I look like you."

"Indeed, you do."

"Will I be able to hold him?"

"Of course you will."

That pleased Susanna immensely. As she stood up and shuffled away from the table, eager to tell Aricia that she would be permitted to hold the baby, Lucien couldn't help reflect on how pleasant it was to have a conversation with her that didn't end in screaming and tears. It was still an amazing happenstance to him, even after all of these months.

Oddly enough, he was coming to feel better about things. With Weston's comfort and Susanna's encouraging words, he did, indeed, feel better. A glance at the mechanical clock on the hearth told him that it had been seven hours since he'd arrived in the hall. Seven hours of not knowing how Sophina was faring.

In fact, he thought it rather ridiculous that he couldn't be at her side when she brought their child into the world. He'd very much regretted not being in the room when Laurabel had passed away. He wasn't going to make that same mistake again.

He was going to see his wife.

Standing up from the table, it didn't take him long to realize he'd had too much of that fine Spanish wine. The room was a bit unsteady. Wiping his hand over his face, trying to square up his equilibrium, he moved away from the table, heading for the entry door, when one of the massive panels opened, creaking back on its hinge. Lucien didn't think much of it until a man entered, dressed in mail, with weapons on his side.

It was dark near the entry and Lucien really couldn't see who it was so he kept walking, knowing at some point he would see the features of the individual. He thought, perhaps, it might be a messenger so he slowed his pace as the figure came forward, into the light. When Lucien finally caught a clear view of the man's features, he stopped dead in his tracks. It was all he could do to catch his breath.

Rafe de Russe had made an appearance.

My son! Lucien thought with disbelief. He hadn't seen Rafe in years. He really couldn't even remember when last he saw him but that didn't diminish the fact that he recognized him. Rafe had grown big; very big. He was as tall as his father, easily. His shoulders were broad and his dark hair was cut short, tussled and curled. He had his father's features down to the shape of his eyes and the moment Rafe recognized his father, those eyes widened somewhat.

In truth, he seemed to have the de Russe ability to conceal his emotions in a crucial situation. Lucien could see it as the young man quickly suppressed whatever surprise he was feeling at the sight of his father. Astonished to the bone, Lucien did the only thing he could do – he walked towards the young man to greet him.

"Rafe," he said, the shock in his voice evident. "It… it is surprising to see you. I did not know you were coming. If you sent word, I apologize that I did not receive it."

Rafe swallowed hard, appearing to brace himself against the sight of the man he'd sworn to hate. "I did not send word," he said. "I came because… because I have been asked to come."

Lucien's eyebrows furrowed. "By whom?"

"Lady Sophina de Russe. Your wife, I presume?"

Lucien's shock only grew. He nodded his head, slowly. "Aye," he said. "She is my wife. I was unaware she had summoned you, Rafe. I apologize if you have been inconvenienced by it."

Rafe stared at him. Truthfully, he wasn't sure what to say. He'd had it all planned out as he'd ridden to Spelthorne, lured by the new Lady de Russe's missive, but now that he was face to face with his father, he'd forgotten everything he'd planned to say. He was weary from his ride, and emotional, for his youth allowed that he didn't yet have complete control of his emotions. The longer he looked at his father, the more feelings and thoughts began welling up in his chest. Old, hurt feelings that were hard to contain.

"I am not inconvenienced by it," he finally said. "I came because I was told to come. My master knew that your wife had sent a missive to me and he told me I must come. So here I am."

Lucien was rather at a loss. He wasn't sure what to say to the young man who, by now, had seen eighteen years. His birthday had been back in April. He wasn't yet a knight but he surely looked like one. He was a de Russe to the core – big, muscular, and dark. Lucien was so proud just to look at him but that pride was tempered by the expression on Rafe's face.

He wasn't happy to be here.

"I do not know what my wife said to you in the missive, Rafe," he said. "I cannot answer for her. If you would tell me what she said, mayhap I can address it."

Rafe just looked at his father. Then, he looked around the hall, seeing the vastness of it. He noticed several people at the far end, milling around. But his observations were merely a stalling tactic as he struggled to speak on the reason why he'd come. He didn't know the reason himself. He could have easily ignored the missive and hid it from his master, but he didn't. So now, he was here.

So many memories came back to him, flooding more and more into his thoughts as he stood there. After several moments, he sighed heavily and shifted the heavy saddlebags from his shoulder to the floor. When he finally spoke, he didn't look at Lucien.

"For so many years, I have hated you," he muttered. "If men asked me, I denied that Lucien de Russe was my father."

Lucien drew in a deep, steadying breath. It hurt him to hear that. "I know."

Rafe's head snapped up, his dark eyes narrowing. "Do you?" he asked. "Do you really? Do you even know why?"

Lucien remained calm but the truth was that he was surprised Rafe began the conversation with this brittle subject. The man was barely in through the door and, already, the subject of their relationship had come up. But in hindsight, perhaps there was no right time for a conversation of this sort, especially if it had been building up. On a lonely ride from Kenilworth to Spelthorne, there had been plenty of time to think about such things. Lucien cleared his throat softly.

"I believe I do," he said. "Would you like to go into the solar? We can speak there, privately."

Rafe shook his head firmly. "Nay," he replied. "What I have to say, I will say it now. You sent me away to foster when my mother was with child and when that child was born, I barely saw you again. Only twice did you come to see me. Twice in twelve years."

As much as Rafe tried to pretend he was angry, the truth was that Lucien could hear the hurt in the man's voice. Such bitter, terrible hurt.

"I am sorry," he said quietly. "Rafe, please understand that I was mad with grief over the loss of your mother. It had nothing to do with you. Throwing myself into my duties was my way of ignoring my grief. I simply could not face it. There were times that I rode to battle and prayed I would never emerge, but I always did. I would charge into the heat of a battle, swinging my sword, begging that God would find a way to strike me down. But it never happened. That is when the men started calling me The Iron Knight. They said I was invincible, but the truth was that it only seemed that way. On the inside, I was dying."

Rafe listened to him, his featured taut with emotion. "You never told me that."

"I never had the opportunity."

"You should have tried."

Lucien lifted his dark eyebrows curiously. "Would you have understood? I am not a great communicator, Rafe. I do not believe my feelings were something I could even bring myself to voice for a very long time, much less tell my young son. I am sorry, but it is the truth."

Rafe listened, digested, and lowered his gaze. Then, he bent over one of his saddlebags and opened it, pulling forth a cylindrical item. Lucien recognized it as a missive of some kind as Rafe held it up, inspecting it without opening it.

"Lady de Russe wrote me this missive explaining much of what you just said," he finally said. "She introduced herself as your wife and went on to explain much of your actions towards me in the past. She said I was your greatest regret. Is that true?"

Lucien averted his gaze. "I am not entirely sure what good it will do to tell you that, but it is true," he said. "I regret how I handled your mother's death. I regret that I kept myself away from you when I should not have. I regret that you have grown up believing your father does not care for you. That is not true, you know. You are my son and I love you. I know you do not believe that, but I do."

Rafe looked at him, then. "You have a strange way of showing it."

"For that, I am truly sorry."

Rafe lowered the missive in his hand. "Your wife asked if I would be willing to mend my relationship with you," he said. "She says that you are a good and wise man, and she hopes that I will be able to forgive you for sins of the past. She further said if I would not forgive you, then she hopes I would at least find peace someday. She wished me peace."

That sounded so very much like Sophina and Lucien could feel a lump in his throat as he thought of her true and noble heart. Although she did not tell him of this missive she had sent to Rafe, he knew her intentions were good. She was far too loving for those intentions to be otherwise.

"My wife is a good woman with altruistic intentions," he said. "She wishes to make things well between us, as do I. But, much like her, if you cannot find it within your heart to understand my failings and forgive them, then I wish you peace as well."

Rafe's gaze lingered on the man. "What do *you* want?"

Lucien lifted his eyebrows in a resigned gesture. "I would like to go back twelve years to when your sister was born," he said. "I would like to think I would have handled the situation differently. Mayhap I would have brought you back for Kenilworth so we could be together. Mayhap I would not have thrown myself into Henry's rebellions the way I did. Who is to say? All I know is that I would have tried to do things differently. My grief over your mother's death was not worth the cost of losing my son."

For the first time since entering the hall, Rafe seemed to lose some of his tense stance. He seemed to relax. After a moment, he looked at the missive again, perhaps pondering the contents in a different way now.

"I have spent a long time hating you," he finally said, his voice soft with emotion. "Mayhap I hated you because I loved you so much, because I was so hurt at being abandoned."

"That is understandable."

"I am not saying that our relationship can be repaired, but I understand more now."

"I am glad."

"May I at least call you Lucien?"

"You may call me whatever you wish."

"I do not think you want me to call you what I really want to."

"I am sure whatever you choose, I will be deserving of it."

It was an unexpected bit of humor and a flicker of a smile crossed Rafe's lips. Lucien responded with a faint smile of his own. Rafe finally lowered his gaze so that Lucien wouldn't see how pleased he was. He didn't think he would feel so relieved to speak to his father like this, but he did. He felt... hope.

"Where is Lady de Russe that I might be introduced to her?" Rafe asked after a moment. "I do not believe she was expecting me to come. She did not ask me to, you know."

Lucien's smile quickly faded. "She is giving birth to our first child," he said. "The last time I faced this situation, it did not turn out favorably. You will understand if I am somewhat on edge."

Rafe's features registered concern. "Is she doing well?" he asked. "What does the physic say?"

Lucien shook his head. "She is being tended by a very good midwife," he said. "But this is a difficult waiting game. If... if it is not too much to say so, I would be pleased if you would wait with me."

Rafe could see the concern on his father's features and, not strangely, he seemed to forget about his own issues with the man for the moment. Rafe de Russe had much of his father's capacity for understanding in him, whether or not he realized it. He also had his father's natural capacity for compassion.

"Would it be too much to ask to wait over a beef knuckle?" he asked. "I have not eaten all day. I am smelling bread and other wonderful things at the moment."

Lucien smiled weakly. "That is because this was to be my wife's daughter's wedding day," he said. "It has been interrupted by childbirth, so there is a great deal of food. Your sister is here, in fact. You have not seen her since she was a baby."

Rafe shook his head, looking into the hall where people were lingering back in the light and warmth. "I have not," he said. "I should like to see her."

"You shall."

They began to move back into the hall although Lucien made no move to touch the young man. He didn't try to hug him or put a hand on his shoulder, although he very much wanted to. He had seen how Weston and Colton were with each other and he very much wanted that with his own son. *Mayhap someday*, he thought. The fact that Rafe was here spoke volumes of the young man's willingness to at least talk, to at least try to understand his father's failings. Rafe's appearance may have been unexpected but it certainly was not unwelcome. It was almost too much to hope for.

Was it possible that they might actually be able to be a family again? God, he hoped so.

They were nearing the tables when the entry door to the great hall opened again. They could hear the great creaking of the iron hinges that secured the door. Lucien turned, casually, to see who it was but ended up bolting for the door when he saw Lady de Royans enter.

Lucien's swift movements startled everyone, Weston and Colton included, and soon everyone was running for the door where Lady de Royans was entering. When she looked up and saw the flood of people coming towards her, including Lucien's anxious face, she merely smiled. Reaching out, she put a gentle hand on Lucien's arm because the man looked like he was about to explode.

"Go, Papa," she said. "Go and see your new baby."

Lucien must have swayed because he could feel hands on him, steadying him. "The baby is here?" he asked, feeling lightheaded. "How is my wife?"

Lady de Royans nodded. "She is doing well," she assured him. "Your son was quite large. It took time for your wife to deliver him, but both mother and son are doing well. Go, now. Do not keep them waiting."

Lucien didn't have to be told twice. As the wedding feast turned into a feast to celebrate a new and healthy birth, Lucien sprinted to the chamber he shared with his wife only to be confronted with a dark-haired, screaming infant with big fists.

It was the first thing he saw, this angry baby. He laughed until he cried as little Achilles de Russe was very vocal with his displeasure at having been born, quieting only when Sophina put him on the breast to feed. In the magical and surreal feeling of the moment, Lucien could hardly believe all was well. Sophina's smile told him that it was, indeed, well, that a son had been born healthy and that she, too, had emerged unscathed. Lucien bent over the pair, kissing his wife until more tears fell from his eyes. He'd never been more grateful for anything in his entire life.

Eventually, he lay down upon the bed, watching his fat infant nurse, his arms gently around both the baby and his wife and thinking that this was, perhaps, the most wonderful night of his life. One son born, another returned, and a great and happy life before him. The vestiges of sorrow that had been his existence for so many years were finally gone, finally erased by a love so powerful that it defied both heaven and earth. What he thought he'd long lost those years ago, he'd managed to regain. For him, there had been a second chance at life.

Now, it wasn't only his love for Sophina, but his love for his splintered family that had finally been made whole again.

He had made it whole again.

The legacy of The Iron Knight lived on.

Cʒ THE END ઠౖ

The de Russe Legacy:

The Falls of Erith

Lord of War: Black Angel

The Iron Knight

Beast

The Dark One: Dark Knight

The White Lord of Wellesbourne

Dark Moon

Dark Steel

A de Russe Christmas Miracle

Dark Warrior

KATHRYN LE VEQUE NOVELS

Medieval Romance:

De Wolfe Pack Series:
Warwolfe
The Wolfe
Nighthawk
ShadowWolfe
DarkWolfe
A Joyous de Wolfe Christmas
BlackWolfe
Serpent
A Wolfe Among Dragons
Scorpion
StormWolfe
Dark Destroyer
The Lion of the North
Walls of Babylon
The Best Is Yet To Be

De Wolfe Pack Generations:
WolfeHeart
WolfeStrike
WolfeSword

The de Russe Legacy:
The Falls of Erith
Lord of War: Black Angel
The Iron Knight
Beast
The Dark One: Dark Knight
The White Lord of Wellesbourne
Dark Moon
Dark Steel
A de Russe Christmas Miracle
Dark Warrior

The de Lohr Dynasty:

While Angels Slept
Rise of the Defender
Steelheart
Shadowmoor
Silversword
Spectre of the Sword
Unending Love
Archangel
A Blessed de Lohr Christmas

Lords of East Anglia:
While Angels Slept
Godspeed

Great Lords of le Bec:
Great Protector

House of de Royans:
Lord of Winter
To the Lady Born
The Centurion

Lords of Eire:
Echoes of Ancient Dreams
Blacksword
The Darkland

Ancient Kings of Anglecynn:
The Whispering Night
Netherworld

Battle Lords of de Velt:
The Dark Lord
Devil's Dominion
Bay of Fear
The Dark Lord's First Christmas

Reign of the House of de Winter:

Lespada
Swords and Shields

De Reyne Domination:
Guardian of Darkness
With Dreams
The Fallen One

House of d'Vant:
Tender is the Knight (House of d'Vant)
The Red Fury (House of d'Vant)

The Dragonblade Series:
Fragments of Grace
Dragonblade
Island of Glass
The Savage Curtain
The Fallen One

Great Marcher Lords of de Lara
Dragonblade

House of St. Hever
Fragments of Grace
Island of Glass
Queen of Lost Stars

Lords of Pembury:
The Savage Curtain

**Lords of Thunder: The de Shera
Brotherhood Trilogy**
The Thunder Lord
The Thunder Warrior
The Thunder Knight

The Great Knights of de Moray:
Shield of Kronos
The Gorgon

The House of De Nerra:
The Promise
The Falls of Erith
Vestiges of Valor
Realm of Angels

Highland Warriors of Munro:
The Red Lion
Deep Into Darkness

The House of de Garr:
Lord of Light
Realm of Angels

Saxon Lords of Hage:
The Crusader
Kingdom Come

High Warriors of Rohan:
High Warrior

The House of Ashbourne:
Upon a Midnight Dream

The House of D'Aurilliac:
Valiant Chaos

The House of De Dere:
Of Love and Legend

St. John and de Gare Clans:
The Warrior Poet

The House of de Bretagne:
The Questing

The House of Summerlin:
The Legend

The Kingdom of Hendocia:
Kingdom by the Sea

The Executioner Knights:
By the Unholy Hand
The Mountain Dark
Starless
The Promise (also Noble Knights of de
Nerra)
A Time of End
Winter of Solace
Lord of the Shadows

Lord of the Sky

Contemporary Romance:

Kathlyn Trent/Marcus Burton Series:
Valley of the Shadow
The Eden Factor
Canyon of the Sphinx

The American Heroes Anthology Series:
The Lucius Robe
Fires of Autumn
Evenshade
Sea of Dreams
Purgatory

Other non-connected Contemporary

Romance:
Lady of Heaven
Darkling, I Listen
In the Dreaming Hour
River's End
The Fountain

Sons of Poseidon:
The Immortal Sea

Pirates of Britannia Series (with Eliza Knight):
Savage of the Sea by Eliza Knight
Leader of Titans by Kathryn Le Veque
The Sea Devil by Eliza Knight
Sea Wolfe by Kathryn Le Veque

Note: All Kathryn's novels are designed to be read as stand-alones, although many have cross-over characters or cross-over family groups. Novels that are grouped together have related characters or family groups. You will notice that some series have the same books; that is because they are cross-overs. A hero in one book may be the secondary character in another.

There is NO reading order except by chronology, but even in that case, you can still read the books as stand-alones. No novel is connected to another by a cliff hanger, and every book has an HEA.

Series are clearly marked. All series contain the same characters or family groups except the American Heroes Series, which is an anthology with unrelated characters.

For more information, find it in **A Reader's Guide to the Medieval World of Le Veque.**

ABOUT KATHRYN LE VEQUE

Medieval Just Got Real.

KATHRYN LE VEQUE is a USA TODAY Bestselling author, an Amazon All-Star author, and a #1 bestselling, award-winning, multi-published author in Medieval Historical Romance and Historical Fiction. She has been featured in the NEW YORK TIMES and on USA TODAY's HEA blog. In March 2015, Kathryn was the featured cover story for the March issue of InD'Tale Magazine, the premier Indie author magazine. She was also a quadruple nominee (a record!) for the prestigious RONE awards for 2015.

Kathryn's Medieval Romance novels have been called 'detailed', 'highly romantic', and 'character-rich'. She crafts great adventures of love, battles, passion, and romance in the High Middle Ages. More than that, she writes for both women AND men – an unusual crossover for a romance author – and Kathryn has many male readers who enjoy her stories because of the male perspective, the action, and the adventure.

On October 29, 2015, Amazon launched Kathryn's Kindle Worlds Fan Fiction site WORLD OF DE WOLFE PACK. Please visit Kindle Worlds for Kathryn Le Veque's World of de Wolfe Pack and find many action-packed adventures written by some of the top authors in their genre using Kathryn's characters from the de Wolfe Pack series. As Kindle World's FIRST Historical Romance fan fiction world, Kathryn Le Veque's World of de Wolfe Pack will contain all of the great story-telling you have come to expect.

Kathryn loves to hear from her readers. Please find Kathryn on Facebook at Kathryn Le Veque, Author, or join her on Twitter @kathrynleveque, and don't forget to visit her website and sign up for her blog at www.kathrynleveque.com.

Please follow Kathryn on Bookbub for the latest releases and sales: bookbub.com/authors/kathryn-le-veque.

Made in the USA
Monee, IL
20 April 2024

57251081R00174